Warily, she eyed the dark knight.

She struggled to stand, her legs tight from her position on the hard stone floor. The dark knight took her elbow. She swatted his hand away and nearly fell back into the fire. Rohan grabbed her to him, laughing at her struggle to be free of him. "I do not bite, damsel."

With reluctance, Isabel allowed him to steady her and guide her upward. "'Tis not your bite that concerns me, sir."

He threw his head back and laughed heartily. He peered at her, a genuine smile gracing his lips. Something shifted deep inside her. The transformation to his face when he smiled was staggering.

He lowered his voice, and as if they were the only two in the great hall he said, "You may well find you would come to crave my bite."

Heat rushed to Isabel's cheeks. Her back stiffened. "I would never!"

His grin widened, and he bent close to her and whispered, "Never say never, damsel. Those words may come back to mock you."

Isabel stepped back from him, shaking her head. Her heavy hair swirled around her shoulders. "Do not speak to me of such things. 'Tis not decent."

His face closed at her words and his eyes hardened. "Nor am I."

ALSO BY KARIN TABKE:

KARIN TABKE

MASTER
of
SURRENDER

Pocket Books
New York London Toronto Sydney

Pocket Books
A Division of Simon & Schuster, Inc.
1230 Avenue of the Americas
New York, NY 10020

This book is a work of fiction. Names, characters, places, and incidents either are products of the author's imagination or are used fictitiously. Any resemblance to actual events or locales or persons, living or dead, is entirely coincidental.

Copyright © 2008 by Karin Tabke

First Pocket Books paperback edition July 2008

POCKET and colophon are registered trademarks of Simon & Schuster, Inc.

For information about special discounts for bulk purchases, please contact Simon & Schuster Special Sales at 1-800-456-6798 or business@simonandschuster.com.

Cover design by Lisa Litwick; Illustration by Larry Rostant

Manufactured in the United States of America

10 9 8 7 6 5 4 3 2 1

ISBN-13: 978-1-4165-5089-1
ISBN-10:   1-4165-5089-5

Acknowledgments

Of course, this wonderful story would never have seen the light of publication had it not been for my agent, Kimberly Whalen, falling in love with the original fifty pages of what was to become Rohan and Isabel's love story. Thank you, Kim: your love and support of this project has been the fuel in my tank.

I would also like to acknowledge all of the regular ladies who stop by my blog, The Write Life, who helped time after time with title suggestions. Though none of them were used, I thank you all for the time and thought. To Jake, Cele, and "hubby": thank you for the many memorable LOL moments with your dueling title contest contributions. Anna Lucia, thank you for answering *all* of my questions!

The great title search was not all for naught, however. Because of my dear friend Lee Lopez's comment regarding the term "Blood Sword" the idea for the Blood Sword Legacy series was born. Lee, thank you!

Of course, I must acknowledge my husband, Gary,

without whose unshakeable belief in what I do, I could not do it. To my youngest son, William; sweetheart, thank you for understanding those many days and nights Mommy stayed holed up in her office growling and snapping while she tried desperately to manage a scene.

I want to thank my entire family for giving up our traditional holiday so that I could write through. The second time was the charm, kids! Thank you for not complaining too loudly.

To Lauren:
Thank you for believing in me
and pushing me to write a better story.
Twice!
Master of Surrender *belongs to you.*

Prologue

The pungent odor of urine, the copper tang of blood, and the stench of terror blended in perfect union with the wailing moans and strangled screams of the multitudes of prisoners begging for merciful death.

In the cell where Rohan hung from iron shackles, the spiked anchors embedded deep in the damp stone wall securing him forever, the stench of death had yet to penetrate. Nay, death was not an option. Vengeance burned white-hot in his heart. It burned as hot in each and every man in the cell with him. All of them proud warriors who would spit in the eye of Atropos as she cut the last thread of life.

A low growl rumbled deep in his throat. Rohan yanked at the shackles, ignoring the pain the gesture cost him. *God's blood! Imprisoned. Condemned to death.*

Jubb, the pit, renowned for its unique and final end to a human life. In ordinary terms it was a dungeon filled with bats. Flesh-eating bats, which over the centuries had grown to crave the taste of human flesh. He'd heard the screams. He heard them in his waking hours. He heard them in his bouts of fitful slumber. The heavy cacophony of thousands of wings, the gurgling cries of the victims as they were eaten alive. His skin crawled. 'Twas no way for a man to die.

Rohan rolled his head back against the wet wall. His long hair was damp, matted, and lice-infested, and it hung in a heavy shroud down his shoulders. How long they had been there, in the hellhole, he did not know. Most days, barely a glimpse of sunlight seeped through the cracks in the higher slabs of stone. He'd lost count of the sparse meals of dark moldy bread and limp leafy vegetables he knew came only once a day.

He closed his eyes, the grittiness of his lids scraping against the dryness. Balancing on his good left foot, he tested his right foot, moving it up and down. The heel had finally healed from a near-fatal cut, compliments of his torturer, Ocba. Had the blade gone further in, he would never walk again. He still might never. Escape was but a dream. He fisted his left hand. Thick scars replaced the ravaged burns he had endured for Ocba's pleasure. He glanced over at his man Ioan. The tall Irishman hardly recognizable under a thick, wooly beard had lost more flesh than any of them. And that was considerable. Ioan was a brute of a man. A worthy second in battle. Rohan's tired eyes fell from Ioan's hollow face down his mud-encrusted body to his right thigh. It still swelled, broken in a wooden vise. Again for Ocba's amusement. Rohan could still hear Ioan's screams in his dreams. Had it healed enough that if by some miracle they escaped, he could ever ride again?

"Rohan," a low, hoarse voice called. He turned his head,

the pain in his neck from hanging suspended so long shooting to his lower back and then to his legs. Rohan bit back the ache and looked to his right. If he could, he would smile. Thorin. Not more than one arm length from him. In the dim light he could count the Viking's ribs.

"Aye, Thorin, I hear you."

"We are next, brother."

Rohan nodded, knowing the cell he occupied with no fewer than a score of other captured knights and a tattooed Saracen would soon see it void of them. Each day the sound of the emptying cells came one closer. His anger flashed anew. They'd been betrayed, the lot of them. Set up like unsuspecting chess pieces in a war where one day you fought beside your fellow knight and the next he slew you from behind.

Rohan swallowed hard, the drag on his parched throat no less painful than the torture he'd endured. He was dying now, from the inside out.

"I swear you this, Thorin: I will take at least a dozen of these Cretans with me before the bats devour me."

"Aye, and I as well."

From beneath his lashes, not having the strength to fight for more, Rohan looked around the cell, at the men, mercenary knights like he who had been captured in an ambush during a raid on a sleepy village in the mountains shrouding the Saracen town of Viseu. Hatred burned as fiercely in their eyes as he felt it in his heart. The men hung from manacles high above their shoulders, clad only in loincloths. The only tenuous balance they had was found standing on their toes to keep them from pulling their arms out of their sockets.

He gazed at the faces he knew from his birth land in

Normandy. Warner, an orphan from his foster father's house; Stefan, the Comte de Valrey's eldest son; and Rohan's old friend and companion since his youth, Thorin. The others—Wulfson, Ioan, Rhys, and the Scot, Rorick— he had met here, fighting in the land of Saracens, now reunited in the pit of death.

They all shared a commonality. By blow each and every one of them. Forced to wield a sword to survive. Aye, mercenary knights they were who pledged a troth to Ferdinand of Castile-León. For a price. And all of them, it seemed, doomed to die a heinous death in this foreign land because of it. Such was the life of his kind.

"They can be beat," a deep foreign-accented voice said from the other side of Rohan. He turned his head to look at the man whose skin rivaled the darkest of moonless nights. In all the days the man had shared this small space with him, he had not uttered a single word. Why now? Did he, too, know their time was near?

With the man's words, the energy, small though it was, rose in the confines of the dank cell.

"Why should you tell us, Saracen?" Rohan demanded.

"I am Manhku. Like you, I do not wish to die."

"Tell us, Saracen. Tell us how we rid ourselves of this scourge!" Wulfson demanded from across the room.

As if summoned by their conversation, keys rattled outside the thick wooden door. The grinding sound of metal on metal gave way to the screeching groan of the hinges opening.

The man who strode through the door, blazing torch held high, was not Ocba, their usual tormentor. This man was better dressed. His robes clean and rich in silk. He practically pranced across the muddy urine-soaked floor.

He pressed a crimson silk scarf to his nose, and Rohan laughed at him when the fop retched in his hand.

"You're not man enough to venture here, Saracen," Rohan goaded. Manhku hissed in a breath, and the surrounding men kept silent.

The newcomer dabbed at the corners of his mouth, oblivious to Rohan's taunt. After setting the torch in the iron ring on the wall, he snapped his fingers. Behind him Ocba and another guard pushed a deep metal cart of glowing coals through the open doorway. Rohan's muscles tightened. Several sword hilts protruded from the coals. One he recognized as his.

Having collected himself, the man lowered the scarf and turned ebony-colored eyes on Rohan. "I am Tariq ibn-Ziyad, second son of Aleyed, Emir of Viseu. I have come at his request, because it appears you Christian knights who offer your sword to the highest bidder have defied the odds of Jahannam." His beady black eyes scanned the lot of them. Purple lips pulled back, showing startling white teeth.

"So now you will torture us further for not succumbing to your hospitality?" Thorin charged.

Tariq smiled, the gesture more a ruthless leer. "It is so." He pulled on heavy leather gloves. "And since you refuse to bow down to Allah, the one and only true god, to save yourselves, be prepared to bear the mark of one who lives and dies by the sword." He pulled Rohan's sword from the coals. It glowed molten orange. He sliced it through the air. His sharp-angled face lit up in delight when his dark eyes rose to Rohan's. "A most worthy weapon, would you not say so, *kafir*?"

Ocba, assisted by the other guard, grabbed Rohan's legs

and pulled his body taut. Rohan steeled himself against the stone wall, knowing full well the Saracen's intention.

Tariq stepped closer to Rohan, swinging the tip of the blade under his nose. The heat of the weapon scorched his skin. "Now, be prepared to wear it for eternity!" Tariq pressed the sword, point down, crossguard just below his throat, full length into Rohan's chest. "In the name of Allah! I brand you for the mercenary you are. Bear the sign of the blood sword to hell!"

Rohan roared his battle cry, the inscrutable pain and sickening stench of burnt flesh pushing him to the brink of sanity. Blackness engulfed his eyes, the pain so intense. In his agony he twisted beneath the sword and kicked at both guards, the velocity setting his legs free for the moment. The blade fell from his chest. Rohan opened his eyes and managed a grimace of a smile when he saw Tariq in his silken robes, arse and hands planted firmly on the slippery mud of the floor.

Rohan's small triumph was short-lived. His breath and strength expelled, his body slumped. He closed his eyes and, for the first time in his life, welcomed the peace of death that his tumultuous life had never brought him.

The last things he sensed were Thorin's hoarse screams beside him and the stench of more seared flesh, then blackness.

He must be dreaming. The soft, exotic scent of a woman filled his nostrils. Cool, soothing hands ministered to his incinerated flesh. An angel? Come from heaven to take him home? Nay, where he was going no angels abided. He was where he was supposed to be, Jahannam, the Hell Fire.

His heavy eyelids opened to light. He was on his back, in the mud of his cell. No longer hanging from the dank stone walls, though he still felt the weight of the shackles around his wrists and ankles.

He looked to his left. Big brown eyes framed by thick black lashes stared at him from behind a black veil. He could tell by the deep creases at her eyes that she smiled. A woman? In a Saracen prison? She nodded and continued to apply the soothing balm to his chest. Rohan moved to lean up on an elbow but fell back to the ground. His shoulder was not properly aligned. He would need the strong arm of a man to set it aright. He turned his head in the mud to see Thorin lying still beside him. To his right the ebony giant. From where Rohan lay, he saw the other men, shackled and lying on their backs. He closed his eyes.

When next he opened them, he was greeted with utter darkness. "Thorin?" he whispered through cracked lips, his throat raw from his screams.

"I am here," came his friend's barely audible voice.

Rohan fisted his hands. He started at a sharp prick in his right hand. What was this? Careful so as not to lose it, he fingered a piece of smooth iron the length of his longest finger. A nail? One he could use to pry open the lock to his shackles? His heart thundered in his chest. Had the angel given him an out?

The grating of metal on metal curbed the elation of his discovery. Rohan closed his hand around the nail and relaxed back to the floor. Light infiltrated the cell, casting weird shadows around them. Rough foreign words were spoken. A soft female voice responded, steel lacing her words. The door closed behind her.

His angel of mercy had returned.

As she had before, she applied the balm to his chest, her soft hands moving quickly over his body. When he looked at her, she lowered her eyelids.

Rohan reached a hand to her face, and she pulled back, a stricken look in her brown eyes. Swiftly she moved from him to Thorin and around the room, tending each man until she came to the hulking giant beside him. Manhku muttered in his native tongue. The woman hissed.

She moved away from him and did something that astounded Rohan. She made the sign of the cross several times before standing. The door was flung open, and Tariq strode in, his eyes flashing in fury. He grabbed the woman. She shrieked and kicked at him. In a defiant gesture, she tore the veil from her face. Rohan's anger flared at the sight. The deep honey color of her skin melted into shiny twisted red scars marring the bottom part of her face.

"Do not look upon her face, *kafirs*!" Tariq screamed.

The woman stood defiant before the Saracen. In one brutal blow to her face, Tariq struck her down. She landed at Thorin's feet. When Tariq reached down to grab her, Thorin pulled her out of his way and glared up at the Saracen. "Leave her!"

"You would dare look at her!" Tariq raged.

"You work your torture well, Saracen. Can you only prevail over chained knights and helpless women?" Thorin challenged.

Tariq pulled his scimitar from his belt. "Now feel the price you pay for daring to look at her, *kafir*." In a movement so quick and so vicious it caught them all off guard, Tariq slashed at Thorin's right eye. Thorin screamed out in pain. He turned his head from the blade as blood rushed from the socket. Tariq brought his sword up to destroy the left eye.

Rage infused Rohan. He roared his mighty battle cry and twisted in his chains. His long legs kicked out, knocking the Saracen from his feet. The scimitar fell from his hand, landing next to Manhku, who grabbed it. As nimble as an ocelot, Tariq turned with a short dagger in his hand and lunged at Rohan.

He stopped wide-eyed in mid-flight; a low gurgling sound followed the slow hiss of air emanating from his chest. Tariq looked down and grabbed at the hilt of his sword, buried in his chest. He looked from it to Manhku, then to Rohan, in stunned silence.

The woman jerked it from his body and pushed him to his knees. "Beware, brother! The seer foretold the coming of the Blood Sword. You are a fool for doubting her."

She turned to Rohan, then to each man in the room. "Be aware of your destiny, bastard knights. Swear your fealty to the other now, for those of you who survive this land of the Saracens to venture over the great mountains to Gaul will have only the other. Much intrigue awaits your future across the water."

She reached down and took the dagger from her brother's grasp. In a movement so quick he had no time to react, she cut a small nick in Rohan's chin. She repeated the move on each man. She moved to the middle of the room, and with both hands she raised the dagger toward the sky. The blood of the knights mingled on the blade, then trickled down her arm. "You bear the mark of the sword on your chest, your blood mingles here on this blade, binding you as knights of the Blood Sword to the end of time, and with it the legacy begins!"

She closed her eyes and chanted unintelligible words. Her body stiffened. When she opened her eyes, a faraway look clouded them.

"Take heed with your seed, Blood Sword knights. It is potent but will strike only the fertile ground of the woman destined to bear your first sons." She closed her eyes and took a deep breath. "But such a womb will not come willingly, and the price for it will be high." She jabbed the dagger higher into the air. "For to claim it, you must spill the blood of her kin!"

One

November 20, 1066
Alethorpe, England

R iders approach!" Bertram the tower lookout called.

Isabel halted just outside the small chapel attached to the magnificent stone manor that was Rossmoor. Her blood quickened. Father! Geoff! Isabel gathered her skirts and ran through the courtyard toward the bailey, her slippered feet barely touching the smooth limestone.

"Armed knights!" the lookout said, his voice a ragged strangle.

Isabel's blood chilled. Just as quickly as her excitement had engulfed her, it plummeted, and dread took its place. A scream congealed in her throat, choking her like a hunk of rancid meat. Skidding to a stop, she turned as quickly on her heels and ran as fast as she could back through the courtyard to Rossmoor. The raiders had returned! *Holy Mother.* They grew bolder each day. Had they not pillaged and plundered the gentle souls of Alethorpe enough?

"To arms! To arms!" Isabel yelled up to the lookout. Why she demanded such an action she had no clue. There were naught but a handful of inexperienced villagers to answer the call. But it mattered not. The warrior spirit in her burned hot.

"Jesu! 'Tis the Black Sword!" Bertram yelled as he identified the leader of William's most notorious death squad, *les morts*. The scream lodged in her throat escaped.

As she pushed open the huge wooden portal, Isabel collided with Russell, her father's squire, who he insisted remain at Rossmoor to protect his daughter and home. "Russell, 'tis the Black Sword! Gather all the servants. Call the villagers!" She flew past him, up into the tower, and out to the rampart. She dared look upon the horizon. The sight that greeted her terrified her to numbness.

Nearly a half-score of fully armored black knights upon equally black war horses, their huge furred bodies as armored as their masters', galloped over the last ridge before the village. Long black crimson-lined mantles billowed like the wings of fallen angels about their shoulders.

Villagers screamed, terrified at this new menace. These were not the hooded raiders who skulked about the forest attacking innocent women, children, and old men. Nay, this menace that moved at breakneck speed toward her home was death on horseback. And Isabel knew with an earth-shattering certainty that once they poured into the village below and then into the manor, lives would forever be changed.

The standard of William Duke of Normandy, two golden lions on a crimson field, ripped mightily in the chill of the morning air, but more terrifying was the standard of *les morts*. Flying arrogantly at the end of each lance a flag with a *gonfalon* blazed on a black field with a blood red sword plunging through a gruesome, grinning skull. Death.

"Sound the horn for the villagers to seek refuge in the woods! Prepare for battle!"

Isabel turned, rushed down the stairwell out to the courtyard, and hurried the panicked villagers into the hall.

Several of her servants came rushing from the kitchen and others from the chambers above. Bertram hurried from the tower, a sword at the ready, Russell behind him. With the help of Thomas the hostler, she threw the thick, heavy bolts into the metal brackets, then secured the braces against the door. "Shutter all of the arrow slits and windows! See to the outer doors! Stoke the fires so they cannot penetrate from above. Bring the knives from the kitchens."

"What of the privy?" Enid asked, wringing her hands.

"There are hooks. They can attempt, but they will find themselves in shreds." Isabel smiled tersely as she imagined William's knights caught up on the hooks designed specifically to ward off any who thought it a good idea to climb up the privy shoot from the cesspool.

Once her orders had been met and the people reassembled in the hall, Isabel took a deep breath. For now, they were safe.

"Milady?" Russell said from beside her. She looked up into the clear blue eyes of the boy on the verge of manhood. She smiled and gave him a reassuring pat on the forearm.

"The bolt will hold. Our walls cannot be scaled. We have enough stores to last us well into the New Year. By then my father and brother will return." The boy gave her a look that belied her words. Anger flared, and she cuffed him. "Believe it, Russell."

Isabel turned and hurried to the wide stone stairway

that led to the many rooms on the second floor of the manor. She turned and called to her people. As she had when the first attack came nearly a fortnight ago, she calmed them by her own calm presence.

As she opened her mouth, the tower lookout called out, "They have scaled the courtyard wall!"

Panic erupted around her.

"Hear me!" she called. "Hear me, now!" The eruption subdued somewhat, but she still had need to raise her voice high. "We have prepared well. The doors will hold!"

"But milady, we have no archers, no pitch. No soldiers to protect us!"

"Aye." Isabel nodded. "And we don't need them." She pointed to the double thick-hewn doors, the impenetrable gateway to Rossmoor. By comparison to the inner richness of the hall, the thick English oak seemed too rustic. But the doors served their purpose. They were designed to pre-vent even the most ardent pursuer's entrance. "Rossmoor has withstood the heartiest of attacks. We will hold until my father and brother return."

The walls were not scalable, save for the tower, but the door at the top and the entrance to the hall were as solid as the front doors. And, she was sure, the enemy would never find the secret passage known only to herself, her father, and her brother.

For now they were safe. The harsh thud of a fisted hand beat on the door.

"I am Rohan du Luc. I come in the name of William Duke of Normandy. Open these doors." The French words rang clear, and while the villagers did not understand them, the tone was clear.

Bertram rushed down from the tower, his face flushed red, his pale, watery eyes open and terrified. "I have battened the door. Should they scale the wall, they will not find a way to penetrate it."

"Open this door, or prepare for the consequences." Du Luc's voice boomed through the timber.

Isabel moved through the crowd toward the tower door.

"Nay, milady!" Russell cried, following close behind her. "'Tis folly. They will surely bring you low with an arrow!"

She flung his hand from her shoulder. "Leave me be, Russell. They are knights, not archers."

She pushed up the heavy bolt from its hold and hurried up the twisting narrow passageway until she came to the equally thick door to the lookout nest. She heaved the bolt up and pulled open the heavy door. The icy November air swirled angrily around her ankles, snaking up her skirts. Her teeth chattered in deference. Isabel hesitated before stepping onto the rampart. What if Russell spoke the truth? Would she die at the hand of a Norman archer? Running her hands up and down her arms to warm herself, Isabel straightened her spine and lowered her arms. Taking a deep breath, she moved to the edge of the stone balustrade.

Placing her hands on the cold, hard stone, Isabel looked down to see each of the black knights save the one leading them, with bows strung and arrows notched, aimed directly at her. She caught the scream in her throat. She would show no fear.

"Would you kill an unarmed woman?" She sneered at the one she assumed was du Luc. He sat arrogantly astride a huge black horse covered in spiked leather armor. As her nervous gaze appraised the lot of them, her blood slowed and chilled. Each destrier was similarly appointed. They looked like the devil's own steeds.

"I am Isabel of Alethorpe. What business do you have with me?"

"Unbolt your doors so that we may *parle*," the knight in front said.

Isabel laughed, the wind carrying off the cryptic sound. "Do I look like a churl? Say what you have to say from your horse."

As one, the knights pulled their bowstrings. Fear congealed in her limbs. She didn't feel the harsh slap of the wind against her face or the way it ripped off her veil and tore at her unbound hair. She stood like a marble statue. Rigid and unyielding. She would not show fear. She would not turn and run. She would never yield the day to this black knight.

"In the name of Duke William, I claim this manor and this land. Now, give us entry!"

His words sliced through her resolve. Fear made a quick, seamless shift into fury. How dare he demand such a thing? 'Twas her home and the home of her ancestors. She would never willingly hand it over to any man, much less a bastard Norman!

Isabel moved closer to the edge of the rampart. "I claim this manor and the surrounding lands in the name of my father, Alefric Lord of Alethorpe, Wilshire, and Dunleavy. You have no right here! Leave us!"

"Harold is dead, damsel. England is William's. Allow us entry." While his voice held a note of contempt, a thinly veiled warning gave it credence. Isabel studied the knight. From her position, she could see only the lower half of his face. Cruel lips were cradled by the harsh cut of his chin. Her gaze moved over the rest of them. Some seven knights and a full score of foot soldiers pouring in behind them. Were there others to come? It mattered not. William himself could be at her threshold, and she would not acquiesce.

"Nay! My father and my brother will return. I will not have them find their home in the hands of foreigners. There are other fiefs to be had. Leave us!"

"I will not ask again, Lady Isabel," du Luc said. "Open the door, or find yourselves with less than I would grant should you comply."

"Nay! I will never open the door for any Norman!"

Isabel turned and hurried from the tower rampart. She pulled the heavy oak door closed behind her and threw the bolt. As she entered the hall, Russell closed the second door and bolted it. Isabel turned to the terrified villagers and her servants.

"Have faith. The manor is strong and will take whatever abuse those barbarians will mete out."

"My lady, what shall we do?" Enid mewled.

Isabel patted her maid's hand. "We shall wait, Enid, for Lord Alefric and Sir Geoff to return. They will rid our land of yonder Normans."

"Do you think those knights plot with the raiders?" Russell asked.

Isabel shot the boy a harsh glare and motioned for him to step aside so that she might have a private word with him. "Russell, speak not of those others. Our people are terrified enough."

He nodded and bowed. "You are wise beyond your years, Lady Isabel. Were you a man, I have no doubt you would best those knights single-handedly."

Isabel swallowed hard and thought were she a man, she might lie stiff and frozen along with other Saxon soldiers on Senlac Hill.

"Keep the people calm, Russell, while I inspect the manor."

Quickly, Isabel set off around the hall, making sure each entrance to the edifice was secured. Rossmoor had been constructed by her great-grandfather Leofric, whom many called Reynard for his wily ways, with the express intention of waiting out a siege and prohibiting invaders from scaling the walls. The roof was pitched at severe angles covered with several underlayers of thin metal sheets topped with treated thatch to prevent fire from infiltrating. It was a chore, but every few years, the thatch was retreated with a special concoction dating back to Roman times to prevent the spread of fire. Should an invader hook a spike, he would have nowhere to climb but up and over.

As Isabel inspected the stores, she counted to herself and calculated how long the occupants of the hall could last. Four months, at least. Longer if they were frugal. She looked over at the thick oak door that led to the courtyard from the kitchens. It would serve as stalwartly as the main portals. The only predator with the strength to penetrate the stone walls was death.

Just as Isabel made her way back into the hall, a loud thump hit the front door. It was quickly followed by another, then another. The cadence was clear. Two battering rams. Isabel hurried to the oak portals and watched as each slam shook the timber. It held. But for how long? A terrible premonition shook her resolve. Her body flinched each time the harsh slam of the wood hit the timber. The villagers cried out, louder with each hit, their confidence shaken almost beyond repair. They had suffered so much.

Isabel forced a smile more to reassure herself than her people. The Normans would learn soon enough that many an attack had fallen useless under the strength of the doors. Should the hinges fail, the braces locked into the stone threshold were thick and sturdy and more than ample to keep the doors upright. It gave her pleasure to thwart such a cunning foe. But she was more cunning. Her smile died when the acrid scent of smoke assailed her nostrils. She glanced at the roaring hearth and watched as billows of gray smoke poured into the hall. "They have blocked the chimney! Douse the fires!"

Several cauldrons of water were poured over the embers of each burning hearth in the manor. Smoke billowed acrid and thick into the hall, stinging Isabel's eyes and sinking deep into her chest. Coughing harshly, she pulled her tunic up over her nose and mouth and motioned for everyone to move toward the front of the hall where the air was clear. When the fire was finally doused, Isabel blinked back the tears. Jesu! Would they die from the smoke?

The rhythmic battering continued on the door.

The small crowd in the hall drew close, eyes wide, bodies trembling, women keening.

"Lady Isabel?" Russell asked from beside her.

"Stand fast, Russell." She moved to the wide stairway and walked up several steps. As one, the small mass of people cleaved to her wake. "Stand fast all of you! Stand fast!"

"They will slay us all! Gouge out our eyes and burn us alive!" Mertred the tanner cried. His wife, Anne, shrieked and tore at her hair. The distraught villagers moaned as one, their fear of a tragic death making them unpredictable. They all knew invasion at the hands of mercenary knights was imminent. Even should they stave them off, their time in the hall would be a living hell.

"My children lie one with the earth from the raiders. I cannot stomach more," Guntha, a village woman, wailed.

Isabel raised her hands and explained. "These knights of the bastard duke are not the same who laid havoc on the village! Those cloaked cowards would not dare come this close." Her voice quieted. "Nay, these knights are of a different breed."

"Aye, the devil's henchmen! We are lost for sure!"

Hysteria rose so thickly in the hall, Isabel could slice it with her table knife. Her mind raced with an alternative plan. Bargaining with the Norman was not an option. He would see his way into the hall, and all would be lost. It would take an army to remove them. Arlys Lord of Dunsworth, her betrothed, had yet to return from his campaign at Harold's side. Yet she heard word he lived. Had she known his whereabouts, she would send word for him to come to her aid.

The sharp splintering of wood crashed into her thoughts, sending them scattering in a thousand different directions. Jesu! The door gave way!

'Twas not possible!

Enid screamed beside her. "Lady! We are doomed!"

Isabel searched out Russell amongst the terrified villagers. She met his eyes over the cowering shoulders. "See them all safely upstairs. Barricade the doors. Do not lift the bolt until you hear my voice, and only *my* voice!"

As the words left her mouth, a full score of villagers stampeded past her and up the stairway. Russell slowly followed. "Milady, what of you?"

"I will stay here, Russell."

"Here? Have you gone—"

Isabel cuffed him. The boy's face turned crimson. "Do not question me, sir squire. I have a ready tongue in my head and know well how to wield words of compromise." She swallowed hard and prayed to the Holy Mother for assistance. For she would need it in dealing with the soldiers from hell.

"I'll see to our people, milady, then stand beside you."

"Nay," she calmly said. "See to them until you hear my word." She pushed him up the stairs as the continual thuds against the cracking timber of the door grew louder. Voices from the other side of the portal were clearly audible. The French words left no doubt they expected to be inside momentarily. The promise of punishment was also clear.

"Go, Russell. *Now!*"

As the boy ran up the stairway to herd the villagers into several rooms to safety, Isabel turned and faced the crippled door. The oak portal shook, the solid wood cracking louder under the violent thrust of another attack. The support braces shuddered. As if struck by the same battering ram, her body jerked violently.

Her determination wavered for the briefest of moments. Had she been a fool to stay and defend Rossmoor? Here, alone, in the hall? What did she truly think a lone woman could accomplish? Was the stone and timber edifice worth her life? The lives of her people?

Her eyes swept the rich tapestries hanging from the high stone walls and the richly appointed furniture, then back up the hall, settling on her father's ornate upholstered oak chair positioned in his favorite spot near the now cold hearth. She had refused to have it moved. It was as he left it some months before.

A bittersweet smile tugged at her lips. Alefric. Her father would never permit another man to sit in his chair. Not even Geoff, who would one day be rightful lord. While the fire of life had dimmed considerably in her sire's eyes at her mother's death some six years past, he still claimed his place as lord and master over his many holdings. He would fight to the death to protect his family and his home. And at three score and nine years, sporting his Saxon glory of a full snowy white beard, he was still a force to be reckoned with.

Her heart beat faster against her breast. Had he succumbed to a Norman sword? Had Geoff? Her fun-loving brother, who had much growing up to do, had just recently been knighted. He had waved as he rode off, promising she would see him home before his November birthday.

The first of November had come and gone with no word of her sire or her brother.

"Milady!" Russell called from the top of the stairway. She turned to find him wild-eyed and pale. "More riders on the horizon!"

Hope swelled for a moment. "My father's standard?"

"Nay, more of the black horses."

Isabel's stomach plummeted to her feet. Hastily, she crossed herself several times. "Go, Russell, keep the villagers quiet."

"But—"

"Nay! Mayhap with words of peace I can stay this threat to our shire. Now go." Before Isabel moved to meet the Black Sword, she reached up behind her father's chair and wrestled down a broadsword from the wall. It rested there more as a decoration, but it was solid and a worthy adversary. It took two hands to bring the great weapon down from the stone wall. But once it was in hand, she moved to stand in the middle of the hall, the only home she had known.

Emotion gripped her heart. She could not imagine foreigners calling the hall home. Call her foolish, but how could she not stand and defend it? She flung the sword from her hands, knowing she could not effectively wield such a weapon. Instead, she fondled the jeweled hilt of the dagger hanging from her chain girdle. And so she stood. And waited.

Let them come.

Two

Prepare for entry!" Rohan called to his men. "The timber gives!"

Thorin, Ioan, Wulfson, and Rorick hurled the thick oak trunk for the death blow. Rhys, Stefan, and Warner wielded its twin. In unison, the two battering rams slammed into the door, and the timber gave way, opening with a sickening screech. Rohan spurred Mordred forward, and crashed through the crippled remnants of the Saxon's defense.

Shield raised and sword at the ready, he maneuvered the huge destrier with his legs into the wide open space of the hall. His body tensed in preparation for a full-out assault. Instead, the sight that greeted him shocked him.

A lone maid, the one who had so brashly challenged him from the tower, stood in the middle of the great hall. A broadsword at her feet, a dagger clutched tightly to her breast. His eyes instantly moved past her to the wide stairway leading to the chambers above. His men fanned out behind him on foot. Rohan urged his horse past the girl and up the wide stairway, the shod hooves making a sharp clicking sound on the stone. He moved down the narrow hallway, certain to find the villagers lying in wait to war against him. Instead, eerie silence met him. Aye, the cowards hid behind the bolted doors, allowing a mere maid to see to their rescue. Rohan sneered contemptuously.

He pulled back on the reins, and Mordred backed up. Rohan allowed the black to move at his own pace down the treacherous stone steps. The woman stood tall and proud before him.

He stopped several strides from her. If she moved, Mordred's spiked leg armor would shred her in half. His blood ran hot in his veins, and it occurred to him that to waste such beauty would be a tragedy. She was no taller than a young lad. Long golden-colored hair hung wildly around her face and shoulders, reaching down to the full swell of her hips. Eyes the uncommon color of heather in first bloom, framed by thick black lashes, stared defiantly up at him. Her skin was the color of fresh-churned cream. Her cheeks were rosy from the chill in the air and, he guessed, from his unwelcome visit. His eyes scanned lower to a full bosom that heaved in her anger. He could already feel the full swell of it beneath his hands, and the soft thrust of her hips as they met his with passion. The spoils of war were gracious this day. He would enjoy her whilst he could. For tomorrow may find him riding the horizon at his liege's call. He nodded, acknowledging her.

"Bow to your new master," he commanded in French.

"I will never bow to you," she hotly replied.

Rohan nodded and looked to his men, who flanked the walls, swords at the ready. They waited only for his word to go deeper into the hall and ferret out the hiding Saxons.

Slowly, Rohan dismounted.

Isabel's breath caught high in her throat as the devil himself strode toward her. All sound stopped, the world grinded to a halt. Tawny gold eyes glittered from behind the black metal helmet. The nose guard split his face in two, making him look all the more menacing. A crescent-shaped scar marred his chin. He was huge. Larger than any man she had come across in her nearly two score years. His shoulders were as wide as half the width of the double oak portal. Legs thick as oak supported a wide chest bearing black mail and black surcoat. She stared at the marking emblazoned on his chest. The black sword plunging through a skull, crimson drops of blood hung from the sword tip. His shield bore no coat of arms. The fate of his kind. The rumors called him bastard nephew to William's mother.

The French called him *la lame noir,* the English the Black Sword.

Her blood ran cold, turning her skin frosty. It was true. The black knight and his death squad behind him were no-torious for their skill at killing. Isabel dared look past him to the equally notorious knights, in search of the ebony giant who it was rumored could slay a dozen men with one swipe of his sword.

The Black Sword's lips twisted into a deadly smile. She felt as helpless as a mouse in the jaws of a stable cat. Yet she stood firm, refusing to back down.

"Strong words for such a small wench," he softly said, the timber of his voice chasing shivers across her skin.

"Do not underestimate me, Norman. I am well schooled in many things."

The black knight advanced toward her, his long stride eating up the small distance. He carried his mail and weapons as easily as she carried a basket of flowers. He stopped a hand span from her, towering a good two hands above her. As if she were as insignificant as the rush mats on the floor, he turned to survey the empty hall. He gave no heed to the dagger clutched in her hand. She had but to jab it at him for it to strike his black heart. She curbed the urge. Her gaze darted past him to the men behind him. Violence swirled around them like a bitter north wind across the northern moors. Should he succumb, there were more to take his place.

Battling her fear of the legendary knight so close to her, Isabel caught his scent. He smelled of leather and horse, of manly sweat. But more prominent was the scent of the kill. Her chest tightened as she realized she stared death in the face. He and his men filled the great hall with doom, and as strong as Isabel had always been, she felt small and insignificant in his presence. A hard tremble wracked her body. Her life was no longer in God's hands but Satan's.

"Call your cowardly people from their hiding places, and I will spare them."

"You cannot harm them where they are."

He looked harshly at her. "Mayhap, but I can harm their lady."

Isabel drew her dagger. An instant later, it clattered to the floor. She cried out in pain, rubbing her hand. The savage grabbed her by the front of her gown. He yanked her hard against him, and her breath rushed out from her chest from the contact. "Would that you were given to more intelligence, lady." He dropped her, and she crumpled to the hard stone floor. He motioned to his men. "Bring the ram, and ferret them out." As two men moved through the open portal and returned with a massive battering ram, the black knight said to them, "Kill any who resist."

Isabel hurried to her feet and rushed ahead of the men as they moved toward the stairway. She stretched her arms out as if she could possibly stop them. "Nay! They do not deserve your wrath!"

The knights pushed past her and up the stairway, lugging up the great piece of timber. The chamber doors would split as easily as twigs in her hand under the combined strength of the men and the battering ram. Soon the loud pounding of mailed fists on the doors echoed through the hall. The terrified screams of her people followed. Isabel turned to the knight who stood calmly watching her as his men terrorized the villagers.

Soon the hall descended into chaotic order. The knights assisted by several foot soldiers dragged down resisting villagers, the women screamed, the men, oddly, were quiet. The sound of the ram battering down more bolted doors echoed throughout the hall. Isabel stood silent and watched, ready to come to the aid of any of her subjects who looked as if the Norman sword might find a home in their belly. Her eyes scanned the terrified faces. By her calm stance against these invaders, she hoped they would gain some small comfort. It would do none of them good for her to rail against these Norman knights. She must be the calm in this storm and see where it would settle.

Isabel's eyes traced the hall before going up the stairway. One face was missing amongst the villagers and house servants. Russell's red head.

"Who lingers, damsel?" the Black Sword asked from behind her.

Isabel whirled around to face him. He stood close

enough to her that all she had to do was reach out a hand to touch his chest.

"None," she whispered.

"If you lie . . ." He stood back and turned to the assembled people, then signaled to his men to bring them closer.

As the terror-stricken people were herded tightly together and subdued, *la lame noir* turned back to Isabel. The same twisted smile he had bestowed on her earlier returned. "Now, damsel, you will bow to me in front of your people so that they accept me as their master."

Isabel gasped at his request. "I will never bow to a bastard!"

The black knight's men gasped in shock. As she spoke in French to the knight, her people had no knowledge of what she said. For that she was grateful, for they would not know what he demanded of her.

The black knight threw his head back and laughed. His hand clamped on her shoulder, his mailed fingers digging deep into her skin. In perfect English he said, "To your knees, damsel. For each moment you refuse, one head will roll across the rushes."

Her pride waged a terrible war with her fear. The Black Sword raised a hand, and one of the knights closest to her grabbed Enid. The maid shrieked. Isabel bit her lip so hard she tasted the hard copper of her own blood. She sank to her knees. But she did not bow her head. She looked harshly up at him, her eyes narrowed. Then she spit at him.

His tawny eyes flinched in surprise. And once again that terrifying smile twisted his lips.

"I will enjoy breaking your spirit, Lady Isabel." He reached down, and as he drew her up, a sharp hiss of air stirred her long hair, followed by the battle cry of a foolish boy. Isabel screamed and stepped back as an arrow struck the dark knight in the chest. When the arrow bounced off and clattered to the floor, her jaw dropped.

In the time it took to blink, the knights surged forward. The dark knight barked an order to his men to hold. The boy was his. Rohan's eyes never wavered from Russell, who stood defiant midway up the stairway. Isabel knew he would pay for the attack with his life. She could not stomach the loss. With cold, hard realization, Isabel moved directly in front of the knight's path up the stairway.

As he reached for his battle ax and hurled it across the hall, Rohan pushed her aside. Isabel stood transfixed in horror, watching the motion of the ax as it hurled handle over head toward Russell in what seemed slow motion. The boy scurried up the stairwell, where the ax bit deep into the scruff of his tunic and into the wooden cross timber pinning him there.

The furious knight rushed up the stairway, pulled the ax free from the lumber cross beam, and raised it to sever Russell's head from his body. Isabel lunged up the stairs, throwing herself across the boy's back.

"Nay! Do not kill him!"

The knight roared his anger and grabbed her with one fist by the tunic, lifting her high off her feet. A storm waged on the sharp angles of his face, but Isabel refused to cower. It was her fault Russell had taken it upon himself to defend her honor. Eye to eye with the son of Satan, Isabel raised her chin, even though she hung from his grip like a scullery rag. His blazing eyes flashed before they steeled again. "Do not interfere, wench!"

She kicked him in the shin. "I am no wench. I am the

Lady of Rossmoor. As such I have some word here. Do not harm the boy!"

Surprise sparked in his eyes. "You demand what is no longer yours. I am master here until William bids it otherwise."

"Are you so demonic that you must murder children as well as their fathers?"

The knight growled low. "I murder those who would murder me."

"He is but a boy trying to protect his mistress. Forgive him his loyalty to me."

"I forgive no one who attempts to cut short my time on this earth. He will pay the penance as those before who have tried and failed before him."

"Nay! You cannot! 'Tis murder!"

"Call it what you will, maid, but I will see it done."

He released her, and she tumbled to the steps, her back slamming hard against the wall. The knight stepped past her and started toward Russell, who had crawled to the top of the stairway. He could have run off and hidden whilst she argued for his life with the Black Sword, but Russell stood his ground. Isabel scrambled up the stairway after the knight and grabbed at his hauberk sleeve. "I beg you, spare the boy. *Spare him!*"

The knight abruptly turned, and she slammed hard into his thighs. Before she bounced off, he grabbed her by her sleeve and pulled her up against the cool hardness of his mail-covered chest. Their gazes locked. Her rage was forgotten as an earth-shattering terror gripped her.

As if she could see her future, Isabel saw it with this man in it. His naked body, glistening with sweat as he thrust himself between her thighs. Her body stilled. For it would be the price he would demand for the boy's life. She squeezed her eyes shut, knowing that as sure as she was Lady Isabel, daughter of Lord Alefric and Lady Joan, this man would see her maidenhead as the price for the boy's life.

And as foreseen, his hand slid down her back, pressing their bodies more intimately together. "What price do you put on the boy's head, damsel?"

With no hesitation, Isabel answered, "I wouldst give my life for his."

His eyes darkened, he pushed her away from him. With a slow, appraising glance, he perused her from the tip of her soft leather slippers up to her hips, then to her bosom. When his eyes rose to meet hers, he softly said, "Your life is unimportant to me." He pressed his hand to her breast. "Methinks, though, you have something beneath your gown that wouldst interest me more."

Although prepared to sacrifice herself for Russell, Isabel would not acquiesce so easily. Let her strike a bargain, but on her terms. "I have only my person, sir!"

He grinned wide, showing straight white teeth. "'Tis what I speak of."

His men hooted and caterwauled, egging him on. Isabel's resolve stiffened. "I cannot give you what you ask for, sir knight. I am promised to another. Would that my betrothed gave his permission, then I would see your request met. But he is not here."

His face darkened. Hope swelled. Isabel pressed the point. "Sir knight, wouldst you defile the lady of the manor only to have my people raise up and take arms against you to defend my honor?"

His eyes flashed. "I would kill any man or woman who raises a hand to me or my men."

"Would you steal then what is not yours to take? Are you a thief as well as a murderer?" she accused.

"I am no thief." His lips tightened, and his eyes turned frigid. His gaze scanned the room to the gathered villagers. "Does one of you call this maid your intended?" he asked in English. It didn't shock her that he spoke her tongue, though it should have.

Wide-eyed, the people of Rossmoor remained silent. The knight turned his attention back to her. "Your gallant is not here. His lands, as yours, are no doubt in the hands of my fellow Normans. Your betrothal is no longer valid, unless William commands it."

"Arlys is one of Harold's most trusted vassals. He will not lie down easily."

"Harold is no more."

"That may be, sir, but Arlys is a nobleman. He fought beside Harold at Stamford Bridge and my father and brother at Hastings. You may rethink your position here. I expect their return any day."

He grinned then. Instead of softening his face, it hardened the angles sharpening them to hewn stone. "I was there. There were few survivors at Senlac Hill. William ruled the day." His eyes swept her person, and she read contempt in the gesture. "Do you not think your kin would have returned home by now should they live?"

Her stomach fluttered as if a swarm of angry bees buzzed inside. She fought the urge to retch. Knowing he spoke the truth made Isabel solidify her resolve. Her father and her brother would not have died in vain. She squeezed her eyes shut, then opened them and peered at the man standing in front of her. He gave no care to her heart, or the hearts of other Saxons, knowing such blood was lost forever and to a bastard conqueror no less! Isabel stood resolved. Until she had proof positive that her kin lay as one with the English soil, she would do everything in her power to keep what was rightfully theirs from the hungry hands of these men of the bastard duke.

Aye, the Norse blood of her great-grandmother Signund ran as hotly through her veins as did the warrior spirit of her Saxon kin. She raised her chin a notch, refusing to give up or give this man before her the satisfaction of seeing her cower. She was Isabel of Alethorpe and the warrior sprit ran long and deep in her blood. "Do not be so sure my kin will not return. Lord Dunsworth will have your head for your trespass, as will my sire and my brother. You have no right here."

"I have every right. William is rightful king. I am Rohan du Luc, his captain." Sir Rohan turned to the gathered people of the hall. "He gives me right to claim land in his name." He turned back to Isabel. "I see no living heir here. By right of conquest, I claim this manor, its people, and all that surrounds it." He stepped closer to Isabel. "That includes you, Lady Isabel. From this moment forth, you and everything tied to this holding are William's property."

The harsh truth of his words penetrated her denial. Should Arlys magically appear, chances were their pledge of marriage would hold no weight with this new reign of terror. And so she would use any methods at hand to sway this scourge to leave them at least to a semblance of their former lives, until such time as they could permanently rid themselves of the Norman yoke.

Isabel looked past Sir Rohan to his men. Clad in black surcoats with the same insignia as their leader, over black mail with black shields and black helmets, only the glare of mercenary eyes and the sharp set of jaws clued her to the fact that they were human and not demon. A more brutal lot of knights she could not imagine. Her people cowered in fear for their lives at their feet. She looked back to du Luc. He was the wickedest of them all.

"Wouldst you rape me then?"

He shook his head slowly. "Nay, but I will take what charms lie beneath your gown in exchange for the young fool's life."

"And ruin me?"

"Never ruin, I assure you."

"I will be unfit for marriage!"

"Nay, you will be a well-schooled lover for your husband."

Heat rose in her cheeks. How dare he speak so casually of what she held so dear? Her eyes darted to Enid, who crouched at the feet of a tall knight. Her maid's eyes beseeched her. Russell was her sister's son. Isabel's heart thundered against her breast. It was no choice. She would use any means at her disposal to save the lives of each and every person in the room.

"No man will have me after a Norman's touch!"

Rohan shrugged his great shoulders. "'Tis no concern of mine."

Isabel struck him. Her hand caught the bulk of his helmet. She winced as shards of pain shot up her arm. Rohan grabbed her hand, yanking her hard against his chest. A low, menacing growl rumbled deep in his chest. "Beware, damsel, I am not above striking a woman for such insolence." He thrust her from him. He stood glaring down at her where she landed in the rushes. "What is your decision?"

Isabel scooted back away from him. "I—I give you what you ask for the life of my squire."

Rohan pointed his sword at her bosom. "What is it you give?"

Her body trembled.

He moved the tip of his sword down her chest to her belly, then lower to her calf. In a slow, unhurried motion, he raised the hem of her undergown, revealing a bare calf. "Tell me, swear your oath here in front of your people and my men. First in my tongue, then yours."

Humiliation rode her hard. She opened her mouth several times to say the words, but they would not come. When he moved his sword tip higher, revealing her thigh, Isabel gasped and choked out the words. "I will allow you trespass on my person in exchange for your oath not to harm Russell," she spit out in French.

"Now so that your people will understand."

Isabel choked out the words in English.

Rohan pushed the hem of her gown back down to her ankles and withdrew his sword. "Aye, for your man's attempt on my life, I will spare him his death in exchange for all that lies beneath your gown."

In a quick fell move, he grabbed her up to him and crushed his lips upon hers. The pain of his assault shocked her. Just as quickly, he released her. His eyes blazed beneath his helmet. He stepped away from her but warned, "I am a man of my word, damsel. Do not disappoint. When this day comes to an end, make yourself available."

The thundering sound of more riders arriving broke the heavy tension in the hall.

Three

Joan, see to these churls. Wulfson, bring me the boy. The rest of you, follow me!" Rohan called, a high note of victory in his voice. He mounted his horse and disappeared from the hall. Isabel let out a long breath she had not realized she held, glad for the moment the arrogant warrior was gone. Russell came down from his place in the landing above.

"Boy!" the one called Wulfson called in English, pointing his sword at Russell. "Come with me."

Isabel moved between the two. "Nay, he is not to be harmed."

Wulfson moved past her and grabbed Russell by the arm. "He has punishment coming."

"Nay!" Isabel screamed.

"Milady, I will go," Russell said. Her eyes scanned the boy's face. He faced her proudly. Yet there was fear in his eyes.

"But—"

"Nay, I will take what punishment the Norman will

give. I thank you for my life." He bowed and took her hands into his and kissed them. "I will regain your honor, milady, if it is the last thing I do."

Wulfson laughed. "Beware, little Saxon, there is none that can best *la lame noir* in battle or wits. Accept your punishment and be done." With those words, the knight pulled Russell through the hall toward the crippled doors.

Isabel flew after them to the courtyard. The sight that greeted her eyes was far from what she expected. New horror filled her heart. Russell's impending punishment forgotten, she stood rooted to the threshold and watched nearly half a score more of battle-ready knights and a score of foot soldiers fill the courtyard. *Les morts* had arrived *en force.* They were a terrifyingly awesome sight to behold. More black as night destriers, mounted by equally dark knights, milled around the crowded courtyard. She watched an equally ebony giant roll off his horse, falling to the rough cobblestone. A loud *whoosh* rushed from his chest as he hit, but other than that, he lay motionless.

Isabel chewed her bottom lip nervously. She looked from Rohan to the downed giant, then back to Rohan, who now moved with amazing agility for one so encumbered.

"Manhku!" du Luc called, pushing his way past armored steeds and dismounting knights. As he approached his fallen man, she lost sight of them both as the other men crowded around them. But his deep voice boomed. "What fell him?"

A deep voice answered. "'Twas a Saxon ax, Rohan. A cowardly ambush just down the way. 'Tis what kept us."

"Aye," another deep voice said, "the head is still embedded."

Confusion clouded Isabel's thoughts. A Saxon ax? How

could that be? The villagers did not possess the backbone to attack mounted knights. Indeed, many had flown to the forests at the first sign of trouble when a band of raiders struck a fortnight ago. They flew no standard or coat of arms; they appeared to be just a band of cowardly raiders bent on destroying.

Rohan knelt by his old friend's still body. He touched his hand to the thick steel ax head embedded deep in his man's thigh. Manhku moaned. Blood ran in a steady stream from the gash pooling beneath on the stone courtyard. "He needs a more experienced healing hand than what I possess," Rohan said, turning to his right hand, Thorin.

The Viking moved past Rohan. "Aye, I'll call for the healer, Rohan."

"I doubt any Saxon will step up to the chore," Rohan's deep voice countered. His men spread out as Rohan moved through them. His gaze searched for the bold and foolish Lady Isabel. He did not have to look far. She stood at the threshold of the great manor. Rohan's blood warmed at the sight of her. The morning breeze pressed the fabric of her garments against her curves, emphasizing each voluptuous turn of her. Her bare head gleamed golden under the morning sunlight. Big violet-colored eyes like a Far East sapphire stared up at him with no hint of fear. Indeed, the damsel looked as if she would take up a sword against him. Would that William had more men with her spirit; he would have taken Senlac with half the loss he had.

"Damsel, my man is gravely wounded. I would have you call for your healer."

"Maylyn fell two days past under the cowardly sword of a raider."

"Who else is skilled in the art of healing?" He watched her face cloud before clearing. For a wench so full of words, she seemed at a loss for them now. "Speak up. My man bleeds to death!"

Reluctantly, she said, "I am versed in healing skills, but I cannot swear to you I can save him."

Rohan grabbed her by the arm and dragged her behind him to the downed man.

Roughly, he pushed her to her knees. She turned a heated glare his way but then turned back to the task at hand. She moved closer to Manhku and placed a gentle hand to the gaping skin around the embedded ax head. The force of the blow had cut straight through his mail chauses. She turned grave eyes up to Rohan. "The wound is deep, and he has lost much blood. I do not know if I possess the skill to save his life."

Rohan knelt beside her. He pressed his hand to hers. "Save him, and I will grant you any request within my power."

He felt her hand tremble beneath his. And if the circumstances were different, he would lay her down then and there and give her innocent body more to tremble about than the mere touch of his hand. For the briefest of moments, he found himself captured by her big violet eyes. The delicate turn of her nostrils flared. He noticed a light spray of freckles across her nose. His eyes dipped to her parted lips. They were full and the color of a blood rose. She licked her lips, glossing them. Rohan clenched his hand tighter over her. She winced but made no sound.

"Sir knight, I am unable to work with just one hand."

Rohan moved back, releasing her.

He stood, and with his right hand on his sword, Rohan

watched her rip a strip of fabric from the hem of her shift and work it through and around his layers of clothing before securing it around Manhku's thigh just above the wound. She twisted the fabric taut, then grabbed the dagger from her belt. Before it was free of the sheath, Rohan's warrior instinct took hold of him. He slapped the weapon from her hand. Isabel yipped and shrank back from him. She turned murderous eyes up at him. Rohan snatched the dagger from the ground. The maid immediately collected herself, retracting her claws to white-knuckled fists at her side. She stood, throwing back her shoulders. As she did, the soft scent of heather swirled around his nose. She held out her hand, palm up, for the weapon. "Foolish knight! To save him, I must form a tourniquet. Give me the knife."

Their eyes clashed. And for the second time that day, something about this woman's warrior spirit moved him. He had invaded her home, taken her people, humiliated her in front of them, and here she was spitting hellfire for the return of her dagger to save his man. His eyes narrowed. Was she a witch? Or was he blinded by her beauty?

Rohan snorted at the notion. There was only one woman on this earth who held any of his affection. And she was dead.

Rohan tossed the dagger hilt over point in his hand. Once. Twice. Thrice. His gaze raked over her face, settling on her heather-colored eyes that flashed angrily at him. He flipped the dagger one last time, grabbing it by the tip of the blade before presenting it to her handle first. His other hand moved to the hilt of his broadsword. The maid ignored his threat, turning her back to him, and bent to her chore.

She twisted the strip of cloth tighter, wrapping the ends

around the dagger and tying them to form a tourniquet. She stood, wiping her hands on her tunic. "Take him into the hall. Have one of your men pull a pallet from the eaves and place it before the great hearth."

The knights hurried to obey. When Rohan assisted her to rise with a hand to her elbow, she flung his arm away. "I require nothing from you, Norman." Isabel strode as quickly as she could from the harassing knight without looking as if she were fleeing him.

Once the ebony giant was settled in front of the newly rekindled fire in the great hearth, Isabel bent to his side, checking the binding. Lifting her gaze to Rohan, she scowled. "I will need another blade, this one heated to a red glow."

She held his hard glare. A shiver kicked and bucked to run across her skin, but she refused to allow it freedom. When he continued to stare at her, unanswering, she threw her hands up. "A blade or he dies."

"Nay."

She shook her head. "Then I cannot help him, sir." She had made a motion to move past the willful knight when his arm shot out and he stopped her. His grip, though firm, neither hurt nor soothed. She looked up into his eyes. His helmet shielded most of his face, but she could see the golden flash of his eyes and the stubborn set of his scarred jaw. His continued silence stymied her. It occurred to her then that this man was not one to change his mind once a decision was made. And whilst she was certainly no supporter of saving the enemy, she could not in good conscience allow a man to die when she knew her skills might give him a chance for continued life. She looked past the stubborn knight to the man he called Thorin and scrunched her brows. On closer inspection, it appeared . . . he had only one eye!

He grinned at her stunned reaction and pulled his helmet from his head, then pushed back his cowl, exposing a full head of long golden hair. But what captivated her most was the contrast of his bronzed skin and the black leather patch that covered his right eye. A jagged scar ran from below the covering straight down his cheek to his jaw. His one good eye was a deep rich hazel color. The same crescent-shaped scar as his master's marred his chin. He was as large as Rohan and carried the weight of his profession as effortlessly.

Her gaze broke from his and touched on each of the knights standing behind him. As did their master, each one faced her unwavering, as if they had more right to be in the hall than she. She looked up to Rohan again, her gaze touching on the small half-moon scar on his chin, then back to the knights who stood closest. Several of them carried the same mark. And while many of *les morts* sported the black surcoat emblazoned with the gruesome skull, only the knights with the scarred chins bore the ones with the plunging bloody sword. These men were more than battle-scarred and battle-hardened warriors. A deep chill settled in her bones as her imagination ran rampant with vicious visions of these knights hacking away at her kinsmen on the bloody slopes of battle.

The giant moaned, disturbing the eerie silence. Isabel gave Rohan her attention once more. "I can stem the flow of blood for only so long with the tourniquet. But after I cleanse the wound, I will only be able to stanch the blood of such a deep wound with a searing. 'Tis extreme, but thread will not hold. I must do it now."

"I do not trust women in general, wench, and Saxon women less. Be sure the blade does not slip." He moved his hand to the hilt of his great sword. "Mark my words, my blade never misses her mark."

Isabel's eyes narrowed. "'Tis no surprise to me, Norman. Your duke's penchant for slaying women and children should only naturally fall to his knights."

Rohan grunted but did not deny her charge.

She moved past him to go fetch the healing herbs. He grabbed her by the arm and pulled her around to face him. "You would learn to ask permission to take leave of me, damsel."

Her hands fisted, her anger sparked at having to ask permission from this man in her own home to aid a man who when once he was up and about would no doubt kill more of her people. 'Twas not right! In her sweetest voice, Isabel asked, "May I have permission to go to the lady's solar for the healing herbs?"

By his nod he gave his permission. She sank into a deep curtsy and said, "You are too kind, sir knight." Then she spun away and hurried up the stairs, only to have Rohan's sharp command to his man infuriate her more.

"Ioan! Escort the lady to her chamber."

Isabel hurried to her task, ignoring the hulking giant behind her. As she hurried back down the stairway, she noted that many of the knights had removed their helmets but continued to fondle the hilts of their swords and keep wary eyes cast about them. Rohan remained helmeted.

Isabel settled her basket and linens by the roaring hearth. As she set about crushing herbs into a simmering cauldron of water, she looked up at the knight and asked, "How did you clog the chimney?"

His lips drew back into a terse smile. "A well-placed arrow with a thick hide riding the head."

Isabel nodded and turned back to her chore. Once the herbs had softened, she pulled a small skin from her pocket and squeezed a bitter-smelling liquid into the pot. Its pungent odor smarted the eyes. She blinked back tears but stirred it well, combining all of the ingredients. Then she soaked clean linens in the brew. From her basket, Isabel pulled a covered trencher of healing balm. She dipped a ladle into the brew and poured a small amount of it into the container, then mixed it together. Without looking up to him, she handed it to du Luc. "Hold this, and give it to me when I say."

He took it, and Isabel bent to her chore. Carefully, she cleaned the area around the wound with the steaming rag she'd dunked in the small cauldron of herbs. When she deemed the area clean, she deftly dislodged the ax head, then pulled it out. The knights moved in closer for a better look. Isabel caught her hand to her throat at the sickening sight. The wound gaped wide, the white of Manhku's bone exposed. It was a wonder he lived.

A heavy hand rested on her shoulder. "Damsel?" Rohan gruffly asked.

She shook his hand from her person and peered more closely at the wound. Her needle would serve no purpose here. Her only option was as she suspected. A searing. Swallowing hard, she grasped the dagger embedded in the embers of the hearth, dunked it into the steaming cauldron to cleanse the ash from it, then plunged it into the gaping wound.

The unconscious giant screamed out, his muscles clenched hard, but he did not pull away. Indeed, his faint deepened.

Isabel swept the flat side of the blade in and around the torn flesh. Although she had seen this procedure done several times, never had she been so close to the stench of seared flesh. It made her stomach rise and fall. She clenched her teeth hard to keep from emptying her gut. Once the task was done, she replaced the dagger in the embers and sat back on her heels.

While the wound cooled, Isabel made a poultice of dark bread and herbs. Setting it to the side, she cut away the bottom part of Manhku's leather bindings and chaussures. She folded the garments into a snug square. When she started to lift Manhku's heavy leg, du Luc leaned forward to help her. She slid the garments beneath his knee and elevated the thigh.

Praying the cauterization would hold, Isabel slowly untied the tourniquet. With each releasing turn, she held her breath tighter. When finally the cloth was limp in her hand, she let out a long sigh of relief. It held.

"The trencher, please," she said. Du Luc handed it to her. She dipped two fingers into the salve, then spread it over and around the wound. Once the wound was dressed, she molded the bread poultice to fit the gouge and gently packed it. She ripped several linens into long bandages and dressed the leg. Before setting back on her heels to survey her work, Isabel pushed back an errant lock of hair from her forehead and noticed the dampness of her skin despite the coolness in the air. She turned and warily eyed the knight who stood several feet from her.

For a long moment, he stared back, his expression hidden behind the shadow of his helmet.

"I can assure you, sir knight, at least for the moment,

you are safe from a Saxon attack. Would you remove your helmet so that I may see the face of Satan?"

"Do you fear that cast angel?"

"Nay, I fear only God."

First, he removed his mail gauntlets. His hands were bigger than they looked encased. Strong hands with long, thick fingers. Hands that killed. Her gaze rose to his face. Slowly, he removed his helmet, then pushed back his cowl to reveal thick shoulder-length hair the color of a moonless night. As he came to squat beside her, his lips quirked. The full impact of his harsh features caught Isabel off guard. Even with the ragged, angry line of a fresh scar along the left side of his face and the one that dug into his chin, she could not say him other than handsome. The aristocratic line of his sire's line was prominent in the wide set of his eyes, the high cheekbones, and the aquiline nose. The blunt cut of his chin carried the line of the scar as if it was meant to be there.

Her belly trembled as the vision of him bending her to his carnal will flashed in her head. Panic tore through her with the fury of a maelstrom. Her body stiffened as taut as a bow string. Until she remembered his oath to grant her any wish should she save his man. Letting out a long breath, Isabel quieted her nerves and turned her attention back to the giant. "Your Manhku will heal so long as he remains down and the wound has time to knit. Once healed, it will not be pretty, and he will have less strength." She pressed the back of her hand to his damp brow. "Pray he does not take the fever. The result, should he survive it, will be a wooden leg."

She struggled to stand, her legs tight from her position

on the hard stone floor. The dark knight took her elbow. She swatted his hand away and nearly fell back into the fire. Rohan grabbed her to him, laughing at her struggle to be free of him. "I do not bite, damsel."

With reluctance, Isabel allowed him to steady her and guide her upward. "'Tis not your bite that concerns me, sir."

He threw his head backed and laughed heartily. He peered at her, a genuine smile gracing his lips. Something shifted deep inside her. The transformation to his face when he smiled was staggering.

He lowered his voice, and as if they were the only two in the great hall, he said, "You may well find you would come to crave my bite."

Heat rushed to Isabel's cheeks. Her back stiffened. "I would never!"

His grin widened, and he bent close to her and whispered, "Never say never, damsel. Those words may come back to mock you."

Isabel stepped back from him, shaking her head. Her heavy hair swirled around her shoulders. "Do not speak to me of such things. 'Tis not decent."

His face closed at her words, and his eyes hardened. "Nor am I."

Her heart thundered against her chest wall. One minute he threatened her life, then the next he made her promises of pleasure? His next action stymied her more. As if she were queen of the realm, he stepped back and bowed ever so chivalrously.

"Lady Isabel, 'twould appear my man's life has been spared due to your experienced hand. What prize do you choose for the life you saved?"

She smiled sweetly and curtsied. "Why, sir knight, my maidenhead, of course."

Rohan's men roared uproariously behind him. Thorin slapped him hard on the back. "Hah, Rohan, the lady does best you at your own game."

With great satisfaction, Isabel watched the dark knight's eyes narrow, the golden sparks barely discernible beneath his stormy brow. She could see him mulling over her demand. He bowed again and grinned wide. "'Tis a price worth paying for my man's life. No woman's maidenhead is worth more."

The smile that played on her lips faded. She suspected this knight, Sir Rohan du Luc, did not have much regard for the fairer sex. She wondered why, then caught herself. It mattered not, for she did not care. Instead, she curtsied and asked, "Sir knight, may I be excused to see to the business of running this keep?"

He nodded. "Aye, prepare a feast. For this eve we celebrate!"

She scowled. "Winter comes, the stores—"

"Are full to bursting. My men will hunt and fill the smokehouse more."

Isabel curtsied again, and this time she did not choose to hide her contempt. "Of course, Sir Rohan, a feast for you to celebrate the blood on your sword."

She turned and had begun to walk away when he called out to her. "Lady Isabel?"

She halted in her tracks, her body tense. Setting her jaw, she turned to face him. He stood rubbing his chest as if a wound bothered him. But his wide grin belied any pain. Indeed, his sprits suddenly soared with the eagles. She cocked a brow in question.

"Before the meal, have a bath prepared in the lord's chamber, and make yourself available to bathe me. I shall be clean for this evening's sport."

Isabel opened her mouth to argue but decided not to. He had made his promise for all of his men as witness. He would not retract it. She swallowed hard. At least, she hoped not.

Four

Before Isabel set about seeing to preparations for the evening feast, she saw to soothing the fears of her people. 'Twas a difficult chore, for she noted that no matter where she went in the hall, a hulking shadow was close by. If it was not one of the menacing knights, it was one of Rohan's foot soldiers. When she ventured out to the courtyard, she stopped short when she saw Russell secured to the whipping post near the stable. He'd been stripped down to his trews. As she ran to him, he looked up and warned her off with angry eyes. "Nay, milady, let me take my punishment!"

"Russell," she pleaded.

He dropped his eyes to the ground. "Milady, leave me my pride. I can survive his hand. Stand back."

Isabel looked up to see Rohan stride her way, a long whip in hand. Furious, she lashed out at him. "How dare you harm a boy for protecting his mistress?"

Rohan strode past her. Isabel followed, grabbing at the

handle of the whip. Rohan turned on her. "You overstep your bounds. Be gone."

Isabel glanced at Russell, who hung his head, humiliated. She did not understand Russell's wish for her to let him be. He seemed almost to welcome the lash. Isabel shook her head and backed away. "After your senseless torture, bring him to me to salt his wounds." She turned and ran to the hall and up to her chamber, where she slammed the door and threw the bolt.

Then she paced the thick woven carpet. The sharp crack of the whip followed by a boy's cry of pain stopped her in mid-step. Unable to help it, Isabel rushed to the slitted window, pushed the heavy tapestry aside, and unhinged the shutters. She had a clear view of the courtyard. A crimson slash marked Russell's fair back. Rohan raised his arm and brought it down again. Russell cried out and pulled against the leather tethers holding him secure against the thick pole. Rohan's arm rose and fell several more times, reducing Russell's cries to gurgling moans. Isabel tore herself from the window, threw the bolt to her door, and rushed down the great stairway out to the courtyard. Rohan's arm rose, and as he brought it down, she lunged at him. "Nay! You have done enough! Leave him some flesh!"

Rohan flung her off. Drops of blood flew from his hand, spattering onto her face. He glowered down at her. "What do you offer this time, damsel?"

Isabel moved to where Russell hung, his back a bloody pulp. "Have mercy on the child. Show you have some decency."

"I have none." Rohan tossed the whip down to the ground, then nodded to one of his men who stood nearby.

"Take him to the stable." He looked down at Isabel. "Tend to him if you must, but see also that my bath is ready."

Isabel hurried to fetch her herbs as Russell was cut down. As she grasped the basket from where she had left it by the ebony giant, she knelt down to him and felt his brow. Warm. But not overly so. Enid came to her, twisting her hands in worry. "Milady? How fares the boy?"

"He will survive; it could have been worse. Have Bert fill a tub for the bastard knight."

"In the lord's chamber, milady?"

"Nay—"

"Aye, it will be mine thus forth," Rohan said from the doorway. She noticed the carpenter had begun to repair it.

"'Tis my father's, and he will expect to use it upon his return!"

Rohan moved toward her, removing his gauntlets as he did. Russell's blood clung to the metal circlets. "Your father is not coming back."

Isabel gasped, her heart tightening at such cruel words. "You have no heart."

He nodded. "Aye, make no mistake of it." He looked past her to Enid. "See to my bath."

Isabel moved past him as Enid hurried to her task. Rohan grabbed Isabel's arm, spinning her around to face him. "See to your squire, but make haste, I expect you to tend me."

Rohan followed the maid's lithe form as she hurried past him into the courtyard. His blood warmed, coursing through his veins. Each time he thought of the Lady Isabel warm and naked beneath him, his cock swelled. He had long ago tired of camp whores. In truth, he had only one reason to seek out a woman. He'd never taken a regular leman. His eyes narrowed as Isabel vanished from view. Mayhap it was time to change that. He doubted he would tire of the wench in one night, and the long English winters were bitter. Though there wasn't much to her, she would be a warm body to spend the long nights with. Besides, when there were no enemies to squelch, he could think of only one sport that gave him the same pleasure as his lust for the fight. Aye, it would be his pleasure to warm the cool heart of the maid Isabel.

He frowned. She was not only beautiful but a wily one. He'd have wagered his horse and mail she would have asked that he not punish the boy for his trespass. Not ask for her maidenhead to remain intact. Rohan smiled then. Ah, but while he promised her her maidenhead, it was not what she swore an oath to him for.

He rubbed his chest where the brand of the sword bothered him still. After all these years, he had not become accustomed to the hard scar, a constant reminder of that pit of a prison.

Rohan strode through the partial portal, glad to see the carpenter making quick progress on the repair. A new permanent door would begin the next morn. He stood at the top step of the large hall known as Rossmoor. A fitting name. Its rich tapestries and fine furnishings pleased him.

Rossmoor was no hovel. The grand manor sat on a slight mound looking down into an open meadow surrounded by thick forest. The village tucked against the bailey walls just down the way once teemed with expert artisans and craftsmen. The granaries were full to bursting, the smokehouse laden with an assortment of meats. The stable boasted several fine mares that would strengthen his line. Rohan's gaze traveled to the lord's table and the great lord's chair positioned by the roaring hearth. If his luck held and William was true to his oath to reward Rohan's unwavering loyalty these past six years, he would one day sit upon it. His blood quickened. Aye, he could see himself as permanent lord and master here. Next his gaze touched on his trusted left arm, Manhku. For Thorin was his right.

He stepped down the next stair, then moved slowly across the woven rush mats. Several hounds sniffed near the kitchen entrance, looking for a morsel. Rohan frowned and cast a gaze about the hall. Nary a servant in sight. No doubt, they huddled in fear in a dark corner.

He'd have a word with the lady instructing them to be more visible. They were useless to him if he could not utilize them. Rohan stopped and squatted next to Manhku. The African slept fitfully. A soft sheen of sweat dotted his brow.

The wound was bad, he admitted, but Manhku had suffered worse. They all had. He would survive to see many more winters. Rohan stood and let the warmth of the fire infiltrate his tired muscles. They had ridden nonstop since Senlac Hill, spending no more than two days at each shire they claimed in William's name.

Rossmoor would see them settled until he received word from his liege that he should join his train in Westminster. He welcomed the respite.

Rohan tilted his head back and closed his eyes. As oft happened, the vision of A'isha sprang into his mind's eye. Their angel of mercy in Jubb. Had she not defied her brother and her father and sacrificed her life for theirs, he and his Blood Swords would all be naught but dust. He owed her much he could never repay.

He had turned back for her. But the bats. They swarmed her in a dark, enveloping death spiral. He'd shouted for them to disperse. But they turned on him, and he had only one course of action. And so he moved as fast as his legs would carry him to the beckoning daylight—and freedom.

Rohan opened his eyes and stared into the fire. A braver woman he had never met. He would never forget her sacrifice for him.

"Sir du Luc?" a timid woman's voice squeaked from behind him.

Rohan turned weary eyes on the maid Enid and scowled. She bobbed her head and stared at the floor. "Your bath is ready, sir."

"Fetch your lady posthaste. Tell her if she dallies, I will see her strung out on the whipping post next."

Enid gasped, bobbed again, and took off toward the portal. Rohan moved slowly up the stairway. With no eyes upon him, he gave way to the soreness in his right leg. Another constant reminder of his time in that cesspit of a prison.

As if she were being led to the gibbet, Isabel walked slowly up the stone stairway leading to the lord's chamber. She pushed the heavy door open and caught her breath at the sight that greeted her. Rohan stood as naked as the day he was born before the firelight of the hearth. His back was to her, and she could not help but admire his manly shape. His buttocks were rounded and hard, the muscles flexing with his movement. His long legs were equally muscled and finely proportioned. His wide shoulders tapered into a narrow waist. Her eyes traveled down his buttocks to his legs and feet. She frowned. A reddish-purple scar marred the back of his right hock.

Steam rose from the copper tub positioned before the fire. Rohan turned angry eyes on her. "You tarry at my expense, wench. My bath grows cold."

Isabel kept her eyes focused on his chest. When she did, a gasp caught her by surprise. Pressing her hand to her lips, she could not help but stare at the large scar marring his skin. As if a burning sword had been pressed into his chest. An inkling of compassion stirred in her chest for this man. For to survive such a terrible injury, he must have suffered unbearable pain. Quickly, Isabel settled her emotions, then, as if she saw such brutal scars every day, she said, "The water still steams. Stop your complaining, and step in."

He raised a dark brow, but she had gathered her composure and was ready to see his bath through. Gathering up a linen towel and a bar of sandalwood soap from the bench beside the cabinet, Isabel noticed several saddle bags and a small trunk set on the floor at the foot of the large four-poster bed. By their presence she knew he meant to stay. 'Twas no wonder. One thing this Norman could not say was that Rossmoor lacked any creature comforts. The hall was renowned for its hospitality and luxurious amenities.

As Rohan sank into the warm water, he let out a long sigh. "By God, this feels good."

Isabel moved to the side of the tub and dipped the cloth into the water, then lathered it with soap. She wrinkled her nose. "By the stench of you, it has been a score of winters since last you bathed."

He settled back against the high rim and closed his eyes. "Only half a score."

Isabel decided not to engage him in further conversation. The sooner he was bathed, the sooner she could leave him. He made her uncomfortable in a way she was not used to. When he'd turned to face her, she caught the heat in his eyes. And she knew he would find a way to get her into his bed.

But try as she may to keep her mouth closed, curiosity got the best of Isabel. She traced a soapy finger from his throat down the indentation of the scar. "How came you by this?"

Rohan's body stiffened at the question. His eyes remained closed, and he did not answer. Feeling most uncomfortable, Isabel chose not to push.

She rubbed the soap into his head, digging her fingers into his thick hair. She poured clear water from the pitcher on the bench and rinsed. Next, she lathered the rag and rubbed it into his chest, mashing the fine hair there. When she moved to soap his arm, he grabbed her hand. She yipped and pulled back.

Rohan opened his eyes. His gaze held hers. "Not so fast, damsel. I would enjoy this moment. It has been a long time since one so fair as you has rinsed the stench of battle from my body."

Isabel lowered her eyes. His intense gaze discomfited her. "I have matters that need my attention," she softly said.

He raised her chin with two fingers, forcing her to look at him. "The only matter you need to see to is me. Should you make haste, I will have you repeat the bath until I am satisfied."

Isabel bit back an angry retort but made no move to continue the chore. His fingers tightened around her wrist, and he pulled her toward him. She resisted, but he pulled harder until she was leaning across the tub nearly in his lap. Her breasts dipped into the warm water. She recoiled, knowing the wetness would show every detail of the swell of her bosom. He pulled her closer so that now to gain balance, she had to rest her left hand on the edge of the tub. His lips hovered only inches from hers. His warm breath caressed her cheek. "I own you, damsel."

"Nay," she murmured, their breaths mingling.

He trailed a wet fingertip across the high swell of her breasts. Her body shivered at the touch. Heat rose in her cheeks.

"Aye, I do, and you would do well to know it." He pressed his open palm to her left breast and softly squeezed. She closed her eyes as shame flooded her. But worse than that, in the very deepest recesses of her body, a spark of pleasure ignited between her thighs. The sensation was foreign, yet it intrigued her more than she would ever admit. Confusion reigned in her head. Arlys had touched her thus, and she had felt nothing but irritated. His kisses left her cold. Yet he was gentle. Not like this barbarian.

"Not only are you a murderer, but you are not a man of his oath."

Rohan would not be waylaid. "Your mocking words do not affect me, damsel. I will do as I please. And at the moment"—he pressed his lips to her throat and pulled her closer, as she stiffened, bracing her arm against the pull of him—"you please me."

"You gave me your word. You would leave me intact," she breathed, trying hard to ignore the way his lips branded her skin and the warm flush cascading through her because of it.

"Aye, I gave you my word not to take your maidenhead." He pulled back from her, and his tawny eyes sparkled. Isabel shivered. He was going to trick her. "But you swore before my men and your people to allow me to explore what lies beneath your gown. And there is more than your maidenhead at stake."

Isabel cried out and pushed back, shoving the linen into his face. He sputtered as the soap burned his eyes. She scurried to the door, intending to leave the chamber, but his harsh words stopped her. "Break your oath to me, Isabel, and see mine broken as well." He grabbed the pitcher of rinsing water from the bench and poured some over his face. When he opened his eyes, they were red, but she could see he was free of pain. "Now, get thee back here and complete my bath."

Isabel knew a deep-seated anger she had never felt toward another human being. Not even Arlys's treacherous cousin Deidre, who took every opportunity to flirt with another's intended.

Isabel set her jaw and returned to the task. She ignored the smooth thickness of Rohan's muscular chest and the way his arms rippled with strength when he brushed back his thick raven-colored hair from his face. She tried to forget the odd sensations his touch stirred. She set her mind instead on the matter at hand. Show a guest, albeit an unwelcome one, the hospitality decorum dictated, then be gone from the room.

"How is it that such a removed shire is so rich in population and appointments?" Rohan asked.

Glad for conversation that did not center on her or their respective oaths, Isabel eagerly answered. "The population has dwindled since the landing of your duke. But the land is fertile, the rivers require tolls to pass, and they teem with fish. My father's stables boast a bloodline coveted by kings and emperors. But more, since my great-grandfather's time, Rossmoor has traded vigorously with the Easterners." She smiled. "And the Vikings. 'Tis how he acquired my great-grandmother Signund."

"He traded for her?"

"Not quite. He borrowed her with no intention of returning her."

"Did not her father demand payment for a stolen daughter?"

Isabel laughed. She felt his body tense at the sound but continued to run the linen across his chest into a rich lather. "Nay, he stole her from a beached dragon ship laden with Danegold. He fled with her and the treasure, saying it was dower money, since he had no use for Nordic lands. He built Rossmoor with his angry in-laws in mind. Until your arrival, this hall has not been breached."

Rohan took the opportunity to remind her of their arrangement. "Aye, and I wager your thighs have not been breached, either."

Isabel sat back and glared at him. "Sir, I am a lady gentle born. Could you not curb your crudeness?"

He shrugged. "'Tis what I am. Crude."

"Does not make it right. If you know these things are offensive, then why not work to change them?"

Rohan sat up in the tub and turned his back to her. "I tire of this conversation. Finish the bath so that I may join my men and hear less waspish words."

Isabel lathered up the linen and scrubbed his wide back. "I am not waspish."

"I said your words were. There is a difference."

From his anxious movements, Isabel knew he was eager to be gone from the tub. Quickly, she rinsed him. As he stood, she wrapped him in a linen towel. He took it from her hands and tied it around his waist. He looked up at the colorful banners adorning the high walls bearing her father's standard. A golden hawk clutching a Viking ax.

"Have these banners bearing your father's coat of arms removed from these walls. And move your possessions in here."

Did he say to move her belongings to this room? "But—"

He turned to face her. "Your sire is no longer lord here."

"Should he swear to the duke?"

"William has no trust of you warring Saxons. He would put his own men, men he can trust, in the power positions."

"What of my brother? He could wed with a Norman. 'Tis what my father did."

Rohan smiled and continued to dry himself. The damp linen clung to his muscular body. Isabel kept her eyes pinned to a spot on the wall behind him. Twice now she had almost dared to look at his full front. "That would explain your knowledge of my tongue."

"I have people in Normandy. Would that they knew a bastard claims their kin's land they would surely raise arms against you! I will petition William myself for leniency."

"Feel free, damsel, but you will lose." He dropped the damp cloth to the floor, and lord forgive her, but she could not help the drop of her gaze to what made him a man. She stepped back and pressed her hand to her mouth. Even dormant as it was, it was manlier than those she had seen before. And she had seen plenty. Not that she chose to, but as the lady of the manor, she had bathed dozens of men over the years, and more than a few had made it difficult for her not to look.

This man stood in all of his naked glory before her like

a bronze statue of a mythical god. Her mouth went dry.
She backed away toward the door. "Sir knight, I beg to be
excused. The servants await my commands for setting the
feast."

She didn't wait for him to give permission. Isabel threw
the bolt and hurried through the doorway, never looking
back.

To her surprise and disappointment, the hall was filled
with many of Rohan's men. The others, she was sure, were
out patrolling the land's edge. Deep voices rose to the rafters, and from the looks of it, someone had discovered the
wine cellar. Several barrels of Aquitaine wine that were set
aside for only the most special occasions had been tapped.
'Tis a celebration, Isabel thought wryly. For the invaders.

Mouthwatering aromas drifted from the kitchens.
Servants hurried about setting the tables. Lacking several
servants at the moment, Isabel hurried to the kitchen to
oversee the preparations. Finding the room bustling with
activity under the capable hands of Astrid, the unchal-
lenged lady of the kitchens, despite the lack of hands,
Isabel nodded in praise. The Normans might think Saxons
lacked courage, and mayhap some did, but her people were
of hearty industrious stock, and even under duress they
found a way to go forward with the day's chores. Seeing
that she was not needed, Isabel looked down at her damp,
soiled gown. 'Twould not do for the feast. Quietly, she
moved from the bustling kitchens up the back stairway to
find her maid.

Rohan stepped down into the great hall, feeling rested and
clean. Since his days lying in the urine- and feces-infested
mud on the floors of Jubb, he had become an aesthete in

his desire to be free of grime. It was the same for the rest of his brothers. They bathed regularly and vigorously. And sometimes, Rohan thought, it was not enough to erase the stench of death. His eyes scanned the hall, looking for the Lady Isabel. He frowned. She was nowhere to be found. An unexpected stab of loss sparred with his anger at her disregard for his authority. It mattered not. He would find her and set a man to guard her. Putting her from his mind since she did naught but cause him ire, Rohan continued to scan the room, his gaze landing on the seven knights who since that time in Iberia six years ago moved together as one with him. They were never far from one another. As they were now. They'd pulled the lord's table down from its spot of prominence and pushed it close to the blazing hearth where their fallen brother lay.

"Rohan!" Thorin called, raising a goblet of wine. "Come enjoy the spoils of our labor!"

Ioan, Rorick, Warner, Stefan, Wulfson, and Rhys raised their overflowing cups. "Aye, to Rohan, may William reward your efforts with this most worthy of fiefs!" Warner called. "And if you should find the Lady Isabel's tongue too sharp for your mail?" Warner drained his cup, the wine flowing down his chin to his surcoat. He slammed the empty cup down and challenged Rohan with his grin. "I'll wager she will find my prick more to her liking!"

Rohan scowled. Of all of them, Warner was the clear cock of the walk. He liked to prattle of love to maids and matrons alike. They seemed to find his pretty words endearing, for he had more bastards than the rest of them combined to his credit.

Rohan strode to the table and took the proffered cup of wine from Thorin. "Warner, should the maid be able to find the prick you boast so fondly of, I will stand back."

The table laughed uproariously while Warner scowled. Rohan slapped him hard on the back. "Come now, my friend, we know of no fewer than half a score of bastards you've left the camp whores with."

Warner grinned and filled his cup. "Aye, but girls all of them!"

"Warner," Ioan said, "you have not yet found the womb worthy of your man seed."

"'Tis a curse we are all afflicted with!" Rorick cried out, and raised his cup but held it high, not drinking from it. His eyes widened, and a small smile twisted his lips. His gaze lay unwavering past Rohan's shoulder. He noticed his men had all stopped their bantering and looked past him. Slowly, Rohan turned.

His body jerked as if he had been struck by a bolt of lightning. Something in his gut did a slow, hard roll. His mouth went dry, and he felt his rod rise against his thigh.

Her beauty rivaled the sun's brightness. And with the realization of how profoundly she physically affected him, Rohan scowled.

Isabel had bathed, and the plainer clothes of her day wear were no more. Now she was richly gowned in a deep crimson undergown with gold embroidery at the hem. Her kirtle was a rich purple and gold velvet with what looked to be jewels sewn into the sleeves. A rich girdle of gold filigree accentuated the full flare of her hips. Her jewel-encrusted dagger hung from it. But what startled him most was her face. Her creamy skin flushed pink, her big violet-colored eyes sparkled even from a distance, and her full lips—Rohan swallowed hard—her full red lips parted as if she waited to be kissed. Her thick golden hair, like fine gossamer, had been brushed to shimmering brightness. It hung long about her shoulders but for two delicate braids entwined with amethyst-colored ribbon framing her face. The edges of the ribbon swirled about her bosom, accentuating the full swell of it. Instead of a veil cloth on her head, she wore a slender woven gold and silver circlet, the form of a hawk crowning it.

When Rohan made no move toward her, Rorick pushed him aside and moved to meet Isabel halfway up the stairway. He bowed deeply, taking her hand. "Damsel, you gift my sight with such loveliness I know not if my mortal self can bear the beauty of such a goddess."

Rohan rolled his eyes and took another long draught of his wine, all while keeping a watchful eye on his man as he prattled on like an ass to the lady he planned to bed.

Isabel smiled, her eyes only for the Scot. "Thank you, sir?"

He bowed again. "Forgive me my manners, Lady Isabel. I am but a battle-weary soldier who has spent little time in court." He brought both of her hands to his lips and looked up to her. "I am Sir Rorick of Moray but more recently knight of Duke William. I am your servant."

" 'Tis my pleasure to meet you, Sir Rorick. I pray your chivalry remains intact. 'Tis such a welcome respite to your brethren's loutish manners."

Rorick placed her arm in the crook of his and led her down the stairway with great care. He looked up at Rohan and grinned. Rohan scowled. When Stefan and Warner made a great show of placing the lord's chair at their table for the lady to be seated in, Rohan had the urge to stick his booted foot up their arses.

"Nay, kind sirs, 'tis my father's chair. Set it aside for his return."

Rohan slammed his goblet down on the table and turned to Isabel. Rorick continued to smile and to pat the lady's hand still resting on his forearm. "Your sire, should he return, will find himself seated with the lesser nobles." Rohan picked up the great chair and shoved it back against the hearth, nearly missing Manhku. He pointed to the spot beside where he stood and ground out, "Now, see thyself perched thus. I tire of this prattle. Call for the food!"

Rorick's good mood fled with Rohan's words. He set the Lady Isabel down and gave his friend a sharp glare. "I must apologize for *Sir* Rohan's poor manners. He was raised in a stable."

Rohan grumbled and poured more wine. He would not allow his man's flirting with a woman he had no intention of keeping to sour his victorious campaign. He caught Isabel's harsh stare and smiled. He raised his cup and turned to his men. "To the conquering of Rossmoor." The rafters shook from the boom of cheers. Rohan turned to look expectantly at Isabel. "And to breaching the shrew's thighs!" While the cheers had been loud before, they nearly split the timbers from the percussion the second time around.

Rohan drank heartily and watched Isabel's cheeks redden. Aye, the maid could play him false in public. But she would see each night who held the power. His blood warmed, and he rubbed his chest where the wound ached. Aye, taming the Lady Isabel would be a welcome repast for the long winter nights ahead.

Five

Isabel stared pensively into her wine. She wanted to tell the arrogant knight he could not command her like some common house servant, but she caught the eyes of several villagers attending to chores. Winston stacked more logs by the hearth, Lyn lit candles along the lower tables, Garth leashed the hounds, and several others carried out heavy trays laden with food.

Steaming platters of roasted boar, fowl, and venison along with poached fish fresh from the river graced the table. Sweetmeats and late vegetables added to the feast. Yet Isabel's hunger waned as her logical mind parried with her emotions. She struggled to come up with a viable means to deal with Rohan du Luc.

If she continued to squabble over small things such as taking a seat next to this unwanted and temporary guest, she would lose precious ground and erode whatever small grip of sanity her people held. So, she would concede the smaller skirmishes. For on the morrow, she might need all of her might to fight a much larger battle.

Isabel looked down at Rohan's large hand holding the goblet of wine, nearly covering the gold and silver chalice. Her body warmed as she thought of his fingers touching her. Her gaze rose to find his tawny eyes steadily watching her.

"Do you think of our time later this eve as I do?"

Isabel's cheeks warmed, and she looked away, not trusting her voice.

"Here, damsel, drink. The wine, as you know, is exceptional. Mayhap it will settle you," Rohan offered, sliding his full cup under her nose.

The last thing she wanted to do was drink from the same cup as he. But she had no choice. It would be a battle she would lose, for if she pressed the point, she would go without drink, and at the moment, she had a strong desire for the rich burgundy wine.

She turned the cup halfway around, making a point of sipping from the opposite side from his. The insult was subtle, but she knew she struck a chord when he stiffened beside her.

"Your insult is well taken, and be sure, 'tis no matter to me, damsel. After you, there will be another, then another after her."

Isabel ignored his jibe and turned her attention to Rorick, who sat to her right. His deep blue eyes sparkled in mischievous humor. She noticed he had the same half-moon scar on his chin as did Rohan. Her eyes moved to Wulfson and the one called Ioan, then to several others. The eight knights sitting at the lord's table all possessed the same scar and the same crimson sword plunging through the skull.

"How came you all by the scars on your chins, and why

do only those of you with the scars bear the blood sword on your surcoats, Sir Rorick?" Isabel softly asked.

The fire in his eyes dimmed for a brief moment before it rekindled. He took her right hand and brought it to his lips. " 'Tis an ugly story not fit for a lady's ears."

"Isabel," Rohan said from her other side, "the trencher is full, and I have cut your meat. Sup. You will need your strength for later."

Isabel turned from Rorick, who chuckled, and elbowed Rohan hard in the ribs. He let out a soft *whuff.* "You have the manners of a boar."

"Aye, and you have the temper of a shrew."

Isabel noticed that he had indeed cut the meat. And from the looks of it, the choice pieces he placed on her side. Though her stomach gnawed in emptiness, she felt no hunger. Instead, a deep fatigue took hold of her. Her coming days would test her character and try her patience more than at any other time in her life. She took another deep drink of the wine and set the goblet down. Rohan grinned and filled it, then turned the lip of the cup to where she had drunk and pressed his lips to it. He looked at her over the rim. When he set the cup down, he softly said, "I have no such reservation placing my lips to yours, damsel." He smiled across the rim. "And if we have the time, you will learn to crave my touch."

Isabel set her hands in her lap, tightly clasping them together. The pain of her gesture made her wince. Rohan speared a large piece of venison with his table knife and bit into it. He chewed thoughtfully and pondered her. After he swallowed, he lowered his lips to her ear and whispered, " 'Tis only a temporary meeting of flesh, damsel. There is no evidence left. If it pleases you to say you have not been breached, so be it. 'Twill be our little secret."

Isabel set her jaw and closed her eyes. The warmth of his breath against her ear startled her in its intensity. As he softly spoke, he made her body react in a way she was not comfortable with. But his words were enough to cool her ardor. For he spoke of something she held precious.

"The proof will be on the sheets on my wedding morning."

"Not all maids bleed."

Her cheeks warmed to hot. She turned to him, beseeching. "Sir, please, such a topic is too personal to speak of."

He raised his hand to her, and she flinched, moving so far from him she bumped into Rorick, who was more than happy to right her.

Rohan's eyes narrowed. But he continued to move toward her. In a surprisingly gentle action, he rubbed his knuckles against her cheek. "I will keep my oath to you, damsel. While I look forward to pleasuring myself with your body, I will not breach that thin piece of skin you cling to so churlishly. You will remain intact for your husband."

"Rohan," Wulfson called from across the table, "what have you planned for the morrow?"

Rohan took a long draught from his cup. "When we slake our hunger, we will gather and speak of the morrow. Until then?" Rohan glanced over to a serving maid, who was more than buxom and who eyed him coquettishly from below dark lashes. "Enjoy the fruits of our labor."

Wulfson laughed and took a long pull from his cup. When the girl, Lyn, came around, he snaked an arm around her waist and pulled her across his lap. She squealed and made as if to be gone from him, but her eyes smiled. "A wench to warm my pallet this eve?" He poured half of his cup of wine into the deep valley between her breasts and drank deeply from her. The table erupted in cheers as Wulfson lapped up every drop of wine covering her full breasts.

Isabel turned her head away, not wanting to watch what would undoubtedly be her turn next. She just prayed Sir Rohan would have more courtesy for her and ravage her behind closed doors.

It seemed that with Lyn's ravishment more girls appeared and found the knights to their liking. Rohan called for another barrel of wine to be tapped, music erupted, and the bells from dancing girls chimed in tempo to the lute and the pipers' tune.

The hall came alive as the knights imbibed the hospitality of Rossmoor. When Sarah, the daughter of Edwin, her father's deceased gamekeeper, came forward, dancing in a tempting way before Rohan, Isabel lost all yearning for food. Rohan turned from Isabel and relaxed back into his chair. She could not see his face, but from the smiles on Sarah's winsome lips and the way she pressed her bosom in his face, she knew the knight enjoyed the show. When Sarah pressed her hands to Rohan's knees and pushed them apart, then moved between them and continued to dance like Salome, Isabel felt as if she would be sick. How could Sarah be so brazen? Isabel looked around to the other village girls. Some of them were recently widowed. Were they so desperate to survive that they would prostitute themselves to these invaders?

Isabel swallowed hard. Had she not done the same? Had she set the example for these girls? Sacrificing her body for Russell's life? Did they feel they must sacrifice themselves as well to stay alive?

A wave of self-revulsion crashed through her. Her stomach rose as if rancid meat festered there. Pressing her hand to her belly, Isabel turned to Rorick, who was the only man at the table not besotted with one of the village girls. She placed her hand on his forearm. "Sir knight, I don't feel well, would you—" Before she could utter another word, he pulled her up.

"Say no more, milady. The fresh air will clear you." He led her to the now repaired front portal and opened it just enough to let her slip through. She saw him turn to look back into the hall, no doubt at Rohan. Rorick's face hardened. Isabel turned and caught her breath. Rohan stood tall, dark, and angry at his chair, poor Sarah desperately gyrating to regain his lost attention.

"I do not wish to bring Rohan's wrath upon you," Isabel offered.

Rorick threw his head back and laughed heartily. "Rohan's wrath? Nay, I fear it not."

He pushed her through and closed the door soundly behind them.

Isabel inhaled deeply, the chilled air hurting the inside of her chest, yet it was cleansing. "Thank you," she softly said. She noted that the torches were lit and burned brightly along the stone walls of the manor. There were several staked torches lighting the way through the courtyard to the bailey and farther beyond to the village. Several shadowed sentinels patrolled the premise.

"More ride warding off those who might try to take from Rohan what he has won this day."

"'Tis not right!"

" 'Tis war, Lady Isabel."

" 'Tis not *my* war." But she knew her words rang false. Alefric had been a staunch supporter of not only Edward but Harold. "My father will—"

"Nay, Lady Isabel. Your sire's time is up here. Your brother's as well. William will be crowned king, and everything will change. 'Tis best to digest it now so that you do not continue to feel as you do."

"But—?"

"If your sire lives and if he is smart, he will go to William and pledge his fealty. William is a harsh man, a warrior at heart, but he is also just. Mayhap he will allow your sire some claim."

"But what of my people? What of me?"

He looked down at her, and for such a fierce knight, he gave her a most compassionate expression. "Your people, should they serve the new lord here, will prosper." He touched a golden curl that blew toward him under the strength of the breeze. He brought it to his nose and inhaled. "You, my lady, will find a husband worthy of your bloodline and live to give him many children."

"I have no dower. I will come to him soiled! What man of means would want a bride such as myself?" The contempt and anger in her voice nearly strangled her. She faced Rorick full on. "Is your master so rigid he cannot see he ruins my chance for any husband?"

"Aye, Rohan is unbending. And with reason."

"Rorick, the men call for you," Rohan said from the threshold. Isabel's stomach lurched at his voice. His eyes burned bright under the torchlight. His jaw was set, and his brows drew ominously low over his eyes.

Rorick turned and bowed. "Good eve, Lady Isabel."

Isabel nodded. "Good eve, kind sir."

As the door closed behind Rorick, Isabel glared up at Rohan. He stood rigid and still, glowering down at her with his hands behind his back.

"You will find no ally among my men. Our bond is unbreakable."

"'Twould seem you are all the same, yet your man Rorick is not the savage you are."

Rohan smiled, and she shivered. It was a smile that said that whatever she thought of Rorick, she was far off the mark. "Does he rape, pillage, and plunder as you do? And what binds you? The scar? As boys, did you play at blood brothers?" She said it contemptuously, demeaning their tie.

Rohan's jaw flexed. "Mock what you don't understand. It matters not to me."

Isabel felt an infuriating urge to strike him. Instead, she started for the stable. "I must see to Russell."

When he made no move to follow her, Isabel picked up her step. She was met halfway by Thomas. "Milady, allow me to escort you," he said.

Isabel started at his appearance but nodded. They both looked over their shoulders to see Rohan striding their way. "He watches you like a hawk watches a mouse, milady. I have news of Arlys."

Isabel's heart lurched in her chest. "He *does* live?"

"Aye, and he prepares to free us from the Norman yoke."

As Isabel entered the stable, she was met by one of Rohan's men. Not a knight but a foot soldier. "I am Lady Isabel, here to see to my man. Let me pass."

The soldier looked past her to where she was sure Rohan stood. She fisted her hands. It infuriated her that she had to ask permission to see her people.

The guard nodded, and Isabel hurried to where Russell lay in the straw. Thomas disappeared.

She knelt beside the sleeping boy and touched a gentle hand to his back. He flinched and turned his head to face her. "Milady," he moaned. "It burns like fire."

She shushed him. "I'll cleanse the area again, then apply more balm. 'Twill soothe the fire."

She set about her chore, and after she pressed the cool compresses to his back, Russell said, "Already the heat vanishes."

"The balm will be better." As she smoothed it over his raw skin, he tried to rise on his elbows. "Stay quiet, Russell, you will need your strength."

"Lady, forgive me for missing my mark."

"You did not. The problem lay with your target. I swear he is the devil's spawn. I doubt a thousand arrows could have hit true."

"I fear for you. He will ruin you."

"Do not worry over me, Russell. I will do what I can to keep my innocence. There is naught you can do."

"I will kill him if he touches you."

"Stop such foolish talk! He will cut you down in your boots. I could not bear to lose you. My honor is mine to maintain. You will need your strength." She bent down and whispered for his ears only, "Arlys comes." Russell turned and tried to face her. She nodded her head. "Now, get rest. I will see you on the morrow."

Isabel stood and turned to leave the stall. Rohan's dark shadow moved forward, intercepting her. She caught her breath. She did not hear him come so close. Had he heard? Her limbs quaked, but she quickly composed herself. "You startled me."

He took her elbow and guided her out of the stable back to the manor. It rose tall and bright in the short distance. Rossmoor. Her birthplace. In the hands of a foreigner. And one who held no regard for her people or their traditions. Her great-grandfather's legacy would die with her and her brother.

"I am not one to give warnings, Lady Isabel. But you are young and inexperienced."

Isabel remained silent.

"I will deal harshly with any and all traitors."

"I am sure you will act first and ask questions after your dastardly deed is done."

"I am a patient man."

"You are a brute."

"It has kept me alive."

As they entered the hall, Isabel expected to see debauchery abound. Instead, the tables were cleared, the maids gone, the torches dimmed, and the knights, the ones with the scars, gathered around the hearth, their voices low.

"Have your men had their fill of my food and maids so early?"

"Wenching and wine do not mix when surely Saxons abound."

Isabel threw him a glare, then pushed off from his arm and moved toward the pallet where Manhku lay tossing and turning.

She pushed past the tall, hard shoulders and sank to her knees beside the African. Pressing her hand to his brow, she recoiled at its heat. She looked up at the men surrounding her. "He burns with the fever. Move the pallet away from the fire."

The men hurried to do her bidding. As they did, Isabel hurried to the kitchen, where she drew cool water from the well and grabbed several clean linens from a cabinet.

When she returned, Rohan scowled, no doubt angry that she had not asked permission to leave the room. She moved past him, sank to the floor beside Manhku, and immediately set about removing his clothing. When she could not pull the hauberk over his head, Ioan and Wulfson helped. As they pulled his last layer of clothing from him, Isabel gasped. Manhku sported the same scar on his chest as did Rohan. And on closer inspection, she saw he also bore the same crescent-shaped scar on his chin.

She pressed her fingertip to the spot at the bottom of his throat where the sword scar began. The mending tissue was hard and heated. Her initial reaction was horror. She wanted to recoil, to turn away, but she did not. A sense told her these men all bore the mark, and if she were to reject them for it as if it were a curse, she would never be able to retake the slur. The pain one endured to benefit from such a scar must have been horrendous.

She turned to look up at the knight who had tossed her world into the air. He stared back at her with hard, cold eyes. Her brow wrinkled. What manner of men were these?

Rohan dropped to one knee and placed his hand to his man's brow as if her word were not good enough. "The fever rages."

"I fear his wound will fester."

Rohan caught her eyes with his. "My ax is sharp should the poison spread."

Isabel's jaw dropped at his nonchalant offer. "How could you be so callous? A knight without a leg is one without an identity. He would have to beg in the streets for his dinner."

Rohan stood. "Manhku will never have to beg as long as I live. I owe him my life. I will see to his."

Isabel turned back to Manhku. She soaked the linens in the cool water and began to bathe him. For a long time, the men were silent as she ministered to their fallen comrade. It was an odd silence. And Isabel found a small comfort in the fact that these men, all vicious killers, would entrust their man into her hands. Hands of the enemy. She looked down at Manhku's face. And since his color had lightened from the blood loss, she noticed for the first time a series of circular tattoos on his cheeks. She turned back to look up at the gathered knights. Each of them different in his own right but all somehow the same.

Too tired to contemplate them more, Isabel bent her full attention to bathing Manhku in the cool water. So intent was she that she did not hear the men behind her leave the hall until she turned to ask Rohan to fetch her more water and realized they were gone.

The water in the bucket had warmed. She picked it up and walked quickly back to the kitchen to refill it with cool water. As she drew up the bucket, a small sound behind her caused her to let go of the rope and turn. Rohan stood in the doorway, filling the space almost completely. "The linens have warmed the water," she said.

He took a step closer. She backed up, the edge of the well biting into her backside. The hard flicker of her heart in her throat nearly choked her. In the low light of the tapers, Rohan's eyes glowed like molten coals. She was trapped.

"I—I must fetch more cool water." Isabel turned quickly around, grabbed the handle to the rope, and began to wind it up.

Rohan's large hand stayed hers. She stiffened, and as she did, he moved closer. So close she could feel the thick column of his manhood against her back. His heat and strength engulfed her. Isabel squeezed her eyes shut and set her jaw, not wishing to experience on any plane the way he made her body feel. "P-please," she whispered.

His free hand slid around her waist, and he twined his fingers with hers on the handle. Bending down, he nuzzled at her ear, and Isabel nearly crumpled to the floor. His greater strength prevented it. When he splayed his big hand across her belly and pressed his groin firmly against her back, Isabel cried out, "Please!"

"Aye, I please, Isabel. I please very much." He turned her in his arms and bent to kiss her, but Isabel arched away from him and turned her head. His lips sank to the warmth of her neck. Despite having no willing part in his mauling of her, warmth spread throughout her body, followed by a low escaping moan. It seemed only to whet his appetite for more. Rohan pulled her tighter against him.

"Yield to me, damsel," he hoarsely demanded against her throat.

"Nay, I cannot." As the words left her mouth, he cupped her breast, and Isabel squeaked in surprise, but her body pressed hotly into his palm.

His thumb rubbed across a taut nipple. Isabel shook from the shock of the sensation. "You play yourself false, Isabel."

She struggled against him, his words biting her pride hard. She opened her mouth to deny his words but stopped when he pressed his mouth to the same nipple he had just taunted. Isabel stiffened, the sensation so intense and so foreign to her she did not know how to react. His mouth clamped firmly onto her through the layers of fabric. Her body shuddered, and she felt a warmth spread between her legs. If he felt so good this way, how would he feel if they were skin to skin? The image shocked her.

"You say nay with your words, but your body begs the opposite."

Shame infiltrated her reason. She was Isabel of Alethorpe, Lady of Rossmoor. Her blood was among the best in Saxony. And here she hung like a spineless ninny in the hands of an invading Norman. And a bastard Norman at that!

Her ardor cooled quickly. "Leave me, Norman! Leave me my dignity!" When he did not move a muscle, Isabel chose another line of defense. "You repay my attention to your man with your dalliance here while he burns with fever?"

Rohan pulled away from her. The air that whooshed between their bodies cooled them both. For that, too, she was grateful. His bright eyes looked deeply into hers. "Your dignity is your responsibility, damsel. Not mine. Mark my word, as it is my oath, I will see our agreement met. Make no mistake of it." He stood back. "Now, tend my man."

He turned and walked away. Isabel stood for a long time, fighting her anger at the man and her fear of his carnal power over her.

Rohan stripped to his braies, washed his face and hands, and flopped onto the feather-stuffed mattress. Its comfort was the best he had had the good fortune to find. The linens were clean and smelled of fresh herbs, and the pillows were soft. Yet he could find no comfort on it. He was used to sleeping on the hard, uncompromising ground or a pallet in a lord's hall. He had his own cutout at William's castle in Rouen, but he spent most of his time with his men, either warring or practicing the art of war.

He rolled onto his back, folded his arms under his head, and stared at the embroidered design in the canopy. A hawk surrounded by smaller birds. The hearth burned bright, casting weird shadows on the fabric, warming the room. But it was the heat in his loins that burned hottest. His cock stirred as he thought of the wench below.

Ha! More like a witch!

Her audacity shocked him. In all of his travels, he had never stumbled upon a woman with so much to lose acting as if she had all the world to gain. Did she not know whom she dealt with? He'd slain men for lesser deeds than her impertinence.

His muscles tightened, and his cock flinched against his thigh as he envisioned her naked and hungry for him in this very bed. A man could lose himself for a fortnight in her lush body. He'd never touched skin so soft. Or a temper so sharp. Rohan smiled despite his discomfort. Yea, she was a bold wench, all right, but his boldness surpassed hers by far. He sat up in the big bed and nearly rubbed his hands together in anticipation of her yielding that ripe body of hers to him. He grinned and moved from the bed, limping to the fire to throw more logs onto the glowing embers. Yea, she would share this bed for more than a night. Mayhap through the winter.

Rohan moved to the tapestry covering the shutters to the window. He pushed it back, opened the wooden closure, and peered out into the night. Stars rose bright and clear in the sky, the full moon lighting the way. His gaze traveled over the distant forests and down to the courtyard and bailey beyond. His sentries moved back and forth, their dark shadows larger then life under the moonlight.

A slight movement from the stable caught his eye. A small figure moving along the courtyard wall to the manor. His blood quickened. Isabel.

As she assured the guard near the kitchen door that she had seen to her chore of retrieving leeches from the bog, he allowed her to pass. It had been a hard-won battle to have the man agree to leave her alone. But when she reminded him that his master, Sir Rohan, slept and would not like to be bothered by a mere girl searching for leeches to save a favored knight, he allowed her to pass. As she came into the hall, she moved to where Manhku tossed and turned on his pallet. His leg swelled, and his only hope was the leeches to bleed the poison from his wound.

Her gaze slipped across the score or more of men bedded down for the night near the far hearth that burned bright and warm. More filled the stable. The enemy. Could Arlys drive these men from her home?

Isabel set the bucket of leeches down next to Manhku, unwrapped the bandage, and slowly applied the slimy creatures to the swollen leg. As she did, she wondered at her own fate. Would that devil sleeping in her father's bed be her undoing? Would he break his oath and force her to spread her legs for him?

She closed her eyes. Nay, he would not! She would hold him to his vow. She opened her eyes and was glad to see the leeches attached. They should be filled by morn.

Isabel sat back on her heels and wiped her hands clean on a wetted linen towel. Aye, not only would she see to it that Sir Rohan kept his oath to her, she would see she kept hers to him. And despite the fear that oath inspired, her body warmed as she wondered what else he would do to her. Would it be more intense than what she experienced in the kitchen? Her hand moved to touch her neck where his lips had pressed. Her breasts swelled, and a tingling sensation taunted her nipples.

Her gaze traveled up the stairway toward the lord's chamber, and she cried out. Rohan stood at the landing, his eyes locked on her.

Slowly, he walked down the wide berth, his gaze not wavering from hers. Isabel's skin heated to rival the flames that she was sure cast an eerie glow about her. Rohan stood naked at the bottom of the stairway save for the braies he wore. The low firelight flickered off the planes and edges of his body, illuminating his old battle scars and those fresh from Hastings. The cloth around his hips stirred, and she flinched, stepping back, her heel brushing the embers from the hearth.

"Damsel, you avoid my bed." His eyes continued to hold her captive. Had they not, she still would have not been able to drag her eyes from him. His long black hair hung wildly around him in the fashion of the Vikings. His wide, muscular chest rose and fell to a quick beat. Power and danger swirled around him. In his presence, while she was terrified, she knew that if she ever required a champion, this would be the man she'd pick. His prowess was legendary.

The cloth around his hips rose as if a serpent squirmed beneath it. Now, instead of fear, something deep and primal moved within her. She didn't question it. Instead, unabashed, she continued to regard him.

"You cannot hide from destiny, damsel," Rohan softly said, approaching her as stealthily as a wolf stalking a deer.

With nowhere to go but into the fire, Isabel held her ground, her chin high and proud. "You are not my destiny."

"This eve I am." Rohan laughed low, the sound husky, provocative, and terrifying.

She sidestepped away from him, her gaze never wavering. "I will not succumb to you."

"'Tis not necessary."

His muscles rippled as he flexed his long arms. Isabel shook her head, terrified of what he could do to her, knowing that if he pressed her regularly, despite her will, he would become as addictive to her as wine had become to her father after her mother's death. Her pride would suffer greatly for becoming his willing leman. Not to mention that should her heart ever become involved, this man would leave it in pieces in the dirt as he rode off to his next conquest.

As if the gesture would stop him, Isabel put her hand out to halt him. "Sir knight, I beg you, do not trespass against my person. It is all I have left to give freely."

Rohan scowled but continued toward her. Taking her hand into his, he brought it to his lips, though he did not press them to her skin. She warmed to his touch even though she feared him. The sensations he wrought so unnerved her she wanted to shriek and run as far into the forest as she could.

" 'Tis not a trespass when struck as an oath. Would your dignity support breaking your word?'

She shook her head, angry that he should turn the table around. She was a woman of her word, and if she swore an oath, she would do everything in her power to uphold it. It did not mean she had to embrace it.

"I see we are agreed at least on this one matter." He pressed his lips to her fingertips. Their warmth, and yes, their softness surprised her. Yet the hot look in his eyes stripped her of her dignity.

Isabel stiffened. "I wish to retain my innocence, sir." Her tone left no room for banter. It was a statement as well as a heartfelt request.

Rohan smiled, and she knew she had lost. And in the next minutes, she would lose more. "My Lady Isabel, you jest if you are to believe I think you innocent."

"Lout!" she hissed, and pulled her hand from his grasp. It was not to be so. He tightened his hand around hers and pulled her toward him, his lips returned to her skin. His tongue slid across the palm of her hand, and she nearly swooned. When he sank his teeth into the fleshy part of her hand, she cried out. But not in pain.

His gaze burned molten, and his nostrils flared with the increase of his breath. "What say you about the way you pressed that wanton body of yours against me earlier?"

Isabel opened her mouth to retort but found nothing to say. How could she argue against the truth?

He laved her palm again and suddenly released her. "As I suspected. You crave me."

Humiliated to her core, Isabel did what any innocent maid would do to an arrogant boor. She slapped him. In a flash, he grabbed her to him, his cock poking her in the belly as he pulled her against the hardness of his chest. He groaned at the contact and surged against her, then pressed harder into her hips.

"Remember how that feels, Isabel. You will beg me for it one day soon."

She raised her free hand to slap him again for his crudity, but he caught it and thrust her away from him. He pointed to Manhku. "Thank him for your reprieve this eve. As it is, I tire of your prickly temper, and the night grows longer. I need my sleep to tend to you warring Saxons on the morrow."

As he walked away from her, Isabel called, "Indeed, sir, we shall see in the end who wins the day!"

Rohan turned full to face her. "Rue the day I find a traitor in my midst. He shall die a traitor's death. By my own hand."

Isabel silently chided herself for her outburst. She held her tongue, not wanting to thwart this man or give him further reason to suspect an uprising. She had said too much already.

"Pray, Isabel, you do not fall into that trap. I would hate to mar such beauty as yours. But fear not. I would." He slid his hand around her neck and pulled her to him, the force of his movement nearly lifting her from her feet. His lips hovered just above hers. "But be sure, first I would take what you so churlishly cling to."

Isabel's lips parted as she struggled for breath, and his mouth dipped closer to hers, almost touching. Her blood quickened, and her body went limp in his hold. Her breasts ached with a now familiar feel. She licked her lips, the tip of her tongue touching his bottom lip. She felt his arm tremble and his body stiffen.

"Jesu," Rohan cursed, thrusting her so hard away from him she nearly fell into the fire. He grabbed her wrist, preventing the fall, but his features gathered like storm clouds on his face. "Be gone with you, witch, before I take you here and now!"

Isabel didn't ask where she should be gone to, she just ran past him up the stairs to the solar, flinging the door closed and bolting the heavy oak door.

Six

Isabel woke to the sound of thunder. "Open this portal, wench!"

Wiping sleep from her eyes, she threw a tunic over her shift, then pulled back the heavy bolt. The door was flung open from the outside. Rohan's stormy face boded bad for all. "My man is awake and screaming for God knows what. Tend him."

Guttural bellows from the hall reached her ears. Other voices attempted to calm him. The more they tried, the angrier the giant's foreign words became. Rohan grabbed her arm and hauled her from the chamber. "Hurry before he destroys the hall."

A snide smile played along her lips as she was pulled along the hallway and down the stairway. It amused her to see this bold and terrible knight so far out of his controlled ways. She almost laughed when she saw the others standing helplessly about like nervous brides.

Isabel's mien changed to serious as she came nearer to the giant. He had pulled off most of the dressings and all of the leeches. The poultice lay in a hunk on the rushes. Anger spurred her forward.

As the African moved to stand, she called out in a sure and steady voice. "Halt!" She spoke in French, doubting he understood English.

Scores of eyes followed her voice, watching her and then the giant for his reaction. Her mood was sorely prickled by her rude awakening and then by this man who would disrupt her healing efforts.

The giant's black eyes widened, then narrowed to dangerous slits. His lips drew back from teeth as sharp as a wolf's, obviously honed to an unnatural point. He growled low and menacing. Undeterred by his posturing, Isabel's temper flared.

She moved toward him and slapped his hand away from the dressing he had nearly removed. "Foolish man! Sit back!" When he did not move, she pressed her verbal attack. "I gave up one of my finest shifts to save your leg, I went to the bog in the middle of the night for leeches, and I lost much sleep last night and this morn." She unwound the tattered dressing, her movements quick and jerky. His damage was thorough. She would need all new linens and to pack a fresh poultice. She raised her gaze to his. "And you reward me this way?"

If she were not so angry, she would have laughed at the shocked expression on his tattooed face. He was not used to being treated thus, she was sure. Isabel looked over her shoulder at Rohan, who stood in equal shock. Her eyes moved from him to his surrounding men. Each of them stood in stunned silence. Ignoring them all, Isabel turned her attention back to the giant and frowned at the gathering storm on his face.

Hands on her hips, she asked, "Do you wish to walk without a tree stump to assist you?" Dark purple lips pulled back from the sharpened teeth. A low growl rumbled deep in his chest. "I will take that as a nay. Now, lie back so that I may repair what you have destroyed."

When he made no move to follow her direction, Isabel expelled a long breath, hiked her skirt, and moved toward him. Placing both of her hands on his chest, she heaved him backward. He resisted. She shoved him harder, nearly sitting on him to have her way. Soft snickers floated around her ears. She glanced up at Rohan, who stood rooted to the floor, his face solemn, his eyes amused. She turned to face his knights, who stood now in eager anticipation of what they assumed was her impending defeat.

Her rancor rose. "You are not honorable men, and I for one look forward to the day you ride off never to return!"

She turned back to the grumbling giant and dug her elbows into his chest. "Give me your word you will not interfere with my work."

His eyes narrowed. A lesser woman or perhaps a fool would have backed off. But Isabel was neither of those women. She was in a most unladylike position on a known slayer of Saxons, amongst battle-hardened knights. When he refused to answer, Isabel changed her tactic. Nodding, she moved off him. "Very well." Once completely off the brute, she extended her hand to Rohan. He raised a brow. "Your ax, sir."

The men behind her chortled, and the giant growled. "What plans have you for it?" Rohan asked, amusement twisting his tone.

"I wish to sever the leg from this most ungracious body.

The cause is lost, and I have my own people to attend to. I have no time for an unwilling patient."

Rohan had the good grace to scowl. He looked down at his man, and the giant growled again, attempting to sit up.

"Milady?" Thorin said, stepping forward. His deep hazel eye glittered in the morning firelight. Her gaze traced his scarred face. She wondered what other scars lay beneath the leather patch. She thought of the pain he must have endured as recipient of such a wound. She looked past Thorin to the others, wondering again what horrible experience bound them.

"Sir knight?" she asked.

"Shall I hold the brute whilst you chop?" he asked with the straight face of a man bent on serious business.

Manhku shot upright and called out to Thorin in rapid, strangely accented French. "Viking scourge!"

The knights doubled over in laughter, breaking the thick tension. Isabel stood, calm, not understanding the camaraderie of men. "You jest with this man's leg." She wiped her hands on her dress. "And so I will leave you to tend him yourselves. I am done with it."

"Riders approach!" the tower lookout called.

Excitement lurched in her chest. Was it her sire come home?

As they were already mailed and belted, Rohan and his men instantly scrambled to attention. Isabel wondered if they slept thus. She warmed as she remembered Rohan's barely clad body last night. Mayhap they did not. As Isabel moved to follow the knights, to see who came to Rossmoor at such an ungodly hour, Rohan turned to her. "Stay in the hall, and see to Manhku."

Frustration strangled her. How dare he command her?

What if it were kin come for refuge? Isabel turned back to look at the abandoned Manhku. "Mayhap I will give you a second chance." She glanced back to the half-open portal. "But first I will see who approaches."

Flanked by his men, Rohan stood with his hand on the hilt of his sword as the score of Norman knights approached. The crimson and black standard bearing the image of the boar flapped arrogantly in the chill of the English winter wind. The same coat of arms caught the morning sunlight on the lead rider's shield.

An anger he had thought long buried rose from deep inside Rohan's belly. He gripped the hilt of his sword so tightly he could no longer feel his fingertips.

"Your brother rides as if he is due the crown," Thorin said from beside Rohan.

"Aye, and if there is a way, leave it to Henri to find it." Rohan stepped down into the courtyard, as one, his men followed.

Henri's big bay destrier skidded to a halt inches from Rohan. He remained motionless. In an arrogant show of confidence, Henri pulled his red plumed helmet from his head. A face much like Rohan's stared back. The one defining difference, at least on the surface, was that Henri bore no scars. His face was clean, and Rohan knew how he would appear had he been the one born to a couple wed in God's eyes.

Henri's contemptuous gaze swept past Rohan to each of his men alongside him before coming back to rest on his brother. In another great show of confidence, Henri dismounted. As his feet landed on the cobblestone, he sneered. "Whores' sons, all of you."

"Take care who you call a whore, Henri. While I have no great love for the woman who bore me, William dotes on his aunt."

Henri scoffed and looked past Rohan to Rossmoor. His eyes scanned for a good long time the impressive edifice. "So, as the bastard's henchman, ye think ye have the right to land?"

"I do my liege's bidding," Rohan answered.

Henri sneered, the twist of his lips so much like Rohan's turning the angled planes of his face into jagged ridges.

"Your liege will see his way to delivering lands and titles in this sodden piece of turf to his nobles, not by blow who have only a sword and horse to call upon."

Rohan pulled his sword and held it high. Sunlight danced off the honed edges. "My Blood Sword has seen well to my needs thus far, Henri." Rohan gestured with his sword to the dark knights flanking him. "While I have grown immune to your insults, my brethren have not. Tread lightly lest you find your tongue a tempting morsel for the hounds."

"Would you threaten me, bastard?"

Rohan stepped closer, the point of his sword pointed directly at Henri's heart. "I never threaten, brother. You of all people know that small fact about me."

Henri slapped at the blade and made as if to move past. Yet the blade barely moved in Rohan's steady hand. His men closed ranks. Henri's men shifted nervously in their saddles.

"It would not sorrow me if you pressed the point."

Henri retreated a step. "I would not argue with you, brother. Besides, this manor is a hovel. There are more worthy lands of a more worthy noble. One whose blood runs true in his sire's line. I'll leave you to pretend, brother, but mark my words. You will not find yourself lord here or—"

Henri's eyes widened, and he looked past Rohan. In that instant, Rohan knew what captivated his brother so. Not trusting the noble-born son, Rohan stepped back and moved toward the open door where Isabel stood. Anger flared in his belly. "I told you to stay in the hall."

"I chose to ignore you." Isabel darted past him to where Henri stood. She looked from the grinning knight back to the scowling knight. "You look to be twins."

Rohan moved forward to obscure her from Henri's lecherous view. But his brother acted swiftly. He took Isabel's hand and bowed regally. "I am Henri de Monfort. Second son of the Comte de Moraine and Belleview and Lord of Moreaux. I am at your service, damsel."

Isabel curtsied. "Lady Isabel of Alethorpe, eldest daughter of Alefric Lord of Alethorpe Wilshire, and Dunleavy. It would please me greatly if you would champion my honor."

Rohan grabbed her from his brother's grasp. His men came to arms. "Go, Henri."

The noble was not to be gainsaid. "What does the lady speak of?"

"Nothing that concerns you."

Henri studied his brother closely. Rohan's temper simmered. It would be just like the noble-born to find a noble reason to take the lady from his care. Yet he knew Henri would use her harshly, then turn her over to his men for more of the same. Isabel knew not whom she temped with her wiles.

"I should petition William on her behalf, brother. He will not take it lightly that his knights, *his most trusted knights,* who have sworn to protect the weak, especially a titled lady, would handle her with less then noble hands."

"Crow to William all you wish, Henri. The maid is in good hands here."

Henri looked at Isabel and smiled. "Do you have other kin?"

"My brother Geoff and my sire, sir."

"Do they reside in the hall with you?"

"Nay, they have yet to return from Hastings."

Henri's eyes softened. He made to move toward Isabel, but Ioan blocked his way. "Irish scourge, move aside!"

Wulfson growled and lunged past Rohan, his double swords poised for attack. Rohan grabbed the younger man's forearm and pulled him back. "He is not worth it, Wulf. Would you waste good steel on a blackguard's heart?"

Rohan pressed his sword to Henri's chest for the second time. "As is your way, you have created a storm in your wake. The lady is no doubt the heiress to this shire, but since it now resides under William's standard, it is not up to us to decide what he will do with the manor or the lady. Until he makes his decision, brother, do not return here. For if you do, I will not curb my men."

Henri stepped back, his bold gaze raking Isabel. The full breeze pressed her garment full against her body, leaving little to the imagination. Her nipples were clearly outlined against the pale blue fabric of her tunic. With her hair unbound and her bare feet peeking from beneath the hem of her garment, she made quite a fetching sight. Rohan's blood warmed. He glanced at his brother. The look on the man's face had the opposite effect on his mood. Rohan's blood cooled to frigid. Henri wanted Isabel for any number of reasons, the foremost as a way to smite Rohan. And

Rohan knew Henri would, as he had always done when Rohan set his sights on something, resort to whatever means were necessary to take it away from him.

Rohan grabbed Isabel's arm and pulled her to stand beside him, making his claim official. "She is my property, Henri. Find your own wench to pass the winter nights with."

Isabel stiffened beside him, and he clasped her arm tighter to keep her from an outburst. He held his breath, praying she would heed him this once.

Henri remounted his horse and turned to look at Isabel. He gave her every opportunity to deny Rohan's claim on her. She must have sensed the darkness that lived in Henri's heart, for she said nothing.

Finally, Henri returned his gaze to Rohan and spoke. "I have not forgotten, you still owe me for Eleanor, Rohan. Had you?"

Isabel trembled beside him. From the cold or from Henri's words, he did not know. "You cry foul for an imagined misdeed. I owe you nothing," Rohan answered.

Henri laughed as he secured his helmet. "Aye, you owe me my heir, brother, and for that I will exact a stiff price." He saluted Isabel and smiled. "We will meet again, Lady Isabel." He turned to his brother. "As to you, brother? I have laid claim to Dunsworth and Sealyham on behalf of Monfort. I hold the nobles as hostages for William. I have no doubt he will bestow the titles on me. I will be in need of a titled bride. And since our father has sent considerable levy to the duke to aid his cause, I am sure he will allow me my pick." Henri's eyes swept to the lady Isabel. "I will pick the fairest flower in all of England, brother. Keep her safe from the likes of yourself until I come for her." He reined his horse and thundered off into the cold morning fog.

Rohan stood rigid as fury infiltrated his body. Henri had a way of making Rohan feel, for all of the achievements in his life, that he was not worthy to clean his spurs. He turned to look down at the lady Isabel. Her cheeks flushed pink. Her full pouty lips parted, her warm breath frosted in the chill of the air. He looked into her big violet eyes as she looked up at him as if gauging his brother's lies. His blood quickened. Henri spoke in half-truths, but it mattered not. She might end up Henri's lady, but she would see his bed first.

Angrily, Rohan clasped her by the arm and dragged her back into the hall. His men followed, keeping their distance.

Isabel tried unsuccessfully to remove Rohan's steely grip on her arm. When they came to the lord's table, he stared murderously down at her. She had not seen his rage reach such heights. "See to the morning meal."

Isabel cast a quick glance at Manhku, who lay quietly for a change on his pallet, his eyes never leaving his master's form. Isabel called for the meal to be served. The knights seemed to converge on Rohan at once, their voices high and their contempt of the noble clear. Whilst she was unnoticed, Isabel slipped from the hall to her chamber, calling Enid along the way.

The maid scampered up behind her, as did Lyn and Mari. Enid threw the heavy bolt into place and stood with her back to the door, trembling like a leaf in the wind. Isabel's temper flashed when Lyn and Mari grabbed each other in the corner and sank wide-eyed onto a pallet. "Do not sit so pathetically like frightened mice!" Was the world bent on looking to her for guidance? Were they all dolts who could not tend to even the meagerest of actions?

"My lady, the Normans, they scare us, and the one who just left? He has the mark of the devil," Lyn wailed. Enid bobbed her head like a chicken, and Mari sniffled in agreement.

Isabel softened. She was not angry at them. She was angry that England for the moment was lost to more than one bastard Norman. That her sire and her brother, if they had not lost their lives on Senlac Hill, were dead or so seriously maimed they were not able to send word to her. Isabel was angry that raiders had decimated the village and the villagers. She was angry that the Norman, de Monfort, thought she would drop for him like some trained bitch because he bore a title and his sire had William's ear. And she was even more angry at his arrogant brother, who went by the name of *la lame noir*, for terrifying her more than any man should.

So if she were afraid, of course her servants were frightened. But as she would, they would have to rise above their fear. Isabel looked sharply at Lyn and Mari.

"Lyn, Mari? Did you not offer yourselves last eve to the Normans?"

Lyn's big brown eyes widened. "I only pretended to like them, milady. I was afraid if I showed contempt as you did, my face would meet with a fist."

A loud knock on the door startled them all. Isabel frowned and flung the bolt back to find Russell, of all people, standing at the threshold. "Russell! What are you doing here?" Her eyes scanned him. He stood, slightly listing, wearing a loose-fitting tunic and rough-hewn trewes.

"I am not one to lie about and cry like a woman, mi-lady."

Isabel smothered a smile. Despite Russell's mask of manliness, he winced when he moved.

"Aye, you are not. What brings you here?"

"The bastard knight has summoned you to break the fast."

Isabel's ire rose anew. "Tell him—" She considered her words carefully. Her impulse was to throw the request in his face. He had no right to ask her to join him. Yet it was her home, and she was lady of the manor. Protocol dictated she invite him. Ha, invite the invader to break bread? Never. Not after his brutal handling of her earlier. And in front of his brother and his men? Nay, she would be no chattel of his.

"I shall present myself when I am ready," she told Russell. His color drained. Being the messenger of such news would not bode well for the bearer. Yet he insisted on acting the man. 'Twould do him good. "Go, Russ, and make as quick a turn as you can when the last word leaves your mouth."

When the door closed behind the boy, Isabel turned to her maid. "See me to a hot bath. The stench of Normans clings too tightly to me."

As Enid poured the last bucket of hot water into the copper tub, Isabel sank into the silky warmth, stealing a moment to luxuriate in the scented soapy water. Normally, she didn't bathe in the morn, but these were not normal times. Indeed, these times were what nightmares were drawn from. She closed her eyes and dismissed her maid, wanting solace with herself and her thoughts before she must face the beast again. The low thud of the door told her she was left to her privacy.

Sighing deeply, Isabel sank deeper still into the calming water. Her mind swirled with the events of the morn. Henri terrified her in a way his base-born brother did not. There was something much darker that drove Henri. Something not human. His eyes held the cold, empty look of a rabid animal. She shivered despite the warmth of the water. She would never consent to being his lady. Another shiver scraped across her skin. It would not matter if she contested or not. If 'twas William's will, then it would be served.

What of Rohan's will? She recognized his claim in front of his men and Henri for what it was. A man's pride at work. Pure and simple. He laid claim to something his noble-born brother coveted. He would see her ruined as well, of that she had no doubt.

The bastard! How dare he use her to bait his enemy? How dare he play with her feelings? How dare he take from her what was not his to take?

She sat upright in the tub, no longer content to relax. The minute the cool air touched her warm skin, her nipples hardened. But it wasn't because of the chill of the air. Isabel drew in a deep breath and locked eyes with the tawny ones across the room. Rohan stood propped against the wall, his arms crossed over his chest, a slow smile tugging at his lips.

"Do not stop on my account, damsel. I am enjoying the scenery."

"Look all you wish, Norman, for it is all you will get."

Seven

Rohan grinned at her words. They both knew they held no truth. As his grin died, the heat in his loins flared at the sight before him. He remained motionless lest any movement make it disappear. She was enchanting. He was not a man of many words, but even if he were, the vision before him would hold him speechless.

Rosy skin flushed under his gaze. Full, ripe breasts he ached to touch trembled just below the waterline out of sight. Blood coursed hotly through him. He had seen enough to know what lay hidden beneath the translucent barrier.

The rush he encountered each time he laid eyes on the Saxon maid unnerved him as much as it excited him. The feeling was the same when he entered battle. Every sense, every instinct, every inch of his body and thoughts were open and aware, anticipation whetting his appetite to ravenous.

Then. Engagement.

And finally. The thrill of victory.

As Rohan saw himself poised and ready to plunder the maid's willing body, Henri's caustic laughter infiltrated the scene. *William gives her to me, brother. Step aside so that I might claim what is mine.*

For a moment, fury clouded Rohan's vision. The depths of his hate for his younger brother stabbed at him with the clarity of a sword plunging into his gut. He blinked, willing the toxic emotion to recede. He focused back on the sight before him. Aye, she was far more pleasant to look upon than any vision of his jealous brother. He and his men were William's most trusted knights. Even Henri could not say it other. Their loyalty was without question. As was William's to his loyal subjects. He pushed Henri's words from his head. He would have this hall, and he would have all that came with it. Including the lady Isabel.

Rohan dropped his arms to his sides and walked slowly toward her, a hunter with his prey clearly in sight.

"Halt," she whispered.

"I am not Manhku." Rohan stepped closer, her scent wafting in the air, tempting him more. As she sank lower into the tub, he walked around her, wanting to admire her from all sides but also to throw her off balance. It would do him no good for her to have his moves clearly in her sights. He smiled, warming to his game. She was as anything he desired but resisted him. A challenge to be had, then used until some other challenge struck his fancy.

Crossing her arms over her chest, Isabel twisted in the small tub, casting a wary eye on him. He grinned wider as he squatted beside her. Her pulse flicked furiously in the vital vein in her neck. He reached out and trailed a finger along the smooth dampness of her collarbone. Her body shivered, the sensation traveling from her body to his.

His cock swelled with anticipation. His grin nearly split his face.

"Admit it, damsel, you are curious. You want me to extinguish the heat you feel for me."

She smacked his hand away, the gesture buoying her breasts for a brief moment. Quickly, she covered herself again. Her eyes sparked fire. He would give his left arm for her to spark like that in desire for him.

"I want nothing from you but to see your backside as you sail home to your country."

Rohan was undaunted. It had been too long since his last woman. And in the very recesses of his mind, Henri's challenge spurred his possessive nature.

He straddled the tub with his long arms, causing the shy maiden to squirm, the movement sending water sloshing over the sides and onto his thighs and the floor. "Until I do, you are mine. Now, lie back and drop your hands. I want a taste of what I shall feast upon this eve."

Isabel's eyes widened. She turned her body as far away from him as she could in the confines of the tub. "I would do no such—"

Rohan slid his hands into the water and wrapped them around her waist, pulling her toward him as he stood. She shrieked and squirmed in his arms, her skin slippery from the soap. He held her tighter. Her breasts plumpened against his chest and her gyrating hips as she sought to kick away from him ignited his fire to blazing. He drew her up, no longer able to curb his hunger for her. Turning her in his arms, Rohan lifted Isabel and clamped his mouth onto an impertinent nipple.

Isabel cried out and went rigid in his arms. He tightened his grip, bringing her closer. A hot rush of desire tore through his limbs, crashing into his loins. His cock thickened to painful. As her body arched against him and her hands pushed against his shoulders, Rohan's lips suckled her like a starving man. Desire clashed with his anger, not only at Henri for trespassing here but at Isabel for being the object of his desire. His fingers dug into her hot skin. It was so smooth and soft it rivaled the silk of the finest robe. His lips left the one turgid nipple for the other, giving it equal attention. He rubbed his face between her generous cleavage, his teeth nipping her mounds as his hands molded over her derriere, his fingers digging into the succulent flesh, pressing her hard against his erection, wanting the succor she was not willing to give but he was willing to take.

Her body heated against his, he could feel it. His right hand slid down her flat belly to the soft mound below. Isabel expelled a harsh breath and loosened in his fierce embrace. He smiled.

Surrender.

He lifted his head, to tell her he could not promise gentleness. But words lodged in his throat. Her fist smashed into his jaw, the blow stunning him in its unexpectedness and, for a woman, its strength. His arms loosened a mite, and it was all her slippery body needed to disengage from him. Like a rabbit, she hopped out of the tub and ran to the door.

"My men will enjoy the sight, damsel."

Isabel turned at the door, more than cognizant of her lack of clothing. The heat of her body warded off the chill of the room. She tried to cover herself, her arms and hands ineffectively shielding her from the tall warrior's hot gaze.

It raked her from head to toe, then up again, leisurely stopping at her hips and the breasts that still burned from the brand of his lips.

He smiled slowly, rubbing his jaw where she had struck him. She had no choice; it was the only action a man like him understood. And with that understanding, another realization dawned. He was a warrior, a mercenary, a man paid to kill, a man paid for his allegiance. Other than coin, he respected only courage.

Isabel drew herself up to her full height, slight though it was, and dropped her hands to her sides. Her breasts trembled as they thrust toward him, but she was determined to stand toe to toe with this knight. He may be able to overpower her by his brute strength, but he would never overpower her will or her heart.

It gave her great satisfaction to watch his expression change from enjoyment to wariness. "What ploy do you seek now, wench?"

Isabel shook her head, the damp tendrils of her hair sticking to her back. "I have no ploy, sir. You have proven to me, and your brother's words confirm the fact, that you are the lout of your reputation. You are no noble knight but a mercenary whose loyalty is purchased. So take what you will from me, and know it will never be freely given. For you could not pay me enough to welcome your touch."

"Were I of noble birth, would your opinion be different?"

Isabel caught herself at his question. "The measure of a man is not if his parents are wed in the eyes of God and king. The true measure of a man is drawn from his deeds."

Rohan scowled and sauntered toward her. Her chin rose higher. And Lord help her, but a hot thrill coursed through every inch of her. That strange feeling had sprung to life between her thighs when his lips touched her breasts in the tub. When he suckled her and dug his hands into her bottom, she—Isabel squeezed her eyes closed.

When she opened them, Rohan stood only a hand's breadth from her. He reached out an open hand and placed it on her right breast. Her heart lurched against it, and she knew he felt it as solidly as she. As if that were not enough, to her complete mortification, her nipple puckered. He smiled softly. "A body doesn't lie, Isabel."

He slipped an arm around her waist and brought her hard against his chest. Her legs trembled, and had he not held her so tightly, she would have crumpled to the floor.

"Make no mistake, the only exchange between us when I take you will be mutual satisfaction." He dropped his head to her throat. Pressing his nose softly against her skin there, he inhaled deeply. "Your scent will ride with me this day as a reminder of what is in store for us both this eve. Make yourself available."

He released her and left.

Isabel held her breath, clenching her jaw to keep her teeth from chattering. Her entire body trembled as if several hands grasped her arms and shook her back and forth. She turned to look at the door Rohan had just walked through and knew with a sinking heart that she was a marked woman.

When she entered the great hall a short time later, forgoing the rest of her bath, Isabel was met with several stares. With her damp hair and high color, she did not have to guess what was on every man's mind. Especially since Rohan's clothes were equally as damp as her hair,

Heat washed across her skin as their eyes clashed. Rohan stabbed a piece of cold meat with his dagger and casually munched it as he stared her down. Isabel threw her shoulders farther back and ignored him. Instead, she stared down his knights, finding for the most part that they were as stubbornly rude as their leader. Every last one of them, including Rorick, met her challenging gaze before turning back to their meal. She turned to find the African's keen eyes watching her raptly.

He scowled when she cocked an eyebrow at him, daring him to add insult to her injury. Haughtily, she strode past him and into the kitchens. When she emerged several minutes later with a modestly filled trencher, she found the one called Warner poking at Manhku's bandages, the same soiled ones he had ripped off earlier. The African grumbled and pushed the man away.

"God's teeth, man, the bindings stink! Shall I separate your leg from your arse now, or will you allow me to tend it?"

Rohan laughed and stood, coming to stand next to his knight. He laid a hand on the man's shoulder as he stood and backed away from the giant. "Mayhap he needs to see the edge of your blade, Warner, to know you mean to help."

"He would cut the wrong leg!" Manhku tossed back.

Warner shook his head and pointed to the maimed limb. "Tend it yourself, then, heathen, and be glad. Like the lady Isabel, I no longer have an interest in you."

Warner strode to Rohan's other side. Isabel continued to the end of the only vacant table in the hall. Unfortunately, it was also the lord's table and the one closest to the hearth. And Rohan.

He turned and glowered down at her as she nibbled a

piece of hard bread. "My man needs his dressings changed."

Isabel shrugged and slowly chewed. She glanced at his hand, then up at his face, her gaze resting briefly on his swelling jaw. "Your jaw may be broken, but it appears your hands are in good order. Do it yourself."

Warner slapped Rohan heartily on the back. "Ha! Smote by a woman!"

Rohan rubbed his swollen jaw. It was obvious he had been struck. He grinned, his humor restored. "She wields her lips as expertly as I wield my sword."

Isabel gasped, choking on the piece of bread she chewed. "I did no such thing!" She coughed.

Rohan made to approach her, but she waved him off. Valiantly, she managed to catch her breath.

"A man approaches!" The shout came from the tower.

Rohan hesitated as Isabel continued to collect herself. She nodded and took a long draught from his cup. Rohan moved past her, accompanied by the scraping sound of leather and metal as his men followed him out into the courtyard. Isabel sat still for a moment, praying the man would have good tidings of her father and her brother. She did not know how much more bad news she could consume without becoming like Lyn and Mari.

Taking a big gulp of air, she inhaled and slowly exhaled and moved quickly to the courtyard. With each step, her heart raced, hoping and praying it was her father or her brother come home.

Instead, the sight that greeted her was truly horrifying. Abel, her father's bailiff, torn, bloodied, and his right arm a stump, stumbled into the courtyard, then fell to his knees in the dirt before planting himself face-first in the hard stone.

"'Tis Abel!" Isabel cried, pushing past the massive shoulders to the man. She dropped to her knees and with Rohan's help turned him over. A white death mask drew his color. His arm, though bound, bled. Emotion washed over Isabel. Abel had been a loyal man. "Abel," she whispered, touching her hand to his blood- and dirt-encrusted brow. "How came you by your wounds?"

His eyes fluttered open, and with a strength that surprised her, he grasped her hand to his chest. "The raiders, milady."

Isabel gasped. "Where, Abel? Where?" He lay quiet, but breath stirred against her hand. She grabbed his tunic and shook him. "Where?" she screamed, her voice on the edge of hysteria.

"The glade, near the river," he murmured.

Rohan stood. "Do you know of this place?"

"Yea, 'tis several leagues from here."

Rohan turned to his men. "To arms." As they set about readying their mounts, Rohan turned back to Isabel. "Tell me of these raiders."

She swallowed hard and bent back to Abel. "They came almost a fortnight ago just after we received word of Harold's fall. They seem more bent on destruction than anything else. They take what they need until they need again. Two days before you came, they were so bold as to come to the edge of the village and attack. They may have been the same who befell your man."

"Do they bear a coat of arms?"

"Nay, they cover their faces with dark hoods, and they fly no standard. I think mayhap they could be Vikings from Stamford Bridge looking for revenge."

"They will find themselves revealed this day."

Isabel stood and grabbed his arm. "Allow me to show you the way to the glade. I have a sturdy mare."

Rohan's eyes widened in surprise. He almost smiled. "You never cease to amaze me, damsel. I will see you stay here."

"But there are several glades. I know—"

"I can show you the way," Russell said, stepping forward.

Rohan scowled, staring down at the boy. But the youth regarded Rohan with quiet strength. "What of your back?"

"It pains me not."

Rohan scoffed but nodded. "If you think you have what it takes to ride with me, then find yourself a suitable mount. Go to Hugh, my squire. He will see you properly outfitted."

Rohan turned back to Isabel, who had sunk down beside her fallen man. She looked up with teary eyes. "Abel gave his final sacrifice for my father." She closed his eyes and crossed herself several times. Rohan helped her to stand.

"Stay within the protection of the hall, Isabel. I know not if these raiders mean to draw us out. I will have plenty of men to guard and protect, but there is too much danger for you to be about."

Isabel scanned his eyes; they seemed to soften. In spite of his harsh words and deeds, did he perhaps hold some affection for her? If 'twere true, it would make her less prickly toward him. When she did not answer, he harshly said, "No argument. For many reasons, I do not wish to have to pay a ransom for you."

Before she could offer a sharp word at yet another of his callous barbs, Rohan stalked off.

Several moments later, the devil's Huns thundered away from Rossmoor. For a long moment, Isabel stood and watched the dark mass of man, horse, and weaponry as it disappeared into the thick forests. If there was one good thing that came of Rohan's presence, it was that the raiders would think twice before engaging again, and she admitted 'twas better they were in Rohan's hands and not in the hands of that devil Henri de Monfort. For had he arrived first, Isabel knew full well she would no longer possess the thin skin between her thighs that made her a virgin. She shivered and ran her hands up and down the thin fabric of her gown. Be that as it may, she knew her days to remain intact were severely numbered. Oath or no, she could see the Norman breeching her in the heated throes of passion.

A harsh wind ripped at her dress, bringing her back to the present. Isabel looked up to see several villagers staring at her. Her eyes went to Abel, then to the group of men. "Take him to his wife, and see to it he is buried." With a heavy heart, Isabel moved back into the hall. A priest. They must have a priest to bless the many graves.

Eight

ilady!" a man's voice cried out. Isabel turned to see Ralph the smithy hurry across the bailey, craning his neck back and forth like a swinging noose. Hunch-shouldered as if trying to make himself small and insignificant, he hugged the stone wall as he entered the courtyard, continuing to look fearfully about.

Several of Rohan's men scowled his way, and one, the knight Warner, kept a wary eye on the smith. Isabel hurried to him. As soon as he could hear, she said, "Act as if you come to the manor every day, Ralph. You bring too much attention to yourself with your skittish movements."

Isabel turned then. As he caught up and fell in step with her in a slow, unhurried pace, she walked toward the manor.

"Forgive me, Lady Isabel," Ralph huffed, out of breath. "But I am unused to these foreigners in my home."

Isabel nodded but kept her pace slow and even. "I

understand, but so long as they are here, let us not give them cause to do more harm than they already have."

Ralph spit. "Had I a sword!"

Isabel shushed him, and they entered the hall, stopping at the forward hearth that warmed the aft portion of the hall. It was also where the villagers ate and came to see to the lord's business and where the hounds were leashed. The upper hall where Manhku rested, along with the lord's table, was where the nobles resided. And, Isabel thought, the Normans who acted as if all was theirs. And William had yet to be crowned!

Isabel bent to let several of the hounds free. As she did, Ralph moved closer and whispered, "Milady, many villagers hide in the forests, near the caves. They are hungry, and many are wounded. You are our only hope."

She turned to look up at him and nearly screamed. Warner stood only a few feet from Ralph. He fondled the hilt of his sword, his dark eyes narrowed, and he stepped closer still.

"Is privacy now against Norman law?" Isabel intentionally asked in English.

Warner's scowl deepened. "It would please me, Lady Isabel, if you would speak my tongue," the knight responded in French.

Isabel nodded, her suspicions confirmed. Sir Warner did not speak her tongue. "I beg your pardon, sir knight. I but asked if privacy was now against Norman law."

Warner nodded and smiled a crooked smile. The scar on his chin tightened with the gesture. He was a handsome man whom under different circumstances Isabel could find herself admiring. Of all of Rohan's men, he seemed the most interested in bridging the great divide that separated

Norman and Saxon, while Rohan seemed to be the one most bent on widening it.

"Nay, Lady Isabel. In times of war, etiquette does not exist. Not even on the battlefield."

Isabel curtsied and smiled a trite, forced smile. "Of course, Sir Warner. How foolish of me to expect more from a Norman." She looked him directly in the eye. "If you will pardon me, my man Ralph brings me news of the village. He speaks only English."

Warner nodded but did not move from them. Instead, he leaned up against the hearth and reached down to scratch a hound behind the ears. "Feel free to discuss your affairs."

Isabel turned from the arrogant knight. She would have the last laugh on them all. In English, she said to Ralph, "He does not understand our gentle tongue. Speak freely to me, but do it in a manner such that he believes we discuss the daily business of Alethorpe."

Ralph nodded, and before he started, he cast a wary eye on the knight, who regarded him with cool disdain.

"Deep in the great forest of Menloc, a group from Wilshire gathers, as well as many people from our village. They fear the Normans. They are tired and hungry, and many have festering wounds."

With the toe of her shoe, Isabel poked at an ember that jumped from the hearth to the stone floor near her foot. In a slow, grinding motion, she snuffed the heat from it. "I cannot bring food, Ralph, but"—she bit her bottom lip and tried hard not to look at the Norman knight—"methinks I have a way to deplete the stores under the Norman's nose. I will gather the healing basket. Then I will meet you behind the stable along the south wall."

"Aye, near the rubble break."

Isabel nodded. Ralph swept a narrowed gaze at Warner, who stood staring at them both as if he understood every word they said. Isabel felt her cheeks warm. It was difficult to remain calm when she was about to defy Rohan's orders.

"The Norman guards you well. How will you rid yourself of this unwanted shadow?"

Isabel smiled and put her hand on his forearm. "Leave that to me. Now, let me sway the Norman."

Isabel turned a serene face up to Warner. He immediately stiffened. She smiled and softly said in French, "You have nothing to fear from me, Sir Warner. I only ask a small favor of you." Skeptically, he nodded for her to continue. "Sir Warner, Ralph has explained to me that there are many villagers who are ailing and have not eaten in several days. Our stores are full. I ask that you give him permission to take from them to feed my people."

Warner scowled, uncertainty clouding his features.

Isabel touched his arm. "Sir, the people require nourishment to survive."

Warner continued to scowl at her. It was clear he held no trust of her.

"Would you and your fellow knights tend the fields and the sheep when there are no churls left to tend them?"

She knew the moment she won. He straightened, and his eyes cleared. "I'll have a man see to it."

Isabel pressed her hand more firmly on his arm. "'Tis not necessary. You Normans scare my people. Allow Ralph to go unsupported so that they may sup in peace." When he gave no further word, she smiled and squeezed his arm, then stepped back. "My thanks, Sir Warner."

Isabel hastened to inform Ralph of what she was about. "See to several families, and when the time is right, slip out the back of one of the huts, and meet me with the cart."

Ralph's eyes danced in humor, but Isabel gave him a stern look. No need to alert the Norman that he was being played for a fool. As Ralph moved toward the kitchen, Isabel moved toward the great hearth and the Saracen. Warner followed close behind.

Isabel stared down at the sleeping giant. His wound gaped, but it did not fester so much. She bent to her task. Several times as she cleaned, packed, then bound the leg, the African stirred. As she wrapped the last of the linens around his thigh, his dark eyes opened, and she frowned at him. "Stay down, Manhku, or lose your leg."

He growled softly, more like a puppy than a great dog, but closed his eyes, and soon his snores filled the hall. Isabel looked up at Warner, who offered his hand to her. She placed hers in his, and he drew her up. "Thank you, Sir Warner. Now, if you will excuse me, I should like to change my clothes and freshen up. I have much that needs my attention this day."

"I have been entrusted to secure your safety this day, damsel. Do not play me the fool in Rohan's eye."

A quick stab of guilt flittered through Isabel's chest. But her path was clear. Her people came first, and did not Sir Warner say only moments before that there were no rules of etiquette in war?

"I doubt, Sir Warner, that you could ever look the fool to Rohan." Isabel grabbed her basket of herbs and hurried up the great stairway to the lady's solar, where she quickly changed into sturdier clothes.

Moments later, with her basket replenished and laden

with herbs, balms, and linens, Isabel slipped out of the room. Casting a wary glance over her shoulder, she held her breath. Warner stood at the end of the hall leading to the stairway. In a slow backward motion, Isabel moved down the hallway. As Warner turned, she pressed back into a shallow alcove. Her heart beat so hard in her chest she thought for sure it would rip her open. The hard, cold stones dug into her back.

After several long moments, when no sound emerged, she dared to peek. With Warner's back once again to her, Isabel darted around the bend of the hallway to the next stairway. On one side, there was a thick wooden door that led to the old chambers of the manor and down to the kitchens. Some were still fit for habitants, but mostly they were used for storage. Across from the door was stone.

Isabel reached up as high as she could on her toes and felt along the protruding ledge of a ruggedly hewn block. She pressed her fingertips up and down until she heard a small snap. She smiled. Several larger blocks moved forward, a door, leading to a secret passageway to the back of the manor and into the forests.

Her smile tightened as she remembered her mischievous brother. Close in age as they were, Geoff had always included her in his adventures. One had been the discovery by accident of the secret passageway. Many a time, they hid from their father in the dark recesses of the dank stairway when he stormed the hall demanding that his children perform loathsome tasks.

Her heart ached for her brother. When he had gone to foster with Harold, she had been devastated. But Geoff had returned regularly, and once he'd earned his spurs, he resided more oft than not at Rossmoor.

Quickly, she slipped through the narrow opening into the dark, dank stairway. Isabel nearly dropped her basket as the odious stench of excrement assailed her senses. The drop to the cesspool ran along the passage. She gagged several times before she managed to gather herself and feel her way down the slippery steps, using the wall as her guide.

Still holding her breath, Isabel came to the bottom of the stairwell. Very slowly, she felt for the latch that would open the door to the outside. Cool air rushed at her, and Isabel gulped great mouthfuls of it. Sunlight filtered through the dense bramble of the mulberry bush that shielded the secret stone door from view.

Isabel crossed herself quickly as she said a silent thank you to her great-grandfather Leofric. When he constructed Rossmoor, he made certain that if his wife's Norse family came to call without an invitation, there would be an escape route. And now it served Isabel well.

Because of where the entry was positioned, all Isabel had to do was move along the manor walls to the high stone wall that surrounded Rossmoor. Hidden behind another overgrown mulberry bush was a passage through the stone wall to the outer fringes of the forest. She found the latch and slipped through the other side to meet with a waiting Ralph.

"You did not encounter any Normans?" Isabel asked, surprised to find the smith waiting so soon with a cart laden with food.

"The Normans may have their own stench, but they cannot tolerate the stench of the tanner's hut. I made that my third stop. They are no doubt still gagging up their morning meal."

Isabel smiled and picked up an even pace beside Ralph as he pulled the cart toward the thick copse of trees. "We may not match the fierce Norman knights in weaponry and horse, but we outman them with our wits. Let us hope the rest of Saxony is as wily as we, Ralph."

Rohan sat astride Mordred, the forest quiet and morose around him, his nose raised in the crisp November air. Like a wolf's, his nostrils twitched, then flared. His prey was near. He could smell the stench of their terror.

There had been nothing left of the small camp the villagers had made. Only blood-soaked earth and cold embers told their story. There was not even the remnant of a cloth or a trencher of food. It was if they had been plucked up by a hand in the sky.

Rohan looked up through the thick canopy of trees. Sunlight filtered through the bleak branches, casting a deathly pall over the eerie silence.

"They watch us, Rohan," Thorin said from his right side.

Rohan nodded, narrowing his eyes to see more clearly into the thick bramble. They were at a disadvantage. His men were best met in the open, where the great destriers could be easily maneuvered. As they were, his Blood Sword knights would be hard pressed to wield their great swords and battle axes in a worthy manner. Their mounts would be climbing over the next man's, and confusion would reign supreme.

Rohan had never backed away from a fight in his life, but his gut told him should they press the point with these marauders on this terrain, the loss of his men would be substantial.

"Aye, they watch and wait for us to pull closer together. 'Tis not the best of positions for us, my friend."

"We would kill each other in our efforts to slay them."

Rohan nodded. "'Tis their folly to underestimate the power of our arsenal." He grinned and said, "So let us give them a taste of what we are capable of."

Thorin grinned in return. "Aye, my bow cries for attention."

Rohan pulled his long bow from the leather sheath that cradled it on his saddle. Instead of one arrow, he drew three and notched them.

His men followed suit. Because the copse was so thick and the cowardly raiders hid low beneath it, Rohan aimed his trio of arrows at an angle that would have maximum impact and penetration.

He released, as did his men. The hissing sound of well-placed arrows stirred the air in a hideous scream, followed by Rohan's deep, gut-wrenching battle cry. Seconds later, human screams erupted from the bramble. Rohan and his men notched more arrows and let them fly.

More screams erupted from the bramble. The forest shook as the bodies of the cowards fell or turned to flee in the thick cover. Rohan sat astride his mount with no intention of following them deeper into the forest. He pulled another three arrows from the quiver and notched them. This time, he aimed at a higher angle, giving the arrows more of an arch to catch up with the fleeing marauders. Once again, his men followed suit. The sweet hissing sound of the arrows as they launched into the sky gave Rohan shivers. While he was knight first and foremost and found the broadsword made for his hand, he and his men were also expert archers and had learned the skill well. It had come to their aid more times than he could count. For sometimes a sword or an ax was not the weapon to see the job met.

More screams erupted, this time from deeper in the forest.

When several more barrages of arrows brought no cries of pain, Rohan nodded, satisfied that while they might not have eliminated the destructive raiders, enough damage was done to prevent another attack anytime soon.

Rohan turned in his saddle and looked down at the upstart squire of the lady Isabel. "You would learn soon enough, boy, that Norman knights are versed in all aspects of weaponry."

Russell swallowed hard and nodded.

Rohan reined Mordred around and raised his hand to his men. "There is naught else for us to do here. Let us patrol this land we have conquered before we return to Rossmoor."

Rohan's blood warmed when he spoke of Rossmoor. But it was not for the impressive stone edifice. Nay, it was for the stubborn wench who called herself lady of the manor. To his utter astonishment, he found himself thinking of the maid and the excitement she wrought from him over the thrill of the kill.

He shook his head in self-loathing. She was but one of many women who could turn a man's head. And there were scores more like her in this godforsaken land.

As Ralph led her deeper into the frigid forest, Isabel noticed the quietness surrounding them. It was as if she stepped through a graveyard. The air here was colder, the color dimmer. The morning frost lingered, marking their

passage with a soft crunch of frozen turf. The birds she
was used to hearing chirp cheerfully in the sunshine were
silent. It was if their joy had been struck from them.

Isabel could well relate. In less then two months' time,
her life and the lives of all of Saxony were twisted inside
out. A foreigner claimed the throne of England. Her father
and her brother gone to war, mayhap both dead, her lands
and people decimated by cowardly raiders and then the
arrival of the Normans.

She shivered hard and pulled her fur-lined cloak tighter
around her shoulders. A sad smile crossed her face. The
mantle was of fine Norse mink. Fully lined, the outer fabric a luxurious embroidered velvet. A gift last Michaelmas
from her father. He had commissioned it for her. Part of
her wedding trousseau. He had insisted she take it as an
early gift from an aging father. She was happy to accept it.

Isabel swallowed hard. Her wedding date was planned
to mark the spring slaughter. Would Arlys come for her?
Would he demand she be given to him as was promised by
her father?

He had been patient all these years. Their betrothal
contract was forged when she was but a young girl. Two
years after her first courses, she was promised as wife to
the earl. But with her mother's passing coming right before
the time she was originally to wed, her father hesitated.
He could not bear to lose his wife and his daughter in the
same year. He insisted that Isabel stay as lady of the manor
until Geoff took a wife. Arlys was not happy and even pe-
titioned Edward to force Alefric to honor the contract as it
was originally written.

But Alefric was godfather to several of Edward's court
favorites. Alefric was also a benevolent patron of the saints

and had stood steadfast beside Edward when Godwin would have stirred up civil war.

And so Arlys was doomed to lose his petition. To show good faith, Alefric gave the earl a portion of her dower lands in Mercia. The balance of her dowry, one of the richest ever to be recorded, would follow on the wedding day. Anger roiled in her belly. Would that she still retained those lands! At least she knew her father's treasury was well hidden deep in the caves. Some months before Edward's death, Alefric being the wise man he was and foreseeing the future, had moved the chest of silver to the caves. When they heard of William's intent to sail to the shores of England and claim the throne, they sighed in relief. Rossmoor may be taken, but the silver would serve them well to buy passage to friendlier climes should the need arise.

But until such time, the coin would await the lord's return deep in the caves of Menloc.

Isabel didn't like the dark, dank caves. The bats were many and ferocious. Tales of the lost souls who wandered the deep crevices crying out for others had terrified her since childhood.

And whispers about the witch there grew with each passing year. 'Twas said she was the one responsible for the lost souls in the first place and that she was mightier than any warrior and wove her clothes from the hair of her victims. Isabel had loudly protested when her father picked the caves as the hiding spot for his silver.

"But Father!" she had cried. "The witch will shear you and pike your head to add to her collection!"

"Nay, child." He had shushed her. "I know of what I speak. Now, let us see to the chore."

And so it was done.

At least, Isabel thought, all was not lost. Mayhap if her betrothal to Arlys was null, she could wag the silver under the nose of a new potential husband. She let out a long breath. It occurred to her then that she was not unhappy she would not wed with Arlys. She could not exactly say why that was, but she knew part of it was that he was older, and he spent most of his time at court instead of tending his shires, but those were silly reasons. Arlys was, or had been, a powerful overlord. He was a good match for someone of her station. United, they would be a most formidable couple. Amongst the most powerful in England.

Isabel sighed and watched her breath darken in the chill of the air. But Arlys did not stir her heart. And his touch did not elicit the warmth that Rohan's did. Aye, Rohan disturbed her on many levels, and Holy Mother forgive her, but on more than a few occasions, her thoughts conjured up his naked, powerful body.

Isabel stumbled, and had she not had a firm grip on the wagon, she would have tumbled to the hard earth.

"Easy, milady," Ralph said, steadying her. "We are almost there."

And so Isabel pushed the troubling thoughts of the dark knight far from her.

Nine

A small clearing emerged from the thick copse of trees. A large fire blazed in the middle. Several small makeshift huts hugged as close to the flames as safety permitted, drawing the meager warmth while forming a snug semicircle around it. Several people looked up, their bleak, forlorn faces nearly as pale as the frosty turf. Those from Alethorpe Isabel instantly recognized, those from Wilshire, a two-day ride from Rossmoor, she barely could.

As recognition dawned on the villagers, their faces morphed from despair to pure joy. "Milady, milady!" they cried in chorus, then enveloped her in a mass of frightened, tired humanity. Isabel's heart swelled with love, and as she hugged them to her, warm tears trailed down her cheeks. She feared to speak lest her voice crack and they would think her weak. Instead, she kept her head down and wiped the tears with the sleeve of her gown.

Once she had collected herself, Isabel stood back and painted on a fierce smile. "Have faith! Lord Alefric and Sir Geoff have yet to return. When they do, we shall see our lands more settled. Until then, let me tend to you, then I urge you all to come to Alethorpe."

Several people cried out in fear. "The Normans!"

Isabel nodded. "Aye, the Normans abound in my hall, but they are not bent on the same destruction as the raiders. At least for now, the Normans will protect us. It is more than what you have here."

"Milady, the Normans would slit our throats whilst we sleep," Ralph said, disdain lacing each word. "I would stay here before returning."

Isabel turned shocked eyes on the smithy. "Ralph! You would desert your wife and daughters in the village?"

He shook his head, his dark eyes hard. "I would bring them here."

"'Tis folly. The raiders are many. They maim and plunder. You would perish here with no food."

"I have a sturdy spear. The others have bows."

"Aye, and you are capable. And whilst I allowed you to hunt two days a month in the lord's forests, the Norman may not be so generous. The stores and larders at Rossmoor are plenty. The Norman has promised to see the smokehouse refilled as it depletes."

Ralph shook his head. His brows furrowed. "Have you been persuaded by the Norman, milady?"

Isabel gasped, shocked at his accusation. "Nay! I think only of your safety and the safety of the others. Out here in the middle of the forest, you are easy pickings for starvation and the raiders. At Rossmoor, you have a chance." Isabel pulled the heavy tarp from the laden cart. "Mildred," she said to the old midwife, "have Blythe help you distribute the food we have brought. Be frugal with it. I have no guarantee when more will be forthcoming."

The woman bobbed her head and set about the chore. Isabel turned back to Ralph. "Show me to the wounded."

She followed him to a larger hut set back behind the smaller ones. As she ducked in, pushing back the tattered fabric that acted as a door, the stench that met her nostrils caused the bile in her belly to rise. She stopped in mid-step and struggled to keep her meager breakfast down.

Ralph steadied her. "Some of the wounds have festered too long, milady. I fear they are beyond saving."

Isabel nodded and motioned to Brice, Mildred's sturdy grandson, to follow her out to the fresh air. "Bring the pallets out here near the fire. Heat two cauldrons of water to boiling."

He turned to do her bidding, but she grabbed his shoulder. He turned dark brown eyes up to her. "And Brice, fetch me a good sharp ax and a dagger." The boy paled considerably, but he bobbed his head and scurried to do her bidding.

"Have you the stomach for it, milady?" Ralph asked from behind her.

Straightening her back, Isabel turned and looked up into his dark eyes, only to find quiet concern for her. "Aye, I have no choice. They can either lose a limb or lose their life. I will give them each the choice."

As so it was to be. When Paul, Ralph's brother, was brought to her and deposited on the pallet, he passed out from the pain of his arm being disturbed. Isabel pulled back the rough fabric stuck into the deep gash in his forearm. The stench that rose from the wound had the kick of a destrier. Isabel breathed in through her mouth. The flesh around the gash was black. Thick green and yellow pus oozed from the swollen appendage. The poison had worked its way up to the elbow.

She touched his brow. It was hot with fever. Isabel pressed her hand to his cheek. He opened his eyes. Bleak and hopeless, he stared at her. "Paul, I cannot save your arm. But I can save your life if you allow me to—" she swallowed hard—"allow me to sever it from you. 'Tis the only way to keep the poison from spreading."

He nodded and closed his eyes. Isabel raised her gaze to Ralph, who kneeled beside her.

"I shall need your brawn, Ralph. If the arm is to be cleanly severed, it will take more than a sharp blade and my meager strength."

"Tell me what to do."

Isabel got to work. She formed a tourniquet several inches above the black flesh and gave it time to numb the poisoned part of Paul's arm. She asked for rope and was given several lengths. She tied one at each of Paul's ankles and the other two on his wrists. The sturdier men would pull him taut so that he could not thrash and impede Ralph's aim. Last, she found a solid branch and gave it to the man to bite down on.

"My pardon, Ralph, for asking such a thing of you. Had I the strength, I would do it myself," Isabel softly said.

"I am honored, milady."

She turned her gaze back to Paul, who despite his dire straits was fully awake. The fear on his face was almost enough to turn Isabel away. But she held fast. She crossed herself and said a silent prayer. "'Tis for the best, Paul. I will cauterize the stump, and the pain will ease as well as the fever."

He nodded. "Do it now!"

Isabel gave the signal to the men, and they pulled his limbs taut. Ralph raised the ax, and in one swift strike, he brought it down, severing the arm in half. Paul's screams disturbed the eerie quiet of the surrounding forest. Isabel could not fight back the bile this time. As discreetly as she could, she released what was left of her morning meal onto the hard earth. She wiped her sleeve across her mouth and bent to the chore of cauterizing the wound.

And so the afternoon went. She did not count the severed limbs, fingers, or toes. She did not count the pale, lifeless faces of those she could not save. She did not count the times she thought she could not stomach another wound or bathe another body raging with fever.

When the last of her people was tended to, Isabel looked up to Ralph, who appeared as weary as she felt. "Ralph, it seems the thieves were more bent on maiming than killing. What manner of man does this?"

The old smithy squatted next to her. He stared into the waning fire for a long time, not speaking. He clasped his gnarled hands, the lines in them deep and cracked. "The men are well armed and skilled in the art of war. Some I would swear were of Viking blood, but they bore no colors." He looked at her. "In truth, I know not whence they came."

Isabel put a comforting hand on the man's sinewy arm. "Viking blood runs deep among our people, Ralph. Could it be kin?"

The smithy frowned and shook his head, but he turned angry eyes on her. "Who kills his own kin?"

Isabel thought of the answer. She did not like what was obvious. "'Tis not so hard to think of in these times.

Harold's own brother sought to slay him for the crown. With the Normans' trespass, I fear we will see many strangers swarm our land, most more than willing to kill for a piece of it. Even du Lac's own brother challenged him." Isabel thought of Rohan, and her body quivered. So involved in her tasks, she had not given him a thought since her arrival in the glen. She looked up toward the darkening sky. He would have returned to Rossmoor by now. She trembled to think of his fury when he discovered her gone.

Isabel smiled sadly at the old villager beside her. Aye, there was no choice. She would take Rohan's wrath a thousand times over. She had no regrets for coming to the glade. Indeed, she would fight to come again. "I pray this knight Rohan will be good for one thing, to rid the forests of this scourge."

Ralph snorted, then spit to the ground. Abruptly, he stood. "Norman swine! Who is this William, anyway? He has no blood tie to our land. He is nothing but a bastard grandson to a tanner."

Isabel nodded and stood with Ralph's assistance. As she brushed the dried leaves and dirt from her gown, she said, "Aye, he is all of that, Ralph, but be warned. The Black Sword who now trespasses our land and claims it is also the grandson of that same tanner. I pray thee tread lightly until we have a firm footing in this war. Let us be patient and see this charade to the end. Much can happen to the two bastards who would rape us of our birthrights."

Ralph's dark eyes flashed in defiance. "Lord Arlys is near, Lady Isabel. He gathers men. I will bide my time and watch. We will yet win the day."

At his words, Isabel's belly slowly churned. "Tell me of Lord Arlys. Where is he?"

"I have only heard he did not have the men to with-stand the assault on Dunsworth, but he escaped with his life. The manor has been reduced to rubble, and the lady Elspeth is being held for ransom. I had heard the young Lord Edward is missing."

Isabel gasped. Poor Elspeth! Arlys's sister was only ten, and poor sweet Edward? Where could he be? Had Arlys hidden the lad? Silently, Isabel crossed herself and realized she was more fortunate than most Saxon maids. Rohan was a brutal warrior. It was true he held no compassion for her or her people. But he had not forced himself on her, nor had he destroyed Rossmoor or the village. Indeed, only a fool would do so. For it would only have to be rebuilt.

Isabel glanced around the quiet camp. The low moans of those surviving wounded had quieted, and the wide-eyed faces of the children now receded into the shadows in fatigued sleep. She noticed a young mother sitting much too close to the fire with her new babe clutched tightly to her breast, trying valiantly to keep the child warm. Isabel reached down and grabbed her fur-lined cloak from where she had laid it and walked over to the young women. Soulful eyes stared up in hopelessness. Isabel smiled, then kneeled next to the girl and wrapped the rich garment around her and the babe. "Here, you will be warmer now." The girl's eyes welled with tears. Isabel's smile widened, and she fought back her own onslaught of tears. "God is watching over you and your babe."

Isabel stood and turned back to Ralph and Mildred, who watched her with shocked expressions.

Isabel shrugged her shoulders. "We are in this together. I hope, should I ever need a kind word, someone will come forward and soothe my fears." Isabel rubbed her hands up and down her arms. "Ralph, have you word of Father Michael? There are too many graves to be blessed. 'Tis not fair that innocents should lie unshriven."

"The good friar has not been seen since the first raid on Alethorpe."

"Do you think him slain?"

"I know not, milady."

Isabel thought on the matter. If Father Michael was indeed gone, then she would have to travel to the abbey at Dunleavy and ask one of the friars there to come bless the graves. 'Twas a two-day ride to the east. But she could not go without an escort. Would Rohan give it to her? Did he even care that her valiant people lay unshriven? Nay, she would not believe such a vile thing, not even of a Norman. She would have her priest, even if she had to sneak out under the cloak of night and find one herself.

Rohan galloped along the well-forged road to Rossmoor, feeling victorious. They had won the day. And with the absence of the raiders, he could encourage those who had fled to the forests to return under his protection.

'Twould be another good day to celebrate. He grinned beneath his helmet. And a good night to taste more thoroughly the sweetness of Lady Isabel. His blood warmed. Aye, he admitted he would be hard pressed not to sink deep between her thighs, but he possessed supreme self-control. There were other ways to find release. And he planned on schooling the reluctant maid in every one of them.

As the thick fog parted and Rossmoor came into view, Rohan's chest filled with pride. The large stone manor was a fine bit of architecture. The luxuries that abounded within were the best he had ever experienced. The surrounding lands were ripe with natural resources. Aye, Alethorpe was a jewel in the crown of England.

Excitement pulsed through him. Should he be so lucky, it and all that cleaved to it would one day be his.

As Rohan skidded to a halt in the courtyard, his mood instantly soured, and his warrior instinct flared. Something was deeply amiss. Warner paced a deep wedge into the stone. Rohan dismounted. Hugh grabbed Mordred's reins and walked off with the huge black. Rohan's eyes scanned the area for Isabel. His ire rose when it was plain she was not present.

"Why are you not guarding the lady?" Rohan demanded, yanking his helmet from his head. As he pushed the cowl back, he knew the moment Warner turned fearful eyes up to him that the lady was gone. A maelstrom of emotion he could not name rushed up inside Rohan. For Warner to show fear of him meant the worst. Had she fallen at the hand of a raider?

Rohan's blood chilled to ice in his body. Had Henri returned?

"Where is she?" he demanded, stepping closer to his man. Never in his life had Rohan thought to strike a man over a woman, but if Warner—

"She gave me the slip, Rohan. She tricked me!"

Rohan grabbed Warner by the shoulders and shook him like a rat. "Where is she?"

Thorin came to stand beside Rohan. He put a hand out, breaking his iron grip on Warner.

"She told me her people needed food. She asked if I would give her permission to take from the larder. I gave it. She then told me she needed to fetch more herbs from her chamber. I watched her go up those stairs, Rohan. I stood at the end of the hallway and awaited her return. She did not pass me by! I turned that keep inside out. She disappeared into the air! Her man Ralph, who was to help her feed the churls, has disappeared as well."

Rohan knew a fury so complete that for a moment he could see only black. In a supreme effort, he leashed his anger. In a slow, menacing voice, he demanded, "Have you scoured the perimeter? She would have had to go over the wall or around it."

"Aye, behind the stable are two sets of footprints and those of wagon wheels. But I lost the trail in the forest."

Rohan whistled to Hugh, who had almost reached the stable. "Mount up," he said to Warner. He turned to Thorin and grasped his shoulder. "Stand guard here, my friend. I will return, God willing with the maid."

As Hugh returned with the black, Rohan sprang onto its back with much enthusiasm for a man who had thought of naught else but resting his weary body and filling his belly. Thorin watched with interest. Rohan caught the look. He smiled grimly. "Do not read more into my concern than what is actually there, Thorin. The maid is a valuable pawn in this deadly game I play with my brother. I would see her here to stack the board in my favor."

Thorin grinned and nodded. "If you say so, Rohan."

Rohan reined his horse about and called to Ioan and Stefan, who also had remounted. "Let us find the maid so that we may return to yet another feast."

Ten

While Isabel stacked what few items she had onto the small cart, she dreaded the long, cold walk back to Rossmoor. Ralph hand-constructed several torches, but she doubted they would see them all of the way back. The sun had set, and with the thick blanket of fog, the path would be more difficult to discern.

"Milady," Mildred said, "mayhap you should not travel. The wolves prowl as hungry as we. 'Tis too dangerous. Wait till morn."

Mildred spoke true. Yet Isabel knew she must return to Rossmoor as soon as possible. Her people would suffer under the angry hand of the Black Sword. She would not have their pain on her conscience. "Nay, I—" Isabel stopped. The ground beneath her feet rumbled as if the earth split in half. A distant thunder approached from where she had come. She looked up, and in the thick mist of the fog, the low glow of fire burned.

The thunder increased in volume, and the fire grew brighter. She cast her gaze wildly about to the villagers, but they had disappeared into the fog behind her. Only she stood in the camp. Alone as hell crashed toward her.

And then they emerged. Four black knights, each holding a blazing pitch torch, on black horses. Mailed and battle-ready, they thundered into the glen. The one in front, the biggest and, she knew, the worst of them all, came to a sliding halt only feet from her.

At that moment, Isabel knew what the hare must feel. Doom settled with a bone-chilling terror gripping her chest. Isabel opened her mouth to defend her action, but words would not come forth. Instead, her gaze clashed with the gold one that blazed from behind the black helmet. A slash of harsh wind blew against her, as if slapping her in punishment for her defiance.

Isabel shivered hard, the spasm wracking her entire body. Her jaw clenched so hard she thought it might break. Whilst she did not look directly at them, she could see Rohan's men fanned out behind him.

As he continued to glower down at her, Isabel found her resolve. "Must you follow me everywhere?"

"You were ordered to stay at Rossmoor!" Rohan bellowed.

Another hard blow of cold air slapped her, this time from behind, as if it goaded her. "You do not own me, Norman."

Rohan turned slightly to his left and tossed the blazing torch he held to Warner, who had a most interesting expression on his face. It was a look of extreme relief mixed with complete fury. Isabel smiled and gave the knight a shallow curtsy. "My thanks, Sir Warner, for the larder."

His eyes narrowed. Isabel turned back to the person who gave her more cause for frustration than any other human on the earth. Rohan urged his mount forward.

As he bent to snatch Isabel up from the ground, a sharp scream rent the tense air.

Like an arrow, Brice shot out of the nearest hut straight for Rohan. Warner swung the torch in a backward swipe. The young man screamed in pain as he went flying backward, landing on his back with a bone-crushing thud. Isabel moved to assist him, but Rohan swooped her up with his right arm. He flung her over the horse's thick neck. Isabel kicked and screamed and righted herself. In a very awkward position, legs astride, she faced the furious knight.

His lips twisted in an amused sneer. Had he not worn his helmet, she would have struck him. Rohan yanked his helmet off and tossed it to Ioan, who had moved closer. Isabel trembled under his angry scrutiny. After he pushed the cowl back with his left hand, he grabbed her with both hands by the shoulders and shook her. "I own you, Isabel. I own everything your eyes can see. I forbade you leave the village today. *Yet you defy me.*"

"I am no man's slave," she breathed.

Rohan's eyes darkened. "Aye, you are mine, and you would fare much better the sooner you accept it."

His eyes seared into hers as if branding her with them. She stiffened when his eyes dropped to her lips. Unconsciously, she licked them.

Rohan groaned. "Yea, I own you, damsel, and so I will claim you in public for all of your people to see."

His lips crashed into hers. Stunned, like a piece of rope, Isabel hung limp in his arms as his lips plundered hers. His large hand splayed across the full swell of her bosom, heating her more effectively than the bonfire. The pressure of his hand increased, and her body reacted as if lightning struck. Isabel opened her eyes and squirmed. The horse pawed the hard earth beneath her. As quickly as it had begun, the kiss was over. Shame heated her cheeks.

And Isabel struck back the only way she knew how, with her tongue. "I will be no leman to a bastard!"

Rohan's eyes flashed, furious. "As my slave, you have no choice." He lifted her high from the horse's neck and turned her in midair, then settled her in front of him. He pointed to Brice, who lay cowering on the cold, hard earth. "Who is he?"

"B—Brice."

"Where does he hail from?"

Isabel half turned in the saddle and caught his angry eyes. "Alethorpe."

Rohan's eyes scanned the huts over her head. "What is this place?"

Isabel stiffened and turned, her eyes scanning the forest edge. Intuitively, she knew her people had not gone far, and all of the wounded still lay in the huts.

"A place of refuge," she softly said.

"From the raiders, damsel, or from me?"

"Both," she honestly answered.

Rohan reined his horse, and in a perfect pirouette the great steed turned on his back hooves, and they thundered to the edge of the encampment. Isabel cried out just as they were about to plunge into the darkness of the forest. But Rohan reined to a halt. Slowly, for great effect, he turned the great steed around. Isabel felt the power of his anger surround her. Nervously, she glanced around the clearing. Not one face showed save for Brice, who did not dare move away from Warner.

Isabel pressed her hand to her throat. The villagers

might be invisible, but she knew they watched. The stallion pranced toward the largest hut, the one housing the wounded. She stiffened. What would he do to them? End their misery?

Facing the forest edge, Rohan stopped next to the hut. "Come meet your new master, Saxons!" Rohan called to the darkness. Nesting birds in the surrounding tress ruffled their feathers. Leaves rustled to the ground. An owl's cry sliced through the tension. When the silence continued, Rohan shouted, "Show courage! Come from your hiding places and hear my words."

As silence continued to meet them, Ioan said, "Shall we torch the huts, Rohan?"

"Nay!" Isabel screamed. She turned as much as possible in the saddle, which was not much, and grabbed Rohan's shoulder. "Please, they fear you. I beg you, no more bloodshed."

Rohan growled low. The vibration of it pulsed down her arm. His arm tightened around her waist. "Once again, you beg for something that is not yours, with nothing to give for it."

Hot tears welled in her eyes. She could not allow him and his men to destroy what she had worked so hard to save this day.

"Spare my people, Rohan. Spare them, and you can take me here, now, in this saddle!"

His eyes narrowed. "Your people are mine now, Isabel. I would do my best to protect them. Yet you are too stubborn to see it."

She caught her breath at his words. "You have no intention of harming them?"

"Only if they attempt to harm me." He pointed to Brice,

who lay as still as a corpse. "What punishment should he receive for coming at me?"

"None. He sought to save me from harm."

"I would not have harmed you. Indeed, why do you think I am here?"

"To find your wench for the night!"

Rohan threw his head back and laughed. The sound was pure glee. Isabel scowled until he had his fill.

"You mock me, sir. 'Tis not wise in front of *my* people."

Rohan sobered. "I fear them not. And they would see themselves spared my blade."

"Tell them you do not wish to harm them."

Rohan scowled. "I will tell them what I will." He forced her around to face the encampment. "Step forward, Saxons, and hear my words! I am Rohan du Luc. I claim these lands and the people of these lands in the name of William Duke of Normandy, who will be crowned king. Swear your fealty to him, and you will have the duke's protection and with his protection, you will have mine!"

Brice was the first to offer his pledge. He was quickly followed by several more villagers, most of them from Wilshire. When Ralph came forward with Mildred, Isabel stiffened. Ralph's eyes held nothing but contempt. And if it were possible, Rohan's body tensed to hewn steel. Many more eyes still watched from the forest. Were they angry enough to attack? A sudden thought terrified Isabel. What if this favored knight, indeed, this cousin to William, should fall under a rebellious Saxon's hand? The terrifying vision of more slaughter erupted in her mind.

"Ralph," she pleaded from the saddle where Rohan enveloped her. "Please, no more blood needs to be spilled today."

The smithy nodded and turned to Rohan. "I am Ralph, smithy to Alethorpe. I pledge my fealty to William, but in return I expect my family should not be harmed."

Rohan nodded. "I accept your terms, Ralph. See to it, though, your family gives no cause for harm."

As each able-bodied man and woman gave the oath to Rohan, Isabel felt more tension leave her body. But every time she rearranged herself in the big saddle, she found herself rubbing up against Rohan's chest and thighs. Several times, she felt him stiffen behind her.

As the last villager came to kneel before Rohan, Isabel could hold her rigid position no longer. She relaxed against the hard chest of mail behind her. Rohan slipped an arm around her waist and pulled her tighter against him.

"Sir Warner," Rohan called to the knight who tossed a crude club onto the very small pile of weapons he had secured from the huts and persons of the villagers. Warner looked up to Rohan. "Since your careless acts have sent us here this night, I bid you watch over these churls until the morn, when I will send more men to accompany you and these poor souls back to Rossmoor."

Ioan snorted his glee. Warner frowned. Rohan turned sideways in his saddle. "He shall need company, Ioan. It is good of you to volunteer."

"But—"

Rohan laughed and reached down to grasp the torch Warner had snuffed. He signaled the horse forward to the fire, where he dipped the pitch-black tip into it. Instantly, it flared. He turned to Stefan. "See to the other torch, and let us ride." Before he turned to leave, Rohan tossed a saddle bag to Warner, who stood scowling in the center of the encampment.

"Good night, my friend." He reined the steed about, and with the torch held high, Rohan thundered into the dark of the forest.

After several leagues, Rohan felt Isabel's body finally relax against his. He knew it was more from exhaustion than comfort. His arm tightened around her soft warmth. He had shed his mantle and wrapped it securely around her shivering body. Now she burned like an ember against his chest and thighs. His groin tightened, and despite his own fatigue, he wanted nothing more than to pull Mordred to the side of the path and lay his mantle down for them both.

He flexed his jaw as he remembered the feeling of pure elation when he rode into that camp to find her standing alone, blood-soaked and defiant, next to the roaring fire, much as he had found her when he broke through the doors of Rossmoor. Once again, her people had deserted her, and once again, she stood fast against William's most notorious death squad. *Les morts* was not a name come by for living a passive life.

After rescuing William from certain death as he attempted to squash a rebellion in Brittany on his return from the harsh years in Iberia, Rohan, along with the surviving knights, was given the highest of honors as William's own private guard. It had been with very grudging reasoning that William dispatched Rohan and his men into the English countryside after Senlac. The duke trusted few men to secure this land, so he weighed the price of keeping Rohan and his Blood Swords close at hand or casting them wide to see to the duke's business. In the end, William opted to send *les morts* as his fist to squash the rebellious Saxons until such time as William was crowned. Once crowned, he would summon his trusted men, and they would decide on the future of *les morts* and England together

Isabel moved closer against Rohan's thighs. Half turning toward him, she rested a hand much too close to his thickening groin. Despite the bittersweet pain her presence caused him, Rohan pressed her pliable body closer to his. With one hand holding the torch high and the other around Isabel, he gave Mordred his head, knowing the beast would get them home posthaste. The call of a warm stall and a full manger was the only guide Mordred needed. Rohan looked ahead to Stefan, who led the way, his torch showing the path.

With each thrust of the steed's powerful haunches, Rohan's hips moved against the back of the sleeping damsel. With each move, his muscles tightened, and with each move, the urge to sate himself between her thighs grew stronger.

As their pace slowed, Rohan could not keep his hand in neutral territory. His fingertips splayed across the bottom swell of Isabel's full breast. When she wriggled in the saddle, her backside pressing more firmly against his burgeoning groin, he groaned.

He moved his hand up higher and cupped the fullness of her. He closed his eyes and envisioned his lips pressed to the sweet rose-colored peak. Aye, she had the breasts of a goddess. Full, ripe, creamy smooth. Perfect fodder for a man's amusement. Rohan pondered that thought. While he was not an inconsiderate lover, he was more bent on satisfying his own needs. Mostly because of time constraints.

There was no time to woo a maid in the aftermath of battle. Yet there had been more than a few winsome maids in William's court who were wont to take things slower when abed. He had lingered mostly for their sake, none holding his attention for more than a night or two. He found himself leaving the bed as soon as the deed was done, having no inclination toward the small talk women were bent on having after the act.

Nay, he was more comfortable conversing with his men, where he knew the words meant what they were intended and there was no speaking in riddles or guessing games such as the maids were plagued with. He found his relief in a woman in the bedchamber and had no desire for further interaction.

Rohan pressed his lips to the delicate shell of Isabel's ear. He nibbled the edge and decided he might want to learn more of damsels and their ways this winter. When her body arched and a soft moan escaped her lips at his touch, Rohan was encouraged to do more. He ran his tongue along the inner edge of her ear and pressed his hand more firmly to her breast. He felt her nipple pucker beneath his fingertips. He answered with a thrust of his hips against her back. Isabel's hand tightened around his thigh. When she moved her other hand to his thigh and pressed into his skin, he pushed harder against her back. His hand clasped her breast, and his lips dropped to the soft spot behind her ear.

Isabel's body stiffened. "Sleeping Beauty awakens," Rohan whispered against her skin. Her body trembled, yet she did not push away from him. He took her lead and kissed her neck, running his tongue along her warm skin.

"I have never touched a woman as soft as you, Isabel. You make me forget we are enemies."

When she did not resist, he did something that surprised him more than it surprised Isabel. He whistled to Stefan. The young knight slowed and turned to Rohan. "Aye?"

Rohan trotted up to the knight and handed him the torch. He would need two hands for what he wanted to do to the damsel. "Take this, and await me up ahead. I will only tarry for a moment."

Stefan looked to Isabel, then to Rohan, but took the torch and nodded. He trotted just up the way, the torches casting a dim glow where Rohan sat astride his mount. He pulled the mantle from Isabel's body and then lifted her and turned her to face him. He wrapped the mantle back around her shoulders. To keep her warm but more to shield her from Stefan's prying eyes.

He moved back in his saddle to give her more room, but for what he had in mind, closeness was required. In the pale light of the waning moon illuminating the path, Isabel looked up at him with startled eyes. Fatigue smudged the skin purple beneath her lashes, but he could not help himself.

He slipped an arm around her waist and brought her hard against his chest. "You will spend this night in my bed, Isabel. And every night until I say otherwise."

She stiffened. "Until you tire of me and cast me out?"

Rohan grinned. With his teeth, he pulled the gauntlet from his right hand and lowered it to her breast. He rubbed a thumb against an impudent nipple that strained against the rough fabric of her gown. Isabel hissed in a sharp breath and squeezed her eyes shut. When he moved the hand to her thigh and pulled her gown up, she opened her eyes. Anger raged. "Would you take me on this horse?"

"Nay, I wish only to slake my hunger a bit." He pulled her roughly against him and seized the moment, crushing his lips to hers.

Eleven

The impact of Rohan's kiss left Isabel limp and breathless. Had she not been so fatigued, she told herself, she would have fought him off, but she used that as an excuse to succumb to his carnal persuasion. Indeed, instead of feeling languid, she sensed a new rush of energy fill her.

Rohan's arm tightened like a band of steel around her waist, pulling her harder against him while his lips plundered and took from her what her mind so desperately wanted to hold hostage. In a slow, sensuous slide, his tongue slid along her lips, dipping into her mouth, softly touching hers. The intimacy of the contact shook her resolve. His large hand moved slowly up her leg to her thigh, his fingers slowly circling her skin, leaving her warm in its wake.

An unfamiliar tightening in her womb frightened her, but more than that, it excited her. She felt liquid, pliable, like warm beeswax in his hands. The space between her thighs grew warmer, and she felt moistness there. Rohan's hand slid farther up her leg, and when he pressed his palm against her sensitive mound, she nearly shot out of the saddle. When she moved against him, he pressed a fingertip to her wet opening. She moaned and grabbed onto his shoulders to keep herself from tumbling to the hard earth.

"Jesu!" Rohan cursed, and pushed her away from him. Isabel opened her mouth to demand to know what she had done wrong, but heat flooded her cheeks. Holy Mother, she had become a willing partner in his carnal game!

Rohan moved her around to face the pommel and away from him. He gathered up the reins and nudged the destrier forward. Without a word, he grabbed the torch from Stefan's hand, set his spurs to the horse's flanks, and thundered toward Rossmoor.

Isabel sat rigid and confused in the saddle. Her lips throbbed from his assault, her breasts felt heavy from his hand, and below? Isabel squeezed her eyes shut. She ached. And despite her ignorance, she knew only Rohan could quell the feeling.

Isabel opened her eyes to the darkness of the night. She pulled the mantle tighter around her shoulders. Confusion reigned in her head. What had just happened? Why was Rohan angry with her? It was he who should feel her wrath! How dare he touch her as he did, elicit the response from her he did, then cast her from him as if she raged with the pox?

Had she responded wrong? Her Norse blood ran hot in her veins, tempering her level-headed, well-bred upbringing. She was a passionate woman by nature. Apparently, she was passionate in this aspect as well.

Her frustration mounted. If she so disgusted him by her response, then mayhap he should not touch her so! Isabel smiled into the frigid night air. *Let him reap more of what he has sown.* To turn the screws tighter, Isabel leaned back into Rohan. Her aim was to frustrate him more, but the residual effect was that his body radiated warmth. The minute she pressed into him, his body stiffened. His anger at her radiated from him like a swarm of angry bees. She would never understand the ways of a man.

For long moments, Isabel contemplated what had happened, but fatigue crept over her, and soon the motion of the horse beneath her and the warm man reluctantly holding her against his chest lulled her into a deep sleep.

He heard the lookout call their approach long before he saw the high rise of Rossmoor. As they passed through the village, several people came to watch Rohan with their lady in hand thunder through the streets and up to the manor. Even after he came to an abrupt halt and tossed the reins to Hugh, Isabel continued to sleep soundly against his chest. Carefully, so as not to awaken her, he slid from the saddle with her in his arms and strode into the great hall. Rohan scowled when his men looked up from their tankards of ale. Several glanced at the burden in his arms and smirked. He could read their thoughts as easily as if they had spoken them out loud. They thought he was besotted by the maid. They were wrong. Yea, he wanted her, he would not argue that fact, but more than that, Isabel symbolized what they all desired. A titled, landed lady. She was England, and to possess her meant he would possess what she possessed. It occurred to him at that moment that he wanted the same respect from her people as they so freely gave her.

He would make a worthy lord. And with a damsel such as Isabel as his lady, his legacy would begin. A'isha's words haunted him. He must kill the kin of the woman who would bear his only sons. He looked down into the sleeping face. Aye, that part of the prophecy was true. And she would never forgive him for it. Regardless of the circumstances.

Rohan strode past his gaping men and up the wide stairway, where he was met by Enid. She followed him into his chamber. Gently, he laid Isabel down on the large bed. "See to your lady." He turned then and descended back into the hall, where he was met with grins and shaking heads.

Thorin thrust a well-filled tankard into his hand. Rohan drank deeply of the robust ale. He poured himself another. Before he sat down at the table, he looked over to where Manhku slept peacefully. Rohan scowled. Another troubled soul saved by the lady Isabel. He had no doubt someone would soon nominate her for sainthood.

With gusto, Rohan sat down to the full trencher Lyn set before him and ate. Stefan, already dining, sat across the table from him.

"Stefan tells us you and the lady stopped along the way for a bit of a tryst," Rorick prodded.

Rohan scowled and stared down the younger man. "Did he now?"

Stefan grinned and chewed a chunk of venison. "Aye, do you think I didn't turn and have a look?"

Thorin slapped the younger man on the back. "A voyeur at heart, are you, lad?"

Stefan tore off a chunk of bread and dunked it into the rich broth the meat stewed in. He chewed thoughtfully and shook his head. "Nay, I prefer to indulge, not watch. But with the way Rohan flutters about the lady Isabel, watching is all we will get, eh, Rohan? Methinks you are not wont to share that one."

Rohan eyed his men. They all watched him raptly for his response. He dipped a piece of bread into the stew, then chewed it slowly. He swallowed and followed it with a long draught of ale. Rohan chose his words carefully. He would not have it said that he had grown soft on a woman. Because a man who was led by his cock was not worthy to lead. "I admit the lady has caught my attention. But trust me, men, when I tell you, 'tis only the thrill of the hunt that intrigues me. Once I have snared the wench, if she will have any of you louts, you are free to pursue her."

Thorin scowled. He set his foot upon the bench across the table from Rohan and rested a brawny arm on his knee. He stared keenly at the younger man. "Isabel is a gentle-born lady, Rohan. In her veins flows the finest blood in Saxony, Norway, and even Normandy. You would do well to leave her be. Sully her, and you wouldst do us all a dishonor."

Rohan choked on his meat at Thorin's words. Rorick pounded him on the back. Rohan caught his breath and took a deep drink of his ale. Finally, through watery eyes, he said, "What say you? That from a man who leaves a trail of maidenheads from Norway to Constantinople and back to England?"

Thorin scowled. "We do not speak of my misdeeds, Rohan, but the prevention of one here. Find another maid to slake your lust. Leave the lady Isabel intact."

Rohan slammed the tankard down on the table, the force shattering it into several pieces. "I have had enough of your fatherly advice. Stefan will give you the details of our travels this eve. Prepare to depart at first light with several carts to retrieve the wayward churls."

Rohan stepped away from the table and stiffly bowed to his men. "Good eventide, men. May your cold pallets serve you well this frigid night." He turned then and strode angrily up the stairway and into his chamber. He slammed the door shut. The action startled Isabel awake.

Wide-eyed, her red lips parted, and her sunburst-colored hair swirling around her, the wild sight of her warmed his blood. He stepped closer and began to discard the trappings of his trade. He noticed a covered trencher of food beside the bed on a table, and a large cauldron of water steamed over the roaring fire with a stack of clean linens sitting nearby. Hugh knew he never slept with the day's grime clinging to him.

" 'Tis only I, Isabel. Go back to sleep," Rohan urged.

He scowled when she shook her head and slipped from the great bed. "I need to change my clothes and bathe. The stench of the dying clings to me." She moved toward the door but turned to him. "May I go to my chamber?"

Having removed his surcoat and hauberk, Rohan moved toward her. "I am not like Warner. I shall accompany you."

Anger flared in her eyes, but Isabel refrained from arguing. After she retrieved fresh clothing, she turned to him and quirked a brow. "I would like my privacy to bathe and change."

"Nay, you forfeited all rights to your privacy when you tricked Warner today. You will be shadowed as closely as a hawk shadows his next meal."

Isabel stalked haughtily past him and back to the lord's chamber. As if he were not present, she set about ladling the hot water from the cauldron into a deep bowl. She poured cool water from the pitcher to temper it. With linen in hand, she turned to Rohan, who stood quietly contemplating her. Even in her disheveled state, she was more beautiful than any woman he had ever laid eyes on. He narrowed his eyes as the thought passed through him. Aye, and while she was a natural beauty, it was her steel belly that attracted him to her most.

His gaze broke from hers and slowly slid down to her full breasts. He smiled when she stiffened. His gaze traveled lower to her slender waist, then rested on her belly. Aye, while she was a slip of a girl, her hips flared with enough space to bear many lusty sons. His gaze traveled back up to meet her glacial stare. His smile widened. Her frown deepened.

Reluctantly, Rohan broke his gaze from hers. "See to yourself first, Isabel. I will bathe at my leisure." His leisure, Isabel soon discovered, was in her father's great chair, drinking ale as he watched her disrobe and wash by the firelight. It could not be helped. There was no place for her to hide from his eyes. So she stood tall and proud before him, daring him with her eyes to touch her.

When she pressed the damp linen to her breasts, she closed her eyes. The pressure of her own hand while under his watchful eyes flustered her. Her nipples hardened, and when she drew the cloth away, Rohan cursed under his breath. He threw the cup into the fire and stomped from the room, slamming the door behind him.

His actions startled her, and yet she felt as if with his departure, the warmth had left the room. Shivering, Isabel completed her bath and slid a clean shift over her head, then slipped between the linens and furs on the bed.

* * *

Rohan was glad to see his men had bedded down for the night. Save for a few torches, the hall light had dimmed considerably. He stalked to where Manhku lay sleeping by the great hearth. Feeling as restless as a lone wolf, he began to pace before the fire. "God's blood!" he cursed, slamming a fist into his open hand. Did the woman not know the effect she had on a man? How could she expect him to sit passively by like a limp rag? And how could she demand such a thing? She had given her oath to him! He was entitled to her body. By her own words, she gave permission.

Then why was he down here with his men and not up there in the lord's bed taking what was his right to take?

Rohan scowled down at Thorin, who snored not far from where Manhku slept. The older man's righteous songs of chivalry fell on deaf ears. There were no rules in war. Survival of the fittest had always been his motto. Had it not been, he would have perished in that hellhole in Iberia.

Resolute, Rohan turned on his heel and took the stairs three at a time back to the torture chamber.

He pushed the door open with more force than necessary. His eyes scanned the room for the maid. When it appeared she had disappeared, he rushed toward the bed. He stopped in his tracks. So great was the bed and so small was she, he could barely see her form nestled deep beneath the furs. But her golden hair spilling out like a halo around her head and shoulders on the pillows gave her away.

Heat rose in his groin. Rohan bolted the door, then shucked his clothes and cleaned himself quickly. Before he slipped naked beside the maid, he threw more logs onto the fire. It flared with renewed heat, much as his cock did.

* * *

Isabel made a valiant effort to keep her breathing and her heartbeat at a regular pace. When Rohan returned to the chamber, her heart jumped so high in her throat at his abrupt entry she nearly choked to death. She prayed he would not press her. So she feigned sleep. She thought the battle won. For when he came to bed, he did not come near her. He lay rigid on the far side of the bed. His actions once again confused her. Did she repulse him so much?

Rohan turned onto his side. She could feel his stare burning into her.

"I know you do not sleep, Isabel," he softly said.

Her eyelids fluttered in her attempt to continue her ruse. He moved closer. Now she could feel the heat of his body caress hers. Isabel continued to breathe as evenly as she could. Rohan pulled the furs and sheets down from where she had pulled them up to her neck.

Isabel felt the quiver of her breasts and knew, unless he was blind, he witnessed it. He pressed a fingertip to her left nipple. Instantly, it pebbled. Rohan moved closer still. Now she felt the soft rush of his breath on her cheek.

"You cannot run away from your own oath, damsel." He replaced his finger with his lips. Isabel stiffened and closed her eyes tighter. The urge to press his head tighter to her chest caused Isabel's resolve to galvanize. Her back stiffened so tightly she thought she would snap in half.

Rohan's lips traveled from her heavy breast up to her throat. He pressed his lips to the thick vein there. She could feel the pulse of it against his touch. "What happened to the firebrand in my saddle?" he whispered against her skin. Shivers of delight coursed across every inch of her. She squeezed her eyes tighter. She bit her bottom lip to keep from crying out in pained pleasure.

Isabel opened her mouth to tell him she would fight him with every shred of might she possessed, but the words caught in her throat. His lips nibbled her chin, and his tongue licked at her bottom lip. "Tell me, Isa, where did she go?"

A deep wave of desire crashed through her at his short naming of her. No one, not even her father, had called her Isa. The sound of it on his lips made her feel so wantonly beautiful she almost cried out. "She—she has disappeared," Isabel murmured, not trusting her voice to speak louder.

"Bring her back."

Isabel shook her head, still refusing to open her eyes. "Nay. She will never return."

Rohan pulled back from her. She could feel his eyes on her. "Why?"

Bravely, Isabel opened her eyes. She caught her breath. Rohan's dark hair fell about his shoulders. His tawny eyes burned so bright they rivaled the north star in brilliance. In the shadows of the fire, he looked like a fierce god come to life.

"She—I—because she displeases you!" There, she said it. A rush of shame flared across her. Her cheeks warmed. By her words, she admitted that displeasing him was something that disturbed her.

Rohan looked taken aback. His dark brows furrowed. "Your meaning escapes me, Isabel. Aside from your waspish tongue, uneven temperament, and refusal to heed my word, there is naught about you that displeases me."

His subtle insult spurred her to reveal what was really bothering her. "Why did you push me away?"

Rohan's expression was confused, but then it darkened as the answer to her question dawned on him. He frowned and moved away from her. Isabel was crushed. She rolled away from him, angry with herself for being vulnerable to this man.

"Isabel," Rohan said from behind her, "'twas nothing you did to displease me. 'Twas my own frustration."

She rolled over and faced him. "You speak in riddles."

Rohan smiled that cocksure smile of his, and warning bells sounded in her head. He moved closer and slid his scarred hand along the curve of her hip and squeezed her. "You were wet for me, Isabel." Her cheeks flamed, and she tried to pull away. His hand gripped her tighter. "Nay, you asked, now hear me out." He took her hand and pressed it to his bare chest. The heat of his body surprised her. The feel of the uneven scar did not repulse her as she thought it might. Rohan pushed her hand down the hard contoured plane of his belly. She flinched when he pushed farther. His hand clasped hers tighter. When her fingertips brushed the head of his penis, he hissed in a deep breath, but hoarsely said, "'Tis painful, Isa, and while there are many ways to relieve the ache, there is only one I crave."

Her eyes searched his face. "What are you saying?"

Rohan ground his teeth and shook his head. "I cannot believe you are so innocent of the ways of men and women, Isabel."

She yanked her hand back. "I am perfectly aware of what a man seeks from a woman and what that act entails. And while I do not see what all of the fuss is about, I know men tend to act rashly when a woman wags her bottom under his nose."

Rohan rolled onto his back and clamped his hand over his eyes. "God's teeth, woman! Sometimes it is more than just a mere wag of a derriere."

"I have not thrown myself at you, sir!"

He lowered his hand, turned his head on the pillow, and faced her. "Aye, you did that and more."

Indignation rose with dizzying speed. "How can you say such a thing? 'Tis a lie!"

Rohan smiled a tight smile. "You responded to me, Isabel. Your body prepared for me."

"Nay!"

"When I touched your mons, you were wet for me. 'Tis how a man knows a woman desires him."

Heat flooded her face. She could feel it travel down her neck to her chest. "You are a lout to say such a terrible thing!" She punched his chest. The hard steel of his muscles bruised her hand. He acted as if he did not even feel the blow.

Rohan rolled back to lie flat on the bed. Once again, he clamped his hand over his eyes and rubbed them as if they ached. "Damsel, you would tempt Saint Michael himself with your wiles." He stopped rubbing his eyes but kept his hand over his eyes and expelled a long breath. "I am but a mere mortal man who finds himself with tight ballocks each time I touch you. Forgive me if I should displease you with my actions."

Isabel shoved his shoulder. "You berate me for your own boorishness? I did not ask you to come into my home and treat me as a common house wench! It is not my fault you find yourself unable to control your lusty thoughts. Go slake your lust on one who welcomes it!" Isabel pushed away from him.

He grabbed her arm and in a quick movement rolled her onto her back and settled himself between her thighs. The base of his thick shaft pressed against her mound. The only thing preventing him from entering her was the thin linen of her shift. Isabel went instantly still.

His eyes blazed, and he worked his jaw in a terrible fit to gain control of himself. Isabel breathed hard. "Leave me," she softly said.

"You make that impossible," he muttered hoarsely, then kissed her.

He was all around her, so much so she felt as if she were drowning. His fingers dug deep into her hair, pinning her to the pillow. His thighs pressed her flailing legs into the furs, and her hands as they pushed hard against him had no effect.

His lips were hot, so hot they singed her flesh. When she arched against him in an attempt to push him away, Rohan groaned, and she thought she had hurt him. She arched again and this time realized she only ignited his fire more thoroughly. He moved slightly away from her and ripped the shift down the front of her. Her breasts popped out, and he latched hungrily onto a nipple and suckled her.

Isabel took in great gulps of air, fighting for control of her body. It seemed every move she made only spurred him further in his headlong intent of ravishing her.

If she lay still, he would take all of her. If she resisted, she would see herself completely dishonored. It was if the Black Sword had lost all control.

Panic tore through her. Under his heated kisses and caresses, her body warmed to his game, and the moistness he spoke of earlier returned with a vengeance. Aye, her body was ready for him, even if her heart was not. Her slick opening would cradle him as a mother would a newborn babe.

The thought of a bastard chilled her to the bone.

"Nay!" she screamed as loudly as she could. "Leave me intact!"

Rohan's mouth descended on hers, silencing her cries. He moved her thighs apart with his knee, and when she felt the wide tip of his cock press for entry, panic ripped through her. She tore her mouth from his lips. "Please! Rohan!" she desperately cried out. "Please, honor your oath to me!"

His body stiffened, and for a long moment he did not move. When he pulled back from her, his eyes had the glazed look of a madman. He shook his head, and lucidity slowly returned to his face. His chest rose and fell as if he had run a great race. The flames in the hearth burned loud and greedy. Heat charged the room, from the fire and from the occupants in the bed.

Rohan touched a hand to her cheek. "My pardon, Isabel. I know not what came over me." His simple apology astounded her. It was the last thing she expected from him.

He rolled off her onto his back and stared straight up. Isabel pulled the remnants of her shift tight around her breasts and peered hard at the man who had just a short few seconds ago nearly ravished her. Instead of fear and anger at him, her curiosity at what drove him overcame her. What manner of man was this?

"Rohan, what demons pursue you?"

He laughed out loud, the sound harsh. He continued to stare up at the canopy. "What makes you think demons haunt me?"

She reached out to his chest and traced the scar there. Without looking at her, he grabbed her hand with his scarred left hand, halting her move. "The scar there on your chest." Slowly, she rotated her hand in his and pressed her fingertips to the thick scars on his palm. "The scars here. Tell me what happened to you."

Rohan turned slightly to look at her. Isabel gasped. His eyes had darkened, and for such a mighty knight, pain clouded his features. It disappeared as quickly as it appeared. Isabel had no doubt this man had been tortured as unmercifully as a man could be tortured and survive. But what of the torture in his heart? Did he leave a lady love behind? A sudden prick of jealousy scratched her belly. Then she remembered he was bastard to the world. Many a sire did not claim a by-blow, but what of his mother? She was aunt to the Conqueror. Surely, she held some compassion for her son. A child was the most innocent of all.

"Did you leave a lady love behind?" Isabel softly asked.

Rohan seemed to stare straight through her. "Nay," he said, the word barely audible.

Isabel felt compelled to move closer to him, yet she was afraid any contact with him would stir his passions. So she settled her head on the pillow next to his. "Does your mother still live?"

Instantly, his body stiffened.

Before he could answer, Isabel said, "Forgive me, Rohan, I was but curious. I did not mean to stir up old hurt."

He rolled over, presenting his back to her. "If she lives, it is no concern of mine," he bit off before sleep claimed him.

Twelve

A harsh voice followed by the shaking of the thick mat-tress woke Isabel from a deep sleep. Were they under attack? She popped up from beneath the warm furs ready to shake Rohan awake. But the voice and the movement on the large bed were from the restless knight. He flailed in his sleep, his fists clenched at his side, his body taut as if some greater force held him down.

Sweat beaded his brow in the chilled air of the room. He had flung all of the pelts from his body and lay naked and exposed upon the bed. Harsh words in a language she did not understand came from him. The cords in his neck stood out as he grimaced in pain.

"I'll see you in hell, Tariq!" he shouted, then flung his arms over his face as if to ward off some evil.

Isabel pressed a soothing hand to Rohan's shoulder. "Rohan," she softly said. He flung her hand away as if she were fire. His eyes, now open, stared wildly at her. "Rohan, it is but a night terror that troubles you," she soothed.

He grabbed her by the shoulders. "A'isha?"

Isabel's chest tightened. "Nay, Rohan, 'tis I, Isabel."

His eyes lost some of their wildness. His hands relaxed, and he let her go, then he lay back among the furs. He closed his eyes, and when he opened them again, the fury was gone.

Isabel slipped from the bed and threw more logs onto the waning fire, then poured a draught of wine from a flagon on the table. She moved around to Rohan's side of the bed and handed it to him. He took it without word and drained the cup. He handed it back to her. His eyes raked her form. "Did I harm you?"

She shook her head. "Nay. I but awoke to your shouts and tossing."

"Battles long fought linger in my head."

Isabel moved around to her side of the bed and slipped between the linens and the furs. "Do they visit often?"

Rohan lay back on his pillow and closed his eyes. "Thank God, they do not."

Rohan woke long before the cock called to the new day. The ache in his groin for the woman who lay slumbering against his side was too uncomfortable to ignore. Yet he pulled her closer to him. Her small, delicate hand pressed his chest. Her warm breath teased his flesh. Rohan stared at the canopy, clenching his jaw. He'd had one of the night terrors again. It had been many years since his last one. That Isabel witnessed it shamed him. Yet she had been a comfort to him. It was the first time he had been able to find sleep so soon after. After the other episodes, he had risen and feared to sleep the next night. It was always the same dream. It always put him back in that despicable cell. It always ended with A'isha's death.

Isabel snuggled closer to him. As she remaneuvered herself, her hand moved down his belly. Rohan froze. Her hand lay over his thick shaft. Jesu! In a slow, shallow undulation he could not control, his hips moved up toward her hand. Her fingers twitched, and Rohan knew he'd spill on her with the next movement. He clenched his jaw. She was too much of a distraction. And after last night, whilst they had not been as intimate as a man and a woman could be on a physical level, he felt somehow they had crossed an emotional bridge together. It unnerved him. Mostly because he didn't understand this newfound feeling of intimacy with a woman that did not involve body parts. And more than that, he feared it would show to his men and they would perceive him as weak. Rohan slipped away from her warmth. Mayhap he should hunt down her betrothed and pay him to take her away. But the thought of her gone from him was no easier to accept than his weakness for her.

Rohan stood naked in the room, staring at Isabel's sleeping form. He didn't feel the harsh chill of the air. His body throbbed, too hot for the woman no more than three feet away. The woman who haunted his dreams at night and his thoughts during the day. The woman who, should he continue with her as they were, would be his demise.

It was war. He could not afford to be distracted.

Rohan shook his head. When she had become his Achilles' heel, he did not know, but he would make sure when next they met that she would understand in very clear terms that the only thing he wanted from her was an obedient slave to do his bidding. He cringed when he thought of the fallout that would ensue.

He moved to the hearth and tossed several logs onto

the glowing embers. In the end, it would be best for them both.

Morning came much too early for Isabel. When she awakened, she knew without even opening her eyes that Rohan was not in the room. For a long time, she lay quiet, thinking of the day and night passed with him. Her entire body hummed. He was a complex man who at nearly every turn maneuvered the tables against her. When she would thrust, he would parry, and he was a much more seasoned warrior than she. She rolled over to look at his side of the bed. The indentation from his head still curved his pillow. She reached out and touched it. Cold. But she brought it to her nose and inhaled the strong, masculine scent of him. It was uniquely his own, and she found herself responding to it.

Isabel turned to face the well-fed fire and smiled, thinking of his thoughtfulness in at least that small way. Though rich woven carpets covered most of the floors and rich tapestries hung from the high walls of the chamber, it was still cold without the help of a fire. Isabel hurried and saw to her morning toilette, not waiting for Enid. As she fixed a finely woven leather belt around her hips, her maid scurried in.

Isabel scowled. "You tarry too long, Enid. I am done here."

"My apologies, milady, but Astrid needed help in the kitchens. The Normans were unusually hungry this morn."

Isabel shivered, knowing full well the appetite of a certain Norman. "Are they still about?"

"Some linger, but most rode out to bring in the villagers from the glade."

Isabel wondered if Rohan was amongst the men who

rode to the forest. She refused to ask. She would find out soon enough. She descended into the hall and found it deserted, save for the African, who scowled at her when she glanced his way. Ungrateful lout. It occurred to Isabel that there was no guard hovering about. Had Rohan lost interest in her so soon? Or had the man he appointed grown lazy? Or worse, did he think he had a hold on her now?

She shrugged. It mattered not. She was grateful no hulking knight followed her every move. She grabbed a chunk of bread and cheese from the trencher and moved to stand next to Manhku, who continued to scowl up at her. "You can look at me as if I am responsible for your wound, Saracen," she said in French. "But if you do not watch your manners, you will wake up one morning to find your leg in the straw next to you."

Manhku grumbled but backed down onto his pallet. She would let him stew for a few more minutes while she broke the fast, then tend to him.

As Isabel sat down at the wide trestle table, the doors to the manor were flung open with such a force she jumped in her seat. Rohan strode in, the morning fog swirling around his great shoulders. His breath curled around his ears. He looked like a fire-breathing dragon. Her body warmed. When his gaze settled on her, she fidgeted in her seat. He scowled. Several of his men flowed in behind him. All of them mailed and armed to the hilt. 'Twas their way. Save for the times in their chamber, Isabel had not seen Rohan in anything but his mail. It was the same with his men.

Isabel turned a shy smile up at Rohan, but his cruel words chased it away. "I give you the lord's chamber, feed your carnal wants, and now you think you are the queen of the realm, not rising until the sun is high?"

Isabel choked on the thick bread in her throat. Rorick scowled, as did Thorin. Wulfson stopped dead in his tracks and gaped at Rohan. Rhys and Stefan shook their heads but continued toward the roaring hearth.

Humiliation rode Isabel hard. Angrily, she stood, shoving her chair back so hard it fell, hitting the floor with a loud crash. Rage infused every inch of her. She spit the chunk of bread into her hand, afraid that if she swallowed it in the tirade that would follow, she would surely choke to death. She flung it to the floor. A hungry hound snatched it up. Isabel squared her shoulders, and, not to be brought low in front of Rohan's men, she moved toward him, stopping only inches from where he stood so cocksure of himself.

"Do *not* speak to me of gifts you bear," she spat. "You have only *taken* from me. Had I not reminded you so loudly this eve past of your oath to me, I might at this very moment carry your child." She moved closer to him and said very low but very clearly for all to hear, "And most, chivalrous knight, your child would not please me at all!"

Rohan's eyes narrowed, and she knew when his skin whitened that she had crossed a line. But she would not allow him or any man or woman to tarnish her good name with half-truths. Hurt, anger, and confusion melded into a big emotional ball in her belly. What she thought was a most intimate evening despite his near rape of her, he saw in an entirely different light.

So be it.

"That you could even bear a child is not known," Rohan said.

Isabel slapped him. "You are a lout and a boor. You are not worthy for me to wipe my feet on!" She reared her hand to slap him again, but this time he grabbed her wrist.

"Beware, Lady Isabel, I am a knight of William, and he does not take kindly to his subjects being assaulted."

She yanked her hand from his grasp and spat at his feet. "I do not take kindly to base-born knights tarnishing my good name, especially one who is not welcome in my home!"

"Your regard of me means nothing, damsel. You are but a slave now."

Isabel gasped at his harsh words. Hot tears filled her eyes. She looked up into his face, searching for a sign that he jested with her. She found none. "You are cruel, Rohan. May God spare you the pain you so freely inflict on others." She turned and started to walk toward the stairway, but Rohan's sharp command halted her.

"Stop, slave."

Isabel stiffened before turning to face him. Through her tears, she saw Rohan's men staring at her, each of them holding the same stony stare as his master. They were all the same, this death squad of William's. There was not one gentle edge to any of them.

"My lord?" she softly questioned.

"You have not been dismissed."

Isabel curtsied. "May I have your permission, milord, to see to the business of the manor?"

"Smoke in the forest!" shouted the lookout.

Rohan turned from her and hurried to the bottom of the tower stairway as the guard came down. "Smoke, Rohan, fresh black billows of it two leagues past the south road to Wilshire."

" 'Tis the small settlement of Siward. The families who excavate the limestone from the caves live there," Isabel said. She wrung her hands. "The huts are made mostly of the stone, but the roofs are thatched. Thatch burns white."

"To arms, men!" Rohan called. He looked down at her and opened his mouth as if to say something, but he jammed his lips together, turned from her, and strode out into the courtyard. Isabel was surprised to see Russell dressed and holding the reins to Rohan's great steed. He was also dressed in similar garb to the knights'.

Before he handed Rohan his weapons, Russell shared a quick smile with Isabel. Confused, she watched the squire's eyes follow the tall knight in something akin to worship. Quickly, Russ mounted a smaller horse behind Rohan and turned with the horde as they thundered off through the village.

Was it not just days ago that the same knight he now so admired nearly stripped his back of flesh? Isabel shook her head, once again stymied by the ways of men and the brutality of one in particular. Her ire rose as she watched the black horses and riders disappear over the crest of the last hill. She kicked angrily at a stone on the ground and in so doing stubbed her toes. She cursed and turned toward the hall and caught the eyes of several of Rohan's guards on her. So, he still guarded her, did he? She would see about giving them the slip as she did Warner. Not because she had somewhere to go but because she wanted to prove she could. Isabel slammed the heavy oak portal closed and strode angrily toward the kitchen. The villagers would be arriving soon with Ioan and Warner, and they would be hungry. She would set about making huts available to them. Once Isabel had the servants hard at work, she came back into the empty hall. Empty except for the African. Anger rushed anew as she watched the foolish man attempt to rise with the aid of a short spear. The wood bowed under his weight. A dull crimson stain marred the bandages. Exasperated and looking to exact some vengeance on Rohan, Isabel chose the next best thing.

She strode up to the man and grabbed the spear from him, knocking him off balance. He sprawled backward toward his pallet, and as he did, he flung a long arm out to her, catching her by the throat as he tumbled backward. The action left her breathless, cutting off her scream for help.

Manhku rolled onto his side, taking the brunt of the impact, but he did not let her go. Instead, he rolled over onto her, his face a murderous shade of purple. He grasped her throat with his other hand, and in a slow squeeze, his hands tightened. Isabel flailed and kicked at him, trying to scream, but no sound would come forth. Still, Manhku did not relent. With the hall empty, there was no one to come to her aid. She saw the spear to her right and grabbed for it. Manhku smacked it from her hand. Then he abruptly released her and moved away. On her hands and knees on the floor, her fingers digging into the rush mat, Isabel coughed and heaved, trying mightily to catch her breath. Her throat burned, and she felt as if it had closed completely. Teary-eyed, she scooted backward away from the giant, gasping and coughing and trying not to lose her precarious grip on her control.

The wooden corner of the table dug into her back. Warily, she watched the man's face morph from wild savagery into uncertainty. He seemed confused and looked around, as if just realizing where he was. His dark brows

furrowed, his sharp teeth flashed. He rubbed his thigh
where the bandage now oozed fresh blood. He mumbled
something in his strange tongue, then looked over at her.

For a long moment, he stared at her. Then he did the
last thing she expected of him. He extended his hand. Isabel shook her head and moved harder into the bite of the
table leg.

She rubbed her throbbing neck. She tried to swallow,
but painful shards pricked her throat. Manhku's eyes narrowed dangerously. He grabbed the spear. She watched
him fight back his pain, but he managed to stand. His grip
was wobbly, and sweat poured from his face, but he did
not fall. She cowered back farther until she was almost
completely under the table.

With a slow, unnatural gait, he hobbled toward her.
When she dared catch his gaze, her panic dissolved. Manhku's pride suffered greatly. She could see it in his eyes in
the way he fought through what must be excruciating pain.
And she had shamed him when she sent him sprawling to
the floor. And more now, witnessing his pitiful attempts to
stand and walk. Aye, he was a man, a warrior, and she, a
lowly woman in his eyes, had shamed him.

Isabel moved out from under the table, her fear set
aside for the moment. She was not one to apologize, even
when warranted. It was a stubborn, prideful streak her father had worked hard to break. But to no avail.

Manhku bent forward, the spear bowing under the
strain of his large body, and extended his enormous hand.
Isabel swallowed hard and searched his face for guile.
There was none. Silently, his eyes repented his deed. Taking a deep breath, then slowly exhaling, Isabel accepted his
offering. She slipped her hand into his. Manhku drew her

up with the ease of a mother picking up a swaddling babe.

Gently, he handed her to the bench, then turned and hobbled back to his pallet, where he tried several times to sit without falling. She jumped to his aid but was immediately waved off.

He would do it himself. Isabel stood back.

Once Manhku settled himself, Isabel went about securing the items she would need to repack his wound.

When she approached him several minutes later, her basket laden with linens and herbs, he scowled at her, and despite the injury she had suffered at his hand, she scowled back with equal force. Clearing her throat and ignoring the tightness of it, she knelt beside him and said, "I will fear you worse as a one-legged beggar. Now, sit back and let me tend your leg."

Manhku nodded and relaxed back onto the pallet. He let out a long breath as she bent to her task. She gave him no quarter as she aggressively cleaned and repacked the wound. Despite his damage, she was content with the progress. It would be months before he had full use. As she bent over him, tying the last of the linen, he reached out and touched a fingertip to her throat. Isabel flinched at the contact, not used to casual interaction with men.

"Hurts?" he asked in French.

A sudden well of burning tears rose in her eyes. Manhku's question combined with Rohan's callous treatment of her and the utter devastation of her people mingled into a harsh balm to swallow. She was no longer in control of her own life but subjected to men who knew not the barest of civilities. She swiped back a tear and shook her head. "Nay. It would take a much stronger man than you to hurt me."

Manhku smiled. A low sound, which Isabel surmised served as laughter, rumbled deep in his chest. "Gooood," he said, then sank back onto the pallet and closed his eyes. Isabel stood, and for a good long time she watched him. When she bent down and covered him with his mantle, she knew she was mad. What manner of Saxon was she to coddle the enemy so?

When the lookout shouted that riders approached, Isabel gave her precarious position no more thought. As it did each time she heard the call of riders, her heart leapt, and her stomach buzzed as if bees swarmed. Could this be the day her father and her brother returned?

She pushed open the great door and rushed out into the courtyard.

Thirteen

The sight that greeted Rohan as they galloped into the tiny hamlet of Siward turned his stomach. The stench had reached him first. The all too familiar rancid smell of burning flesh. Since his branding at the hand of the Saracen, it was a stench that immediately took him back to Jubb and all of the bile-stirring memories that kindled.

Rohan reined his horse to a sliding halt. Aye, even for the battle-hardened warrior he was, the horrific sight that greeted them made Rohan question the hell this earth had become.

A pile of naked, dismembered bodies burned atop thick tufts of thatch. Mordred snorted and pawed the hard earth. Rohan's men fanned out on either side of him. Against the deadly quiet, the sound of Hugh and the up-start squire Russell retching their guts up mingled with the crackle of the fire as it consumed the carnage, sending a hard chill to Rohan's blood. He was in no great rush. There was not enough of a body to save. He urged his mount forward. Arms and legs stuck out from the smoke. Quartered torsos, their innards hanging out, sizzled in the flames. The heads? There were none. Rohan's eyes scanned the perimeter of the hamlet. Vultures circled just beyond. He urged the horse past the human bonfire to the edge of the small clustering of huts to a larger building that appeared to be the stable.

The hairs on the back of his neck rose. There upon a score of pikes were the heads. Men, women, and children, their eyes cut out, their noses slashed off, lay in the dirt at the base of the pikes.

A deep fury simmered in his gut. Rohan reined the horse around back to his men. Thorin and the other knights had dismounted. The squires were still doubled over, their backs to the carnage.

"See to the huts for survivors." As Rohan gave the command, he knew it was for naught. For a long moment, he stood in the middle of the small hamlet and scoured the forest surrounding them. The cowards were long gone. He felt it in his bones. He also knew they were not rid of them yet.

Rohan began to walk slowly around the grounds, searching for evidence of the identity of the culprits. They were not foot soldiers. Several shod hoofprints stamped the softer ground. The size bespoke a destrier. And the only destriers in the region he knew of were those that belonged to knights. Saxons and Vikings, notorious for this type of kill, fought on foot.

Suspicion rose in his heart. Could a Norman have wreaked such destruction?

"Look," Rohan said to Thorin, who strode up to him, pointing to the large hoofprint. " 'Tis as big as Mordred's."

"Aye, there are more on the other side."

Rohan looked at his right hand. "Normans?"

"Mayhap. Or Saxon knights. There were many at Senlac. Mayhap we left a few?"

Rohan nodded. Thorin spoke the truth. While the Saxons were not renowned for their cavalry, they did exist. A sudden thought came to Rohan. "Mayhap the lady's betrothed has made a statement."

"A possibility. There is nothing left here of value. The craven did a good job stripping the hamlet of usable goods. But it strikes me they were bent more on simple destruction than thievery."

Rohan nodded. "Aye, the violence of this screams rage. Whoever is responsible acted in anger."

"Who wouldst be more angry than one whose lady has been publicly shamed?" Wulfson asked from behind Rohan.

Rohan turned to his friend and scowled. Wulfson stood solidly beside Thorin. Both men stared at him, waiting for an answer. "The lady is still intact!" The force of Rohan's words halted the rest of his men as they moved around the camp.

"That may be the truth, Rohan, but it is no secret she sleeps in your bed. Prepare to pay the price for such trespass."

"She is my slave. There is no penalty to pay," he growled. "Now, leave me be on the matter!" He flung his hand at two of the men who had survived hell and back with him. Of all people on this earth, would that they would understand his reservations when it came to a woman, regardless of her comeliness or previous title.

Rohan mounted the great warhorse and said to the squires, "Take the heads down and burn them!" Russell doubled over at the command, and Hugh looked as if he would follow suit. Rohan sneered at their weakness. " 'Tis a man's war. If you cannot hold your spleen, mayhap you should take up the needle and have the ladies instruct you in embroidery."

Angrily, he reined his horse and moved along the perimeter of the encampment until he found the trail he sought. "Let us ride, men. Mayhap with some luck we will find these villains."

Rohan did not await his men's pleasure. He hurtled down the narrow path, bent on easing his fury with his sword buried deep in his enemy's gut.

Isabel ran from the courtyard to the bailey to see Ioan and Warner guiding those people from the glade who could walk to one side whilst they brought the carts laden with wounded up front. She bade Ioan and Warner to bring them to a large hut abandoned by a large family. It would serve as a hospital of sorts. Within minutes, she began to minister again to those she had tended the day before, and with very few exceptions, she was pleased with her handiwork.

Enid, Lyn, Mari, and Sarah made room for the people of Wilshire. They were a sullen lot, not familiar with their surroundings. Most of them having never left their village, fewer still had ventured to Alethorpe. Wilshire was the smallest of all of her father's holdings, but the manor was sturdy and the lands rich with minerals. The forests teemed with game. It was one of Edward's, then Harold's, favored hunting grounds. When the king's train came to stay at Rossmoor, it was always a most tedious time.

There was much to prepare, and the king's courtiers required food and shelter. Yet her father never grumbled at the cost of such visits. He gladly dipped into his treasure trove of silver and was a most gracious host. The last time Harold had been through was in July. It was a short visit. And more than a mere hunting excursion. Harold had come to his most loyal lord, Alefric, to drum up arms and a pledge of soldiers. Alefric had many allies to the north, and even as far south as Normandy on his late wife's side. Harold was counting heavily on them. Her father did not disappoint. He sent almost three hundred men with Geoff to Stamford Bridge, and another one hundred followed him to Senlac Hill. That only a handful of men had returned and with no word of her father greatly disturbed her. As each day passed, Isabel lost hope of ever seeing her sire or her brother alive.

She turned back to her chores. The wounded had been tended to and the displaced families of Wilshire given shelter and food. There were a goodly number of craftsmen among the survivors and several women she would be able to put to good use in the manor. But Isabel waited to press them to duty. They had been so traumatized and walked as if in a fog. They needed time for the scars in their minds to lessen. There was plenty of time to put them to work. A day or two would not matter.

As she stood in the courtyard rubbing the aching small of her back, Isabel gave thought to Rohan. She had deliberately put him from her thoughts for most of the day. Yet, inevitably, he crept back into them. And each time he did, her anger flared.

Isabel felt the overwhelming need for a power greater

than her own or any mortal man's. Having a moment where no one tugged at her sleeve for advice or to clean a festering wound, she slipped into the chapel.

She smiled as she slid into the front pew and saw that some devout soul had lit several candles. Her muscles relaxed in this most sacred of places. She had always found comfort here. She crossed herself and sank to her knees. She closed her eyes tightly and prayed for a priest. She prayed for her father and her brother, and she prayed for all of England, and as she was about to say amen, she crossed herself again and prayed for Rohan's black soul.

As she lit several more candles, the shout of the lookout announcing that riders approached swept away her easing tension. She knew the riders would not be welcome. For the first time that day, Isabel wished for Rohan's hasty return. She moved to the doorway of the chapel and pulled back the door to peek out. Her heart missed a beat. *Henri.*

He strode straight toward her. Isabel turned and quickly moved back to the pew she had just sat in. She sank to her knees and crossed herself several times. Henri would not dare harm her in the house of God.

The door opened with a slam. The sound jerked her around to stare at a man who resembled Rohan in all ways but one. Henri's eyes were almost brown, and his face bore no scars. But there was something more. As he pulled his helmet from his head and pushed back his cowl, his short hair, cropped in the Norman fashion, stuck to his forehead. His eyes smoldered. Yet behind the superficial passion there, a cold evil lurked.

"Milord," Isabel breathed, feigning surprise and also

feigning calmness. She smiled and gave him a short curtsy. "I did not expect to see you again so soon. Rohan rides to the south, but his return is imminent."

Henri took her hand and brought it to his lips. She expected them to be cold like his heart, but they were surprisingly warm. Her hand trembled. Not in the excitement his brother drew from her but in fear.

"I did not come to see my bastard brother, Lady Isabel. I admit, I came for you. I could not wait to see you again, damsel. Your beauty has haunted my dreams."

Isabel attempted to pull her hand from his, but he tightened his fingers around her. He pulled her closer to him. He smelled of sweaty horse and leather and ale, but underlying those scents was the stench of death. Isabel yanked her hand from his and moved away, putting the pew between them.

"I am not one to mince words. Tell me what you desire, and if it is in my power to give you, I will then see you gone."

He smiled. His teeth were as white and straight as his brother's. "I want you," he softly said. Isabel shook her head. "Aye, Isabel. And I want you now. Come to me, we haven't much time."

She shook her head again, not believing what was happening.

Henri darted around the pew with such quickness Isabel cried out. He grabbed her by the waist and pulled her struggling form against his mailed chest. She opened her mouth to scream, and he kissed her. Isabel fought harder. She twisted her head away from him, but he grabbed her hair and pulled her back so hard her back arched and her breasts jutted out toward him. He pushed her arms behind her back and with his left hand clasped her wrists. With his right hand, he grabbed her breast and squeezed. Isabel screamed and stomped on his foot. She howled in pain. His boot was hard.

Henri laughed at her piteous attempt to thwart him. He shoved his knee between her thighs and hiked up her skirts.

"'Tis sacrilege!" she screamed. "We are in a house of God."

"Mayhap your God, damsel, but not mine." Henri moved her toward the altar and cleared it with one long sweep of his arm. He shoved her onto it. Isabel rolled over away from him and silently begged God's forgiveness as she grabbed the goblet used for the communion wine. He yanked her back to face him. Isabel slammed the heavy vessel against his head with all her might. He howled in pain, his hand loosened, and it was enough. Isabel twisted away from him on the other side of the altar and ran for the door.

"Bloodthirsty bitch!" he called after her.

Isabel tore through the courtyard, and instead of running straight for the manor, where he could trap her, she ran for the village. Several of Henri's men who lounged about rose to attention as they saw her running their way.

"Seize her!" Henri screamed from behind her. Isabel was light and fleet, they were heavy and encumbered with mail. She darted between two men as they lunged for her. She would have found their thudding bodies as they crashed together amusing on any other day. Isabel continued to run toward the bailey, where several people stopped to watch the drama unfold. The sharp cry of the lookout announcing approaching riders on the horizon spurred her to move faster. She dared not hope for rescue. It could be more of Henri's men.

In her wild flight, she heard shrill Saxon voices erupt not far away. Dear God, her people were fighting Henri! They did not stand a chance. But she could not help them. She must draw Henri and his men as far from the village as possible.

As Isabel crested a small knoll, she dared to look over her shoulder. She screamed. Though she was half the well-born knight's size and did not sport the heavy mail, even in full battle garb, Henri was a large, strong man with a long, strong stride. He was right behind her. Behind Henri, a swarm of her people descended on two of Henri's men. Two more followed their master.

Isabel zigzagged down the hill and away from more villagers, hoping the others would stay away from Henri and his men. For if they got too close, the Norman would surely hack them to pieces. The tree line was just ahead. If she could get to it, she would have the advantage. Just as she passed the edge of the village and broke for the trees, Isabel stumbled on a stump she did not see. She hit the ground and rolled. Springing back up, she moved to continue her flight. But it was too late. Henri grabbed her. His great weight slammed her into the hard November earth. The force of the hit knocked all breath from her, and she saw only black. Isabel squeezed her eyes shut, then opened them. Henri grinned above her. "I would wager, Isabel, you are more sport than I bargained for." He grabbed a hank of her hair and pulled her face up to meet his. "I will take you here in the wood, as a stag takes a doe."

He dragged her toward the trees. Isabel stumbled as he pushed her harder. Once they had broken through the tree line, he spun her around, and while he held her with one hand, he pulled the slit in his clothing aside. He shoved her to the ground, and she squeezed her eyes shut, not wanting to see his engorged member. "It will give me great pleasure to give my brother my bastard." Henri sank to his knees and flung her over. He intended to take her from behind! He grasped the hem of her dress and shoved it up, exposing her bottom.

"It will give me great pleasure, Henri, to geld you," Rohan said from behind them.

Isabel cried out and rolled from the blackhearted brother. Henri grabbed her and pressed his dagger to her throat. "Aye, but at what cost, brother?"

Rohan dismounted from the great horse. He was not alone. His knights fanned out behind him, all of them with arrows notched and strung in their long bows. They were a most awesome sight.

Henri's men, who had joined the chase, stood back.

"Harm the maid, and you pay with your life," Rohan said quietly.

"It is that simple?" Henri asked.

Rohan nodded. "Aye."

"The life of a Saxon slave is of no consequence to William," Henri proclaimed. "But the son of one of Normandy's greatest families? I doubt there would be a large enough penalty to pay, Rohan."

Rohan pointed his sword at Henri's chest. "If you would like to find out, I am willing."

Henri pressed the tip of the dagger to Isabel's throat. He laughed heartily. "Look at her throat, Rohan. By these marks, I suspect she likes rough play. And 'tis not by my hand." Rohan's eyes narrowed. Henri laughed. "She has played you for the fool. When I found her in the chapel, she was begging your God for forgiveness for her shameful acts."

"'Tis a lie!" Isabel shrieked.

She met Rohan's narrowed stare. She saw doubt there. Did he think she—?

"Aye, she meets her betrothed not far from here," Henri lied.

Though he wore his helmet, Isabel could see Rohan scowled.

"She is no virgin, brother. You have been cuckolded!" Henri threw her at Rohan. "Have her, I do not wish to be third with this piece."

Isabel landed at Rohan's feet. She sprang up and lunged at Henri's back, pummeling him. "Liar!"

He turned, raising his arm to backhand her, but found it seized by Rohan's fist. "For every mark you put on her, I will put three times as many on you."

Henri grinned a nasty smile and flung Rohan's hand from him. "I never thought I would see the day you place a woman above blood, brother. Good riddance. May she spill the Saxon's bastard before she spills yours." Henri stalked past Rohan but turned and gave notice. "I had come by to warn you, Rohan, there are marauders about. Just past the Dunsworth border, there was an attack last eve. The louts seem bent on simple destruction. What was left of my churls was not recognizable."

Rohan faced his brother and nodded. "Aye, I will keep an eye out for them. But should you meet them before I do, give this message for me." Rohan stepped toward his brother, stopping only a horse length away. "When I hunt them down, they will burn alive."

Henri's lips twisted into a sadistic smile. "I would pay good silver to see it."

"You may be present for free," Rohan said, his voice low and threatening.

Henri's eyes sparked, and for a moment Isabel swore she saw a flash of fear. While she did not understand the full scope of Rohan's threat, Henri did.

Henri opened his mouth to retort, but he must have thought better of it, for he turned and strode back to his horse. His men followed.

When Rohan turned back to her, a glower marked his features. He sheathed his sword as he walked toward her. When he stopped, Rohan stood silent, looking hard at her as if to assess the truth of his brother's words.

A hard trembling wracked her. Henri's lies did not affect her half as much as the thought that Rohan believed them.

"I will not defend myself to you, Rohan. You will think what you will."

He moved a step closer, close enough that he could brush her hair from her neck. When he did, his scowl deepened. "How came you by these marks?"

Isabel kept his stare. What would he do to his man if he knew Manhku had attacked her? She shouldn't care. They were all her enemy. Let them kill one another in their bloodlust. But she could not name Manhku. She was overfed with blood and death. She did not want to be responsible for what may follow.

"It has been a long, tedious day. I do not know."

Rohan wrapped his gauntleted hand around her throat

and squeezed. The pressure hurt. Tears erupted. She was so weary of this game of war. "You lie." He released her and stepped back. "And I do not deal well with liars."

He turned his back to her and called to the villagers who had gathered behind his men. "See to your lady." Then he mounted his horse and galloped up the hill to the manor.

Fourteen

Fatigue took over both Isabel's mind and her body, squeezing what little will she had left from her. As she allowed several of the village women to walk her back to the manor, Isabel realized it was the first time since her mother's death some six years past when she wasn't the one seeing to another's needs.

And with that realization, more emotion poured out of her heart. Never once had she complained to her sire or her brother that while they were given the luxury of time to grieve, she was not. She was thrust into the role of lady of the manor before her mother's body was cold. And she did not regret it or resent it; it was what had to be done. Had she not stepped up to the role, Alethorpe and its people would have suffered greatly, for Alefric became a stingy, bitter man after his wife's passing. And only Isabel could soften him. So, for the sake of her sire, her brother, and the people who depended on the lord, Isabel put her own emotions aside. She did the same now. As weary and emotionally drained as she was, she would require only a short time of privacy to collect herself, then once again present the face of a lady in complete control of the manor, to her people and to the Normans who sought to rip it asunder.

When Isabel entered the hall, she caught Rohan's angry stare from across the great divide. Though her energy was severely depleted, she squared her shoulders and presented a hardened front. Let Rohan think what he would of her. In her heart, she knew the truth, and at the end of the day it would be enough, for she had no one else to depend on. That understanding did more to knock her off balance than Rohan's accusing glare.

She was utterly alone.

Rohan's heated gaze followed her up the stairway. His men were quiet, several of them watching her as if assessing for themselves the validity of Henri's words. Isabel leashed the urge to tell them all to go to the devil. How dare they question her virtue!

Having met her in the courtyard, Enid took Isabel's elbow halfway up the stairway, forestalling the eruption the servant knew was imminent. Enid shooed the other women away, and instead of directing her mistress to the lord's chamber, she guided Isabel down the hall to the lady's solar.

Once in the room, Enid threw the bolt. "Norman swine!" she hissed.

Isabel sank to a cushioned hassock at the foot of the large bed. Enid fussed around her. "I'll prepare a bath for you, milady. The blood of the village and the stench of the bastard's brother cling to you like dung."

In a fog, Isabel allowed her maid to undress her. "These

are not fit to wear," Enid scoffed, and tossed the bundle of clothing into the fire. She wrapped Isabel in a thick linen towel and set her back against the hassock. "Lie down, milady, and rest whilst I prepare your bath."

Isabel did. As she closed her eyes and swallowed, the rawness of her throat reminded her of the day. Her chest tightened as she remembered not Henri's attack on her but the way Rohan had looked at her, as if she were not fit to clean his chamber pot. Did he truly believe his brother? *How could he?* Rohan, of all men, knew how desperately she clung to her virtue. A hard sob wracked her chest, and try as she might, Isabel could not contain the tears. In silent protest, they slid down her cheeks. Eyes closed, she sucked in a huge breath and desperately wished for sleep. Wearily, she exhaled and prayed that when she awoke, the nightmare would be over.

Rohan wished for no company. Not even from his men, who having sensed his morose mood moved down to the far end of the hall and the hearth there. He wanted complete solitude. He wanted to throttle his brother for touching Isabel, and more than that, he wanted to force the truth from the maid. Yet he did nothing but stand in front of the roaring hearth and drink another cup of ale. 'Twas his fourth.

Once again, his pride waged a terrible war with feelings he did not understand. When Henri pushed up Isabel's skirts and laid her bottom bare for all to see, Rohan felt an inexplicable rush of fury. And a foreign sense of propriety. He did not want his men or anyone else to see that part of Isabel that only he had seen. Or so he had thought. Did

Henri taunt with lies, or did he speak the truth? Had the maid met with her betrothed? Was she with child?

Rohan cringed at the thought of her lying with another man. He tossed back the last of his ale. Nay, his gut told him. She was not with child, nor had she willingly given away her virtue. Since his coming, she had been watched.

His blood cooled. What of her time yesterday in the forest? She was alone for most of the day and into the evening hour. Mayhap Arlys met her there. The fine hairs on the back of Rohan's neck stood straight up. Aye, she had slipped past Warner with little effort. Mayhap there was a secret passage in the manor. 'Twould make perfect sense. And mayhap they met that way.

Rohan gripped the cup in his hand so tightly his knuckles whitened. And what of those marks on her neck? They were fresh, the mark of a man's hand boldly imprinted. No man in this manor would dare touch her for fear of his wrath. So? How had the marks gotten there? Did Isabel, as Henri suggested, like rough play? He knew of women like that. Indeed, he had had a few. And while he had never left such marks, he could not be sure. For he never stayed long enough to see the face of his evening's tumble. So, it was more than possible her marks had come in the throes of passion.

Rohan threw the cup into the fire and turned, determined to put his doubts to rest once and for all. He strode up the stairway to his chamber. When he flung the door open only to find the room cold and empty, his fury soared.

He left the room, slamming the door open so hard it crashed against the wall. He strode farther down the hall to the lady's solar, where he saw Enid carrying in two great buckets of steaming water. He shoved her aside and burst through the door, intending to have it out with the damsel. He stopped short when he saw her small form curled up in a linen wrap on a hassock. He stepped closer. Her cheeks glistened with tears.

Something moved in Rohan then. Something so deep and so profound it terrified him. He had no words to explain what it was or what it meant. He just knew the woman who lay asleep before him was braver than ten of William's knights combined.

When her body shuddered as she drew in a ragged breath, he stepped closer. She stirred, and the linen fell from her shoulders, catching on the high swell of her breasts.

God's blood, she was beautiful. She moved again just slightly, but it was enough for the thick veil of hair to fall back from her neck. The bruises that marked her jumped out at him, mocking him for a fool.

Rohan moved closer and squatted beside the sleeping maid. Tracing a finger across the bruises, he marveled at the softness of her. Not able to stop, he trailed lower to the creamy rise of her breast. He watched her skin pucker in gooseflesh and her nipples rise below the fabric. His blood quickened, but so did his doubt, and with it his anger welled up again. Setting his jaw so hard he thought he would break his teeth, Rohan wanted to shake her until she told him the truth. He wanted to push up her skirts and ease himself within her body and know for sure that *he* was the first. Rohan stood and moved away from her. Aye, he could take her and know for certain. He'd hang the bloodied linens out for the entire shire to witness *his* taking of her. Not her betrothed, as Henri insinuated, and certainly not that most unnoble of nobles, his brother!

Rohan whirled on his heels, almost knocking Enid over. Damn them all to hell! What did it matter who had had her? She was just a woman.

Rohan found himself not wanting to go near the manor. And with that decision, he found more than a few chores to keep him busy in the stable. As he gave a last brush to Mordred's ebony flank, Rohan glanced down at the straw next to the horse, thinking it would be far more comfortable sleeping next to the furry beast than lying beside the soft and smooth damsel. Aye, he'd take his meals out here as well. He wanted no more distractions. He must focus on what he was to accomplish for William. He expected to be called any day to his liege. And though he tried to push the next thought away, the one about Isabel and leaving her behind, he could not help it. It bothered him greatly that he had concern for her. What if Henri decided to visit again?

While Rohan had complete faith in all of his men, he knew Henri held a deeper fear of Rohan than any of his knights. Rohan tossed the brush into a bucket, then grabbed up a hoof pick. Holding the great hoof between his knees, Rohan began to dig the muck from his horse's foot. The great black turned a head to Rohan and nibbled at his back as if to assure him the woman was not worth his worry.

"Aye, Mordred, you are lucky to be a simple beast. Women are no great mystery to you. Count your blessings." The horse snorted as if in agreement.

"So, you find the maid a mystery, do you, Rohan?" Thorin asked from the aisle outside the large stall.

"I did not invite you into my conversation," Rohan said tersely.

"I could not help but overhear. Thorvald and I were having a similar talk."

Rohan set the great hoof gently down and stood up. Casually, he tossed the pick into the bucket next to the brush. "Oh? And what advice does your horse have for you?"

"He is as confused as we, Rohan. I have no inkling what makes the females of this world think or act. I suspect I never will. And because it only causes me great frustration, I have decided not to try."

Rohan wiped his hands on the leather tunic he had put on over his undershirt. "Good advice."

"Rohan!" Wulfson called from the far end of the stable. "I have come to announce the evening meal awaits your pleasure. Hurry your arse. I am withering away to nothing!"

"Since when do you do the job of a page?" Thorin called.

"Since they are scarce and fear the moody Norman. Come, let us sup together."

"Nay," Rohan said. "I have no hunger for food this eve. Go and dine without me."

Wulfson strode down the aisle and stopped to look at his comrades in arms and in friendship. His green eyes danced in mischief. "I must admit, Rohan, Henri's words today gave me cause to pause." He held his hand up to halt Rohan's forthcoming denial. "Let me speak. As I said, Henri made a good case, but did you not see it for the ploy it was?"

Rohan frowned.

Wulfson smiled. "Come now, my friend, you cannot be so blind to your brother. His accusations were a poor attempt to cover his dastardly deed. He turned the blame to the maid to keep it from himself, where it should have been placed."

"I—" Rohan started.

"Nay, let me finish. In the end, it matters not if the maid is no longer a virgin, or even if she is barren. She is but a stepping stone here. Is she not? A necessary pawn in our game. Take her if you will, and be done with it. I cannot abide your morose moods."

"I gave my oath, Wulf," Rohan said.

"Aye, you gave it, but on the condition that she was a virgin. How else to prove it than to see the bloodstains yourself?" Wulfson countered.

Thorin clapped Rohan on the shoulder. "Wulfson has something, Rohan. Your oath was based on the belief that the girl was a virgin. If she is not, then all oaths are forfeit. Besides, she is but one of ten score more women you will have. Take her, get her out of your blood, and mayhap we can all get along more peacefully."

Thorin winked at Wulfson and said to no one in particular, "Aye, take your fill of her, Rohan, so that we may have a taste ourselves. From what I saw today, you are selfish not to share."

"Hah!" Wulfson shouted, and slapped Rohan on the back. "We have always shared. What makes you think to keep this one to yourself?"

A hard shard of jealousy slashed through Rohan's gut. 'Twas true, if the damsel was obliging, they had on more than one occasion passed the cup, so to speak. It was never a problem. Why was it now?

"She is just another woman, Rohan, and she means naught to you," Thorin goaded.

"Aye, and she is leman to the Saxon," Wulfson added.

"Enough!" Rohan roared. "Do not question her virtue. There is no evidence she is other than virgin. The day I believe any lie my brother spews is the day you can bury me with my sword."

Thorin clasped Rohan's shoulder and leaned toward the younger man. "Aye, and now, listen to your own words, my friend, and give the maid the benefit of your doubt."

"Aye, I am weary of your hostility, Rohan. Mayhap you need to ease yourself somewhere else," Wulfson suggested.

Thorin slapped Rohan on the back. "Or take matters into your own hands."

Wulfson chortled and slapped Rohan as well. He held up his right hand and said, "Aye, 'tis a good way to build calluses." Wulfson turned and strode for the wide double door opening to the stable, "Let us sup, men! I have a great hunger this eve. Mayhap I will search out the fair Sarah or the temptress Lyn." Wulfson threw his head back and laughed louder. "By God, I will seek them both for the evening!"

When Rohan, Thorin, and a grinning Wulfson entered the hall, their hair damp from washing and their spirits high, Isabel let out a bit of the breath she had been holding. She was not the only one in the hall bracing for more storms. Each of Rohan's men looked from him to her, then back to him again. Rohan acted as if he hadn't a care in the world. He did not seek her out. And while that should have made her very happy, it angered her. He obviously believed his brother.

Isabel chose not to go near the lord's table or the hall. Instead, she hid in the kitchen. Until she heard a woman's shriek followed by uproarious male laughter. Isabel hurried to the hall. She stopped in her tracks and watched in horror as Wulfson and Ioan fought over the maid Sarah. Isabel rushed to reprimand them when Sarah turned to face her. Her eyes smiled as she teased the men. Lyn made the mistake of setting a large platter of roasted fowl on the table near Ioan, who ripped a juicy leg from one of the birds, then grabbed the buxom flame-haired maid to his chest. He kissed her full on the mouth. When Lyn bit a hunk of Ioan's drumstick and half chewed it before she kissed him back, Isabel knew they were not in need of her help.

Her gaze rose to where Rohan sat. Her blood warmed. He watched her intently. She quickly turned from him and back to the kitchen, where she found a small bit of solace. As she busied herself with chores, Isabel could not help the wild flutter of her heart, or as the shrill laughter of the village girls mingled with the deep voices of the knights, she could not still the way her blood coursed hotly through her limbs.

The night held the full promise to end in wanton debauchery. Isabel slipped out of the hot kitchen to catch her breath and cool down. She also did not want to listen to the maids giggle and the men chortle. She stepped back against the hard, cold stone of the wall outside the kitchen and watched Wulfson stride with Lyn over one shoulder and Sarah over the other toward the stable. Ioan and Rhys followed, calling out to the selfish knight to share. Isabel shook her head, and despite her morose mood, she could not help a small smile. Mayhap it was good for Rohan's men and her people to ease some of their tension. Henri's appearance today had left a dark, tense pall over Rossmoor. An eruption was imminent. 'Twas good that the men and the women could find pleasure.

Isabel sighed. No doubt, as the summer grew hot and humid, the shire would swell in population. Just as Isabel was about to move back into the kitchen, she heard Rohan's deep voice call to one of his men, "For what I have in mind, 'twill only take a moment of my time, and I am willing to share this piece!" A female giggle followed.

Isabel's stomach lurched. Why Rohan's announcement caused her such pain she could not fathom. Had she not told him to slake his lust elsewhere? She peeked around the corner and saw the recent widow Gwyneth tossed over his shoulder like a sack of turnips, her laughter giving away her excitement. Rohan looked up and caught Isabel's stare in the darkness. The torches burned bright around her, and she had no doubt he saw her. The fire in his eyes faded. Yet he continued his bold stride to the stable. He slapped his hand down on Gwyneth's bottom, and she squealed in delight.

Feeling suddenly lightheaded, Isabel hurried back into the kitchen. She didn't stop her retreat. She moved through the great room and into the hall, where the rest of Rohan's men drank and sang like squires having their first cup of ale. Keeping her head down, she hurried up the great stairway to the lord's chamber, where she quickly gathered her few possessions. Isabel kept her composure until she returned to her solar. She was glad to find it empty. Save for Enid, there were no other ladies to find rest here.

Isabel paced the floor, wondering at herself and the man

who had completely turned her life inside out and upside down. He was a boor, a lout, a knave. He was ill-mannered and brash. He was bold, and he was a Norman! Why, then, did she feel as if he at this moment had betrayed her? She was nothing to him. He was nothing to her. Then why her anger? Jealousy ripped through her like a wounded boar after a hunter.

Dear Lord, he believed she had lain with her betrothed and mayhap carried his child! Then he turned around and insinuated in front of his men and her people that she may be barren! How could she care for such a man?

Isabel cried out. Nay! She did not care for him. He was not worth it! He would be gone soon. Or mayhap not, but either way, what could he offer her? And she him? She shook her head and paced anew. Nay, she could not, *would* not, consider any form of attachment to him. 'Twas only a girl's fantasy. He had awakened the woman in her, and she was drawn to him only for that reason. She crossed herself. 'Twas not holy for a maid to crave a man's hands and lips on her body . . . or more. Most especially if that man was not her husband.

Isabel flopped back onto the bed and stared up at the embroidered canopy. She wondered what Rohan did at that very moment. Did he touch Gwyneth as he had touched her? Did he whisper sweet words of love to her? Would the summer solstice find Gwyneth heavy with Rohan's child? Isabel fisted her hands and punched the mattress. "Jesu!" Jealousy was a bitter balm to swallow. She popped up from the bed and began to pace again. Fury, longing, and sadness warred in her heart, and try as she might to say it nay, it affected her more deeply than any emotion she had ever experienced. She did not like it. And worst of all, she knew there was not a single thing she could do to stop it.

Isabel flung open the door and strode downstairs. She scanned the hall for Rohan, but he was not there amongst his men and several of the village girls. Her stomach roiled. Aye, she knew where he was and what he was about. If she had no pride, she'd march straight down to the stable and yank Gwyneth's blond hair out of her head strand by strand, then geld the Norman she lay with!

Guided by a demon she had no name for, Isabel moved through the hall, and past the giggling women and smiling men, and shoved open the front doors to the manor. Hard chilled air filled her chest, and she welcomed the pain of it.

Fifteen

Rohan stood at a trough outside the stall he'd just stepped from. His loins burned hot. The sounds of heavy panting and women's cries of pleasure crashed around him, like a tight hand around his cock. He clenched his jaw and dunked his head into the icy water a second time. The shock of the cold chased his lusty thoughts of the woman in the manor away for a brief moment or two. He welcomed it. He held his head below the water until he could not breathe. He pulled his head out of the frigid water and shook it, sending icy water everywhere.

The wench he had taken from the hall giggled in the stall next to where he stood. Rohan wiped his arm across his face, drying it some. He hiked up his garters, stepping away from the stall where Thorin enjoyed the spoils of Rohan's hunt. Not that it was much of a pursuit. The wench had fallen into his lap, and when she felt his throbbing cock, she manipulated him to hewn stone. However, he had not been able to find release with the wench. Her scent, her breath, her rough skin did not appeal to him. He had handed her over to Thorin, who had more ale than he and was not nearly as particular this night. He left them to their robust coupling and strode back to the manor.

As he crossed the courtyard, a small, dark body darting toward the bailey caught his attention. He looked up to find the guards, while alert, looking past the bailey to the village. Rohan's blood surged anew. He knew the small form well. He followed.

Isabel met a man near the opening of a large hut. Rohan's blood boiled. Was it the Saxon? She ducked in. He hurried to the doorway and listened.

"How fare they, Ralph?" Isabel asked.

"Most are better, milady, but several rage with the fever. Blythe works hard to cool them with water, but it does not help."

"Milady, the damage is so terrible!" the girl cried.

"Do not stop, Blythe. Sometimes it takes days to break the fever. Come, fetch more water, and show me to those who need us most. I will stay with you," Isabel comforted.

Rohan stepped back as the girl hurried from the hut. He debated whether to demand that Isabel return to him. Yet he knew she would fight him tooth and nail. Especially now that she suspected his romp with Gwyneth. 'Twas his right as a man, and had she not demanded he slake his lust between another's thighs? Rohan growled low. The maid had poisoned him! He no longer found what most men would consider fine fare acceptable. And the flaxen-haired wench was comely. Her teeth were good, and she had a full figure a man could lose himself in for many a night. Yet he wanted another. His desire was so great he could not savor the dish before him. Jesu!

Rohan swiped his hand across his face. He was acting

like a milksop of a boy! He turned on his heel and whistled to a guard who patrolled the bailey wall. "See that the lady Isabel is escorted back to the manor when she is done with her work here."

"Aye," the guard said, and moved toward the hut.

Rohan grabbed the man hard by the shoulder. "Do not let her out of your sight, Robert, or you will pay with my sword buried in your gullet."

The younger man swallowed hard. "You may consider her returned safely to the hall, Rohan."

Rohan debated staying and waiting, but he would be damned if he would let the wench know he followed her.

The hall had quieted considerably since he left it. The torches were dimmed, and sated bodies lay sprawled on the floor and strewn pallets. A likely lot of knights they were. Yet Rohan knew his men had to release their tension. They had fought too long and too hard with no respite. Aye, let them have this night. For tomorrow would find them back on their horses in search of the cowardly louts who destroyed for the sheer love of the kill.

Rohan glanced over at the hearth where Manhku watched him. He nodded to his man, in no mood for conversation, and jogged up the stairs to what he knew would be a torture chamber.

As he lay back on the linens and furs of the great bed, Isabel's heather scent swirled around him like a living thing. He closed his eyes, and instead of fighting it, he opened his senses to her. His cock throbbed with his need for her body. Rohan growled like a wounded animal and took his shaft into his hand. He squeezed his eyes shut at the pressure and cursed Isabel for the witch she was.

* * *

Rohan woke long before the first crow of the cock. He cleaned and dressed. As he stepped down the stairway, he grinned. His men snored happily, no doubt reliving their conquests of the night before. "Rouse yourselves, men!" Rohan called. Muffled groans and pained moans filled the hall.

He kicked several of them in the feet. "Clothe yourselves, and break the fast. We have work to do!" Just as Rohan was about to open the heavy doors, they opened from the outside. He scowled. They had not been bolted?

A weary Isabel slipped through. With her head bent, she moved straight toward him. When she bumped into his chest, Rohan's blood quickened. His release last night had done nothing to temper his want of her.

Isabel cried out, and as she moved away from him, he grasped her by the arm to keep her from falling backward. "What brings you into the hall, Isabel?"

Despite the fatigue that marred her features, she yanked her arm from his grasp. "It is of no concern to you!"

He grinned. So the maid had her dander up, did she? "Aye, 'tis my concern. Why were you not abed?" he asked, knowing full well where she had spent the night.

Isabel stiffened and notched her chin to look up at him. Her violet eyes sparked furiously. "Mayhap I had my own rendezvous."

Although he knew she taunted him with her insinuation, the implication soured his mood. The vision of Isabel hot and panting beneath a faceless man as he pumped into her infuriated him. He yanked her close to him. "Should proof positive be given to me, Isabel, you will feel the lash on that silk-skinned back of yours."

Instead of pulling away from him, Isabel moved toward

him. Her soft scent wafted up to his nostrils. His grip tightened around her arm. "What is good for the gander is not good for the goose?"

His jaw tightened. "Do not jest with me, Isabel."

She moved closer still, so that now the ripeness of her left breast pressed against his hauberk. She slid her hand down the arm clasping hers and moved it to her right breast. Rohan hiked in a sharp breath. Then she moved it up to her neck and pressed his fingers there. "Once I heal from my lover's rough play, I will tutor you in how it is done." She leaned closer toward him, and Rohan thought his body would come apart at every seam. Fury mangled heatedly with his fierce desire for her. He flung her hand away and stepped away from her.

"Who marked you?"

She laughed a low, throaty laugh. The sound of a woman experienced in the game of love. "A lady never divulges such secrets."

"You play a game you will lose."

She smiled and pursued him. "Really, Rohan? What is the prize?"

"Would you have me take you here and now?"

"I would have you take me not at all." With those parting words, Isabel sauntered past him.

Rohan turned, furious, his gaze following the jaunty swing of her hips. He grabbed a stool next to the hearth and flung it across the room, where it shattered into dozens of pieces against the wall. "Name the cur who marked you!" he bellowed.

Isabel hesitated in her step but kept moving toward the stairway.

Rohan strode toward her, his temper nearly out of

control. "You will halt, damsel, and answer me!" He stopped at the lord's table. She was nearly to the stairs.

Slowly, Isabel turned. Her eyes darted to Manhku, who, along with every other soul in the hall, held his breath and watched the storm build.

Isabel swallowed hard, and though she knew she should not, she cast another glance at Manhku, who sat upon his pallet. His eyes remained passive. She dared not name him whilst Rohan raged. He might tear the man apart.

"Du Luc," the giant said. Isabel vehemently shook her head, but the Saracen ignored her. " 'Twas I who damaged the maid," Manhku admitted.

Rohan's jaw dropped. Anger darkened his features. Thorin appeared as if from the thin air and clapped a hand firmly on his shoulder. As if he were asking directions to the nearest shire, he said, "Tell us, Manhku, how that came about."

Rohan shook Thorin's hand from his shoulder and squarely faced his man, his hands fisted at his sides. "Aye, Manhku, tell us."

" 'Twas a simple misunderstanding," Isabel offered, moving between the two men.

Rohan worked his jaw, and Isabel knew a terrible war waged within him. His man had damaged his property. If he allowed Manhku to carry on with no punishment, he would lose face, and his men would see him as weak.

Manhku looked from Isabel to Rohan. "The wench speaks half-truths."

"Then speak the whole truth, Manhku," Rohan bit out.

"The maid came upon me as I was trying to move about with the aid of a spear. She took it from me. To break my fall, I took her with me." Manhku looked to Isabel, who stood rigid, holding her breath. "I begged her pardon. 'Twas not my intent to damage her."

Rohan looked to Isabel, his eyes narrowed, but instead of anger, puzzlement lurked in the golden depths. "Why did you hide this from me?"

Isabel looked up to Thorin and past him to Ioan, Wulfson, and Rorick, who all stood silent in the doorway. "I—I did not want your man harmed."

Rohan shook his head and raked his fingers through his long hair. He laughed, confused. "I do not understand your methods, damsel. You save my man not once but twice. From the looks of those marks on your neck, he nearly snuffed you out, and yet you defend him?"

Isabel nodded. "I am not a barbarian, Sir Rohan."

"Nay, you are—" He sighed and turned to look at Manhku, then back to Isabel. "You are a complete mystery to me. Next you will welcome Henri and his band of thieves to come sup with us."

Isabel quirked a smile, despite the memories the name conjured up. "My civilities only go so far."

Rohan made a gallant bow before her and all of his men. "I beg your pardon as well, Lady Isabel."

His words shocked her. Never had she expected an apology from him, and certainly not a public one. But what worried Isabel most was that she found herself being pulled toward the knight. He was all things bad, but beneath his rough exterior lurked a fair and passionate man. The heat rose in her cheeks as she remembered where he had spent the night. He may be fair, and he may be passionate, but he was as bad as a rutting boar, and she would not be his next conquest.

"You will beg for more than my pardon, sir," Isabel quipped.

Wulfson snorted and chortled. "Nay, Lady Isabel, 'twill be Gwyneth he should beg forgiveness from!"

Isabel scowled, not understanding his meaning, but Wulfson continued. "Aye, the wench was dumped!" Wulfson laughed louder as he made his way deeper into the hall. Rohan scowled heavily at his man. "But 'twas Thorin's gain." He slapped the Viking on the back. "I would have joined you, my good man, but both of my hands were occupied."

"Ha!" Rorick chimed in. "You stingy knight. Could you not share one of your pieces with your brothers in arms?"

Rohan grinned and rubbed his chest. "The way those maids devoured Wulf last night, 'tis a wonder there is anything left of him this morn."

Wulfson's grin nearly split his face. "Aye, I am a bit sore." He poured himself a cup of ale and raised it high. "But not nearly as sore as those two. See for yourselves when they come to the hall." He tossed his head back and drank deeply of the brew. As he finished, Lyn and Sarah brought two large platters into the hall, both walking unnaturally stiffly. The entire hall erupted into uproarious laughter. The maids' cheeks flushed red, and both looked bashfully from beneath lowered lashes at Wulfson. He grinned, and as Rohan was fond of doing, Wulfson rubbed his chest. "Ladies, I am free this eve if you wish for company."

As weary as Isabel was, she was elated at the news that Rohan had not lain with the merry widow. Despite it all, she was filthy from the night's ministries to the sick. But because Rohan pulled her down to sit beside him at the lord's table and because she was famished, she ate. Soon her lids were heavy with fatigue. Enid came to her, and begged her leave of Rohan. He granted it. No sooner had Isabel entered her solar than Enid stripped her of her garments. Too exhausted to bathe, she sank naked between the cool linens. Her last thought was of Rohan's smiling face as sleep found her.

When Isabel woke several hours later, the sun had not risen full up. She stretched and smiled, glad for once not to have the weight of the world on her shoulders. While she still did not welcome the Normans to her home, she welcomed the break in tension. Enid appeared and aided her in a quick toilette, then helped her dress for the day.

When Isabel walked down the stairway, the hall was uncharacteristically quiet. Manhku sat up on a chair with his leg elevated on another. She smiled at him. And while she could tell he would rather she disappeared into the stone walls, his lips twitched in a smile.

"Good morn, Manhku, how fares the leg?'

"The pain eases."

"Good. Let me change the poultice and the bandages."

Isabel set about the chore, and just as she finished wrapping the last linen strip around his thigh, he put his hand to hers. "You are brave."

His words startled her. Isabel raised her eyes to his. "That is very kind of you to say, Manhku, but I only do what anyone would do."

"Nay. Another wench would have run screaming and tearing her hair at the first sight of us. You stayed, and you fought."

Isabel smiled and tied the linen snugly, then sat back. "Aye, and a lot of good that did me."

"Rohan is a fair man."

"He is a man first, Manhku."

"Aye, he is that, but you will not find a finer champion than he. Give him his head. And do not betray him. He would never forgive you that."

Isabel looked closely at the Saracen. "Why do you tell me these things?"

"Your sire and your brother. They will not return." Hot tears flashed at his cold words. "I do not mean to hurt you, Lady Isabel, I speak the truth. They would be here had they survived the bloody hill of Senlac."

Isabel brushed a tear from her cheek. "Aye, I have lied to myself these past weeks. But I still hold hope."

"You can hope, but eventually you will have to put your trust in someone."

"Are you asking me to make Rohan the man I trust?"

"Aye, or any of his Blood Swords. No worthier men walk this frigid island."

"I applaud your loyalty, Manhku, but there is no future for me with any knight here. They are as transient as the wind. They have no name, no coat of arms. The world calls them bastard. The blood of three kings runs in my veins. I was bred to run a great manor. To marry well, to mingle with queens and kings."

His eyes widened. She smiled and patted his arm. "I know how selfish it sounds. But I chose it. I chose that path, for in it I have much at my disposal to help others. Wed to a poor, nameless knight, I might be able to eke out a meager existence for myself and my children, if I am so blessed, while my husband runs off to war. How will I support my family should he fall on the battlefield?"

"Blue blood does not a worthy spouse make."

"I agree, but any blood must come with sustenance."

"Would you prefer Henri over Rohan, then?"

She stiffened. "Nay. Not under any circumstance."

"Riders approach!" the lookup shouted. As she did every time those words echoed in her ears, Isabel first felt a leap of excitement, of hope that her father and her brother arrived, but it was quickly chased by dread. More marauders or, worse, Henri.

Isabel excused herself from Manhku and hurried to the tower door. "Who comes?" she called up to the lookout.

"A laden cart. Mayhap more churls."

Isabel hurried out of the hall through the courtyard and to the bailey and watched as a ragged caravan of Saxons made their way toward her. As they drew closer, recognition dawned, and an emotion she did not like to acknowledge she possessed crept up. It was one thing to feel jealousy at Rohan's taking of a village woman, but a fuller, more potent jealousy gripped her belly. Lord and Lady Willingham of Dover, along with their only child, the renowned beauty and court favorite Lady Deidre, approached.

Isabel smoothed her gown and waited in the bitter cold as they came closer. Had she not known the family personally, Lord Willingham's long, flowing beard and hair gave his heritage away. His lady, Edwina, sat rigid and proud beside him. Deidre, adorned in a fully lined fox cloak, scowled, the gesture twisting her dark beauty. Isabel guessed that they, as were many other Saxons, displaced. And as surely as she could see the future, she knew she could not turn them away.

"Lord and Lady Willingham." Isabel welcomed them as she met the cart where it stopped.

Lord Willingham handed the reins to Bart. "I would

say good day to you, Lady Isabel, but it is a dark day for myself and my family. We come with nothing but a plea for refuge here."

Isabel curtsied and said, "Of course, milord, Rossmoor awaits you. Step down, and let me welcome you and your ladies."

He stepped from the cart and turned to his wife, who, still rigid, allowed him to help her, yet the minute her feet touched the ground, she jerked out of his arms. Deidre continued to scowl at Isabel. Neither lady had much use for the other, and since Deidre strutted around at court as if she should be queen, Isabel had always steered clear of her. Arlys's cousin might be admired by the courtiers, but she was not admired by Isabel. But as she still considered herself lady of the manor, she would be the ever gracious hostess.

Isabel moved to embrace Lady Edwina but was met with a hostile stare. Isabel smiled despite it and curtsied, and when she rose, she embraced the stiff woman. "Lady Edwina, welcome to Rossmoor. Feel free to make yourselves at home."

"At least, Isabel, you have a home," Deidre spat.

Isabel turned toward the angry woman. "I consider myself most fortunate."

Lord Willingham helped his daughter from the cart. As she stood before the great hall, her eyes widened. "The Normans did not burn it down?"

"Nay, the hall is built almost entirely of stone. My great-grandfather planned well, and my father has maintained this great house."

Deidre turned her pinched face to Isabel. Her eyes

narrowed. "How is it you have escaped the Norman's hand?" Her question was loaded with insinuation.

Isabel felt the heat rise in her cheeks.

Lord Willingham shushed his daughter and took Isabel's hand. "It has been a year at least since I have visited here. Rossmoor is a welcome sight to these tired eyes. The Normans burned us out. My lands have been taken from me and my family reduced to beggars. Your father, Alefric, before his death extended his hospitality to me should we need it."

Isabel gasped at his words. Her knees buckled, and had the old lord not held her hand, she would have swooned right there.

He hugged her to him and patted her head. Tears erupted as her worst fears were realized. Hard sobs wracked her chest.

"Forgive me, Lady Isabel, I thought you knew."

He moved her from where they stood in the courtyard and into the hall. He sat her on the first available bench. He knelt before her and took her cold hands into his and rubbed them. The pain of his words was unbearable, her tears so thick Isabel could barely make out his form.

"Alefric fought with the vigor of ten men, lass. He was a sight to behold. Had Harold two more like him, we would have seen the day won."

"Did—did he die swiftly?" She had to know. The thought of her father lying for hours or days suffering on the bloody field was too much for her to bear.

Lord Willingham's eyes glistened as well. The two men had spent many an hour over a flagon of wine. He looked down at his hands clasping hers. "I do not know."

"Milord, please, tell me true. Did he suffer?"

The old man cleared his throat and looked up at her. Softly, he said, "He was struck from behind. When I got to him much later, long after the battle was lost, his throat was slit."

Isabel gasped. "How barbaric!" Then she cried, "What of Geoff?"

The old noble shook his head. "He is not here?"

"Nay! Until you came, I had no word of my sire. Did you see Geoff?"

"Aye, earlier that fateful morn. He fought beside Alefric. I did not see him among the dead, though."

Hope swelled. "Mayhap he lives?"

He nodded. "Mayhap." But his eyes said he doubted it. "Surely, he would have returned by now, Isabel."

Isabel drew the old man's gnarled hands to her. "Were the graves blessed?"

He nodded. "Aye, it took days, but the priests came."

Isabel let out a huge sigh of relief. For that she was grateful. She removed her hands from the old lord's and swiped at her cheeks with her sleeve. She stood. "Come, let us see to your family."

As she turned to go back outside, she nearly crashed into Lady Willingham and her daughter. Their two maids and a manservant stood behind them with heavy bundles and a trunk. Isabel turned to find Enid standing anxiously nearby. "Show Lord and Lady Willingham's servants to the chamber next to Geoff's and Lady Deidre's maid to the solar." She turned back to the family and extended her arm to the hall. "Come and sup. You must be famished."

All three sets of eyes lit up at the mention of food. They

moved eagerly to the lord's table. But Lady Edwina halted. Her sharp hiss caught Isabel's attention. The lady stared open-mouthed at Manhku seated at the hearth. Deidre also hissed in a sharp breath, as if she had touched something unsavory. Oswin, Lord Willingham, scowled at both of his ladies.

Isabel smiled. Though it had been less than a week since the Normans' arrival, she felt a kindness in her heart for the surly Saracen, and as each day passed, it became clearer to Isabel that he might very well call Rossmoor his home. Fellow countrymen or not, she would not have any guests question his right to be here.

Forcing a cheerful tone to her words, Isabel asked, "Do you wish to meet Manhku?"

The women vigorously shook their heads and stepped back. The old man, though not so adamant, declined. Isabel excused herself and went to see to the downed knight. She stoked the fire beside him and softly asked, "Would you like a trencher?"

He raised his black eyes to her, and she read the mischievous glint in them.

"Manhku, the travelers are weary. Leave your rancor for another day." She grabbed a pelt from the pile of them nearby and settled it around his lap. "I beg you, behave yourself."

He growled low, and she could not help a smile when Lady Edwina squirmed in her chair.

After she called for food, Isabel turned to the trio. "I assure you, he does not bite." Deidre gasped, and Isabel added, "At least not today." Lady Edwina mewled, and Manhku laughed.

"Lady Isabel, please pardon my wife and daughter's apprehension. When we heard *les morts* had settled here, we almost did not come." Lord Willingham swallowed thickly. "Dunsworth, it seems, is but a pile of rubble, and the Norman there is mad. We had no choice but to come here."

Isabel nodded, and as she fussed around them, making sure the platters were warm and plentiful, she felt the need to twist the knife. It angered her that this family who had sought her out now turned their noses up to her other guests.

And though her father's death was certain, her brother's was not, and she would hang on to that small sliver of hope. Until then, anyone other than the natives of this shire she would consider a guest and thereby a temporary inhabitant. That most certainly included the Normans. "Aye, Lord Oswin, the Blood Swords will be home to roost before nightfall. They are many, and none so bashful as this one. I would give you a word of warning. Do not offend them, or you will see yourselves cast out."

Lady Edwina harrumphed.

Deidre spoke. "Father, I refuse to seek shelter with a band of thieves and murderers!"

Before Oswin spoke, Isabel did. "Lady Deidre? Should you find a more welcome manor, please,"—Isabel extended her hand toward the door—"be my guest to seek it."

Oswin shushed his daughter and turned tired eyes to Isabel. "Please, our pardon, we are weary and in fear for our lives. We have nothing to offer, and we ask much. Forgive us. And"—he looked to Manhku and managed a smile—"the insult to your man."

Isabel placed a comforting hand on his great shoulder. "These are trying times for us all. Nothing is guaranteed. For now, I can promise you a warm fire and food in your belly and a room with only a few drafts. Now, please sit and sup."

Because of their station, there was no question in Isabel's mind that the Willinghams would stay anywhere else but the hall. She showed the lord and his lady to one of the vacant chambers upstairs and Deidre to the lady's solar. As the maid unpacked her trunk, Isabel caught the dark glare of her mistress. Isabel quirked a brow. "Deidre, you look as if something sour sits on your tongue."

"Aye, the fact that I must share a room with such as you is bothersome."

Isabel's cheeks warmed. Not because of Deidre's insult but for the insults to come when Rohan would demand that she retire with him later this eve. And he would. With the tension lightened, he would no doubt be feeling he had the right to claim her debt to him.

Later when Rohan strode into the hall, his men fanning out behind him, Isabel caught her breath and sighed. He was a most manly man. Tall, handsome, and dangerous on so many levels. He tossed his helmet and gauntlets to Hugh and strode toward her, pushing his cowl back. His face was flushed red, his eyes danced in victory, and she trembled as a warm flush washed over her. She had no doubt she would be the spoils for this victorious knight.

"You look rested, Isabel," Rohan said as she handed him a full cup of ale. Lyn and Sarah handed out cups to the others.

"I feel rested. What of you? Did you find the cowardly raiders?"

"Nay, but we found others who had a covetous eye on the area."

"Did they lay down their arms?"

Rohan drank deeply of the cup, draining it. He set it down on the table, and his eyes met hers. "Nay."

Isabel swallowed hard. She did not ask what became of them.

Hugh bustled back into the hall, followed by Russell. He hurried to his master. "Sir, I will see to your bath posthaste."

Rohan nodded, but Isabel said, "Sir Rohan's bath awaits him already, Hugh."

Rohan smiled. Isabel returned the gesture. Rohan extended his arm and said, "Come then, damsel, and scrub this grime from my back."

Isabel hesitated, then placed her hand on his forearm and let him escort her to their chamber. Beside the hot tub, a trencher of food warmed by the fire along with a pitcher of ale cooling on the other side of the room near the window.

As he often did behind closed doors, Isabel noticed Rohan give in to a slight limp. Without a word, she helped him strip down to his loincloth. She moved away and found other things to occupy her until she heard his heavy sigh as he settled back into the tub.

Isabel filled a goblet and handed it to Rohan. He took it silently and drank. Enjoying the quiet of the moment, Isabel lathered up a linen cloth. Rohan leaned forward and said, "Scrub hard, Isabel." And she did. When he sat back and she lathered his head and dug her fingers deep into his scalp, he closed his eyes and sat back against the high rim of the tub. After she rinsed his hair, Isabel washed his chest. When she looked up to find his warm gaze on her, it unnerved her more than when he stared at her with open

lust. This quiet camaraderie felt more intimate, and there-
fore more dangerous.

"We have guests. I could do naught but offer them refuge here."

Rohan's body tightened. "Who?"

"Lord and Lady Willingham and their daughter, Deidre.
Oswin is uncle to my betrothed."

Rohan grabbed her hand, catching her attention. While
he did not hurt her, his grip was firm. "Why are they here?"

"Displaced." Hot tears welled. "Lord Willingham told
me of my father's death."

Rohan sat up straight in the tub. He released her hand
and trailed a fingertip across her cheek. " 'Twas expected,
Isabel."

Choking back a sob, she nodded, and instead of trying
to control her tears, she allowed them to flow. It was the
least she could do for her father. "Forgive me," she softly
said, and turned from him, not wanting him to see her
cry.

Not understanding what drove him, Rohan stood and,
sopping wet, stepped from the tub. Wrapping the linen
towel around him, he walked over to where Isabel sat by
the fire. He squatted before her and placed his hands on
her knees. "Isabel, I am sorry." He did not know what else
to say.

She raised red-rimmed eyes to him. Her bottom lip
trembled. He slid a hand up her arm to her neck. He
pressed his fingers to her skin, his eyes locked with hers.
Once again, this woman's quiet strength amazed him.
He knew she hung on to the hope of her father returning. Yet he knew the day he thundered up to the doors of

Rossmoor that the old lord was dead. He had his reasons for keeping the news to himself. Reasons he would not divulge now, if ever.

Isabel choked back another sob. When she threw her arms around his neck and pressed herself to him, Rohan stiffened and stood to move away, but she came up with him. His body instantly warmed. She clung to him like a child. Her sobs increased, and he was at a total loss. The only thing he thought to do was slip his arms around her waist and hold her until her tears passed.

Isabel's small body shuddered with sobs, and she mumbled words he did not understand against his damp chest. When she wiped her cheeks across his skin, the warm wetness of her tears stung him. He stiffened. She molded herself more firmly against him, and Rohan responded. His cock filled, his arms tightened, and he pressed his lips to the top of her head. Isabel looked up to him, her violet eyes wet with her tears. For a moment, he lost himself in their depths and wondered how he had allowed this slip of a girl to wheedle her way under his skin. At that moment, when she rose on her toes and offered herself to him, he didn't care.

"Isa," he whispered. Taking her face into his hands, Rohan lowered his lips to hers. The taste of her salty tears reminded him of her sorrow and her vulnerability. He knew all was forfeit when he realized that he wanted this woman's trust.

Warm and soft, her lips parted beneath his. She was warm liquid silk in his arms. When she kissed him back, blood surged through him. He swelled against her belly. Isabel would have to be dead not to feel it. The damp linen clung to his warm skin, and her gown of linen and wool was thin. He felt each inch of her against him. And he wanted more than a kiss. He wanted to take her to the great bed and lay her down and make love to her, slow and unhurried. Her lips clung to his. The heat of her body mingled with his, steaming up the room. The kiss deepened— his tongue, slow and languid, swirled against hers. Isabel moaned and pressed harder against him. His fingers dug into her hair. If she did not stop . . .

Only knowing one way to make a woman feel better, his lips still pressed to hers, Rohan picked Isabel up in his arms and strode to the bed. As he bent with her in his arms over the mattress, Isabel tightened her arms around his neck. "Don't leave me," she pleaded.

"I won't," Rohan breathed against her lips. "I won't."

Sixteen

As hard as he was for her, Rohan's sense of duty overrode his yearning to lose himself in Isabel's body. She needed this time to mourn, and while he was not a man prone to chivalrous actions such as considering another's feelings, he could not in good conscience press her for more than what she gave him. So he lay down beside her and listened to her sobs trail off to soft sniffles, until finally her chest rose and fell in a regular pattern. Her soft body pressed against his side; her warm breath caressed his bare chest. Her tiny hand lay on his chest, her cheek pressed to it. His cock stood straight up beneath the linen that separated him from her. He squeezed his eyes shut and willed his blood to cool.

Before his lust overtook his conscience, Rohan slipped from the bed and dressed. Enid hovered just outside the room. Rohan scowled. Most women irritated him, and the way this one was constantly fluttering about wore his nerves thin. "Your lady sleeps. Leave her be." He strode past her, strapping his sword belt around his waist, then proceeded down to the hall and to much safer ground.

His men greeted him with raised cups. Rohan grinned. They were cleaned up and dressed as he, *sans* their mail, in more courtly garb. Manhku, too, was clothed in his native kaftan and loose-fitting trousers that had been augmented to accommodate his wounded leg. "How does the leg feel, Manhku?" Rohan asked, handing his brother in arms a full cup.

"Better."

Rhys approached and leaned a brawny arm against the stone wall near the blazing hearth. A secret smile twisted his lips. "That confession must have cost you, old man."

Manhku frowned. Rhys explained. "Once healed, you will lose the attention of the wench."

Rohan scoffed. "Trust me, Rhys, Manhku does not have the fortitude to manage a wench such as she."

Rhys raised his cup. "We are in awe of you, Rohan. 'Twere it any of us"—he flung out his arm to encompass the rest of the Blood Swords, who all listened intently— "the wench's virtue would have been a thing long gone, and she would no doubt feel the burden of yet another bastard to carry on the line." Rhys raised his cup. "Your balls must be purple by now. I bow to your superior self-control!"

Rohan laughed and raised his cup and drank deeply. As if on command, several village maids, some of them new faces to Rohan, and the widow Gwyneth appeared.

Ioan chortled along with Rhys and the quiet Stefan. Once again, the ale flowed, and the easy camaraderie that was the essence of the Blood Swords filled the hall.

Rohan sat before the hearth and drank and watched his men behave like the conquerors they were. The women did not seem to mind. Heat burned in his loins. His belly growled, and if he could not feed his lust, he would see to his belly. He debated whether to send someone to fetch the lady of the manor but decided he would see to the chore of waking Sleeping Beauty himself.

Rohan stood and called to Astrid, who stood frowning at the doorway to the kitchen. "See to the meal, woman!"

Rohan took the stairs three at a time and stopped abruptly as he saw Isabel move toward him, her maid fussing over her. Rohan shot the maid a hostile glare, and Enid scurried past him. He strode up to Isabel and smiled. She paused before him.

"You seem rested," Rohan softly said.

Her cheeks pinkened, and his cock swelled. Her long golden tresses hung lose around her shoulders, a delicate golden circlet on her head. The crimson velvet of her overgown accentuated the high color of her cheeks.

Shyly she looked up at him. "I—" She searched for words. As she did, Rohan maneuvered her against the stone wall. He placed a hand on either side of her head and moved close to her.

"You what?" he whispered as he lowered his lips to hers.

Isabel struggled to control her racing heart and her warming body. The hardness of the wall pressed into her back; the hardness of the man surrounding her pressed into her breast. "Please," she whispered, not knowing what she pleaded for. This knight's gentle handling of her earlier had confused her. She was not used to allowing her weakness to show. She was the person everyone came to for succor. While she found the situation foreign, she did not find it altogether unpleasant.

Rohan's eyes blazed in the torchlight. He watched her as a hawk watched its prey, seeing deep into her soul. She licked her lips. He swelled against her and groaned. "Isabel, you tempt me beyond my will." His lips crashed down onto hers, and she did not fight him. Indeed, she pressed back against him, finding his strong warmth revitalizing.

The power of him surrounded her, his passion, his strength, and his ardor fueling the flame he had ignited the first time he touched her. She gave in to it because she chose to. Just this once, she would allow another to ease her burden.

Isabel did not think of her losses; she thought only of how safe she felt at that moment in this man's arms. She opened her mouth wider, and as he had done earlier to her, she touched her tongue to his. Rohan groaned and pulled her against his chest, arching her back, taking what she offered.

The sheer force of his pursuit left her breathless. Her breasts grew heavy, her nipples hardened, and Isabel found herself wishing he would ease the ache between her thighs.

"Du Luc!" Thorin's voice thundered from the hall. "The Blood Swords starve!"

Isabel broke her lips free from Rohan, trying valiantly to collect her racing pulse. Rohan groaned again and pressed his forehead against hers. "I will sew that Viking's mouth shut."

Isabel smiled and slipped from his arms. "Come, Sir Rohan, let us slake our hunger."

His eyes glowed as he presented his arm to her. "Aye, but 'tis my hunger for you that I will slake later this night."

Isabel's cheeks flushed hot. And to her utter horror, she looked forward to his carnal promise more than the promise of the food downstairs.

As they descended into the hall, the Blood Swords whooped and cheered as if the Conqueror and his duchess made an appearance. Isabel instantly noted that all of the knights, while armed with their swords, were dressed in more courtly garb, as was Rohan. They were clean, and their faces beamed, mostly, she decided, because of the maids, who were red-faced, and the tapped kegs near the tables. If they continued their regular wenching and feasting, there might not be enough larder to see them through the next month!

Isabel also noted that there were at least four more maids come from the village. Rohan grinned and escorted her to the lord's table. As soon as she was seated, the knights followed. And soon the evening meal was under way. Rohan cut several choice pieces of meat from the platters for her and put them in the trencher they shared. He smiled down at her, and she smiled in return. He sipped from his cup and handed it to her. Very aware that his men watched, Isabel sipped from where Rohan's lips had touched.

"You tamed the shrew? Eh, Rohan?" Wulfson asked as he chewed a hunk of roasted lamb.

Isabel rose to the challenge. "'Tis not I who has been tamed, sir knight."

Rohan choked on his food, and Thorin pounded him on the back. Red-faced, Rohan drank a swig of his ale. He turned red eyes to Isabel, and while he scowled, mischief danced behind his eyes.

Isabel's words had been a randy comeback, but his men

did not think it so amusing. The mood of the room shifted. They watched Rohan intently. Isabel's throat tightened as she swallowed a tender piece of capon.

Not to be bullied by his men, Rohan took Isabel's hand and raised it to his lips. He grinned and looked at her first, then at his men. "I have found that in love and war, sometimes the force of a sword must be tempered with a firm but"—he bit into Isabel's palm, his intimate action shocking her; his eyes burned into her, and heat rose in her cheeks and spread to her thighs—"gentle stroke." He kissed her where his teeth marks showed in her skin.

Isabel drew her hand away. "Rest assured, sir, your sword will never breach me."

His men roared in laughter. Rohan was undaunted. "Would you like to wager on that, damsel?"

Isabel glowered at Rohan's men. "Continue your jesting. Take these willing maids, and spread your seed to replenish Alethorpe." She turned to Rohan, and while she wanted to pierce his cocksureness with her words, she chose to ease the sting. "Is the life of a bastard so enjoyable, Rohan, that you would see a son of your loins endure what you have?" His face clouded in anger. She looked from him to his men. "What of you? What of the children spawned from nights of debauchery? Do you not think of them? What manner of men are you to continue such a hardship for one of your own making?"

Isabel took a deep breath and continued. "I do not condemn you, Rohan, or any man here, for what you had no hand in. But you do have the power not to continue the legacy. Is it such a burden to marry and bring legitimate children into this world?"

"I would claim any by-blow I should produce, Isabel."

"And what means do you have to support such a child? Your life is not your own." Isabel looked around the table. The Blood Swords frowned, but she could see her words had struck a chord. She let out a long breath. Fatigue gripped her again.

"What of you, Isabel? Should you find yourself with child and no husband, would you cast it to the streets as something ugly and disgraceful?" Rohan challenged.

She gazed up at him and saw his own pain, for it was clear this man found no love from his mother. Slowly, she shook her head. "Nay, a child is a gift. I would never cast him away."

"But how would you support a child with no husband to provide for you?" Rohan turned the tables on her. She straightened and looked past him to his men, then up to Rohan, who regarded her keenly.

"I would do whatever was necessary."

Rohan nodded and took a deep drink of his ale. As he set the cup down and nodded, he said, "As would I, milady. As would I." She opened her mouth to comment, but he raised his hand. "Enough! I weary of this talk. Let us sup."

Even had she wanted to fight his edict, she did not, for the Willinghams decided to make an appearance. She knew the minute Deidre broke into view. Rohan's men, sitting across from her facing the stairway, grinned like idiots. Isabel rolled her eyes and shook her head. Men. They were led not by the head that sat upon their shoulders but by the smaller one that hung between their legs.

As lady of the manor, and despite their bad manners for not appearing before the feast was set, Isabel rose and introduced the guests. She was not surprised to see Lady Willingham not in attendance.

"My wife is not feeling well," Lord Willingham offered.

Isabel was not stupid. She knew the great dame would rather sit with a pack of wolves than sit at the same table as a Norman. Isabel shrugged. "I will see that a tray is sent to her."

Lord Willingham took her hand as he raised her from her short curtsy. "Thank you, she will appreciate that." The old man turned to his daughter and took her hand.

Isabel looked up to Rohan, then to his men. "Sir Rohan, sir knights, may I present Lord Oswin of Willingham, formerly of Dover, and his daughter, Lady Deidre."

Rohan nodded his head, not giving the Saxon the full respect of a bow. He did the same to the daughter. Isabel watched Deidre's eyes widen in surprise. Did she think the Norman sported two heads?

"My lord," Warner said, slipping between Isabel and the noble lady. He bowed to the lord and turned smiling eyes on the daughter. "My lady, I am Warner de Conde. I am at your service."

Deidre smiled and extended her hand. "I am pleased to meet you, Sir Warner."

Thorin snorted and poured himself another draught of ale, as did Wulfson. Rhys shook his head and said to Ioan, "Next thing you know, he'll be singing to her."

"Milord?" Isabel asked Rohan as she inclined her head to the lord's table.

Rohan nodded, and with his permission, Isabel invited the lord and his daughter to sit with them and sup. Isabel was glad to see that when Deidre made a move to sit to Rohan's left, Thorin directed her farther down the table and to the other side, where her father sat beside her. They were given a trencher to share. While the old man looked rather nervous surrounded by his enemies, Deidre fastened her gaze onto Rohan. Isabel was not surprised. 'Twas her way. It was clear to everyone in the hall that Rohan held some claim to Isabel; whether that claim was returned Deidre did not know, and apparently she did not care.

Once the ladies were seated, the men followed suit and the meal continued.

"Tell me, sir, what news have you to share?" Rohan asked.

The old man's hand shook as he raised his cup. He set it down and looked directly at Rohan. "Edgar has been crowned king."

Rorick snorted. "The lad is not fit to wipe his own nose."

"Aye," Rohan agreed. "Besides, it is of no matter. The Witan has no power. William will be crowned as rightful king." He speared Willingham with a glare. "What are your thoughts on the matter?"

"I believe Harold should have been named heir over your duke. He is a Saxon, and the people's choice."

"What of Harold's twice-pledged oath to William to uphold Edward's naming of him as king? He swore the second time on the bones of a saint."

"He was coerced," Deidre offered.

Rohan set down his piece of bread. "Coerced? Nay, he was not. I was there. Harold freely pledged his oath." Rohan turned to Isabel. "And I assure you, when a Norman gives his oath, he sees it through, even to his death." He turned back to Deidre. "Do not talk to me of coercion. William saved Harold from Guy of Ponthieu's dungeon. Besides, William is nephew to Edward's mother. There is blood."

"Edgar has more right to the throne than Harold or William," Willingham interjected.

Rohan nodded and stabbed a tender piece of capon from the platter and cut it into smaller pieces, which he set on Isabel's side of the trencher. He took a heartier piece for himself. "By blood that may be true, but by a king's decree William is heir."

"What will become of us?" Deidre asked sharply.

"William will expect a pledge of fealty," Wulfson said. "From there it is up to him."

"'Tis not fair!" she continued to rail. "My betrothed is dead. My dowry taken by bloodthirsty—" she stopped, realizing she was about to insult her host. "By invaders. We have nothing but the few meager possessions we brought with us."

Rohan shrugged. "Your cry is heard across this land. 'Tis the way of war. Had Harold held to his oath, I would no doubt be playing dice with these wretches in a garrison in Westminster."

"Have you no kin?" Warner solicitously asked Deidre. Ioan snorted, and Thorin rolled his eyes.

"My cousin Arlys Lord of Dunsworth has been displaced," she answered angrily.

At the mention of Arlys, Rohan's body tightened. Isabel watched several of his men look to him.

"Is that not your be—" Warner stopped. He had the decency to look properly chastened. "My pardon, Lady Isabel."

"Isabel, have you word of Arlys?" Willingham asked.

Now every eye in the hall focused on Isabel. Her cheeks flushed at the attention. She raised her eyes to the man who would have been her uncle-in-law. "Nay, but I hear he lives to see the return of Dunsworth."

Rohan laughed. "Henri will see to it there is nothing left of Dunsworth."

Willingham shook his head. "'Tis a tragedy what that devil has done."

Rohan nodded and chewed another bite of meat. "Aye, my brother has a way about him."

Deidre gasped. "That devil is your brother?"

"Aye, we share the same sire, and little else."

Deidre wrinkled her lovely brow. "But I thought you were a bastard."

Isabel stiffened. Rohan seemed unaffected by her statement.

"If you look closely enough, Lady Deidre," Wulfson said, "you will see every one of us Blood Swords sports the horns and pointed tail of a bastard."

Deidre knew she had pushed. Isabel watched the wheels turn in her head. Aye, she was regrouping and would cast her net far and see what she could land.

"You all are knights of William?" she asked demurely.

Isabel rolled her eyes and picked at her meat. When none jumped to answer her, Warner the gallant spoke for them all. "Aye, Lady Deidre, we are all Blood Swords in our own right and known as *les morts*, William's elite death squad."

"The deaths?" She shivered delicately. "That seems so—" She dropped her eyes before raising them and smiling coquettishly at Warner. "Barbaric. Surely you are chivalrous."

Thorin choked on his ale, and Stefan nodded. "Aye, Lady Deidre, we wrote the code of chivalry. I wouldst be most happy to demonstrate all of its properties for you."

"Sir knight," Willingham interjected, "my daughter is a maid of virtue."

Stefan's dark eyes simmered as he caught the coy maid's darker eyes. "Of course she is. I beg your pardon."

Deidre continued to play the coquette, this time setting her dark eyes on Rohan. Isabel pushed the trencher away from her, suddenly losing her appetite.

"Sir Rohan, does William promise you this shire?"

"Deidre!" Willingham hissed. "Mind your manners."

Deidre ignored her father's plea. Rohan held her gaze. Isabel watched the small tic of his jaw flare. The sign did not bode well for the inquisitive Deidre.

" 'Tis no concern of yours," Rohan boorishly answered.

Isabel hid her smile, and Deidre blinked as if she did not believe her wiles had been rebuffed. Just as Deidre opened her mouth to continue her questioning, Lyn leaned between Deidre and Warner with a bowl of steaming water and lost her footing. The bowl poured directly onto Deidre's lap. The women screeched. "Churl!" Then she slapped Lyn hard across the face. Wulfson rose, as did Ioan and Stefan, so abruptly their chairs scraped hard across the stone floor.

Lyn howled. Isabel rose and came around to the maid, and as Deidre raised her hand to slap her again, Isabel grabbed it. "Lay a hand on her again, and I will see you cast from this hall."

"How dare you?" Deidre railed. The lady's dark beauty morphed into something very ugly.

As she placed a comforting hand on Lyn's shoulder, Isabel moved directly into Deidre's space. "I would dare anything I like."

"Because you service the Norman?" Deidre spat.

If the hall had been silent at Deidre's eruption, now it was as if they all stood in a tomb.

"Nay, Deidre, I dare because 'tis my right as lady of the manor." She poked a finger into Deidre's chest. "Do not forget whose daughter I am. I am not above taking arms against anyone who would damage my people."

Lord Willingham took his daughter's arm. His old blue eyes beseeched her to acquiesce.

Deidre took a big breath and slowly exhaled. She smiled first to Rohan, who stood silent, allowing Isabel to handle the affairs of women. Then she turned to Isabel. "I beg your pardon, Isabel. I fear I am not at my best these days." She turned to Rohan. "I beg your leave, sir."

Rohan nodded. Isabel moved aside as Deidre collected what dignity she could and hurried from the hall up the stairway to the solar. Her father followed on her heels.

The hall breathed a collective sigh of relief with the guests' departure.

Isabel caught Rohan's gaze across the table. He seemed unperturbed by the incident. Miraculously, Lyn recovered and bustled about the table and the knights as if nothing had happened. It was then that Isabel realized the bowl of hot water in Deidre's lap was no accident. She smiled as she looked up to catch the wily Lyn's eyes.

"Your servants are a vindictive lot," Rohan commented.

Isabel turned a wicked smile up to the knight. "As is their lady, and do not forget it."

Rohan rubbed his chest and smiled just as wickedly. For her ears only, he said, "I am counting on it. Come, let us retire now."

Isabel trembled, partly in fear but mostly in excitement.

"I must see to the wounded in the hospital hut. Would you escort me?"

Rohan nodded and called for Enid to fetch the lady's cape. "I do not possess one, Rohan. I will brave the chill."

"I find that hard to digest, Isabel. A lady of your rank should have ten of the finest fur-lined cloaks in the land."

"Aye, and I did, but another needed it more. I have a wool one in the solar but will not intrude on Deidre. Indeed, she may gouge my eyes out."

Rohan smiled. "Aye, she is full of vinegar." He cocked a brow. "Much like you."

Isabel slapped his hand. "I may possess vinegar, as you say, but at least I only use it on you Normans and not my own people!"

Rohan extended his arm, and when Isabel took it, he pushed her hand snugly into the crook of his elbow. "I do not know what magic you possess, damsel, but your wish is my command."

Isabel smiled as they started for the door. "I wish you to rescind my oath to you."

Without missing a step, he replied, "Impossible."

Isabel stiffened. "Your chivalry only extends to those things you choose."

"Chivalry is for poets and swains, Isabel. I am neither. Never mistake me for one or the other."

"You disappoint me, Rohan."

He squeezed her hand to his side. "You will take those words back this eve. For I will show you just how undisappointing I can be."

For the tenth time that night, Isabel shivered, knowing the morning would no longer find her so innocent, and also knowing that unless she could command herself to die, there was nothing she could do to prevent Rohan from touching her in the most intimate ways a man could touch a woman. For she had given her oath that he could.

Isabel sucked in a deep breath and held it. The price, she told herself, was not too high. Each time she saw Russell's smiling blue eyes, she knew she made the right choice.

So be it.

Seventeen

Isabel took as much time as she thought she could get away with. But she had misjudged Rohan's patience. As she was refastening a bandage, he strode into the makeshift hospital, grabbed her arm, and pulled her away and out of the dwelling.

"Rohan!" she cried, but he did not heed her. She resisted, and he swept her up into his arms. As if she were but a sack of turnips, he slung her over his shoulder.

Isabel shrieked indignation at his action. "Put me down!" she demanded.

Rohan slapped his hand across her bottom. "Nay."

She could not bear the embarrassment of having his men or her people see her in such an undignified position. Luckily for her, the hall was quiet and most of the torches doused when they entered.

Rohan moved with great, powerful strides up the stairway and kicked open the door to the lord's chamber.

He kicked the door closed and with his free hand threw the heavy bolt.

Rohan pulled Isabel down, pressing her body against his. His passion was clearly on the rise. His arms locked around her waist, and he lowered his head to her lips. Isabel turned her face from his.

Clasping her to him with one hand, he grasped her chin and forced her to look up at him. "I am weary of your games, Isabel. 'Tis time to pay."

Wide-eyed, she shook her head. Her time had come. There were no more chances, no more distractions, no more outs. Isabel stepped back, and he moved against her.

He dropped his arm from around her waist and softly said, "Go stand before the fire."

She hurried from him, wanting as much space as possible between them.

When she reached the fire, he said, "Now, turn around."

When she did, he was seated in her father's great chair near the small table several paces from where she stood. The fire burned brightly behind her, warming her. It reflected off Rohan's tawny eyes, casting a molten sheen. He unstrapped his sword belt and hung it from the high back of the chair. He removed his tunic and then his linen chemise. When he sat back down, the planes of his muscular chest glowed in the firelight. Isabel didn't dare look lower than his waist, afraid she would see his erection. She sucked in a desperate breath, knowing he would not break his oath to her but unsure just how far he would go this night. For while she knew of the act of procreation, she was sorely ignorant of what other means a man had of pleasuring a woman.

"Take your circlet off," he said hoarsely.

Startled by his command, Isabel slowly removed it and set it on the cabinet.

"Remove your girdle."

Isabel caught his gaze. She felt for the clasp and un-hooked the belt. She let it fall to the carpeted floor.

"Now your shoes."

Isabel kicked them from her feet.

Rohan was seated back in the chair, his hands on the edge of the arms. "Now, remove your clothes, one layer at a time."

Unhurried and feeling oddly in control, Isabel lifted her kirtle and let it fall to the floor. Her nipples hardened under his hot gaze.

"Now the other."

Just as slowly, she raised the undergown up her legs, to her hips, then up to her breasts. Rohan's breath hissed, and as she pulled it over her shoulders and let it fall in a heap at her feet, she glanced at his lap. He rose mightily against the fabric of his braies. Isabel stood bathed in the firelight, the only thing separating his eyes from her naked-ness a soft silk and linen shift.

Her body was fully outlined, and despite the warmth of the room and the heat of his gaze, Isabel shivered.

"Remove the shift," Rohan said hoarsely.

With trembling hands, Isabel raised the fabric up and over her shoulders.

"Jesu!" Rohan whispered.

She stood proud and unflinching before him. Yet in her excitement, her breasts trembled. As Rohan's gaze caressed her, Isabel's breathing came faster, and her heart thudded harder against her chest.

Rohan stood, and as if she were an apparition, he moved slowly toward her, afraid the vision would disap-pear. In his twenty-five years on the earth and through all of the lands he had traveled, he could not remember ever seeing anything so lovely as the vision before him. When she shook her long golden hair and it shimmered about her, he caught his breath. For the first time in his life, Rohan questioned his self-control. If he touched her, he would take her. And if he did, she would hate him.

"Touch your breast, Isabel," he whispered.

Her lips parted in shock; her eyes widened.

"Do it now."

With a trembling hand, she pressed her fingers to her right breast. He watched her nipple pucker and wished it were his hand that caused the change. "Harder," he said.

Isabel closed her eyes and squeezed her breast. Rohan groaned and stepped closer still. Isabel moved her head back, exposing her neck to him. Her scent swirled around him. Rohan's body throbbed, his cock straining against his clothing. His hand reached out and touched her hair. Its silky smoothness mesmerized him. He knew her skin to be as soft.

"Touch the other," he softly commanded.

Isabel's free hand moved up to cup her other breast. On her own, she squeezed them both and pressed the full mounds together. She moaned, and so did Rohan. He moved closer to her still, fighting the overwhelming urge to lay her down on the floor and seek refuge deep within her.

"Rohan?" Isabel whispered, her eyes still closed, her breathing almost as heavy as his. "Touch me."

He groaned. "Isa," he breathed, "I cannot."

She opened her eyes, and he nearly lost himself in their amethyst depths. "Why not?"

"Because I will break my oath to you."

Isabel took his hand and pressed it to her breast. "Nay, you will not. I will not let you."

Rohan trembled. The heat and velvety smoothness of her against his calloused hand amazed him. He slipped his left arm around her waist, drawing her to him. His lips crashed down on hers, and Isabel felt her world tilt.

She'd pressed Rohan, she told herself, to get it over and done with, but if she told the truth, it was because her desire nearly matched his, and her curiosity overrode them both.

Though he told her he would break his oath to her if he touched her, she did not believe him.

Ravenously, Rohan kissed her, his hand caressed her breast, he rubbed her nipple between his thumb and forefinger. Isabel arched toward him. Heat and moisture welled between her thighs. Rohan's hand around her waist slid to her bottom, and his hand on her breast slid down her belly. Isabel stiffened. Rohan moved her backward to the wall. The cold of the stones shocked her, but Rohan pressed her harder. His lips clung to hers.

Isabel's head spun. She was caught up in a heated sexual frenzy. Rohan surrounded her. His hands, his lips, his shoulders, his hips, and his legs. His erection pressed hard against her belly. She could feel the heat of it.

Isabel tore her lips from his, gasping for breath. He trailed his teeth down her throat, to her shoulder, where he nipped at her skin. His hand on her belly traveled lower. In a bold move, Rohan pressed his lips to a nipple and suckled her like a hungry babe. His hand cupped her mons, and Isabel lost her balance. Rohan held her against him. His fingertip touched her hardened nub and slid slowly back and forth against it. Isabel cried out, the sensations his touch elicited unlike any she had ever experienced. Like a wanton, she found herself spreading her thighs for him and pressing her breasts harder against his mouth.

The pressure between her thighs increased, and Isabel had no idea how to make it better. But she knew Rohan was the answer. "Rohan," she whispered, "I ache with a fever. Make it go away."

Rohan moaned, and if it were possible, he pulled her tighter against him. What he did next shocked her. He slid his finger along the wetness of her opening. And as nature intended, Isabel moved against him. When he slid the finger into her, she cried out and clasped her thighs tightly around him. She closed her eyes as tight as she could and knew she had crossed a line with him she should not have. Yet he had become an addiction in such a short amount of time. Her body craved him. He was the only one to ease her ache.

"Jesu, Isa, you are so tight and so warm."

Isabel clung to his shoulders, writhing against the movement of his hand. He moved his finger in a slow slide in and out of her, pressing the heel of his palm against her hardened nub. Her body glazed in sudden perspiration. Her hips bucked in an uncontrollable tempo against his hand. Waves of desire swelled between her thighs. Her skin heated almost unbearably. Rohan's body, slick with desire, slid up and down against hers.

A sudden storm gathered between her thighs, taking Isabel by surprise. It swelled hot and wet, with the velocity of a summer squall. And just as suddenly, it crested and crashed deep inside her. The tempest in her swirled out of control, taking her high up before dropping her in an out-of-control dive back to earth. "Rohan!" she cried. He silenced her with his lips, as her body jerked and spasmed. The shock of what had just happened numbed her brain. Rohan slid his finger from her, and Isabel cried out again. Her body undulated toward him, and even though the feral ache in her had subsided, she wanted more from him.

He pulled back just enough to look into her eyes. His blazed. She licked her lips, and, still panting she asked, "What just happened?"

"'Tis the right of passage for all women."

Isabel contemplated his answer. "What of men? Do you—?"

Rohan pressed his erection against her belly. "Aye, 'tis the only way to take the stiffness from me."

Isabel reached out and pressed her fingertips to him. He sucked in his breath and trembled from her touch. "Isabel, you play with fire."

She pressed her palm against him. "Does it ache as I ached?"

"Aye."

"Would you like me to release you?"

Rohan groaned and pulled down his garters. Isabel looked innocently up at him. "Tell me what to do."

"Jesu, Isabel, you would tempt a saint. Push down my clothing."

She did, and when she moved the fabric over his erection and down his thighs, Isabel could not help but admire the smooth, thick length of him.

"Touch me, Isa."

Tentatively, she touched the wide head. In the firelight, she could see it glistened. The warmth of him surprised her. She gasped, pulling her hand away. Rohan grabbed it back and pressed it to him. He groaned and undulated against her hand as she had against his. "Wrap your fingers around me, Isa. God, yes, like that."

He surged in her hand. He wrapped his hand around hers, and in a slow up-and-down motion, he showed her the way. Isabel was a quick study. Rohan dropped his hand from hers, and she added her other hand. Wrapping it around him, she squeezed, and Rohan nearly spilled into her hand that moment.

Fervently, he thrust into her hands, and Isabel squeezed him tighter. She boldly maneuvered him around so that now his back was against the cold stone. He grinned down at her. A saucy wench she was. Rohan grabbed her breasts with his hands, and as she pumped him, he massaged her mounds. Rohan closed his eyes, pressed his head back against the stone wall, and let the wild, hot rush of their play take him to paradise.

He sucked in a harsh breath and gritted his teeth, erupting with a force he had never experienced. He grasped her tightly against his chest as his hips slowed. Isabel kept at her slow, rhythmic milking of him until he was depleted of every drop of his seed.

Finally, he relaxed back against the wall, not feeling the hard cold of the stone. Indeed, all he felt was hot and sated. For the moment. Isabel wiped her hand across his belly. Rohan laughed, coming down slowly from the storm Isabel had created, and slipped his arm around her waist, drawing her to him.

Once their breathing resumed a normal cadence, Isabel moved away from him and grabbed a linen towel from the cabinet. She dipped it into the pitcher by the hearth, and with care she cleaned him. And damn if he didn't rise beneath her ministrations. She looked him boldly in the eye. "Your hunger is voracious, Rohan. Is this normal to want again so quickly?"

"My desire for you, Isabel, is insatiable."

She leaned against him and touched his erection. In a slow trail, she traced the full head of it. "I will admit, I have a hunger for you as well."

He looked down at her, wanting her to grasp him tighter. And God, put her lips to him. The vision of her doing just that swelled him.

"Rohan, I cannot stay in this chamber with you indefinitely."

Rohan swooped her up into his arms and tossed her onto the bed. "Do not talk to me of tomorrow."

"It will come whether we wish it or not."

"Aye, 'twill come, and with it"—he plopped down onto the bed beside her, sweeping his hand down her belly and cupping her damp mound as she closed her eyes and pressed against him—"we shall come together."

"Rohan," Isabel breathed. "Take me there again."

"Isa, I—"

She pressed her hand to his and cried out. Her slick, swollen folds teased his fingers. "Do not deny me."

He pressed his lips to hers and slid a finger deep into her. She arched and moaned. Rohan's head reeled, overwhelmed by her passion for him. He had known the minute he saw her up on the rampart, the icy November air ripping at her hair, that she was a tigress. The vision of her soft and yielding beneath him flashed in his mind at that moment as it did now.

Rohan knew that if she gave him the slightest signal, he

would be buried to the hilt in her. Not trusting himself, he withdrew his finger. Isabel cried out, "No!"

"Isabel, I cannot watch your face as I touch you and not want to fulfill my desire in you." He kneeled and flipped her over, pulling her hips up with his left arm. The vision of her firm creamy derriere and what he wanted to do to it caused him a moment's pause. Rohan sucked in a deep breath, wondering if he had made a mistake turning her over. His rod swelled against her cheeks. He could so easily . . .

Groaning, he slid his middle finger deep into her hot, wet opening. Isabel sucked in a deep breath. "Oh, God, Rohan," she breathed. He closed his eyes, steeling himself. She moved back against him, and he hissed.

"Nay, Isabel." It would be so easy to replace his finger with his cock. She was so hot and slick for him, would she forgive him his loss of control in the throes of passion? He told her he could not promise . . .

"Rohan," she begged as she pushed her bottom against his hand.

"Jesu, Isa, I am not made of stone."

Rigidly, he kneeled behind her, afraid he would not be able to control himself if she moved against him again. She must have sensed his battle. Her body trembled. "Rohan," she softly said, "please, ease my ache."

Rohan thrust his hips against her bottom, his cock slid between the firm cheeks, and in a slow, rhythmic movement, he moved his finger in and out of her.

Isabel closed her eyes and reveled in the erotic charge of him. She'd no idea such sensations existed. His finger was large and thick, and Isabel knew if he were ever to press her with his cock, she might not be able to accommodate him. He hit a spot deep inside her each time he pushed into her. His cock had stiffened to capacity and slid back and forth against her bottom. Still slick with his previous ejaculation and her perspiration, he moved between her cheeks. Rohan bent over her and nipped at her back and whispered, "Isa, you make me forget my promise." He bit the back of her neck, and Isabel shot off like a shooting star. She screamed as a hard wave of release slammed into her, then shuddered through her body with the force of an army.

Her muscles clasped tightly around his finger.

"Isa!" he cried hoarsely. His hips slammed against her, and she felt the warm spill of him against her backside. Slowly, their breakneck ride came to a panting halt. Isabel dropped to the bed, breathing heavily and knowing she was forever lost to this man. She also knew that if she continued on this path with Rohan, she would lose not only her maidenhead to him but her heart.

Rohan wiped his seed from her back with the linen she had used, then slipped into the bed beside her.

Isabel turned over, her body still warm and slick with sweat. Rohan slid up against her and kissed her deeply. She wrapped her arms around his neck and brought him closer to her. For it would be their last kiss. As she realized that, she suddenly felt cold and empty.

She closed her eyes. Aye, it was already happening. She had feelings for this knight that she should not have.

Breaking away from his kiss, Isabel caught her breath, and in the firelight she looked up into his hooded eyes. He smiled the smile of a happily sated man. Her heart swelled. It made it all the more difficult to separate from him. She pushed back a heavy lock of his hair the better to see his face. Scars and all, he was the most handsome man she had ever laid eyes on. Even at court, the nobles garbed in rich silks and velvets did not compare. His wide, muscular shoulders hovered above her, and she knew he would slay one hundred dragons should she but ask him to.

She should be angry with herself. For now she was truly a wanton. But at least she was still intact. And, she reasoned, many noble Saxon women were praying this very night that they carried no bastard Normans. Ravishment 'twas but a casualty of war, the maidenheads taken as a trophy. She was spared. For now. Because this knight had given her his oath. An oath that she would break if she continued to sleep in this bed. Isabel smiled.

"Ah, such a rare and beautiful sight," Rohan said softly.

"In these times, there is not much to smile about."

Rohan rolled over and pulled her with him. "But this eve we forget the war. Forget our sorrows. Here with you, I care not what is happening outside that door."

Isabel rose on an elbow and traced a finger down the scar on his chest. "How came you by this?" she softly questioned.

Rohan pressed her hand to the scar. "A brand."

Isabel gasped. "A brand? How barbaric! The person who did this to you also did it to Manhku?"

Rohan nodded and closed his eyes. "Aye, and Thorin and Wulf and Rhys—"

"All of your knights?"

"Aye."

Isabel pressed her lips to his chest just below the point where the cross bar was burned into his skin. Rohan stiffened and grabbed her hand. "What are you doing?"

"Kissing the hurt away."

Rohan squeezed her hand, then brought it to his own lips. "The physical pain is long gone, Isabel."

"Mayhap, but what of the memories?"

"They are few and far between."

Isabel searched his face. "Was the man who did this to you and your men named Tariq?"

Rohan sat up in the bed, his eyes flashing wildly. "How do you know that name?"

Fear shot through her, but it subsided just as quickly. "That night you awoke from the night terrors. You called out the name."

Rohan jammed his fingers through his hair. And the wild look left his eyes. He lay back on the pillows, drawing her with him.

"Aye, Tariq was the sultan's son, sent to hone his torturing skills on Christian knights."

"Rohan, I'm sorry. I should not have asked."

" 'Tis truly but a vague memory." He yawned and pulled her tightly to him. "I am fatigued, wench. You have worn me out with your demands; now, cease your talk so that we both might find some sleep."

Isabel nodded and snuggled close to him, amazed at her comfort with him. She cleaved to him as if he were a lover known for years instead of just recently.

"In the morn, we must talk about this thing between us," Isabel said as she yawned. "It cannot continue."

Rohan's soft snore told her he had not heard a word. She pulled a thick fur blanket up around their shoulders. Isabel closed her eyes and dreamed of Rohan taking her in the final way a man takes a woman.

* * *

The pounding on the door startled them both awake. Rohan shot out of the bed and grabbed his sword. Isabel moved back against the huge headboard, the fur blanket pulled up to her chin.

"Lazy lout!" Thorin bellowed from the other side. "Your men grow restless while you dawdle in bed."

Rohan heaved the bolt and pulled open the door. Isabel gasped as he stood naked, wielding his sword before his man. Thorin grinned and looked past Rohan to where she huddled in the bed. He scowled, then looked to the younger man.

Rohan turned away and faced Isabel. Her eyes grew huge. Rohan's manhood hung heavy and stiff against his belly. "As if it is any concern of yours, Thorin, the maid is still virtuous."

Thorin looked to Isabel for affirmation. Hurriedly, she nodded. "There are no bloodied sheets for display."

"You are a stronger man than I, Rohan. We await your pleasure below." Thorin backed out of the room, closing the door behind him.

Rohan turned and grinned at Isabel. "Wouldn't you ease my ache this morn?"

She shook her head and kept her eyes from his glorious erection. Her dreams of him thrusting that weapon in and out of her sheath until she screamed for mercy had her tossing and turning most of the night. Each time she awoke, Rohan slept. She had used the quiet to study him more closely in the firelight. He was a most magnificent specimen of a man. And a bolder one she had never met. Several times she had pressed her hand to him to feel him surge in his slumber.

Finally exhausted, she found sleep.

Isabel climbed from the bed, dragging the fur blanket and wrapping it around her nakedness. Rohan scowled. "Isabel, we have gone beyond—"

She put her hand up. "Rohan, my oath to you is paid. We must stop now before it becomes impossible to do so."

Confusion clouded his features. "Your oath paid?"

"Aye, for Russell's life, I gave you free rein with my body except for my maidenhead."

Rohan poured water from the pitcher beside the hearth into a deep bowl and began to wash. "The terms were free rein to explore what lies beneath your gown. And while I agree that last night I did so"—he pressed the linen to his face, then looked at her—"I have yet to explore *all* that lies beneath."

"What else is there?" she demanded, suddenly feeling as if she had been duped.

"You will see this eve."

Frustration flared. "Rohan, I will not be your leman!"

"You already are."

She grabbed the cup from the table by the bed and hurled it at him. "You bastard! How dare you? I met my part of the bargain, now let me go!"

Rohan strode over to her and grabbed her by the hands. The fur fell to the floor. His erection jutted up angrily between them. "The bargain is not yet met. I will tell you when it is."

"I will not stand for this!"

He let her go and returned to his bath. "It matters not. I will see you in this chamber tonight. Whether I have to hunt you down or not."

"I will leave Rossmoor!"

He turned quickly and pinned her with a narrow-eyed glare. "You will not."

"My betrothed is near, Rohan. He will take me thus. Leave me some dignity!"

He grabbed her again, and this time he shook her. "Betray me to another man, Isabel, and I will personally take the lash to your back."

Eighteen

Isabel scowled as she descended the wide stairway.
Seated next to Rohan at the lord's table and hovering
over him like a camp whore was the lovely Deidre. Rohan's eyes rose to meet and clash with Isabel's. Her back
stiffened when a small smile wound its way around those
lips that had so recently scalded her skin. As it always
did when Rohan scathed her with his attention, Isabel
warmed. She dragged her eyes from the scandalous knight
to the woman beside him.

Deidre looked up and smiled. The gesture reminded
Isabel of one of the stable cats that had just snagged a fat
mouse from the hay.

A hard jolt of jealousy speared Isabel, piercing straight
into her heart. It felt as if she had been hit in the chest, the
reaction was so strong. She nearly missed the second-to-
the-last step. And as much as Isabel told herself it was for
the best, her heart continued to interfere. As she wrestled
with these harsh feelings, Isabel knew that if she stayed at
Rossmoor, she would end up heartbroken.

Taking a deep breath, she smiled. Let Rohan find succor in another woman's arms. It was how it should be. There was no future for them together. Yet the vision of Rohan's dark head buried deep in Deidre's ample bosom made her sick to her stomach.

Isabel looked past Rohan to Manhku, who sat quietly in his chair with his leg hiked up on another one. He nodded silently to her. Her eyes traveled around to the rest of the lord's table. As one, *les morts,* rose as she approached. Isabel was relieved to see Rohan had the decency to stand in her presence as well. And despite her resolve to steer clear of him, she had some small feeling of victory when he took her hand and seated her to his right. Though she had no appetite, Isabel sat.

With her presence, the morning meal commenced. Grateful that Rohan separated them and feeling the need to lighten the mood, Isabel asked the Viking who sat across from her, "Where do you hail from, Sir Thorin?"

He smiled, the crinkle at his one eye deep. "In truth, milady, I have no place to name."

"What of your people?"

Thorin shrugged and stabbed a coddled egg with his table knife. " 'Tis hard to say."

Isabel nodded, realizing the man had no interest in speaking of his family.

But despite his short answers, the Viking laughed. "My lady, would your curiosity be satisfied if I told you I am the product of a coupling between the late Hardrada and a Byzantinian gypsy?"

Isabel was surprised at such a revelation. She cocked her head and looked at the man in a different light. On second thought, mayhap she should not have been so surprised. Thorin's regal bearing and aristocratic features melded in a ruggedly handsome harmony with his gypsy mother's exotic lineage. Despite his injury and the black leather eye patch, Thorin was a striking man. Taller than Rohan, which was no small feat, and as muscled, he was no doubt as experienced on the battlefield. When Thorin rubbed his chest as she had seen Rohan and Wulfson do, her heart thawed more for these fierce warriors. Their suffering was unimaginable, the scars only a glimpse at what they must have endured.

Isabel smiled and nodded, understanding that had the coupling been sanctioned by the church, Thorin would be sitting not among them but upon a throne somewhere in a distant land.

"How fortunate for us a royal prince sits amongst us," Deidre said, the scorn lacing her words almost indiscernible. Isabel's rancor with the women was on the rise.

Thorin smiled grimly at the displaced Saxon. "A royal bastard, Deidre. A distinct difference."

Isabel choked on the piece of braised meat she'd just chewed at Thorin's blatant insult. Had he held any respect for the lady Deidre, he would have addressed her as such. That he did not gave Isabel a supreme sense of satisfaction. And to further confirm why Deidre did not deserve his respect, the woman blundered on. "What of your mother?"

"She is dead," Thorin said softly. Isabel gasped. And while he did not say it in such a way that asked for pity, she felt her heart swell for this man.

"How?" Deidre persisted.

Gwyneth, who had just a moment ago batted her lashes at the Viking as she set a large platter of meats before him, gasped at the audacity of Deidre's question.

"Methinks, Lady Deidre," Isabel began, "it would be more courteous if you minded your own affairs."

The entire table fell silent as if waiting for a cat fight to ensue. Before Deidre could stick her foot further down her throat, Isabel looked across to Thorin, who seemed unaffected by the line of questioning. "My apologies, Sir Thorin. Such subjects are better left unsaid."

The proud Viking smiled. "My thanks for your concern, Lady Isabel, but I assure you, the topic, even so baited, does not cause me pain."

Isabel nodded her head but knew he lied. The look of fury that had crossed his face when he spoke of his mother's death did not escape her. And while Isabel was intrigued by this mysterious Viking's story, she had the good manners to let it rest.

Feeling the need to set Deidre further back on her heels and quell the woman's barbed insults once and for all, Isabel asked, "Does your mother still ail, Deidre, or does she find the company here not to her liking?"

It was Rohan, Wulfson, and Rhys's turn to choke on the food they were chewing. When Rohan could not catch his breath, Isabel pounded him on the back until he raised his hand for her to stop. She poured him a full cup of milk from the pitcher and handed it to him. Gratefully, he drained it. Isabel looked over at Deidre, who looked as if she had just drunk a goblet of vinegar.

The entire table stared at Deidre, as if daring her to speak against the lady of the manor. When she bent to her single trencher, Isabel sat back in her chair, satisfied that for now the wasp would keep her stinger retracted.

The conversation turned lighter and concluded in that tone. As Isabel moved to see to Manhku, she felt Rohan's heated gaze on her back.

"How fares the leg today, sir knight?" she asked.

At Deidre's sharp gasp behind her, Isabel bristled. Was the woman bent on alienating herself from everyone?

Manhku nodded, a small smile twisting his lips. Isabel pulled up a chair and sat beside him. "Let us have a look."

Several minutes later, the wound lay exposed. Isabel smiled and looked up to Manhku, who looked expectantly at her. She smiled wide. "You are healing very well. If you promise not to exert yourself, you may join your men at the table for the next meal."

This time, Manhku smiled wide, revealing his sharp teeth.

"Blessed Mother!" Deidre gasped from the table. "To what lengths will you go, Isabel, to save yourself from the slightest of hardships?"

Isabel stiffened, Deidre's words biting hard into her pride. That she shared a bed with Rohan was bad enough, but to insinuate that she did it to escape hardship was a crueler blow.

Isabel scowled and turned to the woman, who was there only by Isabel's goodwill. Rohan stepped between Isabel and the wanton. He laid a hand on her shoulder and softly squeezed it. The warmth sent a shiver through her body. Isabel set her jaw, not knowing whom to concentrate her anger on, the waspish Deidre or the knight beside her.

"Your healing skills are admirable, Lady Isabel. My thanks for saving my man. Will he ride again?"

She did not look up at Rohan, or over at Deidre, or to anyone else but Manhku, who fairly stewed in his chair. She sighed. She did not regret saving this man's life. "Mayhap. But as I explained to your man, he may be up and about in a day or two with the aid of a sturdy stick." Isabel scowled at the Saracen. "But be warned. If you overexert yourself, you may cause further damage. Damage I do not have the skill to heal."

"Why do you have this heathen amongst Christians?" Deidre boldly asked, coming to stand beside Rohan.

Rohan tore his gaze from Isabel and frowned down at the woman. "I do not answer to anyone here. Do not ask questions on subjects that are of no matter to you." He brushed past her and said to his men, "Let us survey more of this promised land."

As the men stood, the dreaded shout from the lookout pierced the morning tension, hiking it higher. "Smoke, four leagues south of the crossroads!"

In less time than it took Isabel to blink, the knights stormed out of the hall. Isabel let out a long breath she had held. She faced Deidre. The woman was an awesome sight in all of her fury. Her black hair and green eyes sparked with fire. Isabel stiffened.

"You may find yourself his favorite for now, but when it comes time for him to take a wife, he will not choose a soiled dove such as yourself but a woman of pure virtue."

The words struck deep into Isabel's heart. For while she had no dreams of marriage to the bastard knight, she knew he would want a wife pure. And if what had happened between them last night was any precursor to what he intended to do to her later that eve, she was doomed to find herself no longer a maiden.

"Deidre, that you have not been prey to a Norman thus far is a miracle in itself. For your sake, I pray your good luck continues."

"I do not throw myself at the first Norman who strides through my door, as you seem to have done."

Isabel smiled and bowed her head. "That I have a door is another miracle."

The barb hit home, and Deidre sneered. "I would never trade my virtue for a manor."

Isabel continued to smile. Aye, nor would she, but she would for the life of a squire who sought only to protect her from the very thing she offered for his life. And as she remembered her sacrifice, Isabel no longer felt ashamed. She looked closer at the woman. Aye, even for the surly Deidre, Isabel would make the same sacrifice.

Without further adieu, Isabel moved past the woman and into the kitchens to see about opening the stores to the villagers. When she returned to the hall, she felt Manhku's eyes on her. She poured him a cup of ale and took it to him. Silently, he took it and drank deeply from the cup. "Keep watch over the hall, Manhku. I have much to do in the village."

She opened the great doors to the manor and stepped outside, stopping short to find Wulfson's dark scowl on her.

She scowled in return. "Why are you here?"

"I am relegated to tiring woman today."

Isabel laughed while Wulfson's scowl deepened. She placed a hand on his mail-clad forearm and tried in vain to suppress her merriment. "The honor is all mine, Sir Wulfson. A fiercer maid I cannot think of." She laughed louder and stepped past him. "Come, let us go pick posies and chat and giggle of things maids find so consuming."

Wulfson glowered down at her, a low rumble in his chest. Isabel smiled as she looked up at the sun. It had begun its rise in the cool, crisp morning air. Not a cloud hung in the clear blue of the sky. The village teemed with activity, and as Isabel looked around, it occurred to her that more villagers had returned from the glade. Some even were new to her. Her heart swelled. Word had begun to spread.

And so the morning progressed until after a rather lengthy conversation with Mildred on the different locations of different healing herbs, Isabel stopped in mid-sentence to find Wulfson's dark green eyes, the color of fresh moss, narrowed at her. Isabel regarded him as scrutinously. "Does something ail you, Sir Wulfson?"

He shook his head and grumbled. Isabel smiled at the reticent knight but ended her conversation with Mildred, who gladly scampered off.

Whilst Wulfson was certainly not bashful when it came to the maids in the village, he was quieter than most. His dark bay-colored hair hung in the same fashion as that of all of the Blood Swords, long like that of the Vikings. She noticed that Wulfson's hand continually fondled the hilt of his broadsword. Unlike the other knights, who did the same, Wulfson had double scabbards attached to a vest of sorts on his back. The blades were nearly as long as a regular broadsword but thicker. When he had drawn them in honor of Henri's visits, her blood had curdled. He wielded them expertly, and she could only imagine the carnage they created.

She further regarded him. Aye, these knights of Rohan's

were a suspicious lot. Like great wounded beasts who held no trust for mankind. Her limbs trembled in the chill of the late morning air. Her imagination was rampant with thoughts of what these men had endured.

Isabel scrutinized Wulfson more closely and decided he reminded her of a troubled angel. The golden flecks in his green eyes pulsed. While he sported the same crescent-shaped scar as the others, his face was free of other scars. Her heart did a slow tumble. He was a man a maid could get into trouble with. His dark and brooding face posed a challenge to any woman.

"Sir Wulfson, your name is Saxon. Why do you ride for a Norman?"

He scowled. "I am of Norman extract." Isabel raised a brow. He bowed and clicked his heels together. "Wulfson of Trevelyn, at your service."

For the second time that day, Isabel hid her surprise. "Trevelyn? Is that not—?"

"I was raised in Wales by foster parents. I took their name."

Isabel pressed her hand to his forearm. He stiffened beneath her touch. "I do not bite, sir."

Wulfson growled low, obviously not comfortable with the conversation. Isabel enjoyed knocking these men off balance. So controlled were they in every facet of their lives except this one. "Did you leave a lady love behind in Normandy?"

When he only scowled in answer, Isabel continued to question him. "Did your sire recognize you?"

His scowled deepened. "Cease your prattle."

Isabel returned his scowl with an exaggerated one of her own. " 'Twill be hard, 'tis what women do."

" 'Tis why I avoid them."

Isabel laughed. "Do not tell that to Lyn and Sarah."

Wulfson looked past her shoulder as if something interested him more than their conversation. Isabel looked closer at the troubled knight. She had been correct with her first impression of him. Troubled angel was an apt description. Like Stefan, he was dark and brooding. "Did you escape the prison with Rohan and Manhku?"

Wulfson hissed in a sharp breath, and his hand tightened around the hilt of his sword. His green eyes flashed. Isabel instantly regretted prying, but she had a burning hunger for information regarding Rohan. And knowing that these men had been to hell and back together, she hoped through them she could better understand the man who had changed her entire world.

Isabel set her hand over Wulfson's. "Sometimes my curiosity causes me to speak out of turn. My apologies."

The knight finally looked down at her. Pain and fury clouded his eyes. When he spoke his voice was low and throaty. "Your question reminds me of things better forgotten."

Giving him a trembling smile, Isabel nodded. "Come, let us see to the rest of the villagers." He nodded, and they set off.

Isabel was happy to see so many familiar faces. While at first many of the churls hesitated to pay their respects to her because of the hulking knight by her side, when they realized she held no fear of him, they were more bent on approaching her. Their tales of fleeing the raiders and also de Monfort set Isabel's nerves on edge. The tales of de Monfort's actions were gaining epic size. Isabel feared if the man was not stopped, he would single-handedly destroy Norfolk. She felt Wulfson's reaction more than he voiced it.

As Wulfson escorted Isabel back to the hall for the noon meal, she was surprised to see Aryls's unwelcome cousin strolling toward the stable. "Does that not strike you as unusual?" Isabel asked Wulfson.

He followed her gaze and frowned. At that moment, Deidre looked up to find them regarding her. Her step faltered, but she quickly recovered and made her way toward them.

"You there! Sir knight, I request a mount. This filthy hamlet has me bored. Be a good man, and escort me so that I may get some much-needed exercise."

Isabel's rancor rose. The woman acted as if she were the Queen of England, not a refugee.

"Nay, Rohan's instructions were clear. No one is to leave the village for any reason."

Deidre changed her tactic. Her body loosened, and her smile turned inviting. In a slow, sensuous stroll, she sidled up close to the Norman knight. Placing her hands on his forearm, she looked up at him with deep blue eyes and softly cajoled, "Please, sir? I will assume all responsibility for my person. Your master will understand."

Wulfson removed her hand from his person and shook his head. "Nay. I have my orders." He extended his arm to Isabel, who took it and they walked off, leaving Deidre quietly cursing them both. Once in the hall, Isabel saw to the meal. As several of the soldiers, including Wulfson, sat down to eat, Isabel quietly slipped from the kitchen and into the courtyard, then hurried toward the stable, to see a flash of yellow fabric disappear into the thick edge of the forest. Deidre.

Isabel glanced over her shoulder and found no suspicious eyes on her. She had a fleeting twinge of guilt. Wulfson would be furious with her. But she had no intention of being gone too long. Taking a deep breath, knowing the Saxon woman was up to no good for anyone at Rossmoor, Isabel, too, disappeared into the forest.

Nineteen

ollowing the scent of smoke and with Russell's directions, Rohan and his knights made quick time to the
small clearing by the river. What met their eyes would have
disturbed most men, but after the previous pyre of bodies
and what he had seen in his short time on earth, nothing
affected Rohan so deeply he could not function.

But that did not mean he had no compassion. Nay, his
blood chilled at the sight before him. His anger festered
deep and hot in his belly. He scanned the blood-soaked
earth from astride his great horse. Several women, their
skirts flung up around their heads, their most private parts
exposed, no doubt horribly abused, lay scattered across
the hard ground, most in unnatural positions. Several
men, their body parts hacked to pieces, dotted the scenery. And stuck into the ground, though battle-battered,
the black and white raven standard of the Norse king
arrogantly taunted him. Rohan's blood boiled. He looked
to his friend, knowing the standard would conjure up bitter memories.

" 'Tis a ruse," Thorin said softly, his voice barely perceptible. "My sire is dead."

"Aye, mayhap you have kin who seek revenge."

"My kin shame me with this carnage. Wouldst the chance present itself, I would show them real torture."

Rohan looked at his one-eyed knight, knowing full well of what he spoke. "The Norse have gone too far."

Warner approached, his steed prancing, chomping at the bit, sensing the blood in the air. "It appears to me, Rohan, these demons seem bent on taunting. Do you think their game is to draw us out?"

Rohan nodded. "I am sure of it." He raised his hand to the silence. "Listen," he said.

Warner looked to Rohan, then to the thick forest around them. "There is no sound."

"Exactly. Even from deep within the forest and along the river bank, there is no sound. The creatures that inhabit it are silent. Our enemy is near." Rohan urged his mount forward to the edge of the river. The trail was clear, as if an open invitation to follow. Rohan turned to Russell, just as the boy recovered from retching his guts up at the sight of the ravaged bodies. "Is this the shallowest spot to cross?"

"Nay, down further. By the small bend."

"What awaits us on the other side?" Rohan asked.

The boy blanched to white. "The haunted caves of Menloc."

Rohan threw his head back and laughed. "There will be more hauntings when we are done with them." He turned to his knights. "After we cross and pick up the trail, fan out two abreast at ten horse lengths apart."

The great destriers picked their way through the brush

and bramble, their ears laid back, their muscles bunched, ready to crush the enemy. Deeper Rohan and his men moved into the forest, following the well-marked trail, their eyes and ears on high alert. "Beware, men," Rohan softly warned. "The trail of crumbs is clearly marked for us."

Moments later, Rohan put his hand up and knew his quarry was near. He suspected they had moved right into their trap, as he intended. In a quick motion, Rohan circled his hand, and his men formed themselves into an impenetrable half-circle. His short lance drawn, Rohan's great battle cry rang out, the sound sending the birds, squirrels, and foxes diving for cover.

As the death cry trailed off, the knights charged, and the ghosts in the forest rose, answering with their own battle cry. What moments before had been a quiet forest now swarmed with battle ax–wielding Norsemen, accompanied by several of Harold's men still bent on winning the day.

As Isabel broke through a small clearing and stopped, she scanned the forest. Though barren, there was still much brush and bramble to muddy the view. Nowhere did she see the yellow muslin cloth of Deidre's dress. Shivering in the cold, Isabel looked over her shoulder, debating whether to return to the manor or continue her search for the Saxon woman. An inner voice told her the woman was bent on betrayal.

Isabel forged forward until she came to a well-worn path. As she turned a bend, she stiffened. A man approached. By his long hair and beard, she knew he was Saxon. From his rich clothing, she knew him not to be a churl.

When he spied her, his face lit up, and his pace quickened. Caution prevailed. Isabel stood, hand on the hilt of her dagger, ready to defend herself.

"Lady Isabel!" he cried, coming closer. Isabel scrunched her face in confusion. She did not recognize the Saxon. He continued toward her, his face beaming. " 'Tis me, Cedric, Lord Dunsworth's reeve."

Memory dawned and with it more confusion. Why was he not with Arlys?

He crossed himself several times and made a deep bow. "Praise God you are here. I have come for you."

More confusion reigned in her head. "Why?"

"Milord bade me bring you to him. He wishes to see you married posthaste."

At Cedric's words, Isabel's heart stumbled in her chest. "How fares your lord?"

"He is well. He makes plans. Support rallies for the young Edgar. We pray for your support. Come with me now. He grows anxious for you."

As much as she wished to be free of the Normans, Isabel hesitated. "I cannot leave my people, Cedric."

"But your betrothed wishes you to come to him."

She shook her head. "I am afraid that is not possible right now, Cedric. I—"

"My lord has news of your brother, Geoff."

Her head snapped back, and her heart raced in her chest. There were no sweeter words to her ears. "He lives?"

Cedric grinned and nodded. "Aye, but he is wounded, and at least a day's hard ride from here. Come with me, Lady Isabel. Come with me to your lord, and he will take you to him."

Isabel nodded but still hesitated. Indecision waged a war inside her. Desperately, she wanted to see her brother and tend to him. To bring him home. But what of Rossmoor? And what of Arlys? She shivered, the cold having nothing to do with her chill. Nay, it had to do with thoughts of the dark and brooding Norman. Would her people suffer under his wrath?

"Come now, there may be little time left for him," Cedric urged.

Isabel took a tentative step forward, then another and another. She had only one brother. She would see to him.

As they moved down the path, a bone-chilling cry from deep within the forest stopped them both. Cedric turned pale and wild-eyed toward her. It sounded as if death arose and was on the prowl for souls. Isabel wrapped her arms tightly around herself, having no mantle. "What was that?" she breathlessly asked.

He grabbed her hand and pulled her toward the blood-curdling sound. "The devil's battle cry, milady."

She allowed him to drag her down the path, then deep into the wood, away from Rossmoor, away from the people who needed her most. Closer to the raiders even Rohan could not altogether quell. Her step slowed, but Cedric pulled her harder. If what Cedric said was true and her brother lay wounded, she would go to him, but not like this. As much as she yearned to see him and bring him home, the odds of her arriving safely at their destination were slim. But more than that, her people needed her. And if she were honest with herself, she did not want to see Arlys. Not yet.

She yanked her hand free from the reeve's grasp. He turned abruptly and grabbed it back. "Nay," she said, shaking her head. "I cannot go with you now. My people need me. More hide in the forest. 'Tis my duty to coax them out."

Cedric's tawny brows knocked together. "But milady, do you not wish to see Sir Geoff before he meets his maker?"

Isabel swallowed hard, and her hands trembled. "Aye, I do, more than anything, but if he lives now, he will live long enough for me to come to him. I must return to Rossmoor. Cedric, give my regrets to Lord Dunsworth. Tell him I wish him well and look forward to seeing him soon."

She turned and stepped away from him, but Cedric stopped her with his hand wrapped around her arm. Isabel whirled and stopped short. Cedric's eyes morphed from warm and friendly to dark and dangerous. Slowly, he shook his head. "My instructions were clear. Do not return without the lady Isabel. I will not disappoint milord."

Isabel pulled her hand, and he pulled back. "Arlys will understand my loyalty to Rossmoor. Surely, you can make him understand."

"Nay. There is more to it than that. He requires your treasury. Milord builds an army. Many come from the north to fight for our cause. When he triumphs, his lands will be restored, as well as all of Saxony."

"'Tis madness right now! William storms London. His knights prowl the English countryside armed to the hilt. 'Tis rumored he has thousands more mercenaries on their way. The time is not ripe!"

"Aye, it is! The Witan is strong. The nobles rally. The time is now! Wouldst you stand in the way of Edgar, the rightful king?"

Isabel shook her head. "Nay. I support Edgar and will do my part to see him rightfully take the throne, but I am not so naïve as to believe William can be quelled now. His rampage is without mercy. He will see the entire island wiped clean of Englishmen."

Cedric shook his head. Isabel persisted. She grabbed his hands and pleaded with him. "These last nights *les morts,* his elite death squad, have resided in Rossmoor. I have heard their talk. Not only does William have support in Westminster, but his army is still strong. He has coffers to back his claim. He will prevail if challenged now."

"There is more at stake."

Isabel eyed him. "What more?"

"You are worth a hefty ransom."

Isabel laughed, the sound bitter. "Who would pay good silver for me? I have been reduced to a slave."

"De Monfort has shown interest."

Isabel gasped as realization dawned. "'Tis a ruse! Arlys does not send for me! Cedric, how could you play me false?"

As she backed away from him, he moved toward her. "For the cause, milady. De Monfort has money, and he is willing to part with a goodly sum of it to have you."

Isabel shook her head. "Nay! I will not go to him. You would have to kill me first!"

In a violent reaction to her challenge, Cedric struck her in the face, the force of the blow landing her on the forest floor. The shock of his action and the searing pain in her jaw stunned her. The copper taste of blood filled her mouth.

Cedric yanked her up by the arm and pushed her forward. "Be warned, milady, we are desperate men in desperate times. If the devil Norman wants you and is willing to pay, then he shall have you!"

"You lied about Geoff!"

Cedric nodded. "Aye, and I am sorry to give you hope, but I knew of no other way to have you come with me." He drew a short sword from his belt and poked it at her belly. "Go, and do not try to flee from me. You will regret it."

Isabel turned in the direction they had been walking. She held fast to the knowledge that while Cedric may have leverage with his strength, she knew the lay of the land. Indeed. She caught a small sob. She and Geoff had slain many an imaginary dragon in these woods, and not far off were the caves. She shuddered but decided she would fare better with the witch than with Henri de Monfort.

Several paces ahead of Cedric, she stumbled and dropped to her hands and knees. As the reeve moved to right her, Isabel rolled hard into his knees. As he tumbled backward, she hurried to her feet and ran for her life.

Cedric shouted for her to stop, promising her glory should she side with him and Arlys, promising that once the ransom was paid, they would rescue her. And it occurred to Isabel at that moment that Arlys was as involved in the ploy to see her ransomed as was his reeve. Though she did not wish to wed the earl, his betrayal of her caused her great pain. She was but a pawn to every man. Anger spurred her forward. She would be no man's passage to greater glory. She would rather live a life of solitude. Isabel plunged headfirst into the wood. As she crested a knoll, she lost her footing and plummeted in a steep fall. She rolled endlessly, twigs and leaves biting into her skin, the hard earth forcing the breath from her chest.

When her body finally came to rest against a large boulder, she lay with her face planted in the cold, loamy earth. The sound of heavy footsteps from above pushed her forward. Ignoring the pain in her limbs, Isabel scurried to her feet, looked up, and screamed.

Twenty

More than a score of armed men charged the Norman knights. Rohan ran the first one within range of him through with his lance. He pulled the weapon free from the listing warrior and with his right hand drew his sword and brought it down for the final blow, separating the man's head from his body.

Rohan roared as a raider chopped at his calf, the blade biting into the thick leather surrounding his boots and mail. Enraged, Rohan kicked the attacker from him. He hurled his short lance at the Viking. It hit true through his neck. The man gurgled, blood bubbled from his mouth, and he fell dead to the forest floor.

Rohan pressed the stallion deeper into the fray. Two ax-wielding Saxons rushed him. Mordred chopped through them, his spiked armor tearing into the men's thighs. Rohan hacked one down, and the other, now behind him and having managed to regain his stance, found Rohan's blade backhanded deep into his gut.

Wheeling the stallion around, Rohan charged into three

Vikings bent on hacking Russell into bits. As Rohan swung his mighty sword around his head, chopping at the assailants, their heads tumbling to the ground, Russell blanched white.

Rohan scowled and reined in his horse. "Man up, boy. William will want able Saxon knights."

Russell's eyes widened, and immediately Rohan whirled around in his saddle just as the blade of a battle ax swiped in front of his face. He felt the breeze of it too close. He jabbed his sword into the chest of the man wielding it. He turned back to Russell to find him engaged with a man who had come up on the other side of Rohan. While this was no immediate threat to himself, Rohan's knights having sufficiently quelled the attack, Rohan called to Warner as he saw several men flee into the wood. "See that those cowards do not see the break of the next day!"

Rohan turned back and watched as the young squire thrust and parried his short lance against the last of the Norsemen who had chosen to stand and fight. Russell was outmanned, outweaponed, and outseasoned, but Rohan held his position. There was no better experience for a young warrior than actual battle.

And as the knights gathered around the dueling pair, the Norseman knew he was doomed, and not by the red-haired boy he fought but by the black knights circling him.

In a last-ditch effort, the Viking let out a blood-curdling battle cry, and knowing he would soon meet Wodin, he brought his battle ax down for the fatal blow just as Russell gave one last thrust of his lance. It fell short of its mark. The boy's blue eyes widened in terror.

Rohan swung his blade, severing the Viking's hand from the ax. The Norseman screamed in pain, then stood in stunned silence as he looked at the bloody stump that was once his hand.

Rohan dismounted and strode toward him, his blade raised. Casually, he pressed the tip to the man's chest. "Who leads you?" he demanded.

The Viking shook his head, his eyes wide.

"Tell me, or you will lose a limb each time you deny me." Rohan moved closer, his blade digging into the fur pelt that covered the man's chest. When he refused to answer, Rohan hacked off his right arm.

The man screamed and sank to his knees. Blood spurted in a high arch from the stump. Rohan raised his blade again, this time intending to hack off the left arm. "Hardrada!" the Norseman screamed.

Rohan pressed the sword into the man's belly. "Hardrada is dead."

The Viking looked up through narrow eyes, violence burning hot in them. "And so shall you be when the devil is through with you!"

Rohan roared and hacked off the left arm. The Viking fell back onto the earth. Blood spurted from both stumps. He closed his eyes and breathed, "The devil wants his due."

With both hands, Rohan took up his sword and plunged it deep into the warrior's chest, skewering him into the ground like a spitted boar.

Russell choked when Rohan withdrew the blade and raised it high in the air. The blood of half a score of men mingled on it.

Rohan turned shrewd eyes on the squire. "Your lady has sacrificed much for your life, boy. I would see you home alive this day."

Russell nodded and swallowed hard. He bobbed his head and murmured, "My thanks for my life, milord."

Rohan bent and wiped the blood from his sword on the Viking's leg. He turned back to Russell. "You would do well to train more often with my men. Next time, I may not be so available."

Russell hastily nodded, his color returning. The crashing of horses' hooves broke into the carnage-laden clearing. Warner raised his blood-soaked sword and saluted Rohan. "We gave the cowards the ride to hell they deserved."

Rohan nodded and sheathed his sword. He mounted and rested his gauntlet-encased hands on the high pommel and leaned forward to survey the carnage. "Methinks, my good fellows, we have two different groups of raiders amongst us. Armed knights and these foot soldiers."

Thorin moved closer to Rohan. "Aye, these men are led by more than revenge."

"Rohan," Ioan said from behind him, "the devil is indeed at work here."

A hard shiver wracked Rohan's body. The hairs on the back of his neck stood on end. "Aye, and who else bears the name with such aplomb?"

"Henri?" Warner said.

Rohan nodded. "Aye, my brother's heart is filled with hatred. He seeks to destroy everything that I covet."

Warner shook his head. "But Rohan, he does not have the coin to pay these men."

"He can promise it," Thorin interjected. "He can also give promise of land. Is it not why we are all here?"

Warner nodded. "He is foolish to think he can best you, Rohan."

Rohan urged his mount to where one of the Saxons lay

slain. He dismounted and raised the man's leather hauberk to reveal his tunic. A red fox on a green field stared back. "'Tis the colors of the earl, the lady Isabel's betrothed." Rohan ripped the patch from the garment and stuffed it into his hauberk, then mounted. Anger seethed. Did the maid have a hand in this? Was she in contact with the earl?

Rohan whirled his mount around and said to no one in particular, "Let us ride and seek out my brother."

As Isabel pushed back, Cedric's body slammed hard into her, sending her sprawling forward, where she fell once again into the hard earth. The soft, loamy smell of the forest floor mingled with the stench of rotten flesh. She screamed again, the sound buried in the dirt. Cedric yanked her up by the hair. He raised his hand to strike her again, but his arm froze high in the air. His eyes widened, and he froze.

Isabel followed his gaze, knowing he saw the sickening sight that had caused her to scream. In a large semicircle before them, several pikes with decapitated heads in varying degrees of decay stared gruesomely down at them. The warning to trespassers was clear.

"'Tis the work of the witch," Cedric breathed. Grabbing her tighter against him, he slowly backed away from the awful sight. Her wits regained after the shock, Isabel yanked her hair from his grasp. Surprisingly, Cedric did not fight her action.

Isabel used his fear to strengthen her position. "Aye, 'tis Menloc. Shall I call to the witch?"

Cedric paled and vigorously shook his head. "Nay!"

Isabel smiled, fighting her own fear. Cedric was now

concerned for his own welfare. Slowly, Isabel edged away from him toward the pikes. "She prowls this forest in search of rapists and looters, 'tis said, for revenge against her own raped daughters and slain husband."

"Shut thy mouth," he hissed, not wanting to draw the witch.

Isabel raised her voice. "Would that I could tell her you were willing to sell me to the devil himself for the right to land!"

Cedric implored her with his eyes to keep silent. She would not. Isabel pointed to a fresh head. One of a Viking. "One of your hired men, Cedric?"

He shook his head but not with the conviction of an innocent man. His plot began to take fuller shape, and her fury built.

"Did you and Arlys promise the Norsemen land and wealth for their part in terrorizing your own people?"

He remained silent, but the hatred in his eyes spoke the truth.

"Why, Cedric, why kill your own people?"

"'Twould rally those who chose not to fight against the Normans."

Isabel shook her head. "You are wrong. 'Tis the Normans they look to now for protection!" Her hands fisted at her sides. "You are a fool!"

He stepped closer, the witch forgotten. "Nay, your father's treasury is well known. With it and the ransom from the devil Norman, we will be able to buy the best mercenaries. With them, we will win the day!"

He grabbed her arm and yanked her back toward the hill. "I do what I must for the good of England. If it means a few of us should fall to save the throne, then so be it."

"You are mad to think so, Cedric. England is lost."
As Isabel said the words, she knew them to be true. The
Normans were fierce and determined, the Saxons as well,
but the difference was that while a few such as Cedric and
Arlys were willing to sacrifice some of their countrymen,
the Normans were willing to wipe the entire race from
the face of the earth. Her chest trembled as a hard sob
wracked her. Hot tears followed. The battle was lost; to
continue to fight meant more misery. She straightened,
throwing her shoulders back, and sniffed. "I will not abet
you, Cedric, on any level. My oath is to my people, and I
will keep them safe at all costs, and that includes keeping
them safe from you. If that means accepting William, then
so be it."

Cedric's face turned a murderous shade of red, and
Isabel knew she was in deep trouble. He had lost his
tenuous grasp on sanity. She kicked him hard in the shin,
then punched him with all of her might in the groin. He
grunted, bending over, and Isabel kneed him hard in the
sensitive spot. She turned to flee in the direction of the
caves, but he grabbed her long hair and pulled her back
so hard she fell flat on her back. For a moment, Isabel saw
only black. She closed her eyes and caught her breath,
then opened them to the meager light filtering through the
heavy canopy of trees above her.

Cedric reached down to grab her, but the far-off thunder
of hooves stopped him. A sharp cackle added more tension
to the air. Isabel sat up and turned toward the sound just
beyond the piked heads. The blood cooled in her veins.

The whispers were true.

An old crone, hunched and clad in ragged garments,
shuffled toward them. She chanted softly in a foreign

tongue. Her long white braid was unkempt, but fringes of silver shrouded her face.

She pointed a long, bony finger at Cedric and cajoled him. "Come, Saxon, come to me so that I might add your head to my collection." For one so old and feeble in looks, her voice was clear and strong.

Surprisingly, Cedric held his ground. "Be gone, hag! Do not concern yourself with my affairs!" he shouted, but took a long step backward just the same. He pulled Isabel with him. Grabbing her hair at the base of her skull, Isabel yanked it hard from his grasp. In what she was not sure would be the correct action, Isabel darted toward the old woman, who paid her no mind but instead kept her black eyes focused on Cedric, who did not follow her.

"Come, Saxon," she wheedled, her clawlike hand outstretched in invitation. "Come to me, and live the pain of those you have betrayed."

Cedric swallowed hard but squared his shoulders. "Give her to me, crone, or I will return with an army to take her."

The woman cackled. "There is no army with the might to breech my magic." She looked up at Isabel, the dark eyes glowing not in madness but with complete lucidity. At once, Isabel lost her fear of the woman. Had her sire known she meant them no harm? A surprising calm filled her. As addled as the woman appeared to be, with her speech of magic, Isabel knew she was in no danger from her.

"Who are you?" demanded Cedric.

The woman cackled again. "I am Wilma, guardian of Menloc and those true hearts who abide nearby." Her eyes narrowed, and she pointed her finger at the quaking

Saxon. "And your heart is black with lies. Innocent souls cry out for revenge." She stepped closer. Cedric backed up a step. "I see all that happens in these woods, Saxon. I know your plots. I know who plots with you." She laughed, the cackle cracking in her throat. She was consumed with a fit of coughing. Once it died down, she turned watery eyes up to Cedric. "I know who plots against you!"

Cedric took a brave step forward. "If you know all, Wilma of Menloc, then you know the devil will have her at all costs! Give her to me so that others may live!"

"Nay, Saxon. She belongs to another, and when he discovers your trespass, you will feel the bite of his sword deep in your gut."

"Lord Dunsworth would never take up arms against me! I am his loyal servant."

Wilma laughed again and moved a step closer to him. "Fool, what makes you think I speak of him?"

Isabel gasped. If not Arlys, then who?

Wilma shared a grim smile with Isabel, then turned back to the Saxon. "Aye," Wilma crooned, moving closer. "The legacy will begin in her womb. Much blood will be spilled to see the final result. But mark my word, Saxon, no blood of England will spring forth from her loins."

Isabel trembled in the chilled air, Wilma's words causing her great concern. If she was not to wed a Saxon, then—? Her heart leapt in her chest. Nay! She would not bear a bastard!

Cedric stood silent for a long moment, contemplating the woman's words. Fury clouded his crimson face. His hands fisted open and closed at his sides. As if a decision had been made, he nodded. Slowly, he drew his short sword. "Then I will spill her blood now to end the legacy before it begins!"

He leapt at Isabel. But Wilma threw herself between her and the crazed Saxon. "Run, girl, run to the caves!" she screamed. Isabel turned to flee, but she could not let the old woman fall for her. She grabbed a large rock from the ground, and as Cedric raised his sword to plunge it into Wilma's gut, she brought it down with all her might on his skull. He moved his head in time to escape the brunt of her blow, but it was enough to cause him to lose his grip on Wilma. Isabel grabbed her up and turned to flee with her. The ground beneath her shook. Riders!

"Hurry, Wilma, we must flee now."

The old woman didn't budge. Instead, a smile twisted her thin lips. "Nay, lass, stand and face the devil."

Isabel gasped as Henri crashed through the bramble to their left, several of his men following close behind. Cedric rolled out from under the hooves that would have shred him to pieces had he not acted so quickly.

Henri's bay stallion reared and pawed the air with his hooves. When he dropped to all fours, he blew nervously, stomping the hard ground. Henri removed his helmet, his grin, so much like Rohan's, screaming victory. "So, we meet again, Isabel."

Henri dismounted. Isabel move backward. Cedric, in an act of submission, bowed low to the devil. "My lord," he said. "As promised, the lady Isabel."

Henri gave him a cursory glance, then motioned to one of his men. The knight dismounted and drew his sword. Cedric read his death in the knight's eyes. He dropped to his knees, then lay supine, grabbing Henri's ankles. "I pray you, do not do this! I know the hiding place of the lady's treasury!"

Henri held up his hand and kicked Cedric in the chin, rolling him over. He placed a heavy foot on the reeve's chest and drew his sword. He pressed the tip to Cedric's throat. "Tell me now, or die."

Cedric opened his mouth, but no words came. "Nay! Do not slay him!" Isabel screamed, tearing away from Wilma. "Enough Saxon blood has been spilled for silver. End it now!"

Rohan galloped furiously toward the screams. The hairs on the back of his neck rose at the first cry. It was too familiar. When he broke into the clearing, his eyes went directly to the devil knight and the woman he clasped tightly to his chest. The Saxon at his feet groveled like a mewling bitch. Not far from the trio stood a grizzled old woman who seemed to have command of the situation. Farther back still were several of Henri's men.

Rohan reined his horse to a grinding halt several horse lengths from his brother and his minions behind him. Rohan knew his own men were ready to lay down their lives at his slightest command. And, Rohan thought as his blood began to boil, the end of the day might very well see his brother's blood fertilizer for the hard English soil. His patience was at an end.

Henri grinned, and with Isabel clasped to his chest, he bowed and extended his arm to the piked heads. "Welcome, brother, to hell!"

Rohan's men flanked him, their hands on the hilts of their swords. Henri's men mirrored the action. "What goes on here?" Rohan demanded.

Henri threw his head back and laughed. "It appears, dear brother, you have been cuckolded."

Rohan scowled at the implication. His angry gaze locked onto Isabel's wide-eyed stare. Slowly, she shook her head.

"Your lady was off to meet her lover. How fortunate for you I discovered her ruse."

"Nay!" Isabel screamed, twisting in Henri's arms. "'Tis a lie!"

Rohan sat quiet but alert in the saddle. Anger burned hot in his belly. His eyes dropped to the Saxon cowering at Henri's feet. Henri pointed his sword at the man. "Ask him. He will tell you."

Rohan contemplated the man as an unexpected spear of jealousy stabbed him. While the man appeared to be nothing but a coward, his rich clothing spoke of his higher standing. Was this Dunsworth? "Who are you?" Rohan demanded.

The man rolled over to face Rohan. He started to crawl away from de Monfort, but the Norman placed his booted foot on his back, planting him hard into the ground. "Speak from there, Saxon, and speak clearly so we all may hear the truth."

Rohan stiffened. The Saxon swallowed hard, and his body shook violently beneath Henri's heavy foot, but when he spoke, he spoke clearly and strongly. "I am Cedric, reeve to Lord Dunsworth. I came to take the lady to my lord."

"Why did he not come himself?"

Cedric looked up at Henri, then to Isabel, then to Rohan. "He—he had pressing matters to attend."

Rohan laughed coldly, not believing the reeve. Nor Henri. He speared Isabel with another glare. He did not believe her, either. There was far more afoot than Isabel simply going to meet her betrothed.

"Did the lady go with you willingly?" Rohan softly asked.

The reeve nodded, not making eye contact with Rohan. "Aye, she did indeed."

The old woman cackled. "The Saxon speaks in half-truths, Norman."

"Shut thy mouth!" Henri shouted.

The crone moved toward Henri, no hint of fear in her eyes. Indeed, her calm boldness impressed Rohan. "Your lust for revenge will be your undoing, Norman. Leave this island now, and you will live to see yourself lord over all your sire claims."

"You are addled, crone! My brother Robert is heir to all my sire holds sacred!"

She smiled, her lopsided, snaggletoothed grin unnerving. Rubbing her hands together the old woman cackled again. "Aye, you, sir knight, are the least-favored son." She turned to Rohan, then looked back to Henri. "The sire even favors his bastard above his noble-born second son!"

Henri roared in anger and moved forward with Isabel in front of him, using her as a shield, with his sword pressed across the vital vein in her neck.

"How do you know this?" Rohan demanded.

She turned dark eyes up to Rohan. "The forest whispers her secrets to me." The old woman's eyes darted from Henri to the reeve, then to Rohan and beyond. She moved at an angle away from the noble-born son.

"What madness do you speak, woman?" Rohan demanded.

She stopped her sideways movement and looked long and hard at Rohan. Despite her crazed ranting, her eyes were clear and lucid and held a deep wisdom he saw in few men and fewer women. His skin flinched as he thought of A'isha. She'd had the same knowing eyes of this sage.

"I am Wilma of Menloc, seer of the ignoble." Her eyes moved past Rohan to Thorin, touching on each of his men before landing on Isabel, then back to Rohan. She raised her hands to the sky. "In the dungeons of hell, you have sworn your oath to one another. For the oath to take root, each of you must sow your seed deep between the thighs of England. But before each coupling, blood must be shed, for only the blood sacrifice will assuage the fury of the Blood Sword!"

Her words stunned Rohan. When he looked to his men, he saw they were equally stunned. When he looked to Henri, he saw murder in his eyes.

"Norman knight, bastard kin of the bastard duke, strike your mark, and make it sure, for if you do not, the legacy will die before it breathes life!" Wilma turned and looked to Isabel of Alethorpe. "Your destiny is clear, virgin daughter of Saxony. Prepare yourself!"

With those last words, Rohan felt as if he had been struck by a bolt of lightning. His chest heaved toward the sky as if a rope pulled it, before being abruptly released. With a clarity he had never before experienced, he understood his destiny was with the maid. He had known the moment she challenged him from the tower rampart that she was destined to be his. Now he could no longer deny it. Nor did he want to.

His body frosted, before his blood thawed, then warmed to hot. He turned to face Isabel, who stood blanched white in Henri's arms. A fierce possessiveness grabbed hold of Rohan's heart. Yet a calm determination held on tighter.

"Henri, release the maid," Rohan said, his voice barely audible yet laced with tempered steel the noble could not deny.

When he did not release her, Rohan dismounted. He silently signaled his men, and in the time it took to blink, the knights had arrows notched and bowstrings drawn. Henri's lips twisted in a maniacal smile. He nodded as if warming to this deadly game, then lifted his foot from the reeve and moved Isabel backward away from Rohan, toward the piked heads.

"My men never miss their mark. Release the maid," Rohan said again.

"Men!" Henri shouted. In answer, his six knights drew their swords.

Rohan laughed, unfazed by Henri's threat. "You will be dead before they can thrust." He moved toward his retreating brother. "Release the maid."

"Release her, second son!" the crone cackled. "If you do not, your head will grace my pike."

Rohan watched the cowardly reeve skulk to the edge of the clearing.

It took the words of the witch finally to get to Henri. Wildly, he looked around. Rohan's men had two arrows notched in each of their bows, aimed directly at his head.

"You are doomed, brother. Release the maid," Rohan softly said, moving closer.

Henri smiled, his eyes clear. Then, in a swift move, he ripped Isabel's dress down the middle, exposing her naked breasts. "The hag's prophecy will die here and now!" He pushed Isabel's back with his knee, forcing her to arch toward Rohan. When Isabel tried to shield herself, Henri slapped her hands away and pressed his sword harder into the white flesh of her throat. Rohan roared and moved toward his brother. When Henri grabbed a breast and rubbed a nipple between his thumb and forefinger, Rohan saw red.

"She is quite the prize, brother. Much sweeter then Eleanor. Did you know this lady's betrothed is willing to pay for her?"

"Release her," Rohan ground out.

"I will, but first, brother, I will take from you what you stole from me."

As he moved to push Isabel back into the thick forest, he was suddenly hurled high up into the air.

Rohan and his men stood wide-eyed, their jaws agape. Henri hung by his right foot, swaying back and forth and upside down from a thick rope attached to a high limb of a sturdy oak. His screams of frustration echoed throughout the forest. The crone laughed so hard she coughed. Henri's men swarmed below him, looking up, not sure how to free their lord. With all eyes on de Monfort's dilemma, Isabel darted to Rohan but was grabbed by the reeve, who had kept his focus solely on the maid and had grabbed Henri's sword from where it fell on the ground. As Henri had done before him, the reeve pressed the blade to Isabel's throat.

Though he stood fast, the man's eyes implored Rohan for understanding. He would get none. "Forgive me, Sir Rohan, but my loyalty lies with my lord first, and he insists I bring his lady to him at all costs."

Rohan strode toward him, his body heated and taut. He saw nothing but the shaking pale hand of the Saxon and the blade at Isabel's throat. The vision of her flesh slit and her life's blood slowly oozing from her clouded his sight with rage but more than that, a gut-twisting sorrow. He would go to hell first before he allowed Isabel to be taken from him.

"Forgive me, Saxon, but my loyalties are to the lady!" Before the Saxon knew what he was about, Rohan grabbed Isabel with one hand and plunged his sword deep into the man's gut with the other.

Isabel screamed.

The crone laughed in self-satisfied glee. "'Tis as I foretold!"

Twenty-one

Rohan jerked his surcoat off and placed it over Isabel's head. She shivered from the cold but more from the shock of all that had just unfolded. Numbness kept her from going completely hysterical.

Wilma moved toward Henri, who had quieted from his humiliating upside-down position on the rope. Instinctively, Isabel knew he realized that his life was in his brother's hands. When Wilma pulled a short knife from the inside of her garment, Rohan stepped between her and his blackhearted brother.

"Nay, Lady Wilma. My brother will not die by your hand today."

She raised dark eyes up to him, and her lips twitched. "Allow him to live now, Norman, and he will cost you more."

Rohan nodded and hacked the taut rope in half with his sword. "So be it."

Henri tumbled to the hard earth with a sickening thud.

His men rushed to him. Rohan's knights still held bows drawn, aimed directly at the ignoble.

Wilma threw her hands up and tore at her hair. "I cannot control your destiny, bastard Norman!"

Rohan sheathed his sword and walked to where Isabel shivered uncontrollably. He picked her up and carefully placed her in his saddle. He mounted behind her and turned to the seer. "Nay, you cannot, but I can."

The ride back to Rossmoor was long and silent. Rohan's arm clasped Isabel possessively to his chest. The powerful thrust of the great horse beneath her ate up the turf and his body steamed, keeping her warm. Isabel's thoughts and emotions whirled from relief at not going to Arlys, not succumbing to Henri, and surviving Cedric's attacks to fear and despair at what Wilma prophesied. Her body trembled violently at the implication of her words. Rohan pulled her tighter against his chest, and try as she might to deny that she wanted a life with the Norman, the prospect excited her. Being wife to a man such as he would be a constant challenge.

But he did not offer marriage.

Even if he did, as his wife, she would no doubt see him off fighting beside his duke more than he would stay and be husband, for while England was crippled, there were those such as Arlys and her father so passionate about keeping a Norman off the throne that they would die for the cause. What would Geoff want? Would he lay down his arms and swear to the Norman duke, or would he stand and fight him?

Isabel shook her head, still unable to bend her mind around exactly what was expected of her. Was she to bear the bastard a bastard? Nay! She would not. She would not give herself to any man but her wedded husband. She looked up at the set jaw of the man who had since his arrival turned her life inside out. Aye, she could admit she lusted for the man. Her cheeks warmed. She would not lie. But he was a landless knight; there was no future for them.

Isabel sighed heavily. And she was a landless Saxon noble. She had nothing but the remains of her father's treasury at her disposal, and that she would not touch, for in truth it belonged to her brother now. And she would never take from Geoff.

So, like Rohan, she had nothing. Was nothing enough? Mayhap it would be if there was love between them, but there was really only the ramblings of an addled old woman in the forest.

Isabel's chest tightened as grief and despair engulfed her. For the first time since the Normans' landing, she felt the urge to give up. To go away and lick her wounds. To be left completely alone. She was tired of taking care of everyone. She wanted someone to take care of her.

She settled back against the hard chest of the man who dominated her every thought, and she closed her eyes. Mayhap when she awoke, the world would be brighter.

It was not. A dark gloom hung over the manor, giving it a dull, sad pall. Whereas the villagers had looked cheery and carefree that morning, now they looked forlorn and sullen. Wulfson met her stare with a furious glare. Isabel's cheeks flushed hot. 'Twas not her intention to shame the knight in the eyes of his master.

Rohan tossed his reins to Hugh and dismounted; he turned to Isabel and extended his arms. She moved easily into them, and as he drew her from the horse, her body pressed against his. She caught her breath at the heat that radiated from him. She looked up into his stormy eyes. Her heart beat so hard against her breast she felt as if it would break out. The storm passed in his eyes; he turned and extended his arm to her. She took it.

He ignored Wulfson, who did not look nearly as afraid as Warner had when she gave that knight the slip. Indeed, Wulfson's face twisted in furious anger. Rohan ignored his man. They swept into the hall, and despite her fatigue, she perked up when she saw it was vacant of any Willingham. She did not have the strength to trade barbs with the peevish Deidre.

Isabel sat quietly throughout the meal, the day's events unfolding again and again in her head. She was tired, confused, and afraid. But she also felt a different, more ready tension. She watched Rohan's large hand cut meat in their trencher, then grasp the goblet of fine wine and drink heartily of it. He had killed with no compunction today. Yet those hands could be gentle. And had been with her. She trembled. What would he expect from her this eve?

She looked up to see his tawny eyes quietly contemplating her. While they burned, there was a serene sheen to them. Isabel dropped her gaze to her food and nibbled on a piece of spiced capon. Emotions collided in her heart. She would not succumb to him. She could not.

She would come to her husband a virgin. She could not bear the thought of bearing a bastard. 'Twas not fair to the child, and 'twas not fair to her. She knew Rohan would press her for complete yielding. She would not bend. On this matter, she was steadfast in her resolve.

"Isabel, what plagues you?" Rohan softly asked.

A sudden wave of hot tears welled up in her eyes. She shook her head, but a big tear plopped onto her hand. She moved to wipe it on her sleeve, but he brought her hand to his lips and kissed it away. He raised his lips, hovering just above her skin, and said, "Your bravery today was commendable. Do not despair overmuch, damsel. This war is coming to a close, and you will benefit from the outcome."

"Rohan." She choked as emotion overcame her. "I must know of my brother. Too much hinges on his life."

He squeezed her hand gently. "Nothing changes between us should he return."

Isabel withdrew her hand from Rohan's. "You are wrong to think that. He would be a worthy ally to you and your duke. I cannot think William would relieve him of his lands and title. He is rightful lord here."

"This land is still unsettled, Isabel. Much can change. William is a man of his word and not one to change his mind with the direction of the wind. He will see his loyal subjects where he will. And we are all subject to his discretion." He smiled, plucked a piece of succulent capon from the trencher, and waved it beneath her nose. "Eat, Isabel, you will need your strength."

She looked up to see a flash of fire in his eyes. Her belly did a slow roll. She opened her mouth, and he popped the meat between her lips. When she closed her mouth around his finger that lingered against her bottom lip, a hard, sensual jolt nearly unseated her. Rohan smiled and slowly withdrew his finger.

His action surprised her. The erotic charge the soft brush of his fingertips across her lips elicited shocked her. Just

moments before, she sat determined to end their physical
liaison. But now, a different hunger consumed her.

She watched him watch her, and when he understood
her thoughts, his lips turned up into a slow, knowing smile.
Heat infused her cheeks. She turned and looked away from
him. She had fought so valiantly to put carnal thoughts of
this man far from her mind. But with this one, single, innocent touch, her body flamed for more.

"May I be excused, Rohan?" she asked softly.

"You do not hunger for food, Isa?"

She refused to look at him. Instead, she shook her head.
"Nay. I am weary. I seek a bath and my bed."

Rohan stood and offered her his arm. She took it, and
he led her to the bottom of the stairway. Without looking
back, Isabel ran up the stone steps to the chamber she
shared with him. Once inside, she closed the door and
pressed her back against the hard timber. She caught a
hard breath and pressed her hand to her belly. Her entire
body flared hot with desire.

A soft knock on the door pulled her out of her thoughts.
She opened the door to Enid, who stood wringing her
hands. Isabel bid her maid come in, and Enid quickly set
about preparing a bath for her. As she bustled about the
room, several times she cast an eye toward Isabel. Finding
the maid's actions annoying, Isabel said, "What pricks
your mind, Enid?"

Once again, the tiring woman stood wringing her hands.
"There is word of others lurking in the forest. The branded
souls from Dunsworth."

Isabel's heart went out to the poor people. Henri was a
menace. He would see every Saxon and no doubt some of
his own countrymen dead. Indeed, Isabel knew it was only

a matter of time before the two brothers clashed, and one would not rise. The thought of Rohan lying on the cold, hard English soil as his life blood drained from him terrified Isabel. Her heart squeezed so tightly she could not draw a breath. The unexpected emotion that claimed her at the thought of Rohan's death terrified her as much as his death itself. She sat perfectly still. What did it mean? Did she—did she have feelings for the dark knight? Isabel pressed her hand to her throat and swallowed hard. The buzz in her belly and the heat in her loins told her what her head did not want to acknowledge. Somehow, in the last week, a man, a sworn enemy, had found his way into her heart.

How could it be? She tried to swallow but the dryness in her throat hurt. Nay, she could not care for a man such as Rohan du Luc! Could she?

"Milady?" Enid softly questioned. "What ails you?"

Isabel blinked and shook the crazy thoughts from her head. She looked up to Enid and smiled. "Forgive me. I am weary. What did you say of the people of Dunsworth?"

"They band together in the forest."

"Do they seek refuge here?"

Enid shrugged, still holding back.

"Tell me where they hide, and I will alert Sir Rohan to fetch them."

"'Tis rumored they are marked by the devil's brand now. They conjure spells and are more bent on revenge than rescue, milady. They hold no trust for the Normans."

Several boys brought in steaming buckets of water and poured them into the copper tub, filling it. Once they left the room, Enid helped Isabel undress. As she sank into the steamy water, Isabel closed her eyes, and as much as she did not want to think of her feelings for Rohan, the buzz in her belly made her smile. "Enid, Sir Rohan is not like his brother. Rest assured, he means the villagers no harm. I will talk to him on the matter. Now, please leave me to my bath."

Enid made haste to leave the room.

Twenty-two

Sometime later, when Rohan ascended the steps, the weariness he had experienced as he and his men planned for more harassment from Henri and what was left of the marauders disappeared. His blood warmed as he thought of the soft and creamy maid in his chamber. And for the first time since their return to the manor, he gave his mind over to what the seer had proclaimed. While he was not one to believe in spells and magic, he believed A'isha, and he believed Wilma. And he believed the fire that burned hot and strong in his heart for the maid upstairs. Aye, she was his destiny, and she would know it before too much more time passed.

He rubbed the scar on his chest and hastened to his chamber, where Hugh had set up his bath. He looked forward to the hot, steamy soak, but what he looked forward to more was stretching his tired limbs out beside the smooth warmth of Isabel.

When Rohan entered the room, it glowed in the low halo of firelight. The copper tub steamed near the hearth.

Several tapers were lit on the cabinets. Fresh linens sat folded on a stool next to the tub. Isabel was curled up asleep in the large chair he surmised had been her father's on the other side of the hearth.

He was careful not to disturb her. As he closed the door, Hugh materialized. Rohan shook his head, not requiring the squire's assistance. He closed the door, bolting it. He moved quietly toward the hearth and the maid who slumbered beside it. A tenderness he had never experienced, not even for A'isha, overcame him for the brave girl. Quietly, Rohan unstrapped his sword belt and set it aside. He continued to undress. Once free of all clothing, he stepped into the tub and sank into the welcoming water. As he rested back against the rim, Rohan let out a long, heavy sigh. He closed his eyes for several long moments, and when he opened them, he found two of the most mesmerizing eyes softly watching him.

His belly made a funny quivering movement. He scowled, not liking the feelings infusing him at that moment. Isabel smiled and began to rise from her seat. "Nay, Isabel, rest. I will see to my bath." When she sank back into the upholstered chair, he let out a long breath of relief. The way he was feeling at the moment, if she so much as touched him, he would come apart at the seams. And while he intended to keep to their bargain and indulge in that ripe body of hers, he wanted so much more.

As he washed and then rinsed himself, Isabel's gaze never once left him. Finally, feeling most uncomfortable under her scrutiny, he demanded, "What ails you, woman?"

She smiled and shook her head and continued to watch

him. When Rohan stood to complete the rinse, she boldly refused to cast her gaze away. He rose hot and thick before her. "Do you desire me, Isa, as much as I desire you?"

With no hesitation, she nodded. Rohan growled and stepped from the tub, not caring that he dripped water over the rugs. He strode to Isabel and swooped her up in his arms. He carried her to the bed, where his body followed hers into the thick fur pelts. He dug his fingers deep into her damp hair, and before he pressed his lips to hers, his gaze scoured her face for protest. He found none. "Isa," he breathed, "what spell have you cast upon me?" Not waiting for an answer, his lips descended onto hers, and he felt her, warm and pliant, open up to him. He took everything she offered.

His head spun as her fingers dug deep into his hair and she pulled him tighter against her. Her body arched, the hard tips of her breasts digging into his bare chest. A hot, crazy sexual inferno engulfed Rohan, and suddenly he could not get enough of her. He tore his lips from hers. His hand pulled at her shift, ripping it in half, exposing the most glorious breasts he had ever laid eyes on. Voraciously, he plundered them with his mouth.

Isabel squirmed and arched, pressing her body hotly against his. As if he were drunk, his eyelids were hooded, his limbs became heavy, his head swirled. His loins filled with hot blood. He would have her this night and every night thereafter.

"Isa," he breathed against a nipple, his breath ragged, "you make me forget everything."

She moaned in response, and when she slid her hand down the hardness of his belly to his rigid cock and wrapped her hands around him, Rohan shuddered against her. "Jesu, Isa, you make me insane."

He moved his hand down to cover hers, and in unison they moved up and down the thickness of him. His hips undulated against her belly. Their hot, moist breaths mingled. In one great thrust, unable to contain himself, Rohan spilled his seed into her hand. He groaned, his body stiffening as she pumped him, milking him dry of all his seed. When he shuddered against her for the last time, Isabel scooted out from under him. She grabbed a linen from the stand next to the bed and wiped herself clean, then him.

Rohan, while sated for the moment, was not done with her. He pushed her back onto the pillows. "Isa, 'tis not what I wanted." He kissed her long and deep, and his hands traveled down her belly to her soft curls. Isabel moaned beneath his lips. When he dipped a thick finger into her waiting wetness, she cried out, arching toward him. "Let me make love to you," he whispered against her lips. "Let me love you all night long."

His lips traveled from her lips to her chin, and then he pressed them to her throat. His hand moved slowly back and forth, the sheen of sweat erupted on Isabel's skin, and the sultry scent of her sex swirled in the air, heightening Rohan's senses. His lips tasted each pink-tipped nipple, and when he pressed his lips to her belly, Isabel hissed in a breath.

She felt as if she were caught up in a wild, wanton vortex. The heat and velocity of Rohan's assault made Isabel forget herself. All she wanted was total consummation. He moved another finger into her, and the slick sound of her juice as she moaned and thrust against his hand added more fuel to her out-of-control flame. When he nuzzled her mound, Isabel stiffened in shock. "Relax, Isa," he softly said, the percussion of his breath against her swollen lips driving her mad with want. "Let me love you this way." Slipping his fingers from her before she could answer, his tongue breached the seam between her loins. Isabel strained against him. As his tongue lapped her there, his fingers swirled slowly around her creamy, straining nub, and the wave she had craved emerged, gaining full force with exhilarating quickness. He suckled her nub, and with his middle finger, he pressed deep into her, tapping that sweet spot. In one liquid wave, she came into his mouth. Grabbing his hair, she trembled beneath him and truly thought she had died and gone to heaven. As each spasm wracked her straining, sweaty body, Isabel cried out.

When he took all of her into his mouth and suckled her nether lips and nub, she lost all control. Her thighs fell wide open, and her hands slipped from his hair. She lay hot, wet, and panting, cradled in the fur pelts, unable to catch a decent breath. Her chest heaved as she sought to breathe a regular breath. Rohan moved back up her belly, his long hair trailing softly against her sensitive skin, heightening her experience. When he kissed her, she tasted herself and nearly died of shame, but he did not give her the chance to dwell on it. His shaft had filled and pressed against her moist curls.

Isabel shook her head against the pillow, squeezing her eyes shut. If she looked at him, she would not be able to resist the call of his eyes.

He pressed the head of his cock to her thigh. "Allow me entrance, Isabel.'"

She moaned and shook her head. Though her hips moved against his and her breasts quivered wanting his touch once again, she could not.

He pressed her, his hot breath mingled with hers. Isabel opened her eyes and gasped. Rohan's eyes burned with the brightness of a thousand suns. His wide, muscular shoulders hovered over her. His dark hair shrouded him, reminding her of a fallen angel.

She opened her mouth to deny him, but no words came forth. A terrible battle raged. Her desire and, yes, her love for this man wreaked havoc with her morality. She squeezed her eyes shut and shook her head. "Nay, Rohan, you cannot."

If 'twere possible, his body stiffened further to steel. She felt him tremble against her. But he did not press her. Instead, he moved to her side, releasing her from his touch. Though he lay only inches from her, she felt as if he were leagues away. Her body yearned to follow his, to give him what they both so desperately wanted. But she could not do it. The thought of him casting her aside after he had what he wanted from her tore through her with unimagined pain, and just as harsh was the vision of her begging in the streets of Alethorpe with his bastard strapped to her breast.

Isabel took several minutes to collect herself. She wanted him to understand, she needed him to. Finally, after long drawn-out moments, her body was once again quiet and free of the liquid desire for the man lying beside her. She rolled over to find him facing her, his eyes bright in the firelight. He looked not angry but perplexed.

"Rohan," she began softly, not trusting her voice. Her

emotion ran high, and she felt once again as if she would burst into tears. When he did not respond, she scooted closer and reached out to press her hand to his chest. He flinched and pushed her away. "Do not touch me, Isabel. I cannot control my body."

She closed her eyes and sank back into the furs. Taking a big, deep gulp of breath, she continued. "'Tis the same with me, Rohan."

"Then why do you deny me?"

She let out another long, pensive breath. If she told him of her fear of him casting her aside, he would deny it and promise the moon to get between her thighs. 'Twas what men did, was it not?

She smiled sadly. Mayhap, but not Rohan. He did not strike her as the type to play a man or a woman false. He told her days ago there would be another after her. So instead of delving into emotions where he would think she held a love for him and mayhap use it against her, Isabel gave Rohan a reason he could respect and, more than that, relate to. "The man I give myself to will be my husband. No bastards will I bear."

He moved toward her, careful not to touch. "Would my bastard displease you much, Isabel?"

She swallowed hard. For if the truth be told, she would welcome his child, but not the unhappiness that would follow for the babe.

He pressed his hand to her belly and spread his big fingers across her. Her skin immediately warmed. "We would make lusty sons together, Isabel. And daughters full of the same fire as their mother."

Isabel closed her eyes, and her heart rose high in her

throat. She pressed both of her hands to his. "I believe you," she whispered. He moved over her and pressed his lips to hers.

"The prophecy marks you as the womb to bear my sons, Isa. I would have no other."

Had he gotten down on one knee and professed his love to her, she could not have been more shocked. Fear gripped her. Fear of the power of love, fear of conceiving his child, fear of Henri and Arlys, and fear of the unknown. Her destiny was not in her hands but in God's, and she feared he had more heartache in store for her. She could not bear it with a bastard child and no husband to support her.

"What the old woman said today was addled prattling."

"Nay, Isabel, it was foretold by a seer in Iberia. Wilma only reminded me of my destiny here in England."

Isabel's eyes flashed open in disbelief. Rohan smiled and lay back on the pillows, drawing her with him. "'Tis the truth." As she settled against him, he pulled the torn shift from underneath them. He held it up and looked at her. "Methinks I owe you several of these."

She swatted him. "And a gown or two."

He tossed the torn garment over the side of the bed and pulled her tighter against him. "I will press you no further, Isabel. Our bargain is met." He closed his eyes, and Isabel went still.

His disclosure should have elated her. It had the opposite effect. She had grown accustomed in this short time to his warm and powerful body beside her in the bed. She drew strength from it. She slept soundly knowing he would protect her from any intruder save illness.

Her mind ran out of control with scenarios of who

would next share this great bed with the Norman lord. Would it be Deidre? Or would he go to William's court and bring back a titled Norman heiress?

His arm tightened around her as if he read her disturbing thoughts. She sighed and loosened her body, molding it tighter to his. He had said he believed the prophecy. Even if she did not, he was convinced she was the only woman to bear him sons. With that small comfort, she drifted off into a troubled sleep. Visions of Henri standing over his dying brother with his sword raised high in the afternoon sunlight, Rohan's blood dripping from it, interrupted her slumber. Visions of Wilma cackling and telling Isabel she had made a mistake, that it was the noble-born brother she was to couple with and spill his sons on English soil. She tossed and turned, throwing the pelt from her body. Each time, Rohan pulled her into his arms and soothed her with his kisses and caresses.

Isabel woke to thundering on the door. Rohan was up, sword drawn, demanding to know who dared interrupt his sleep. "'Tis I, Rohan. We have visitors. Come at once."

Rohan lowered his sword and pulled open the door. "Who?"

Thorin did not look into the chamber, but his dire eyes looked at his longtime friend. "'Tis a standard bearing a red fox on a green plain."

Isabel gasped, and both men turned to her. "'Tis Arlys."

Rohan scowled heavily and turned back to his friend. "See that he and his men are disarmed. I will be down directly."

As he shut the door, Isabel slid from the bed. "I will go as well."

Rohan strode past her to the bucket of water warming near the fire. He poured half of it into a bowl and cooler water from the pitcher. Quickly, he washed and dressed. Isabel washed the sleep from her own face and the overnight taste from her mouth, and she, too, quickly dressed.

"I would prefer you wait for me here. I know not what your betrothed is about. I have much suspicion of him."

"I have my own suspicions. And like you, I wish to know what he seeks."

She helped him don his mail, and as he strapped on his sword belt, she searched the room for her shoes. Finding them under a bench, she hastily donned them.

Rohan took a deep breath and looked meaningfully at her. "I have no loyalty to this man. And while he may not support the bands of raiders who have sorely plagued the shire, we found a man bearing his colors amongst those we killed yesterday."

Isabel's eyes widened.

"Should he challenge me, I will not back down on your behalf," Rohan said softly.

Isabel nodded and felt confident that the meeting, while it would not go well for Arlys, would enlighten them all. "I would not expect you to decline on my behalf, Rohan." She strode over to him and placed her hand on his left forearm. "Let us go and see what the fox is about."

Rohan looked down at Isabel and smiled. She never ceased to amaze him. He realized at that moment that had A'isha or Wilma not prophesied the maid as his destiny, he would still move heaven and earth to make it so.

She was a rare treasure in his dark and tarnished world. He would always welcome her smile, her touch, her gentle heart. He grinned. And her nails in his back. A livelier maid he never had the pleasure of bedding. His blood quickened. He would give her her wish. He would not breach her. For when he did, she would be his wife proper.

And there would be naught but William to say him nay. Rohan would dispatch the messenger after he dealt with the errant Dunsworth.

As they walked down the hall, Rohan gave Isabel one last appreciative look. While she had bathed and dressed quickly, she was still a sight to behold, begowned in a heavy sapphire-colored velvet, the intricate golden girdle from which her jeweled dagger hung accentuating her waist. Her long, golden hair hung thickly and freely about her shoulders. He would beg her to wear it thus even after they wed. He grinned down at her. But the smile faded as a terrible thought crossed his mind. Would she choose the ousted Saxon over him?

Did she burn for Dunsworth the way she burned for him? Jealousy tore through him, and Rohan decided then and there that he would retain her at all costs.

Twenty-three

As the couple descended the stairway, every eye in the hall was riveted on them. Rohan scanned the visitors with the scrutiny of a hawk and immediately singled out Dunsworth. He felt Isabel's hand tremble on his arm. He squeezed it subtly to his chest in reassurance. Once again, a fierce possessiveness he was not familiar with engulfed his being. He did not want to lose Isabel, not when he had just found her.

For a displaced noble, Dunsworth was dressed in rich garb. His aristocratic features were sharp, but his eyes danced with joy as they settled on Isabel. But only briefly. For next they clashed with Rohan's. Instinctively, Rohan knew the lady beside him blushed, for every person either knew or suspected where they both had just come from. And at that moment, Rohan felt ashamed for the position he had placed her in. He had no right to strip her of her dignity. He would beg her forgiveness.

Once again, foreign emotions toyed with his stiff resolve. It irritated him beyond belief. He was a warrior, a knight of William, captain of *les morts*, the most deadly fighting force known in Christendom, and he was thinking how at his first chance he would beg a maid's forgiveness for trespassing upon her person, a trespass he was rightfully entitled to!

He scowled heavily, his mood becoming morose. Aye, Dunsworth was everything Rohan despised in a man. Fat, titled, and legitimate.

"My lady!" Arlys cried, and moved toward her, extending his hands to hers. Rohan allowed her to move away from him when they reached the bottom of the stairway.

Arlys grasped her hands, reverently kissing them as he bent down on one knee. "My lady, how fare thee?" Arlys asked ogling up at her as if he were a nursing lad.

Isabel gave her betrothed a short curtsy. "I am well, milord, how fare thee?"

Their polite talk with so many waiting with bated breath for complete havoc to ensue seemed ridiculous to Isabel.

"I am much better now that your beauty once again graces my eyes." He pulled her away from Rohan, but only so far before Rohan moved his hand to the hilt of his sword. Arlys looked up at the Norman, his eyes narrowed. "I am Arlys, Lord of Dunsworth. I wish no war with you, Norman. I have come here with the sole intention of claiming my betrothed, Lady Isabel."

Rohan nodded and looked past Dunsworth to his handful of assembled men. While they looked battle-weary, they stood erect and proud. He wondered how many of them had partaken in the slayings.

"Indeed, for a man who no longer holds land or title, you are very bold or very stupid to show yourself here."

Arlys's face puffed red. "You are as boorish as your brother, du Luc. But rest assured, while de Monfort drinks my wine, eats my food, rapes my sister, and shouts to the world that he killed my brother, I have confidence I will regain what is rightfully mine."

Isabel gasped at Arlys's declaration. Poor sweet Elspeth and young Sir Edward. "Arlys! You must take Elspeth away!" Isabel cried.

He looked down at her and slowly shook his head. "Dunsworth is well guarded. Should I return and get found out, I will suffer greatly." His blues eyes hardened. "I will petition William for my rights."

Rohan laughed. "Your petition will fall on deaf ears, Dunsworth. While my brother is the scourge of the earth, our common sire has sent heavy levy to William. De Monfort is a powerful ally to the duke and one he would not want to displease. Henri will hold what he has plundered here. Make no mistake of that."

Arlys swallowed hard, visibly paling. His eyes darted to Isabel, then back to the Norman. "All is not lost to me, du Luc. I still have my betrothed. Allow her to pack her belongings so that we may go."

Rohan fondled the hilt of his sword. "What makes you so sure the lady wishes to go with you?"

Arlys looked at Isabel. He smiled, and when she did not return the smile, his lips tightened. "Isabel, tell this man you wish to be released from his care."

"I—I cannot leave Rossmoor, Arlys," Isabel said softly.

The noble looked hard at her, then up to the towering Norman. "Cannot or will not?"

She shook her head. "I will not."

Dunsworth's face colored dark crimson, and for a man

who had everything to lose and very little to gain, he pushed. "Does this man violate you? Has he forced himself on you, Isabel?" he demanded.

Isabel struggled for words. Her eyes lifted to Rohan's, then turned to her betrothed. Slowly, she shook her head.

Arlys struggled for words, for a thought, for a way to persuade his lady love to fly with him. "I sent Cedric to bring you to me. The forest whispers that this man slew him. Is it true?"

" 'Tis true," Rohan answered for Isabel. "His life for those lives of Alethorpe your men have slain."

Arlys's head snapped back, his eyes narrowed. "What lies do you spill, Norman?"

"Your colors were on one of the raiders we slew yesterday."

Arlys stepped back, shaking his head. "Nay, I never sanctioned such a thing."

" 'Tis not what Cedric said to me, Arlys," Isabel challenged.

The noble-born Saxon shook his head. "I am afraid, my love, Cedric had his own agenda." His eyes softened for a moment. "I only asked him to bring you to me."

"And so you will not have her. The maid has given you her answer," Rohan reminded him.

"Nay!" Arlys insisted. "She is mine. I will not leave without her!"

Rohan was at the end of his patience. "You have nothing left to offer the lady. You are landless and without title. Your betrothal is null and void."

The color drained from Arlys's face as Rohan's words hit home. Yet he persisted. "I may have lost all, Norman, but I give her the promise of my love and respect and to pledge my troth before God. What do you offer her? The chance to be your leman?"

Those in earshot gasped at the Saxon's bold words. Rohan drew his sword.

"Nay, Rohan!" Isabel beseeched him, pressing her hand to his arm. "Leave him be."

His hot gaze pierced deep into her heart. Her hand trembled on his arm. "Please, leave him."

"Isabel," Arlys said softly, " 'twas your father's wish we were to wed. Would you deny him that wish?"

Isabel looked stricken for a moment before she turned to the earl. "My father is dead, and mayhap my brother. When our betrothal contract was signed, Edward was king. He is dead, as is Harold. The contract is null, Arlys. It cannot be enforced."

He dropped to a knee and grabbed her hands into his. "But what of you, Isabel? What of our love?"

Rohan stood so stiffly beside her he thought his back would snap in half. Yet he would have the maid's answer. Not, he realized, that it would change anything. She was his. No man, contract or no, would take her from him.

Isabel wrestled with her emotions. She did not want to hurt Arlys further, but she also did not want to give him false hope.

"Arlys, I do not love you. Not as you would have me love you. Take this opportunity to find a lady who would make your happiness her happiness." She shook her head. "I am sorry. I am not that lady."

He squeezed her hands. "I do not believe you, Isabel. This Norman intimidates you. Come with me! Edgar has been crowned king! There is hope for England!"

Rohan pressed the tip of his sword into Arlys's chest,

moving him away from Isabel. "'Twill be rectified soon, Saxon, I assure you," Rohan said.

Arlys threw his shoulders back and looked Rohan hard in the eye. "If that is to be the case, is your duke so ignorant as not to understand he will be met with far more resistance should he strip everything from us? Does he not have the slightest understanding that should he be crowned king, there are many Saxons who will pledge loyalty to him?"

Rohan's eyes narrowed. "Are you such a man, Dunsworth? Do you swear here and now your oath to William?"

Arlys sidestepped the question. "My loyalties are to the king of England."

Rohan was more direct. "To the current king or the rightful king?"

"I served Edward and Harold. I will serve the king."

"You play with words, Dunsworth. Which is it? Edgar or William?"

Arlys shot Isabel a glance, then looked hard at Rohan. "I serve the king."

Rohan smiled and nodded. "You are swift, Dunsworth. But a subject who switches loyalties as frequently as my men switch women is of no value to myself or William. As a former lord, what would you suggest I do with someone such as yourself?"

"Under the circumstances, I would ask that you allow my lady to come with me so that we may find shelter in a clime where we are welcome and not looked upon as slaves."

Rohan turned and looked down at Isabel. She returned the look, and while he saw she was tense, he felt she wanted the Saxon gone from the hall for fear he might take a ride on Rohan's sword. "Do you feel unwelcome here, Isabel?"

Isabel looked around the room and saw so many familiar faces. Faces filled with fear of the unknown, faces looking to her for guidance. Faces that looked to her for hope. Her duty was to her people first, and despite her newly discovered feelings for Rohan, she would not leave her home. She shook her head.

"Do you feel set upon by me or my men?"

Slowly, she shook her head.

Rohan turned back to Dunsworth. "The lady has denied you thrice. The subject is no longer open for debate."

Arlys stood, furious, his hands opened and closed into fists at his side. His men, though unarmed, pressed closer to him in defense. Isabel trembled. She had never seen Arlys so angry.

"You choose this bastard over me?"

"I choose Rossmoor, Arlys."

"Would you choose the man who now owns Rossmoor if you knew he slew your sire?" Arlys triumphantly flung at her.

Isabel's body jerked as if she had been hit in the chest with a club.

"What say you?" she whispered.

"Du Luc is the slayer of your sire!"

Rohan's gut twisted as he watched a part of Isabel die before his eyes. She turned toward him, and he watched her features crumble. Her big violet-colored eyes turned up to him, tears making them shine like precious gemstones. Silently, she beseeched him to tell her it was not so. His body stiffened.

For as fierce a warrior as he was, and as many men as he had slain and the unspeakable horrors he had survived, Rohan did not have it in him to crush this woman's heart with the truth. For with the truth he would lose her forever. And he realized that while he could take her hate for the bastard he was, he could not bear to see the incrimination in her eyes every time she looked at him, knowing his was the final strike that drew her sire's last breath.

But it had to be so, and if presented the situation again, he would repeat it one hundred times over. Honor bound, he had no other choice. But she would not understand the ways of men or how dying with honor on the battlefield by the hand of your enemy was the Holy Grail in a true warrior's heart. And Alefric was a warrior Rohan would respect on any battlefield.

So be it.

Isabel choked back a sob and asked, "Does he speak the truth?"

The hall was deathly quiet as a tomb, every ear straining to hear his answer.

"I slew many Saxons on that bloody hill, Isabel. It is possible your sire fell beneath my sword."

"Nay!" Arlys screamed. "I saw with my own two eyes, you slit his throat!"

Isabel crumpled to the floor. Rohan bent to her. Isabel cried out and waved him off. Her cheeks turned ashen; her eyes held a far-away look in them. She turned to Arlys and asked, "What of Geoff?"

"I watched him fall, Isabel, beside your sire. He is dead."

"Why did you not tell me this sooner? Why did you not send word?"

Arlys shuffled his feet and looked down at the floor. "I wanted to tell you myself and would have once we flew from here."

Isabel nodded weakly in understanding. Rohan squatted beside her. Her shoulders shook as great sobs wracked her. Her great, luminous eyes turned up to his, and Rohan felt the earth shake beneath his feet. "He is bent on swaying you to his favor, Isabel. He has much to gain from his words."

She shook her head as tears streamed down her cheeks, her golden hair stuck to her face. She lay down on the floor, as an animal crawling off to die would lie. "Leave me be, both of you." She closed her eyes and murmured once more, "Leave me be."

Rohan turned to Wulfson, who stood nearest to his lady. "Take her to my chamber." He then gestured to Enid. "See to your lady."

As Isabel was carried up the stairway, Rohan turned to the unruly Saxon. "You have wounded her to the soul. For that, you will get your chance to see William sooner than I am sure you expected. And"—Rohan smiled grimly—"in chains."

When Rohan gestured to his men, pandemonium broke out as Arlys and his men attempted to make an escape. But *les morts* were always prepared, and within minutes, the Saxons were subdued. Just in time for the Willinghams, who came down the stairs with their meager belongings in hand to witness.

"Arlys!" Deidre cried out, flying down the stairway. "What is happening?" she demanded of Rohan. He ignored her and strode past her to the wide portal, which he flung open, allowing the chilled December air to swirl in.

"Take them all to the stable." Rohan commanded.

As they were dragged out, Rohan ignored Deidre's hysterical screams and Lord Willingham's demands for explanation. Rohan strode to the stable himself to saddle up his horse. At Deidre's repeated demands for explanation, Rohan heard Ioan explain in no uncertain terms that Dunsworth and his men were now war captives of William and that if the Willinghams would like to join him, he would gladly see to it.

Seconds later, Rohan threw open the stall door and flung the bridle around his great horse's head. He drew him from the stall and hopped onto his back. With a swift kick, Mordred dug his great hooves into the hard earth, and away they thundered.

Isabel collapsed onto her father's bed, and if she had been more coherent, she would have demanded that Enid move her to her solar. Her heart was torn in half, and she knew not how to mend it. The vision of Rohan standing over her father, pressing his blade to his throat and watching him die, tormented her soul. How could he do such a thing?

Her sobs tore through her, great, wracking sobs that shook her entire body. And Geoff. Sweet, funny Geoff. He was a lover of the arts and of women; he was not a warrior. She would never hear his laughter or his teasing voice as he called her more a boy than a girl.

She would not see nieces and nephews, and he would never be lord of Alethorpe. Isabel dug deeper into the furs, her body so cold she felt as if she rested on a block of ice. She did not know which news affected her more darkly, her brother's death or that Rohan had slain her sire.

She did not hear the knock on the door until Enid asked if she should answer it. Isabel did not respond. Several moments later, she recognized a deep voice as Thorin's. Enid's voice rose in argument, only to be silenced by Thorin's much deeper and much angrier tone.

Isabel rolled over, her eyes so swollen she could barely make out the one-eyed knight. He approached her and bowed. For a long minute, he did not speak, and when he did, his words were slow and measured. "Lady Isabel, subterfuge abounds. I beg you, do not believe what a desperate man says when he has nothing to lose. Rohan is many things, but he is first and foremost a noble warrior on the field. Unless he had good cause, he would never kill a downed knight with a dagger to the throat. He would use his sword and pierce his heart. 'Tis his way."

Isabel cringed at Thorin's graphic description. She sniffled and nodded. He bowed and hurried from the chamber.

Long into the afternoon, Rohan rode. He rode hard, he rode angry, he rode confused. His heart had swollen to twice its normal size in his chest. The pain of it was unbearable. Just as painful, he felt Isabel's heart against his own heart, beating in agonized rhythm. He knew not what to do. The deed was done. He had slain Alethorpe there on the bloody slopes of Senlac Hill. As the old man lay dying, he'd begged Rohan to finish him off, for he had been stabbed in the back by one of his own. He did not want to die by a treacherous Saxon hand.

Long after Harold fell and the battlefield was laid to waste, Rohan had been clearing the field of bodies when he heard a man call to him.

"Norman!"

Rohan had hesitated but turned back in answer. His eyes had scanned the thick copse of bodies before he located the one where a bare hand waved slowly in the chill of the air. The late sun had begun to lose its light. Rohan had squatted down and squinted for a better look. He had knelt beside a Saxon knight, much as Rohan foresaw himself in many years: a hardened warrior, forever loyal to his king and country, fighting to his last breath.

The Saxon had grabbed Rohan's hand. "Finish me off, Norman. I will not die by the coward's hand that slew me from behind." His voice, still strong for one so aged and so wounded, had continued, "Do not let the vultures pick my eyes out. See to it that myself and my fellow Saxons are shriven."

Rohan had nodded; not being a man of God, he had more interest in the sword lying beneath the old warrior. He slid it out from under his back. The hilt bore Edward's symbol. 'Twas a Saxon sword. Rohan had scowled but held it up. " 'Tis a Saxon sword, milord."

The old man had nodded. "Aye, a coward's sword." Taking in a shallow breath, he'd continued, "I am Alefric of Alethorpe, lord of the great manor Rossmoor. I fear my son has fallen by the same cowardly Saxon sword as I." He'd coughed, bloody spittle foaming from his mouth. Rohan had doubted any force could take him until he'd said what he had to say. "I leave a headstrong daughter and a treasury worth a king's ransom. Slay me, Norman. Allow me to die by my enemy's hand, not the one of a coward." He had coughed harder that time, more blood bubbling up from his throat. His faded violet eyes so much like his daughter's had beseeched him. "Swear your oath on your sword that you will see to the future of my daughter." Alefric had grasped Rohan's hand tighter. "Do not let her fall prey to the fox in sheep's clothing."

So close to the old man, and understanding a warrior's wish to die with honor at his enemy's hand, Rohan had slid his short sword from its sheath and placed his right hand on it. "I swear an oath to you, milord, I will do my best to see her safe." Then, in a quick motion, Rohan had slit the vital vein in his neck. The old warrior had closed his eyes, and Rohan had watched him quietly leave this earth. Whether he went to heaven or hell, Rohan did not know. If 'twere the latter, he was sure they would once again meet.

And so that was how the old man had met his maker. By Rohan's hand, to be sure. He turned his horse around and gave the beast a quick kick. His chest and flanks already lathered, Mordred gave more for his master. Rohan came to a decision. He would tell Isabel all, and he would live with her decision. His love for her was too strong to force her to bend to him. He would take her only if she wanted him, scars and all.

And while he felt a great weight lift from his shoulders, it was replaced with a heavy load of trepidation. While he wagered all, the odds were not in his favor.

He smiled grimly and nodded to the wind. He had learned much in his short time with the maid. To gain the respect and honesty of these Saxons he so desperately yearned for, he would in turn have to give it to them. And there was no better place to begin than with their lady, and if she would have him, their union would be an honest and blessed one.

The chilled wind blew full in his face as the steed ate up the space between him and the woman he loved, and excitement mounted in Rohan's belly. Aye, he would plead his case to the lady, and she would see his love for her was true.

And so she would not deny him!

Twenty-four

"Milady!" Enid cried, shaking Isabel awake. "You must come. 'Tis a messenger from the duke!"

Isabel heard the words, but they did not make sense in her fatigued mind. Her face felt as if it had swollen to the size of a wineskin. When she tried to open her eyes, they stuck closed. Her chest hurt, and her throat felt raw. In one torrid rush of pain, she remembered why.

Fresh tears, hot and salty, burned her eyes as they seeped from beneath her closed eyelids.

She rolled over away from Enid's insistent voice. "Leave me be, Enid," she cried into her pillow.

"Nay, milady, you must rise. The messenger demands to speak to you and the Norman together. Do not tempt William's wrath. Rise!"

Her limbs had no strength, her heart had no will, but somehow Isabel managed to sit up and throw her legs over the side of the bed. Enid pressed a cool damp cloth to her face and fussed about combing her long hair and working two small braids down each side of her face while leaving the bulk of her hair free.

Enid slid Isabel's shoes on, and when she was satisfied with the results, she pulled her lady up and helped her to the door. Once over the threshold, Isabel stopped. A sob wracked her chest. Valiantly, she fought back more of the hot, stinging tears. She met Enid's calm eyes, and her resolve strengthened. She was Isabel of Alethorpe, daughter of one of England's most noble knights and granddaughter of kings. She was as much a warrior at heart as her sire and his sire before him. And as much as the man who slew him. She would see what the duke demanded of her and see it done.

Isabel swept down the stairway just as Rohan burst through the portal. He stopped in his tracks. Over the long expanse of the hall, their eyes met. Isabel turned to look down at the messenger bearing the duke's crimson and gold colors. He was surrounded by several armed knights also bearing the royal colors.

Rohan hurried toward the messenger. He bowed, then demanded, "What news do you bring of William?"

The man held a sealed scroll in his hand. "Duke William makes a proclamation, Sir Rohan." He broke the seal, unrolled the parchment, and began to read, "In the name of William Duke of Normandy and heir to the English throne, I do hereby command my captain Rohan du Luc and his brother Sir Henri de Monfort to meet two days from the reading of this edict on the grounds of Rossmoor in a duel of swords, but not to the death, for the rights to the lady Isabel of Alethorpe and the lands that come with her."

Isabel gasped, and her knees buckled. Rohan moved to her and set her down on a nearby bench. "The lady is to be separated from both knights, with no interaction until such time as the tourney. It is my express desire that this not be a duel to the death, as I have great need for my knights. But let the outcome of this tourney never be disputed again. William."

The messenger rolled the parchment, and not one person uttered a word. Indeed, everyone in the hall stood in shocked silence.

Isabel looked from where she sat, anger hot and bright burning in her eyes. "Tell your duke I will die before I go with either of these knights." She stood up, and the messenger, shocked by her outburst, seemed lost for words.

"Isabel," Rohan softly said, "you cannot thwart the duke."

She turned bright eyes up to him; tears hovered at the edges. "I will kill myself then."

As she turned to leave the hall, the messenger shouted, "Halt!"

Isabel hesitated in her step but continued toward the stairway. At the bottom, she turned to the assembled crowd. "Tell your duke he will have to find another bitch for his knights to fight over. I am not available." She turned and walked with as much dignity as she could up to her solar. Enid hurried behind her.

The messenger motioned to one of his men to go after Isabel. Rohan stopped him with a brawny arm. "Do not, Rodger. She learned only today that her brother is dead and just a few days before that of her sire's death. If you press her, she will make your life miserable." Rohan grinned. "To that I can attest."

The messenger shook his head. " 'Tis of no matter to me, Rohan, but William will have his due." Rodger reached behind his surcoat and handed Rohan another scroll, this one smaller but with the duke's seal marking it as unopened. "His grace asked me to give you this after I read his order."

Rohan took the scroll, slipped his thumb beneath the wax seal, and read silently to himself: "My good friend and comrade in arms, it is with a heavy heart and much irritation I have had to take time from warring with these ungrateful Saxons that I write to you. Have heart. The duel is not to the death, and if I had any doubt as to the outcome, I would not have issued the order. For as you know, I could not turn de Monfort's brat away. Too much levy is dependent on Henri feeling I do not play favorites. Win the day, the damsel, and the lands, and there will be much to celebrate at my coronation. William."

Rohan moved to the hearth, where the hungry flames yearned for more fodder. He tossed the scroll into the flames and watched as it was consumed.

Rohan smiled. He would see the day won and his brother once and for all off his back.

He bowed to Rodger. "I beg only a moment with the maid and to retrieve my belongings from my chamber."

Rodger started to shake his head, but Rohan persisted. " 'Tis urgent I speak with her, Rodger. Do not deny me this."

"Aye, go, Rohan, but do not push. I will not have it said I favored du Luc over the house of de Monfort."

Rohan hurried past the king's man to his chamber. His blood ran cold when he found it empty. On impulse, he ran to the lady's solar, where he found Isabel pacing the room and Enid fussing about her like a fly around a horse.

"Leave us," Rohan said.

Wide-eyed, Enid stopped her movements but made no move to leave the chamber. "Now!" Rohan boomed. She squeaked and rushed from the room. When the door slammed shut, Rohan flung the bolt into the brackets. He turned to face a murderous Isabel.

She launched herself at his chest, her fists pummeling him with everything she had. Rohan allowed her her attack. She screamed and railed against him, using words not fit for a lady, but still he took her wrath. As her strength waned and her fists no longer hit with such force and he knew she was beat, he swooped her up into his arms and strode with her to the bed.

He laid her down and sat on the edge next to her. Her sobs tore his heart in half, and knowing he was directly responsible for her pain pained him.

He smoothed her hair back from her face. "Isabel, let me tell you of that day."

She shook her head, and her eyes closed. "Nay," she gasped, barely able to get the word out. "Leave me be."

She rolled away from him, and Rohan felt his world slipping from his grasp. He inhaled a long breath, then began his story. "We all fought for our lives that day on Senlac Hill, Isabel. Both Saxon and Norman. From early morn to late in the day, the tide of battle changed back and forth. William would repel the Saxons only to have Harold regroup and move us back down the hill. Blood from both sides ran like a crimson river. The stench of it clogged our noses and chests. It made breathing difficult. I did not think they would, but the Saxons impressed me. Harold was a good man, though one who did not keep his oath. He would have made a good king, but the throne was promised to William, 'twas, as you know, why we were there. To claim it."

He reached out a finger and touched her shoulder, wanting contact.

"Once the day was won, William sent word he would not have his men defile the fallen dead. He was adamant. He sent many of us forth to see that the bodies were not desecrated."

Isabel rolled over, the violet of her eyes barely discernible beneath her red, swollen eyelids. Rohan smiled and brushed hair from her cheeks. "As I made my way among the fallen, a voice speaking my tongue called out to me, but he called me Norman. I knew it was an Englishman who spoke my language. I moved in that direction, Isabel. I could not ignore the desperation in his voice."

Her bottom lip trembled, and Rohan touched his finger to it. "When I approached the old man, he was on his back and struggling for every breath. He bade me come closer. He grabbed my hand and told me his name and how he and his son had fallen from a cowardly Saxon sword."

Isabel gasped. Rohan nodded and took her hand. "He spoke the truth. I pulled a Saxon sword from beneath him. He also spoke of his defiant daughter. He demanded my oath to see to you and protect you from the fox in sheep's clothing. I gave it."

Fresh tears trailed down her cheeks. "He then demanded I give him the death of a warrior."

Isabel shook her head. "Isabel, 'tis unworthy not to die by the hand of your enemy on the battlefield. Alefric had been brought low by a cowardly Saxon. He desired a warrior's death. One of honor, at the hand of his enemy. I gave it to him. He died peacefully with the knowledge that he would see God as an honorable knight of the realm."

Isabel closed her eyes. Tears slid from beneath her lids down her cheeks. Rohan bent over her and kissed them away. "You of all people know I am a man of my word, Isa. I promised your sire I would see to you, and I promise you now, you hold my heart in your hands." Then he stood and left the chamber.

Isabel could not comprehend Rohan's deed. Honor was not gained by who slew you on the battlefield. Honor was gained by how you lived your life. Did her sire feel he had not lived the life of an honorable man? Was he so sure of his demise that he insisted a stranger, a Norman, make the final strike? Sobs welled up in her chest, and she rolled over, smashing her face into the pillows. Aye, it was exactly what her father would have demanded! Honor was not a word to him but a way of life. He had taught his daughter well. Honor above all.

She drifted off into a troubled slumber. When she woke, the room was dark, but in the small hearth a fire burned brightly. A covered tray of food sat on a nearby table, and watching her from the corner of the room was Enid. Her maid smiled but made no move toward her. For that, Isabel was grateful. She wanted no interaction on any level with anyone. Her wounds were raw, and she wanted more time to heal from the shock of her life. She closed her eyes and drifted off to a more solid slumber.

When she woke, Isabel felt the urge to use the garderobe, and her stomach gnawed in protest. But she felt no hunger for food. Indeed, she felt no hunger for anything. Not even revenge. She was completely and utterly depleted.

After taking care of a few necessities, Isabel managed to eat some stew and a piece of bread. She removed her clothes but did not bother to bathe. Once again, she allowed sleep to claim her. It was far easier than facing the reality of her world.

The next time Isabel woke, she knew she could no longer hide. As her father was honor bound to die a warrior's death, she was honor bound to her people to lead by example and accept the duke's edict. Her stomach roiled with such velocity at the thought of lying with Henri de Monfort that Isabel could barely breathe. But if she did fly, he would take his wrath out on the gentle souls of Alethorpe. She sucked in a deep breath and refused to think of Henri as lord here.

"Enid," she called, her voice thick and rough. "See to a bath for me, and find out when the tourney is to commence and where Sir Rohan resides."

Enid smiled and bobbed her head, scurrying from the chamber to see about her lady's business.

As Isabel soaked in the steamy water, Enid came back into the chamber. "The tourney is set for noon tomorrow, milady, and Sir Rohan and his men reside in the huts surrounding the stable."

Isabel closed her eyes and asked, "Is the reeve's cottage still vacant?"

Enid bobbed her head, but her eyes were full of question. "Aye, 'tis."

Still keeping her eyes closed, Isabel said, "See that it is thoroughly cleaned by nightfall and that a thick goose-feather mattress with clean linens and furs is placed within. Along with enough wood to heat the meager place."

"But—"

Isabel opened one eye. "No buts, Enid. See to it."

And with that resolve, Isabel rose from the bath and dressed herself. She could no longer deny Rohan's last words after he told her of her father. And she could no longer deny her own love for the man. Despite the heavy burden of what was in front of them, she loved and cherished him over all men. It was the only thing she had left to give freely. Isabel smiled. Well, she did have one other thing. And that thing she had so stubbornly clung to she would give to Rohan this night. Aye, she would join with him as one and celebrate their love and what might be their last night together. For on the morrow, she might have nothing left to give.

When Isabel entered the hall, several of Rohan's men milled about, but she noticed none of his Blood Swords. She nodded her head to each man as they acknowledged her with short bows, and she made her way to Manhku, who sat before the hearth playing a game of chess with the duke's messenger.

They both stood as she approached. Manhku smiled and bowed, holding tightly to a thick walking stick. "How fare thee, Lady Isabel?"

She smiled in return. "I fare well, sir knight. How fares the leg?"

"Good. The Viking has seen to it."

"'Tis good to hear Thorin is multiskilled." To the messenger, she said, "Do you have a name, sir?"

He grinned despite her forwardness. He bowed and clicked his heels. "I am Rodger fitz Hugh. At your service, milady."

It seemed bastards abounded amongst William's entourage. Isabel gave him a short curtsy and inclined her head toward the door. "Tell me of this tourney in which I am the prize."

The hall grew quiet, but after Rodger seated Isabel in a chair beside him, he explained in a low tone for her ears only. " 'Tis not to the death, I assure you, milady. William has much need for his knights. In truth, methinks he is more annoyed by de Monfort's demand, especially as my duke has much on his hands at the moment. Immediately following the tourney, the papers will be drawn naming the victor and the spoils—er, um, my pardon, milady, the name of the disputed lady."

As he spoke, Isabel's anger resurfaced. "How does your duke think to win over Saxons when he treats them as one would sheep for breeding?"

Rodger reddened. "I know not, milady—I—" He looked down at his shoes and shuffled his feet.

"Aye, 'tis as I thought. There is no honor in a man who would force a maid to lie with a man she despises."

Rodger's head snapped up, and anger flashed in his dark eyes. "Do you dishonor his grace?"

"Aye, as he dishonors me."

She turned from the stunned messenger and made her way to the lord's table, where Lyn immediately set a loaded trencher before her. Since the afternoon meal had passed, the serving maid brought what she thought Isabel would enjoy. Isabel smiled at the girl, and as she chewed and swallowed a piece of meat, she nearly choked as she thought what horrible things Henri's men would do to her and the other women of the village should the devil win. Suddenly, her appetite was gone.

Isabel stood, and with one of the duke's men behind her, she moved out into the courtyard. The ringing sound of clashing steel echoed in the quiet chill of the air. Isabel followed it. As she passed through the bailey to the open meadow used for sheep along the east side of the village, she stopped.

Her heart thudded hard in her chest. Bare-chested, Rohan wielded his sword against Thorin, then Ioan, then Wulfson, to Rhys, and Stefan, then Warner, ending with Rorick.

In mid-swing, he stopped his sword held high above his head. Even in the cold, his great muscles glistened in manly sweat. His tawny eyes caught hers across the small meadow. All eyes turned to her. Isabel's cheeks warmed.

Rohan brought the blade down. In a slow, shallow move, he bowed to her. She turned from him, and instead of going into the hall, she looked for sanctuary in the chapel, where she fell to her knees and prayed to the almighty for the strength to live through yet another ordeal, for her personally the most trying.

As the shadows of yet another day began to work their way into the westerly sky, Isabel still prayed. She did not want to leave the calm of the chapel. She did not want to face the world. She wanted to turn into mist and float away unseen and unaccosted.

For the third time, she crossed herself, then pushed off from her kneeling position. The horn had blown for the evening meal sometime before. Deliberately, she ignored it. She did not want to take part in the revelry that was sure to be going on in the hall. Rohan and his men would no doubt be speaking of how the ignoble would fall.

Instead, Isabel slipped from the chapel, only to be followed by the large shadow of the duke's guard.

She entered the hall through the kitchen door, and

through a back stairway that led to the second floor, she entered not her solar but Rohan's chamber. She let the bolt fall into the brackets and stood for a long moment in the empty room, her back pressed against the smooth wood of the door, and inhaled his manly scent. It was everywhere. She opened her eyes to see the cold hearth, but instead she saw it blazing with fire and warmth, Rohan standing before it, his naked body gleaming in the firelight like a great Norse god. She looked to the fur pelts scattered on the bed where last they had left them. Her body warmed as she remembered their last tryst in that place. She closed her eyes and allowed her body to feel his hands, his lips, his hot skin pressed against hers.

Aye, Rohan had moved her as no other man had. She was sure she could live one hundred years more and never find a man such as he. As it did when she thought of Rohan, her father's face sprang into her mind's eye. Instead of the anger she felt at Rohan's hand in his death, a calm peace filled her. While she did not understand the workings of a man's mind, she understood honor. She nodded and walked deeper into the room. She trailed a hand along the soft fur of a pelt. God willing, this space would find Rohan residing in it with the next rise of the moon.

She moved to the slitted window and pushed the tapestry that covered it to the side. She opened the shutter. Moonlight streamed in. The courtyard below and the bailey farther down were quiet. She had felt the anxiety of the entire hall. Not only did she fear the outcome of tomorrow's tourney, but the villagers did as well. Would they flee back into the forest?

She could not blame them if they did. Would they take

up arms against Henri? The thought sickened her. Henri would hack them down where they stood. And what of the branded group from Dunsworth that Enid spoke of, the ones who conjured spells against the devil knight?

Her heart swelled with pain, hope, and, yes, love. She was honor bound should Henri win the day to keep his bloodlust from her people. And she would do everything in her power to see it happen. She swallowed hard. Or die trying.

And with those thoughts, the decision she had made earlier in the day was solidified. Until noon tomorrow, she would be in charge of her own destiny.

Twenty-five

"Sir Rohan," Russell said, coming in on Rohan just as he finished his tepid bath. He scowled. These baths from a bucket were not to his liking. But at least the water was clean, and the soap gave a good lather. As Rohan rinsed his hair and flung it back, he eyes rested on the young squire. The boy had shown his mettle. He would make a worthy knight.

"Aye, boy," Rohan said as he dried his hair and shoulders. He stood in a small hut he and his men used as a bathing room of sorts. He stood naked, the low fire in the hearth keeping the room warmed against the chill.

"I—a—lady—"

Rohan's body flinched, but he continued to rub his hair dry. "Speak up, boy."

Russell straightened his shoulders and looked Rohan in the eye. "There is a message from Lady Isabel. I am here to take you to the person who carries it."

Rohan slowly lowered the towel and stared hard at the squire. "Is this some trick?"

"Nay, I would not play you false, sir. The messenger is just down the way. Dress, and I will take you."

Rohan hastened to do just that. He left his mail, but he did strap on his sword belt. Hastily, he followed the squire, his eyes wary as he watched for the slightest hint of subterfuge. While he had come to trust the lad, he did not completely trust anyone.

As they moved past the stone wall to the village and slightly beyond to a stone cottage just off to the side, Rohan frowned. The cottage was abandoned. Who had word of Isabel? And why here? He slowed his step. Russell bobbed his head and opened the door. "The messenger awaits."

Rohan drew his sword. "Stand back, squire, and await me."

The boy nodded and stood ramrod-stiff beside the open portal. Rohan ducked in, and before he could rise to his full height, his heart clogged high in his throat. In the low light of the hearth, a vision stood. A golden angel. He tried to swallow, but his throat had thickened and his limbs would not move him toward her. The soft fabric of her shift illuminated in the firelight silhouetted her ripe curves.

His rod filled. His blood coursed hotly through his body. When she turned and her violet eyes looked to him with adoration and love, and her full red lips smiled, Rohan knew he had died. For only in heaven could this be true.

As if gliding in the air, she moved past him, closed the door behind him, and threw the bolt. He dropped his sword and stood rooted to the floor, afraid that if he moved any more, he would wake from his dream.

She pressed her body against his. "I am real, Rohan."

His entire body quaked; he raised a hand to her face

and brushed her gossamer hair from her face. She smiled up to him. "Give me your child tonight, Rohan."

Her words shocked him to his core. "Isa?" he asked, taking her face into his hands. "What are you saying?"

She moved backward away from him. He followed, still holding her face between his hands. She backed up to the mattress and sank to her knees on it. She lifted the shift from her golden body and lay back on the linens and furs. Her body glowed like alabaster in the firelight. Her eyes twinkled in soft seduction. Rohan dropped to his knees. She pulled him by the hair on either side of his head toward her as she maneuvered herself to lie back. "I am saying I want you to make love to me. And in the process, give me your son this night."

His entire body trembled, his emotions too stormy to describe. So he did not try. "Isa," he whispered, "it is my heart's desire to give you my son."

In slow, unhurried fashion, Rohan kissed her lips, her cheeks, her nose, her ears. His hands worshiped every smooth inch of her, touching as a blind man would. Softly, savoring every part of her, burning her curves and planes into memory. Her skin smelled of roses, and her hair was thick and soft like silken strands. Her soft red lips kissed him back with a fervor he had never known.

Miraculously, his clothes disappeared, and when he pressed his heated body to her equally heated skin, he knew he was in paradise.

Isabel luxuriated in Rohan's dark, powerful warmth. His fingers and lips worshiped each inch of her body, reverently as if she were a cherished possession. When she stripped his clothes from his body and he laid her back onto the furs, she could not wait to feel the full weight of him inside her. He was gentle at first. Digging his fingers deep into her hair, he looked into her eyes. "Isa," he whispered, "you own my heart, my body, and my soul. Do not ever cast me aside."

Emotion so powerful built with his words that tears momentarily blinded him from her view. She arched against him and closed her eyes. Biting her bottom lip, she tried to quell the rush of emotion that threatened to overwhelm her senses. The wide head of him nudged her swollen folds. She opened her eyes and sobbed. "Rohan, you are my heart, my body, and my soul. Do not ever cast me aside."

His lips lowered to hers. "Never, my love. Never."

He entered her then, slowly, reverently. She opened for him, giving all of herself with all of her heart.

As he breached what now mattered not to her, a sharp prick of pain came and passed so quickly she was barely aware of it. Rohan's powerful body surrounded her. The heavy feeling of him inside her as her body accepted him caused her a moment of panic. He overwhelmed her. His size. His power. His passion for one brief moment terrified her.

Rohan soothed her, raining soft kisses on her cheeks and eyelids. "Isa, the pain will pass," he promised, then kissed her deeply, his hungry lips washing away any vestige of discomfort.

And with all the love she felt for this man, Isabel kissed him back. Wrapping her arms around his neck, snaking her fingers into his thick hair, she strained against him, opening wider for his entry.

Her body had prepared for him. Her muscles relaxed, and slick and hungry, Rohan moved inside her. The feeling of him filling her was more than she expected, so much more. The sublimity of him made her want to cry out with joy. The heat he generated from his slow, rhythmic thrusts caused a familiar tide to rise deep with her, but this was different from the others. This was deeper, richer, more powerful.

Wanting to crest, to feel that ultimate feeling of ecstasy with him, uniting them, to feel his seed erupt deep within her, Isabel could no longer contain herself. A wild frenzy for more of him, for harder and faster, overcame her. Her body was slick with sweat. Rohan's body glided in and out of her. The tide built to dizzying heights before crashing with the force of a thousand exploding stars inside her. Isabel hung suspended in his arms as her body spasmed, and one wave of pleasure slammed after another. "Rohan," she gasped as her body convulsed against his. She gulped for air, hardly able to breathe. Her body had melted like warm wax around him.

Rohan followed her bliss. His lips crashed down on hers as he thrust hotly into her. His body tightened. His hips tensed.

"Jesu, Isa," he muttered as his hips shuddered and he spilled deep inside her.

Isabel wrapped her legs around his thighs, holding him tightly to her, wanting him to spill until he gave her the child of his she so desperately wanted.

His body slowed, but his breathing matched hers in velocity. He collapsed against her. For long moments, their bodies spent, they lay entangled in each other's arms.

Their sweat-soaked skin glistened in the firelight. Their chests rose and fell in great gasps as they tried to regain control of their breathing.

Isabel felt more womanly at that moment than she had ever felt. She had no idea a man and woman could share such bliss and intimacy.

Rohan pulled her into the circle of his arms. "Isabel," he said softly.

She smiled and luxuriated against him. "Aye?"

"I have no intention of losing you on the morrow."

She smiled, but fear overshadowed it. "I have no intention of losing you, either, milord."

He rolled her onto her back, and his eyes searched her face. "We will wed as soon as a priest can be found."

Her heart filled to bursting. She smiled and looped her arms around his neck, bringing his lips down to hers. "I expected nothing less."

Her young body craved more of what he had just given her. "Make love to me again."

As hungry for her as she was for him, Rohan obliged her.

Isabel woke to the mournful song of the lark. With a start, she realized where she was. Rohan snored softly beside her. Isabel pulled the furs up to her chin to ward off the chill of the room. The fire had died down, but what chilled her more was the call of the lark. 'Twas morning. And a bad omen. She slipped from the bed and threw more wood on the hearth. As she returned to the bed, she saw the bloodstained linens.

A sudden worry terrified her. What if—what if Rohan

fell this day, and Henri found her to be impure? Would he beat her? And what if she were with child? Rohan's son? Would the brother kill him?

"What troubles you, Isabel?" Rohan asked from the bed.

She smiled and hastened back to his warmth. As she snuggled against him, she shook her head. "Nothing. I was only angry the lark began his song so early."

For long moments, they lay there. Together, heart to heart, wishing with all of their hearts that there was no Henri de Monfort.

A soft knock on the door disturbed their silent revelry. "'Tis time, milady. The guards will be searching for you soon," Russell called from outside the door.

Isabel cried out, "Nay, 'tis too early."

"The light breaks, milady. Make haste."

She turned in Rohan's arms, burying her face in his shoulder. His long hair was soft against her cheek. "Rohan, let us leave here. Run away to where we both will be safe!"

He kissed the top of her head and shook his head. "I cannot believe I am hearing those words from your lips, Isabel."

She smiled sadly and rubbed her cheek against his shoulder. "'Twas but a passing thought." Rising on an elbow, Isabel traced the scar on his chest with a fingertip. "We are both foresworn to honor our king and our people. We could not run away even if 'twas our true hearts' desire. We are honor bound to see this day to its end."

He rolled her over and kissed her deeply. "I love you, Isabel. Keep that with you this day, and this night I will see you back in the lord's chamber tending to my hunger for you." He smiled and moved from the bed and slapped her heartily on the rump. "Rise, woman, and go back before Rodger comes searching for us both!"

Isabel hurried to dress, and as she brushed her long hair, her eyes caught sight of the colored ribbons on her gown. Hastily, she untied several and handed them to Rohan. "Wear these today tucked into your mail. May they serve as a reminder of what you have to lose this day."

He took the silk ribbons and pressed them to his heart. "I will win the day, Isabel, and in so doing a place for us both here." He grabbed her to him, and by his fierce kiss Isabel knew he would die before he would allow Henri to trespass on her person. She swallowed hard as he released her. She searched his stormy eyes for the slightest doubt. She found none.

"Godspeed, Rohan."

He kneeled before her, took her hand, and kissed it. "I will not disappoint you, my lady."

He rose and was gone.

Isabel could not eat. She could barely breathe. The tension in the hall was so thick it was suffocating. When Henri and his entourage arrived shortly after Rohan and she had parted ways, the tension escalated. The villagers booed and hissed at him and his men, and several times Isabel was sure they would take up arms against the Norman. But they did not. Even when Henri and his men taunted them.

When he strode boldly into the hall, he stopped to leer at Isabel as she chatted with Manhku. "I hope you have prepared our bed for this eve, Isabel. Be sure to strip my brother's linens and put fresh on for me." He grinned and strutted close to her. "I like my bed neat and my women dirty."

Isabel gasped at his crudity. Manhku stood without the aid of his stick and pressed his sword to Henri's mailed chest. "If milord Rohan does not kill you today, I will."

Henri's color paled by several shades. "You will see my brother in hell at the end of this day!"

"Gentlemen, gentlemen," Rodger said, coming to stand between the two knights. "There will be no duel to the death today. William is adamant. No death. He has need of living knights."

"Shut thy mouth, fitz Hugh. We have no interest in your blatherings."

Rodger stood rigid but did not continue. Thorin stepped into the hall. "We are ready, Rodger. Bring the ignoble forth so that Rohan may make quick play of him. We hunger for the noon meal!"

Manhku sheathed his sword and grabbed his walking stick. He presented his arm to Isabel. She looked up into his dark, intelligent eyes. He smiled and said, "Have faith in Rohan, milady. He would never allow Henri to touch you."

She nodded. Manhku threw his head back, and his laughter rang through the rafters. "Besides, he has grown soft on this place!"

Twenty-six

As Manhku led her toward the knoll where just yesterday Rohan had practiced with his men, she was shocked to see so many gathered. Every villager from every corner of Alethorpe, Dunleavy, and Wilshire appeared. She even saw a few faces from Dunsworth. She had forgotten about Arlys. Was he still being held hostage in the stable?

As she looked closer at the throng, Isabel's heart clenched. She looked upon the group Enid had spoken of. A more pathetic assemblage of churls she had never seen. Some two score of them, all shaven, even the women and children, but more noticeable and frightening were the X's burned into their foreheads. They huddled as one, their dark, murderous eyes locked unwaveringly on Henri and his men.

When the devil knight beheld them, he stopped in his tracks. He waved to Rodger, who walked beside Isabel and Manhku. "Seize those churls! They are under arrest by my order!"

"Nay!" Manhku shouted. "Sir Rohan has given them safe haven here. They are no longer your property."

Henri threw his head back and laughed. "My brother has become Saxon overnight?" He smiled at Isabel. "What magic do you work with that addled crone Wilma?"

Isabel smiled. "You will see shortly."

Henri's face fell at the implication of her words, but he turned around and continued toward the knoll, where Rohan stood in all of his mailed glory, ready to take his brother down once and for all.

Once they were all assembled, Rohan made brief eye contact with Isabel. But when he pressed his hand to his chest, she smiled. It was all she needed from him. He would be her champion. She had known the first time she laid eyes on him that cold morning not long ago.

Rodger's heralds blew their horns, and soon the gathered crowd was quiet.

"In the name of William Duke of Normandy and heir to the English throne, I hereby give notice. A tourney between Henri de Monfort . . ." The crowd jeered, and scores of missiles in the form of rotted fruit and vegetables sailed from its midst. Rodger raised his hands, calling for order. The crowd quieted. "And Sir Rohan du Luc." The crowd roared in approval. Isabel smiled and looked to Rohan, whose face she could not see behind his helmet, but the outpouring from the villagers filled her heart. Their acceptance of the man she loved was more than she hoped for.

Once the crowd settled, Rodger continued. "The tourney rules are thus. Each knight will use his own sword. No other weapons will be allowed. Should one appear, then all is forfeit, and to the other go the spoils, which in this case is the lady Isabel." If the crowd had cheered for Rohan, they nearly lost their voices in their zealous cheers for her. She smiled and waved, her chest swelling with pride. She would never forsake them. *Ever.*

"The prize is the lady Isabel and the lands she is heir to. At the conclusion of this tourney, the last knight standing will be declared the winner, and for that he shall never again be challenged for the lady or the lands."

Rodger turned to both knights. "William has expressed deeply, he does not wish for death for either of his knights this day. Do not aim for any vital organ. This is a test of strength only."

He looked to Henri, then Rohan. "Do you accept the terms of this tourney?" They both nodded. "Choose your seconds."

Rohan chose Thorin, and Henri chose a knight Isabel did not recognize, but apparently several villagers did, for there was a buzz amongst the crowd when he stepped forward. Isabel looked to Manhku in confusion. He shook his head, unable to give her an answer.

The two warriors faced each other at a distance of no more than four horse lengths. Their eyes, like those of a hawk eyeing its prey from on high, never strayed from each other. Rohan knew his brother was not invulnerable, but he was a more than worthy opponent.

As he expected, Henri moved first, stepping around Rohan in a circle. Matching his motion, Rohan moved in the opposite direction. And as Rohan also expected, his impatient brother raised his sword and rushed him. Rohan met his blade steel to steel. Their swords sang out in a single howl above their heads. Rohan parried Henri, sending him flying past him. Rohan turned, and the two changed directions.

"Surely, you intend to do battle face-to-face, brother." Rohan grinned through clenched teeth.

Henri did not reply but charged once again. His sword, striking downward, was met by a defensive counterstrike, and the toe-to-toe battle was on. Long before the rift that drove them apart and divided them, as boys, the brothers had practiced regularly together using wooden replicas. Each had become so accustomed to the other and his tactics that their sessions often lasted well past the expected time, resulting in a draw.

But much time and emotion had passed between them. Rohan knew with clarity that there would be no draw today. One of them would not get up.

The angry sound of steel on steel rang out as the two fought for advantage. Henri struck down upon Rohan's sword, then raised his sword and struck down again from the opposite direction, all the while moving his feet in a small circle. Forced into a defensive position, Rohan could only muster protective blows. Sensing that the weight of the sword would soon take its toll on Henri's arms, Rohan hoped to bide his time for a counterstrike.

Yet Henri continued to move with lightning speed, his barrage of potentially deadly strikes unending.

Sweat poured down Rohan's face. He blinked rapidly to keep his devil of a brother clearly in his sight. He ignored the sting as well as the increasing fatigue in his arms and shoulders. Strike after strike, blow after blow, brother to brother, they prolonged their dance.

Suddenly changing his tactic, Henri swiped at Rohan from the opposite side. Planting his steel blade deep into the earth, Rohan pushed off from the weapon and leapt skyward and away from his brother's attack. His weight above the sword gave it additional resolve against the strike; the ensuing reverberation stung Henri. He could barely maintain his grip.

Sensing the opportunity before him, Rohan wasted no time in going on the offensive. In one upward motion, he yanked the sword from the hardened soil and swung it like a club at Henri. Clods of earth trailed its motion through the air as the tip of the blade narrowly missed Henri's chin, and he stumbled backward. Rohan swung again from the opposite side and advanced on his adversary.

Rohan grinned beneath his helmet. Advantage Rohan, and Henri knew it. Struggling against his own fatigue, Henri managed to deflect the onslaught of strikes barraging him. He continued to retreat while looking wildly for a way out.

But Rohan was a man possessed. Striking from every direction, he was consumed by his advance. Henri realized his brother had more reason to win than he did himself. Henri's heel caught on a rock protruding from the soil. Suddenly, he fell onto his back while thrusting his sword upward at the juggernaut before him. Rohan's momentum carried him uncontrollably forward and into the cold steel of his brother's sword. Heat seared his side.

All motion ceased as the reality of what had just happened struck them both. Rohan's eyes widened; his heart screamed for retribution. He could not die, not by Henri's hand, not when Isabel would suffer for his folly.

"Nay!" he cried. "You will not have her, brother!"

He heard Isabel's scream, but he could not look to her. Instead, he looked down to where blood slowly ran down the blade of the great broadsword stuck in his left side. He grabbed at the site of the wound. A slow burning worked its way across his midsection as he tried to wrap his mind around the scene before him. Henri had won? Nay, it— could not be so . . .

Rohan looked to Henri. A slow, maniacal grin twisted his face as he drank in his victory. His hand still on the hilt, Henri slowly dragged his weapon from the wound, reveling in the additional pain it caused his sibling.

Tiny pinpoint stars danced in front of Rohan's eyes, and his legs quaked, no longer able to support his weight. Still gripping his sword before him with his right hand, he dropped to one knee, while trying to hold back the tide of crimson with his left. He struggled to catch his breath, with his shoulders rounded and his chin pressed against his chest. He fought simply to stay conscious.

"Struggling, brother?" Henri taunted from nearby. "Stay with me for just a moment longer. While your pain will soon disappear, I want your eternal memory to survive. Go to your grave, brother, with the knowledge that while you sleep in the cold of the earth, I sleep between the warmth of your woman's thighs!"

Isabel's scream rang out, slicing the cold December air. Rohan pressed his hand to his chest, remembering the ribbons there.

A droning like that of a buzzing hive of bees filled his ears, but slowly Rohan's vision cleared. He willed his body to rise and defend itself against the wound. With each breath, he became more cognizant of his surroundings. He still held his sword in his right hand. Henri's feet and legs were poised before him. He lifted his head and gazed at Isabel. Manhku held her back; the horror twisting her beautiful face wrenched his gut.

That Henri thwarted William's decree of no fight to the death, Rohan was not surprised. It had to be this way. Only one of them would rise.

"It is done," Henri crowed. "To the victor go the spoils, and to the dead the afterlife. Haunt me no more, brother." Henri stepped toward Rohan and, with a wide base, dug his feet into the ground. Grasping the broadsword with both hands, he slowly lifted the weapon above his right shoulder and over his head. His chin rested on his left shoulder as he looked down on his brother. "For Eleanor, Rohan, and for our sire, who could not see past his by-blow to his noble son, who would have given him the world had he but paid the slightest bit of attention!"

As Henri brought his blade down, Rohan let out his chilling battle cry and thrust. Henri's body jerked but hung as if suspended by an invisible string above Rohan. Henri's eyes widened, and his chin quivered. His legs shook, and his hands slowly broke grip with the sword he still held. It fell to the ground behind him. His arms slowly dropped to his sides. Poised on his toes, he looked in confused astonishment at Rohan.

Rohan let out a long breath. In that single moment of superiority, dominance, and victory, Henri had been vanquished. Consumed with his triumph, Henri had failed to notice Rohan take his own sword with both hands and thrust it high into his groin. Rohan wasted no time in withdrawing the blade, ensuring a wide and fatal wound.

Falling to his knees, Henri came face-to-face with Rohan. "You have killed me, brother."

Rohan nodded. "You left me no option."

Henri fell to Rohan's right no longer able to maintain himself. Rohan turned to the man fate had determined should be noble born but unloved. Henri's head rolled to one side facing Rohan. He seemed to struggle for words, but none came. Slowly, the life force drained from his body, and his eyes turned hard and lifeless. They stared blankly up at him. Rohan closed them with his hand.

The final chapter to Henri's unhappy life closed, while another chapter opened for Rohan. As he turned to find his lady, he squinted in the sunlight, sure that he was hallucinating. For while Isabel stood, she stood with Dunsworth. What was this? His men swarmed him, but Rohan shook his head and pointed toward the woman two seers had prophesied would be his for eternity.

Isabel wrestled against Arlys's grip. But the more she wrangled, the harder he pressed the tip of his short sword into her back. "Be still, Isabel, or your knight will have a corpse for a leman," he hissed in her ear.

As it occurred to Rohan's men that he was directing them back to Isabel, they stopped their mad rejoicing. Dunsworth, along with his men who had accompanied him to Rossmoor several nights before, stood armed and holding the lady Isabel as hostage. A Willingham no doubt had a hand in their escape.

"Stand back, Normans!" Arlys cried out. "Stand back, or the lady will pay the penalty for your trespass!"

Les morts stopped.

Using her as a shield, Arlys moved Isabel toward the gathered throngs of Saxon villagers. "Take heart, my countrymen. We will win the day here. Take up arms now so that we might clear this scourge from our midst!"

When they did not respond with gusto, Isabel saw her chance. "Nay! Do not listen to him! He would have sold me out to de Monfort! He is not worthy to lead you!"

Isabel turned and pointed to Rohan, who had been helped up by his men. The wound at his side bled heavily. Tears blurred her vision. She twisted out of Arlys's grasp but was caught by one of the X'ed Dunsworth churls. He held her to him. When Arlys made a play to regain her, the man raised a spiked club.

Isabel turned to her people. "William may not be rightful king in our eyes, but he will be crowned. He has the mighty arm of seasoned knights; he has the treasury to fight us. He is a vindictive duke and will bring suffering to all who rise up against him." She looked at their faces and saw fear and indecision. She pointed to Rohan and his knights, who stood battle-ready. "These knights have not pillaged or plundered our home. They have not raped our women. Nay, they have gone out daily in search of the cowardly raiders who seek only to kill and maim. They hunt and replenish the larders with fresh meat." Isabel took a deep breath. "Sir Rohan is a fair man; his men are fair; he is strong and has the ear of the duke."

She turned and pointed an accusing finger at Arlys, who stood, furious, not two steps from her. "He is a liar." A hard sob caught high in her throat as sudden realization dawned. "Beware of the fox in sheep's clothing," her father had told Rohan.

" 'Twas you who slew my sire!" She broke free from the churl's grasp. When Arlys's face twisted in fury, she knew she had touched the truth. "Did you slay Geoff as well?" By his silence, she knew she had hit home. "Was it you,

Arlys, who led the marauders into the forests, destroying the people and the lands?"

He shook his head and backed away from her. "Nay, not all." His eyes darted to Henri's second, who stood listening intently. Arlys pointed a finger. "'Twas Henri's idea. He wanted to kill as many of Rohan's churls as possible and make them fear all Normans. He hoped to instigate an uprising."

"It had the opposite effect. For Rohan pulled them together and protected them." She spat at her former betrothed. "You are no man in my eyes. You are a coward and a traitor to your own people, your country, and me, your former betrothed. Did you think to gain my lands by doing away with my sire and my brother?"

His silence once again confirmed her allegations. As she spoke, she did not notice how the branded churls closed in around Henri and Arlys's men. The man who had grabbed her from Arlys pushed her aside. "Milady, move far from here. We have unfinished business to conduct with several of these men."

Isabel turned and ran to where Rohan stood with the help of Thorin and Manhku and in silent horror watched as the branded people of Dunsworth hacked down Henri's men and Arlys.

No Norman made a move to save them, and while Isabel would not have wished the feeding frenzy on any person, she understood the value of not interfering. The mob had turned ugly, and as soon as she and the good people were gone from it, the sooner it would subside. She waved to Russell and several of the village elders, signaling them to do just that, and with the help of his men, Rohan was taken back to the manor. Isabel hurried to clear the lord's table near the hearth.

"Lay him down here. Enid, stoke the fires and boil water. Wulfson, go to my chamber and fetch my basket. Manhku, help me remove his clothing."

Rohan had passed out from blood loss by the time he was stripped. But clutched in his hand were the colored ribbons. Tears rose in Isabel's eyes, but she fought them back. *He will not die!*

Once the wound was cleaned and she had a better look, Isabel's concern rose. While it did not seem to go directly into his gut, as it was off more to the left side, it went clean through. As she pondered her approach, the doors opened, and a sudden hush fell over the hall. Isabel turned to see Wilma scurry into the great hall. Her hair rose on her neck, but she welcomed the woman. Isabel hurried to her and dragged her back to Rohan. "Milady, the wound is thorough. I know not if it pierces any vital organs. My skill in sewing is only for superficial cuts. I fear for his life."

Wilma cackled and patted Isabel's hand. "He will survive, lass. I will see to it."

And so Isabel stood back and watched as Wilma expertly sewed what she assumed was more than just skin and muscle. Isabel did not question the seer's methods. But when she was done, blood no longer seeped from the wound. Indeed, Rohan's death pallor had pinkened up. She pressed her hand to his brow. It was cool.

"The healing has begun." Wilma smiled her snaggle-toothed smile and took Isabel's hand into hers and patted it. "The prophecy has only just taken root. It is too soon for any of you to perish."

Wilma looked past Isabel's shoulder to the assembled

Blood Swords. She threw her head back and cackled. "'Tis to Mercia one of you will go, and 'tis there you will meet a warrior to match you in skill and spirit!"

She skittered off, leaving them all looking at one another in question.

Epilogue

R iders approach!" the lookout called from the tower. Isabel hastened from her chair by the hearth and motioned to Manhku, who rarely walked with the aid of his stick now. She hurried to the door, flung it open, and squealed in happiness. Ignoring the bite of the February wind, she ran across the courtyard to the knight who dismounted from his great warhorse and ran equally swiftly toward her. He grabbed her up in his arms, twirling her around, hugging her close, showering her with kisses.

Breathless, Isabel pulled slightly back from him, her .eyes scanning his body. She threw her arms around him. "You came back!"

Rohan laughed and carried her toward the hall. "Did you doubt it?"

"It has been two months, Rohan."

He nodded but smiled down at her. "Aye, two of the

longest months of my life. But the king required much of me."

"We heard the news last month. I am glad for you. Mayhap now this isle can return to order."

Rohan scowled and shook his head. "'Tis not likely. Many plot to take what is William's. There is much treachery afoot."

Isabel's heart sank. "Will you be joining William?"

"Nay, he returns to Normandy with Edgar and other prisoners of war. I have been given the title here as well as overlordship of Dunsworth and Worster. You will tire of seeing this scarred face of mine."

Isabel happily circled him, making doubly sure no wound afflicted him. She looked past him and did not see the rest of his men.

"Where are your Blood Swords?"

"They see to the king's business."

A sudden jolt of sadness hit Isabel. Their absence would be felt by many.

Manhku clasped Rohan's arm in friendship.

"Manhku, you will be my right arm now that Thorin is off scouring the north lands for subterfuge. Are you up to it?" Rohan asked.

The giant nodded and smiled. "Aye, 'tis my honor."

Rohan pulled Isabel into the warmth of the hall. Those now familiar to him raised a cup in welcome, and Rohan felt for the first time in his life as if he truly belonged. He looked down at the woman by his side. He still could not believe his good fortune.

She moved the lord's chair from the hearth and held it for him to sit upon. His eyes caught her soft gaze. She nodded. "You are more than worthy to sit upon it, Rohan." She took his hand and pressed it to her belly. "As one day your son will as well."

Joy erupted in his chest, filling it. Taking Isabel into his arms, he hugged her close, and for the first time in his life, the hot sting of moisture in his eyes made him blink. " 'Tis glad I am I made an honest woman of you before my departure. There are too many bastards in this world as it is. Our son will be born with no blight on his good name."

Isabel looked up into his eyes, her own moist with tears, and smiled.

As two hearts, two souls, two bodies became one, the prophecy was realized at that moment. And with it a legacy that would live for more than a thousand years.

POCKET BOOKS
PROUDLY PRESENTS

MASTER
of
TORMENT

KARIN TABKE

Coming soon
from Pocket Books

Turn the page for a preview of the next book
in the Blood Sword Legacy series . . .

Ornate sconces burned brightly along the stone walls of the opulent chamber, illuminating it and all of its vivid colors like a gem encrusted crown. Velvet appointed furniture a king would envy graced the thick wool rugs, but what caught the eye when one walked into the chamber was the enormous bed. Though the heavy curtains of the elaborately carved four poster bed were drawn, a sharp, frightened gasp permeated the lavish chamber, alerting anyone near to the debauchery afoot.

The bile in Lady Tarian's belly rose. She breathed in slowly and exhaled slower, listening intently, waiting in breathless anticipation for the most opportune time to strike.

"Please, milord, I beg you—" a high, strained voice pleaded.

"'Tis what I desire," a deep male voiced cajoled. The sharp sound of a hand slapping bare flesh startled Tarian. A muffled voice cried out. "Beg me for more," the deep voice commanded.

Once her circumspect inventory of the room showed

there to be no other escape route but the thick oak portal she had just come through and that her men were in place, Tarian glanced over to Gareth, her captain of the guard, who held the lord's manservant. The honed sword blade leveled snugly against the servant's throat and his ashen face behind it told Tarian he was properly subdued. She nodded to her captain before turning back to the shrouded bed.

Despite the encumbrance of her mail Tarian glided a step closer to the bed. She pressed the tip of her sword into the slitted fabric and slowly pushed it aside. Only the orange blush of a tallow candle and the pale skin of a man's back glowed within the darkened space.

"Please, milord, do not—" the boy begged.

Shocked at seeing a young boy as Malcor's newest victim, Tarian almost missed the well muscled arm rise up from the darkness. What looked to be a studded leather strap dangled from the fist holding it. Revulsion rose higher in Tarian's throat and with it the knowledge that in the very near future it could be her blood, not this boy's, that stained the leather. 'Twas past time someone removed this dark, twisted predator from the mist of the innocents he terrorized. And she, it appeared, was the chosen one.

"Malcor, did you think I would not come for you?" Tarian demanded.

Without the barest hint of surprise or concern for his wellbeing, Malcor rolled over, the leather strap grasped defiantly in his fist whilst he speared her with a malicious glare. The linen sheet rode low on his thighs and for all that he was a well-muscled man, the view repulsed her. Tarian set her jaw and stood fast, her motives for her appearance unwavering despite the lewdness of the man who had run like the coward he was.

"Did you think, Lady Tarian, that I would care?"

Tarian forced a blithe smile. She did not feel so carefree as her gesture may indicate, but this man would only see her for the true warrior she was. Too show him weakness on any front would find her a victim of the earl's sadistic nature. Carefully, her gaze held the glittering angry one of her betrothed. She did not look at the boy who shivered on the fur pelts beside the man her stepfather, Lord Edmund of Turnsly, had chosen for her to wed. It was marriage to Malcor, the perverted Earl of Dunloc, or the convent. For no other mortal man would have her to wife.

The cloister did not want her, nor she them. Her God-wineson blood, while a curse, was also her salvation. She was bred to fight, bred to lead, and despite the sins of her father, bred to breed with the finest blood of Europe, not spend endless days and nights on her knees praying for forgiveness she seriously doubted any god, even one so forgiving as hers, would grant.

Malcor was her destiny, and she would control him through their children. Despite the recent change in sovereignty, the earl continued to hold title to some of the finest land in England. And while Malcor and his uncle Rangor had fought valiantly beside their king, her uncle Harold, their loyalties appeared at least on the surface to stand with William, when in actuality, like so many English, they supported Edgar.

And if she were true to herself, in her heart she did as well. But Tarian was not so blind not to see the foreshadowing of the gloom and doom the Norman born king could elicit if sufficiently provoked. Nay, she would swear to the man who slew her kin and bide her time. At least then, there was a chance for her and her line to survive.

Unfortunately, the perverse Malcor was a most necessary pawn in her game of survival.

Her smile tightened. She required only one thing from this man, and despite his preference for squires she would extract it from him at sword point if necessary.

"How remiss of me, Malcor, to think a noble such as yourself would hold sacred a betrothal contract. 'Tis well I know the character of the man I will marry."

"There will be no marriage," he ground out.

Barely perceptibly, she inclined her head toward her betrothed. From behind her a score of armed soldiers fanned out, their swords at the ready. Tarian pressed the honed tip of her own sword, Thyra, to Malcor's chest. Pale lips pulled back from long, yellow teeth. She controlled her revulsion. With God's blessing 'twould take only one time for his seed to strike fertile ground. Provided of course she was fertile. How ironic would it be then, that she conceive a child of a man who despised women? And she the daughter of a royal rapist. Was she not following in her illicit sire's footsteps? The sins of the father will repeat in the sins of the daughter. She had heard the words all her life, now she would breathe truth into the curse.

"We will wed this night, milord, or you will not wake to see the morn." She looked up to her right just past her shoulder and smiled at Gareth who had handed off the servant to another of her guard. "See that Earl Malcor is a properly dressed groom."

She turned back to her intended. He may not fear her, which was foolish, for she was well schooled in the art of war, but Gareth was a force all of his own to be reckoned with. He would not stand back should Malcor decide to get heavy-handed with her. Tarian grinned up at the enormous man and shrugged, suddenly not caring a whit for what Malcor desired. "Or not, if he doth protest too much."

"You will regret your action, Lady Tarian. Your guard cannot always be within reach," Malcor softy threatened.

The edge of steel in his words alerted her. A small ripple of apprehension skittered down her rigid spine. Her gaze rose to his. Stark contempt filled Malcor's pale blue eyes. His pallid skin blanched whiter beneath his flame-colored hair. She would find no succor from this man soon to become her husband. She would find only hardship. But with a child and the title of Lady of Dunloc much could be forgiven. For life in a convent that cringed at the mere mention of her name would drive her mad. She nodded ever so slightly to her intended. "Your own priest awaits us, milord, pray do not dally."

As she swept regally from the chamber she said to Gareth over her shoulder, "And, Sir Captain. Be sure he washes all traces of the boy from him. I would see my husband clean in my wedding bed this night."

"Thou art the devil's spawn! I will not wed with thee," Malcor screamed.

"Aye, you will," Gareth said as he pressed his point with his sword.

"Nay, she is cursed!"

Tarian turned at the door, her sword raised. Stepping back into the chamber she leveled it at her reluctant groom. "Make no mistake, Malcor. This eve will find us both in that bed as man and wife. And should you continue to resist me?" She glanced at Gareth and smiled. "I am not above forcing myself upon you." She stepped closer. She could see the wild dilation of his pale eyes. "Try now for once to be a man of honor. Honor your vow to me."

Malcor moved back into the furs. "Nay! *Never.* I will not have the mark of the witch upon me!"

Tarian smiled tolerantly and nodded. "So be it then. You will not be the first reluctant spouse."

A fortnight later Tarian knelt beside the embroidered pall that covered her dearly departed husband. The priest's low voice droned one prayer after another. The dull ache in her back throbbed. But 'twas not from the endless hours of kneeling, then standing, only to kneel again. It was from the force of her dead husband's foot on her back as he kicked her from their bed three days past. For him it was the last time for all things earthly. Where his soul traveled at this moment she could only guess. And she did not care. There would be no alms to the churls of Dunloc, and there would be no alms to Hailfox Abby just down the way for the priests to pray. Nay, Earl Malcor deserved where he was going, and she held no guilt in watching his speedy decent to hell.

Finally Father Dudley's murmuring came to an abrupt end. Silently he signaled to the gathered few that prayers were at an end. The body would be taken to a prepared place just outside of the chapel doors. As was the custom, Tarian, nor any others, would witness the internment.

She was helped to her knees by her stalwart guard, Gareth. "Milady?" he softly said awaiting her direction. She smiled up into his concerned blue eyes. His unwavering devotion to her was her only salvation in these dark days. Had he not been the mouse under the bed since her arrival at Draceadon, she would be the one being buried, not Malcor. Her gaze darted across the pew to Lord Rangor, Malcor's ambitious uncle. His arrival the day before Malcor's death had been a blessing in disguise. When questioned on

the state of their marriage, Malcor had unbelievably confirmed not only were they wed, but the relationship was *in
facto comsume.*

Only she, her dead husband, and Gareth knew the truth.

Rangor, dressed in rich scarlet and saffron velvet, ges-
ticulated toward the altar and the dearly departed, then
presented his arm to his niece-in-law. "Lady Tarian, do me
the honor of accompanying me back to the hall." It was
not a request but a command. And since she was curious
as to what he was about, Tarian nodded her head to Gareth and took Rangor's professed arm.

As he swept her down the long aisle and out into the hot
August breeze, her black hair whipped around her head.
She had not bound it as a wedded woman, nor as a widow
should. Indeed, she left it down and beribboned. Nor did
she wear a widow's black. She could never be accused of
false emotions. The relationship she had with Malcor was
not veiled for the sake of propriety. They despised each
other. That he was dead was of his own making.

Wordlessly they approached the stone fortress known
far and wide as Draceadon. Dragon Hill. It was a worthy
structure and one she would call home for many years to
come. She chewed her bottom lip and wondered just how
she would orchestrate such a maneuver. Whilst she had the
law on her side, England was a swirling cesspool of intrigue
and anarchy. The old ways may not hold sway.

At the threshold of the manor, Rangor stopped and
took her hand into both of his. "My Lady, I would have a
most private word with you if I may," he entreated.

Once again Tarian acquiesced to him. Not because he
demanded it, but because she did. He looked past her to
where Gareth, along with half of his garrison, stood. A
most formidable sight to any man or woman. Once again

she was grateful for their presence. "Completely private," Rangor insisted.

"My man will stand back."

Rangor's manservant appeared from inside the manor as well as Ruin, Malcor's sniveling manservant. The two were a matched pair. She'd see Ruin gone from Draceadon post haste. Easily Rangor lead her through the wide threshold of Draceadon. No sooner had she stepped into the coolness of the great hall the heavy doors clanged shut behind her and the bolts were thrown. She whirled around to find a half score of Rangor's men blocking her retreat. She turned to Rangor who stood too full of himself beside her.

Gareth's loud voice called to her from the other side, and he pounded on the door demanding entrance.

"What is the meaning of this!" she demanded.

Rangor smiled. It held no warmth. "I have a proposition for you, Lady Tarian, one I wish you to think about with no council from your man Gareth or anyone else for that matter. And I would have your answer post haste."

Dread churned in her belly. Yet she would hear him. "Ask me what you will."

Rangor bowed, then stood erect and faced her. "I propose we see the priest after my nephew is secured in the ground."

Tarian frowned. "For what purpose?"

"To wed."

Tarian gasped, the continued pounding on the door behind her rattling her steely nerve. Marry Rangor? Never! Inconspicuously her eyes darted around her for the closest weapon. While her jeweled dagger hung from her woven girdle, a sword would better suit what she had in mind. She could wield the weapon as well as any man, yet none was in her reach, and Rangor's men were many and fully armed.

Her best defense then was her shrewd mind. Her initial reaction was to tell the man under no circumstance would she wed him, but the game must be played with a level head. She was well aware she treaded on very thin ice. "I am honored, milord, but I am a widow of only three days. 'Tis not decent to wed so soon."

Rangor's smile widened. He bore the same long, yellow teeth of his nephew. Involuntarily, Tarian shivered as she relived the pain of Malcor's teeth in her back.

"I promise you, milady, I do not covet boys in my bed. I am a man on every level and would make a lusty groom."

Tarian kept her cool. "Be that as it may, sir, your nephew had no problems in the marriage bed. Indeed, for as virile as he was, I should be heavy with child by the New Year."

Rangor's smile faded, but he pressed further. "I do not believe you. I know my nephew, and I know he could not stand the sight of a woman. I would have us wed by sunset on the morrow."

"Nay, I cannot."

"You will," Rangor pressed.

"Nay, I will not. You cannot force me."

"You forced Malcor."

"I but reminded him of his public and private oath to wed with me."

"Would you give up title here?"

Tarian stood her ground. "My title here is not contingent on my wedding with you, Rangor."

"It will be when I inform the king you murdered my nephew."

Tarian's blood cooled. "I did not murder Malcor."

He inclined his head toward Ruin. "He says different."

Tarian narrowed her eyes at the simpering fop. "He lies."

She turned back to the noble, and despite the continued pounding on the door, she spoke calmly and played her hand. "But it matters not. I anticipated your intervention here. I have sent word to Normandy. I would have William decree me Lady here over you. The messenger left the day of Malcor's death."

Rangor's pale face flushed crimson, his cheeks puffed, and his fists opened and closed at his sides. "You will rue the day, Lady Tarian! Draceadon and all that belong to it are mine by rite of blood. I will not have a murderess sit upon the dais while my nephew molds in the earth by her hand!" He turned to his guard. "Take her to the dungeon!"

Tarian drew the jeweled dagger from her girdle. She stabbed the closest man to her, then backpedaled to the door that quaked under Gareth's wrath. The guards pressed upon her. She would not go down without a fight. She whirled around to attack the next closest man, when her hand was caught from behind. A fist squeezed her fingers until the dagger dropped clattering to the stone floor. Unceremoniously she was hoisted onto a set of wide shoulders. "I will kill you for this, Rangor!" she screamed.

The ignoble stalked toward her. It took three men to subdue her sufficiently. "You have time to change your mind. Either we wed by the time William's messenger arrives, or I will instruct him you are dead."

"You had better have a body, Rangor, for I have Malcor's will. He leaves all to his lawful wife!"

Rangor blanched white. "Where is it?"

She spat at him. "You will never find it!"

In a slow swipe, he wiped the spittle from his cheek. "Enjoy your stay with the rats, milady. I hear they have a taste for human flesh."

Discover the darker side of passion with these bestselling paranormal romances from Pocket Books!

Kresley Cole
Wicked Deed on a Winter's Night
Immortal enemies…forbidden temptation.

Alexis Morgan
Redeemed in Darkness
She vowed to protect her world from the enemy—
until her enemy turned her world upside down.

Katie MacAlister
Ain't Myth-Behaving
He's a God. A legend. A man of mythic proportions…
And he'll make you long to myth-behave.

Melissa Mayhue
Highland Guardian
For mortals caught in Faeire schemes,
passion can be dangerous…

Enough desire for a lifetime... and beyond.

Gena Showalter
Savor Me Slowly

Her mind is programmed to kill—
but her heart tells her otherwise.

Sharie Kohler
Marked by Moonlight

When a good girl goes werewolf, attraction can be lethal.

**Susan Sizemore, Maggie Shayne,
Lori Handeland, and Caridad Piñeiro**
Moon Fever

Passions suddenly turn primal in this unforgettable
collection by four of today's hottest writers.

**Allison Brennan, Roxanne St. Claire,
and Karin Tabke**
What You Can't See

Three dark and dangerous tales from rising stars
in paranormal romance!